DEEP DEVIL

THE DEEP SERIES - BOOK FOUR

NICK SULLIVAN

Cover design by Shayne Rutherford of Wicked Good Book Covers
Cover photo by Martonio Paleka, photographer in Split, Croatia
Copy editing by Marsha Zinberg of The Write Touch
Proofreading by Gretchen Tannert Douglas and Forest Olivier
Interior Design and Typesetting by Colleen Sheehan of Ampersand Book Interiors
Original maps of Cozumel & W. Caribbean by Rainer Lesniewski/Shutterstock.com

ISBN: 978-0-9978132-6-5

Published by Wild Yonder Press
www.WildYonderPress.com

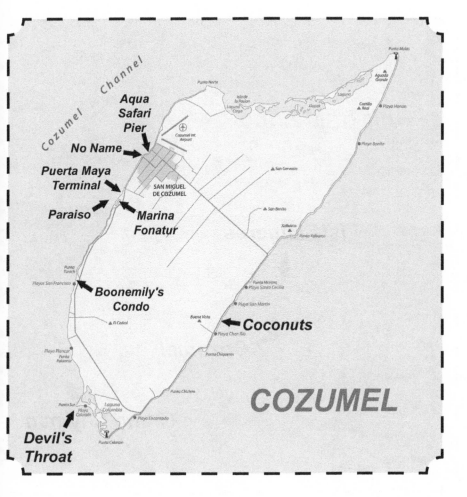

COZUMEL

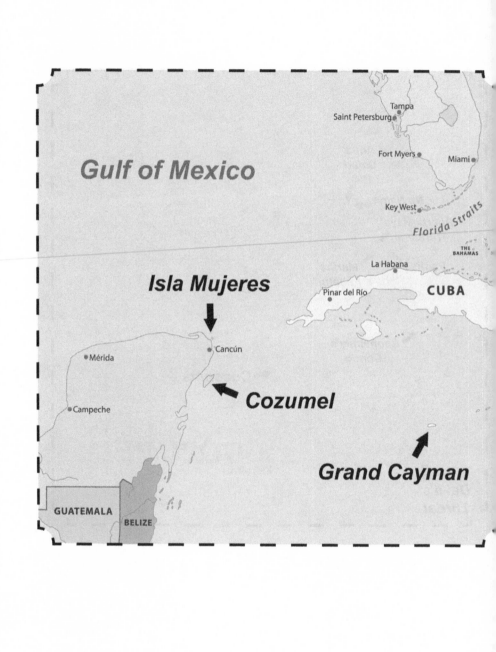

To Dawn Snow of the Caradonna Adventures travel agency. You booked my first dive trip ever… and the majority of the ones that followed. Thank you for introducing me to new worlds, both above and below the water.

In Memoriam
Dawn "Shelley" Snow—March 18, 2020.

AUTHOR'S NOTE

I conceived the guts and bones of this story while writing my previous book, *Deep Roots*—before the arrival of COVID-19 and the unparalleled disruption it has brought to all of our lives. As you might guess, the virus has greatly affected the travel and diving industry. Many of the places I base my books around will look very different when I return.

When I sat down to write *Deep Devil*, it didn't take long for me to decide that my fictional world would depart from the reality we now find ourselves in. For one thing, many of the events in this story could not take place in our current environment. For another, I'd like to think that one of the services I provide to you, the reader, is escape. And I, for one, hear enough about COVID-19 during my day-to-day life. Boone and Emily will enjoy their lives in a world without this virus... and I hope you enjoy living it with them, if only for a while.

Nick Sullivan
August, 2020

1

"Anything biting, mister?"

The man in the multi-pocketed fishing vest looked up. "Nope. Slow night." He played the line in the water before squinting at the kid beside him. "You're out late."

"Fishing pier's open twenty-four hours."

"Yeah, but you ain't fishing. And you're a bit young to be out here on your own at one in the morning."

The teen shrugged. "I'm eighteen."

The man laughed, reeling the line in a few yards. "No, you're not."

The youth was sixteen, at best—more likely less. There was enough light spilling from the nearly empty pier parking lot to make that crystal clear. The Sunshine Skyway Fishing Pier was actually two separate piers that ran along the western flank of the Sunshine Skyway Memorial Bridge. Situated at either end, the piers were the remnants of the approaches to the original bridge, which had been destroyed in 1980, when a freighter had struck a support during a sudden storm. High above the fishing piers, the four-mile expanse of the new bridge rose above Tampa Bay, connecting St. Petersburg to the north with the suburbs of Sarasota to the south. This southern span of the fishing pier was quite a ways from any residential areas.

The fisherman eyed the kid. "How'd you get down here?"

"Bicycle. That's a cool tattoo. You in the army or something?"

"Retired."

"Thank you for your service."

"Thank you for your thank you. Now run along home."

"Nah, it's boring there. What's in your ear?"

The man adjusted his fishing cap, adorned with a spare hook and several iron-on patches. "Earbud. I like to listen to audiobooks when I fish." Unseen by the youth, the man dropped a hand to his side and waggled it in the direction of the nearby bait shack, a "closed" sign hanging across its door.

"What're you listening to?"

"Harry Fuckin' Potter."

"Really?"

"No."

A throat cleared behind them. "Hey, kid… your parents know you're down here?"

The fisherman turned and tipped his head in acknowledgment of the newcomer, a fit-looking young man in an orange reflective vest.

The teen squared his bony shoulders. "Who wants to know?"

"A Florida State employee who's gonna have the cops call your parents if you don't head on home."

"Okay, jeez, I'm going." The kid grabbed his bicycle, which was leaning nearby. As he slung a leg over his bike, he paused, looking at the newcomer. "You listen to audiobooks, too?"

"Beat it."

As the kid wheeled away toward the southeast, the fisherman reeled in his line. There was no bait on the hook. "Thanks, Baker. If that pipsqueak asked me one more question..."

"Handled it like a pro, Angler," a voice said over the earpieces. Both men heard it, the speech distorted by some form of voice changer.

Baker snorted. "Yeah, you had a real 'get-off-my-lawn' vibe going there, grandpa."

"I'm thirty-nine, you drummed-out bullet sponge."

"Can the chatter. Target is two and a half clicks out, just increased to ten knots. Saddle up."

"Roger," the fisherman said to the air, hefting the rod and a nearby bait box. Handing the fishing gear to Baker, he crossed the parking lot beside the darkened bait shop, thumping the wall twice with his fist as he passed, before heading for a black Chevy Tahoe with tinted windows. Behind him, the door to the shop opened and four figures moved smoothly toward the SUV. One was dressed in Florida casual, but the remaining trio were most decidedly not, their silhouettes black-clad and bulky in the dim light.

Twenty yards away, Baker tossed the fishing gear into the back of an official-looking Florida Department of Transportation pickup. A close inspection might reveal that the FDOT labels on its white flanks were magnetic decals, but at this hour of the morning, Baker wasn't worried. He hopped into the truck, putting it in gear and heading for the on-ramp that would lead to the southern bank of the bridge. Two miles away, on the north Sunshine Skyway fishing pier, a similar truck would be making its way to the other side.

The fisherman, call sign "Angler," slid into the passenger side of the Tahoe and exchanged his fishing vest for a black tactical one, its pockets containing no jigs, hooks, or spare line. Instead, it was packed with spare magazines, electronics, and inset ballistic plates. Angler swung his legs outside the SUV to slide portions of a harness into place on his thighs before seating himself and closing the door. The other doors opened, and two men and a woman joined him, the man in plain clothes cramming into the rear.

"Let's get this show on the street," the black-clad driver said in a thick Russian accent.

"It's 'road,' borscht-for-brains," the woman in the rear quipped. The lanky man beside her brayed a loud, equine laugh just as their earpieces crackled.

"Pipe down, Stallion!" the fisherman barked. *That guy's laugh is inhuman.* Indeed, with those bulging eyes, Angler wondered if there wasn't some frog in the man's DNA. "Say again, Palantir." God, he hated these stupid call-signs. He knew "Palantir" had something to do with *Lord of the Rings*, an all-seeing crystal ball the evil wizard had... but why not just go with "Eagle Eye," instead of something some mom's-basement-dwelling nerd would dredge up.

"Target is inside of two klicks. And I see you're still stationary." The last sentence may have held a hint of disapproval, but the electronic distortion made it hard to tell.

Angler smacked the driver on the arm. "Tolstoy, you wanted to drive, so drive!"

"Pedal to the steel!" the Russian crowed, and the SUV lurched forward, heading for the southern end of the bridge. As they reached the shore, Tolstoy swung left under the overpass of the bridge, turning onto the service road that ran alongside the

Manatee County Rest Area before feeding back onto the bridge on the northbound side.

Ahead, the FDOT truck was parked on the shoulder and the SUV flashed past it. Angler glanced down at the Tahoe's passenger-side mirror and watched as the truck's orange roof lights flashed to life. It followed them to the bridge before turning broadside across the roadway and coming to a stop. Road flares sparked as Baker got out and blocked off the northbound lanes. If all was going according to plan, the second doctored truck would be doing the same on the other side of the bridge. If questioned, they were there because a horse had somehow made its way onto the bridge and they were closing it off until they could catch it. Once the team had completed their task, the bridge would be reopened, leaving no trace behind.

"Bridge is sealed. CCTV feeds disabled. Four minutes."

"Roger." A black bag was handed forward and Angler took it, swiftly opening the zipper along the side and checking the safety on the compact H&K SP5 submachine gun within. Satisfied, he strapped the bag containing the compact weapon across his chest before retrieving a pair of gloves from a breast pocket and pulling them on.

"Three minutes."

"Check harnesses," Angler rumbled. Clinks and clicks filled the interior of the SUV as the team adjusted lightweight harnesses, ensuring everything was secure. Glancing out the window toward the waters of Tampa Bay, Angler could see a majestic ship approaching the bridge. Nowhere near the size of the newer, gargantuan cruise ships operated by the major cruise lines, this vessel was still substantial, almost a cross between a mega-yacht and a smaller cruise ship. Just as well: this bridge only had 180 feet of clearance, and the larger cruise ships couldn't pass beneath it.

"Helmet." A hand came forward, holding a lightweight helmet with night-vision goggles mounted above the brow.

Angler took it and strapped it on. Overhead, the greenish glow of the bridge's nighttime lighting shone on the support cables as they reached the apex of the span. Angler flipped down the optics, exchanging one eerie glow for another.

"Two minutes."

The Tahoe skidded to a stop. In seconds, the four figures in combat gear spilled out and vaulted the concrete barrier that separated the northbound lanes from the southbound, moving low as they crossed, coils of rope in hand. Behind them, the man in the T-shirt exited the still-running truck and followed, standing by to retrieve their rappelling gear.

"Hook up," Angler said, leading the group to the pre-selected spots where they would attach their rappelling ropes, splitting into pairs and lining up on either side of a red crisis-counseling phone mounted at the edge. The Sunshine Skyway Bridge had an infamous reputation that belied its sunny name: it was a popular spot for suicides. The Florida Department of Transportation had begun preparations to implement the Skyway Vertical Net, a barrier to prevent jumpers, by extending a net eight feet out from the center span. This would have made their current plan impossible, but construction had moved with the glacial speed of any government project, and only the initial stages had been installed. Ironically, the very thing that would eventually prevent jumpers now assisted them: the sturdy framework for the nonexistent netting made an ideal place to attach their primary carabiners.

"One minute. Descend to hold point."

"Roger. Descending."

As one, the group glided down to the base of the bridge and waited.

Now came the moment that Angler was most nervous about. They'd drilled this step the best they could, using an old railroad trestle as a stand-in for the bridge and a flat-bed semi driving underneath to simulate the boat. He wasn't worried about their execution; it was the fact that the timing depended on someone who named himself "Palantir."

"Ten seconds."

Below their boots, a glow shone across the surface of the bay. A moment later, the sleek bow of the ship slid into view… then the foredeck… the roof of the bridge with a bulbous radar mast, and then…

"Now. Now. Now."

With a near-silent whisper of rope against metal, the four figures glided downward, only an occasional application of their belaying devices needed to bring them down smoothly. They all landed on their feet atop the helicopter landing pad, situated behind the hangar nestled aft of the bridge. Swiftly detaching lines from harnesses, they moved in a low crouch, heading for a single pulsing light inside the hangar, an infrared strobe that their contact had left for them. Invisible to the naked eye, it winked on and off in their night-vision goggles. Much of the interior was occupied by an Airbus ACH160, its rotor blades folded for storage.

"Hangar's clear," Angler whispered.

"Good. Wait one. Incoming."

A buzzing sound approached and after a minute, four glowing pinpoints of red light came into view, a dark shape slowing to a hover near the hangar entrance. A small quad-rotor drone slowly sank to the deck, gently bumping onto its skids.

"Fetch the drone. Pocket the strobe. Enter the maintenance locker on the left."

"Roger. Stallion, get the drone. Potluck, strobe." As the woman on the team retrieved the flashing device from under the tail boom of the helicopter, one of the other men lifted the drone. Angler swung a metal door open and slipped into a small workroom, the others on his heels. "We're in."

"Excellent work, Angler. You should see four suitcases at the stern end."

"Affirmative."

"Each has a sticker with the first letter of your call sign and suitable attire inside. Put your gear into each suitcase and wait. At 0300, I will direct you to where you'll be staying for the next few days."

"Better 'n' this, I hope," Stallion muttered, looking around the cramped space, the scent of lubricating oil hanging in the air.

Palantir's electronic voice barked a laugh. *"There's a very select passenger list for the maiden voyage of this ship, and half the rooms are unoccupied. Our employer has given you one of the best suites."*

"Is hot tub?" Tolstoy inquired hopefully.

"And more. Be sure to enjoy it all. After the payoff we'll be getting for this gig, you'll all acquire a taste for the finer things."

"Just keep Tolstoy out of the mini-bar," Potluck warned in her upper midwestern twang.

"I'm afraid that's one amenity you won't be able to avail yourself of. Our employer has locked up the in-suite bar."

Tolstoy groaned, then winked at Angler, patting a pocket on his tactical vest as he unzipped it.

Angler laughed as he began stripping off his own gear. In addition to his hacking abilities, Tolstoy was also an expert lockpick.

As the team stowed their gear and donned fashionable attire, the 542-foot giga-yacht *Apollo* sailed into the night, bound for its first port-of-call, 507 nautical miles to the southwest.

2

"I think we're gaining on them!"

The excited tourist from Kansas was squinting toward the south. In the distance, a small dive boat was churning up an impressive wake.

"We'll get there first, Greg, don't you worry." Boone Fischer sat in a half-sprawl across the portside bench on the flybridge, calmly plucking another slice from a half-consumed orange and popping it into his mouth. "Em's not even at full throttle."

Emily Durand glanced back from the flybridge wheel and gave Boone a shining grin, wind-blown locks of blonde hair tickling the top of her bright green sunglasses.

Cecilia, Greg's dive buddy, pointed off the port bow. "But their boat is... I dunno... so much sleeker!"

Boone chuckled. "This boat's blessed with inner beauty." Admittedly, the *Lunasea* didn't seem like the kind of vessel that could pour on the knots. A 38-foot Delta Canaveral, she was designed for an easy, stable ride at cruising speed, but unlike most boats of her type, she had a bit more under the proverbial hood. Originally named the *Alhambra*, her dive op in the Honduran Bay Islands had been a front for a local cartel, who used her and her sister ship to smuggle drugs in the area. When a failed run resulted in her capture by the Honduran Navy, the *Alhambra* changed hands again at a police auction in La Ceiba. After her second police seizure—this time in Belize—she had been gifted to Boone and Emily for their assistance in the retrieval of a priceless Mayan artifact, the jade bust of Ix Chel. Along with the boat had come a sizeable amount of money.

Greg bit his lip. "So, he's not gonna beat us to Maracaibo?"

"Nope." Boone popped the last two slices of orange into his mouth and unfolded his long legs, rising to join Emily at the wheel. In Cozumel, the most spectacular dive sites were off to the south. That morning, they were headed for Maracaibo, a breathtaking wall dive near the southernmost tip of the island, sixteen miles from Cozumel's town of San Miguel. Boone and Emily prided themselves on getting to the best sites before the "cattle boats" had even left their dive ops, leaving earlier than most of their competitors. On Coz, many dive ops operated a variety of boat types. Fast-boats took smaller groups of divers, striving to get to the best spots first for an additional fee. Cattle boats took larger groups, often gathered from the numerous cruise ships that flocked in droves to the piers of the Mexican island.

Ahead, the rival dive boat bounced across a wave. Typical of many six-pack fast-boats on Coz, she had a pair of outboards and a rudimentary canopy to shield the crew and six divers from the brutal tropical sun.

"It's Marino Mundo's fast-boat, *Barco Rápido*," Emily noted. She snorted a laugh. "I love that they named it that. '*Barco*' is actually a name for a *big* ship, which just makes it funnier." She reached back and pinched a blonde pigtail from under her green paisley do-rag, popping it into her mouth for a contemplative chew. "She can hit upwards of thirty, I think."

"On a choppy day, that'd be a problem for us..." Boone began.

"But not today." Em grinned, her perfect teeth pinching the pigtail. She spat it out. "You lords 'n' ladies wanted a fast-boat? You got one!" Em nudged up the throttle. Below, the Caterpillar C 12.9 rumbled and the *Lunasea* leaped forward. The engine was capable of 985 horsepower, but the Delta's hull wasn't designed to take full advantage of it unless the seas were calm. Fortunately for today's group of divers, the seas were glassy.

Boone fished his binoculars out of the compartment beside the wheel and leveled them on the horizon, bracing himself beside Emily. The *Lunasea* typically put to sea a full half hour before most other ops, to better compete with the ones that operated out of the resorts in the south. Most of those were only half the distance to the most popular dive sites. "No one else yet. Looks like we'll be first on site."

"Natch." Em increased speed, ratcheting the *Lunasea* up a few more knots to ensure they overtook the *Barco Rápido*. In minutes they were alongside. Across the way, the skipper sagged and shook his head, a smile on his face. This wasn't the first time "Boonemily" had blown by them. He gestured toward Emily, beckoning as if he were requesting something. "Take the wheel for a tick, Booney."

"Aye aye, *mi capitana*."

Em stepped to the port side as they passed the Marino Mundo's fast-boat. She struck a pose and started pulsing a fist, bobbing her head to a silent beat.

"What is she doing?" Greg asked, his face a tapestry of rapt confusion.

"Interpretive dance." Boone throttled down a bit to give Emily a more stable platform. "Jorge over there took her out dancing and they had a ball. Now, every time we pass them on the morning run, he requests a dance."

"Oh... I thought you and she...?" Cecilia began.

"I'm taking a sabbatical from night clubs," Boone remarked with a half-smile. "I farm those dates out."

Em burst into a flurry of dance moves, spinning expertly as she swung her arms and pulsed her petite body. All the while, she kept her balance on the boat's pitching deck. Over on the *Barco Rápido*, the skipper clapped to Emily's inner beat and the divers aboard hooted and hollered, with more than a few cameras and GoPros capturing the performance. Abruptly, Em stopped and took a bow as Boone throttled up again.

"Budge up," Em prompted, hip-checking Boone aside and taking over the wheel. When Greg and Cecilia applauded, Emily dipped her head to them. "Thank you, thank you, no autographs please."

"You threw in some new stuff this time," Boone said. "But I'm a little sad we didn't get any twerking."

"How dare you, sir!" Emily huffed. "I would never debase my performance with such primitive bum-twitching. Also, I'd likely faceplant on the deck if I tried that while underway."

Boone turned toward the stern railing of the flybridge and called down to the other four members of Greg and Cecilia's group. "All right, folks, start gearing up! We'll be there shortly." Below, the other divers began pulling on wetsuits. At the stern, a local divemaster named Ricardo gave him a thumbs-up.

The *Lunasea* was rated to carry up to twenty-two divers and crew, but Boone and Emily liked to keep things chill, usually booking smaller groups of six to twelve. Many ops were not in a position to make that choice, but the young divemasters weren't hurting for money after their "endowment" from the Belizean government and several cultural institutions. They'd moved to Cozumel six months ago, and rather than signing up for another company and being beholden to someone else's schedule, Boone and Em had struck out on their own, filling out the company with locals and bringing on Ricardo as part-owner. They offered themselves up as a "sub" to other dive ops; if one of them had a boat go down with maintenance problems, or if they simply overbooked, a quick call to Bubble Chasers Diving would bring the *Lunasea* from the Marina Fonatur, south of town. In addition to subbing, they chartered their own dive trips several times a week, catering to groups seeking an uncrowded experience on a roomy dive boat with fast-boat speed.

As Greg and Cecilia climbed down the ladder, Boone slipped up beside Emily and traced his fingertips across the back of her neck, eliciting a shudder. "You wanna stay up top, or shall I?"

"You and Ricardo can get wet on this one," Em said. "I'll do the second dive."

"You sure?"

"Maracaibo can have tricky currents. Can't have you running over our divers. I'll be on bubble duty."

Situated off the coast of the Yucatán Peninsula, the Mexican island of Cozumel was renowned for its drift diving. In most Caribbean islands, dive boats would moor themselves at a site and the divers would enter and make a circuit, heading out from the mooring line against the current before turning around and making their way back to the boat. In Coz, the dives were made on the leeward side of the island, where the channel between the island and the mainland made for strong currents. Rather than mooring, dive boats here would drop the divers at one end of the dive site and then follow their bubbles and a surface marker buoy, picking them up as they surfaced. Some days, the current was strong enough that kicking was scarcely necessary; you reached your depth, adjusted your buoyancy, and just enjoyed the ride.

"You want to do the briefing?" Boone asked.

"I think you and Ricardo can handle it. I already drew the dive site on the whiteboard."

Boone descended the ladder to the deck and grabbed the whiteboard, clipping it temporarily to the ladder rails. Using a rainbow of dry-erase markers, Emily had drawn an elaborate representation of the dive site they had scheduled, complete with eagle rays, turtles, and a blacktip. True to form, she'd added a little fancy, in this case a bright green mermaid with a gold crown, hanging out at the bottom of the arch they'd swim through.

"Okay, we're coming up on Maracaibo! Anyone here dive this before?" Boone was pleased to see all the hands go up. "Well, all right then… I'll give the abbreviated version. This is the southernmost dive site on Cozumel. It's a wall dive, and it's a deep one, so everyone stick close to me or Ricardo. I know you're all advanced divers, but the current can be tricky down here. Fortunately, it's been pretty manageable this week, so we'll give it a shot. There's plenty to see: some big green morays, lots of turtles and stingrays. Since we're at the tip, there's a decent chance you'll see some bigger life down here, so check the blue from time to time. Emily saw some dolphins last time we were here."

That elicited some excited murmurs from the group; many a diver might dive every year for decades and never see one underwater.

"Em will drop us here"—Boone tapped a spot on the drawing—"and we'll descend against the current, heading south along the wall. I'll ask you to stick to the edge of the wall and not drop down until we near the arch."

Cecilia pointed at the mermaid. "Is that…?"

"I have no idea what that is," Boone deadpanned. "This, however, is the arch." He tapped the drawing just above the fish-woman. "We'll descend along the wall to the arch. The base is at 120 feet and that will be our max depth. Ricardo will swim down and up through the arch, following the fissures in the coral that ascend from it. I'll stay above the arch, since I'll have the dive float on a reel, so anyone wanting to remain shallow can stick with me."

Boone went on to detail the remainder of the dive plan while Ricardo scanned the ocean with a practiced eye, looking for any unusual eddies that might indicate unexpected currents. Above, Emily throttled down as the *Lunasea* neared the entry point. With a final flurry, the divers finished gearing up. Minutes later, the group slipped beneath the waves.

"How'd it go?" Emily called down from the flybridge, her voice pitched above the thrum of the engine, as she made adjustments to keep the boat near the ascending divers.

"Great!" Boone brought his gear aboard and turned back to toss the dragline aft, then stepped onto the swim platform to assist the divers who were breaching the surface alongside the boat. Ricardo remained under, Boone having passed off the dive buoy to him. The orange tube bobbed in the waves a short distance off the starboard quarter. "No mermaids, though."

"Oh, they were there," Emily shouted back, mirth coloring her voice. "You just aren't as in tune with nature as I am."

Boone brought the divers up, one by one. They were all experienced, and it didn't take long before everyone was aboard. Ricardo was the last to reach the stern ladder.

"You see the dolphins?" he asked, handing up his fins to Boone.

"Are you kidding me?"

"I guess you didn't, then." The divemaster laughed, climbing up the ladder. Ricardo had been working for Cozumel dive ops since he was a boy, and Boone and Emily had been lucky enough to hire him. Although "hire" was probably the wrong word; Mexican labor laws were strict, and they'd actually brought Ricardo on as co-owner, asking him to staff the rest of the tiny company with locals he knew.

"How many dolphins were there?"

"Only two, in the blue. And they went *wshhht!*" He made a gesture to indicate they'd skimmed past.

Boone had logged thousands of dives and had only spotted dolphins a handful of times. "Oh well, something to keep looking forward to," he said.

"Where do you want to go for the second dive?" Ricardo asked.

"Paraiso. That right, folks?" Boone raised his voice for the dive group. "Paradise Reef, for the shallow dive?"

"Yes!" Cecilia confirmed. "We want some photos of the splendid toadfish."

"Best place to find them," Ricardo said.

Boone ascended the ladder to join Emily at the flybridge helm.

"Paraiso, yeah?" she queried.

"Yep." He began stripping off his wetsuit. "Hope there aren't too many cruise ships in today."

"It's a day that ends in 'Y,' so..."

"Yeah, but maybe it'll be a four-boat day, and not an eight."

"Aren't we the optimist?" Emily throttled up and the *Lunasea* headed north.

After a leisurely trip at a fuel-saving cruising speed of fifteen knots, the southernmost of the three cruise ship piers, Puerta Maya, came into view. There was one cruise ship there currently, and Boone could see a pair at the International Terminal to the north. Paraiso Reef was just to the south of the piers. Boone checked his Aquinus dive watch and went to the stern side of the flybridge so he could address all of the divers, since half were up top, and half below.

"Last dive was a deep one, so we need another twenty minutes of surface time. Just relax for a bit, and I'll let you know when to start gearing up."

"*¡Ay, caramba!*" Ricardo exclaimed. "Look at that one!" He pointed out to sea at a vessel on the approach to the piers, about a half mile out.

Cruise ships coming and going were such a common sight that Boone hadn't given this one any scrutiny, but now that he focused on the newcomer, his jaw dropped. The ship was sleek, long glass windows gleaming across the multi-leveled superstructure, the decks stacked in sloping tiers that climbed toward the bridge, and what were likely some impressive accommodations above that. Reaching down to a compartment beside the wheel, he retrieved his binoculars.

"Is that a cruise ship or a yacht?" Greg asked, shading his sunglasses as he squinted west.

"A little from Column A, a little from Column B," Boone remarked, scanning the ship. "A bit small for a cruise ship, nowadays... but awfully big for a yacht." He focused the binoculars amidships, scanning the ship's side. "She's named the *Apollo*." He swung the lenses toward the stern, where he could make out a blue and white flag fluttering in the ocean breeze. "Greek registry."

"Well, Apollo's a Greek god, right?" Greg pointed out.

"Yeah, but that's probably a 'flag of convenience,'" Emily interjected. "A lot of ship-owners will register their vessels with other countries for fewer regulations or lower taxes. Take that one there." She pointed to the ship docked at the pier nearest to the dive site. "*Nordic Starr*... but that flag's Liberian. Not very 'Nordic.' We see a lot of Liberian flags... Panama and The Bahamas, too. And Greece."

"That looks like a Mexican flag, to me..." Cecilia said, shielding her eyes with her hand as the *Apollo* grew closer.

Boone shifted his binoculars to the superstructure of the newcomer. "That's the courtesy flag," he said, spotting the flag in question flying from the starboard halyard, situated alongside a bulbous radar dome and radio mast. "Ships coming into port fly that as a sign of respect."

Emily pointed. "And below that, you can see a yellow flag, yeah? That's the Q flag. You fly that when your vessel is free of any quarantinable disease."

"So, if you were one of those cruise lines with an outbreak of norovirus on board... you wouldn't fly that." Greg surmised.

"Three points to Greg!" Em said.

"She's got a helicopter pad," Boone noted, as the *Apollo* angled slightly to port, aiming toward the berth opposite the *Nordic Starr*. "Looks like a raised pool area, too... just aft of the..." He trailed off.

Underneath a canopy and alongside some deck-planted palm trees, a stunningly beautiful woman stood with a pair of binoculars of her own, their lenses pointed right at Boone. The *Lunasea* and the *Apollo* were close enough now that the binos weren't necessary, and as Boone lowered his pair, she did the same.

She appeared quite tall, with jet black hair, sunlight shining off it in places. Her lightly tanned skin stood out in sharp contrast to a cobalt blue bikini. As the ship angled toward the pier, the woman turned slightly, stepped down to the rail, and waved to Boone. When he lifted a hand in reply, her face broke into a brilliant smile.

"Give me those." Emily snatched the binoculars from Boone's nerveless fingers. After tucking her lime green sunglasses into the neck of her shirt, she raised the binos to her eyes. "Cor blimey, she's fit 'n' tidy," she breathed.

Greg looked over at her. "She's what?"

"Gorgeous…" Boone said, translating.

Em lowered the binoculars and slapped them to Boone's bare chest. "Right, well, enough gawping. Rehinge your jaw and take the wheel. Time to get wet!"

As Emily descended the ladder to wrangle the divers, Boone looked back toward the *Apollo*, whose bow was now partially obscured as it passed behind the end of the pier. Another woman was standing beside the raven-haired beauty, and apparently she'd done as Emily had with Boone, snatching the pair of binoculars from her counterpart. This one stood a full head shorter than the other woman, her face obscured by a floppy sunhat and oversized sunglasses. The *Apollo* swung slightly to starboard, water frothing from the side of her stern as transverse thrusters below the waterline aided the captain in maneuvering the vessel against the pier. Suddenly both women turned, seeming to speak with someone before walking away from the edge, vanishing from view.

3

Lyra Othonos breathed out an audible sigh as the *Apollo* neared the dock, and the shirtless young man on the gently rolling dive boat below came into better focus. He was exceptionally tall and lean, his well-defined musculature evident even from a distance. An unruly mop of brown hair was frosted with blond highlights, no doubt from his time working in the sun. That this man was a divemaster for the boat was an assumption, of course, but Lyra was fairly sure she was right. As she watched, the man raised a pair of binoculars to his eyes.

"What are you looking at?" a young woman in a floppy sunhat asked from poolside, a note of petulance in her voice. "You've been staring through those things for the last ten minutes."

"He is beautiful," Lyra murmured, her speech kissed with a light accent. *And he's looking right at me.*

Calypso craned her neck around to glance at her older sister. The statuesque beauty had lowered her binoculars and was walking

29

down from the raised pool area toward the starboard rail. With an impatient sigh, Calypso rose from the deck chaise and followed.

Lyra reached the rail of the promenade deck and lowered the binoculars. She waved to the young man and after a moment he raised a hand in reply. Quite of its own accord, her face lit up into a smile.

"Oh, Lyra… found another one, have you?" Calypso said, her voice half-teasing, half-not.

Across the way, a petite blonde snatched the binoculars from the young man's hands and trained them up at the sisters.

Calypso snorted a laugh. "If I'm any judge of character, your Romeo-of-the-day is already spoken for. Quite a tasty little thing, too."

"Oh, Callie," Lyra said, shaking her head.

The blonde on the dive boat pressed the binoculars into the young man's chest and made her way to the flybridge ladder. It was clear to Lyra that she was a divemaster as well, as she began to address the divers, and everyone gave her their attention.

"You know…" Lyra mused dreamily. "I believe I'd fancy a little diving during our stay."

"Maybe they charter." Calypso took the binoculars from her and scanned the boat's flank, bow to stern. "*Lunasea*. Ah, very droll. Behind that it says Bubble Chasers Diving, which I'm assuming is the business. I suppose it could be fun."

"Lyra! Callie!" a voice bellowed from behind them.

Callie groaned and the sisters turned toward the voice. Her brother Achilles was across the pool, dressed in stylish slacks and a crisp white shirt, his arms bulging beneath rolled-up sleeves. The shirt was open to the navel, displaying an expanse of waxed pectorals, his hairless chest sporting a number of gold chains that would make the most egregious stereotype shake his head in disapproval.

"We're over here," Lyra called out from behind the tropical plants that fringed the pool area. Their brother crossed over toward them.

"What do you want, Chilly?" her younger sister asked.

Lyra stifled a laugh. Achilles was so proud of his pompous name and Callie loved to wind him up.

"Stop calling me that, Calypso!"

Lyra sighed. "Callie, be nice." The youngest Othonos had been teasing him with that nickname for as long as Lyra could remember, yet Achilles reacted as if each time were the first. Their eldest brother wasn't the deepest thinker in the family. "Do you need us for something, Achilles?"

"Nicholas has called a meeting."

This time it was Lyra who groaned. Her younger brother, Nicholas, was always assembling them for one thing or another. "What is it about this time?"

"I don't know, but Father's going to be there. The nurses are getting him ready. Nicholas talked him into it."

"I swear, it's like Nicholas thinks he's running the family business..." Calypso said, a half-smile on her lips.

Lyra turned to the side and could see her sister watching their eldest brother intently from behind her overlarge sunglasses.

Achilles reddened, the blush managing to penetrate his carefully cultivated tan. "*I'm* the one who will be running the business once Father passes. Me! It's in the will! That nerd can play at board meetings all he wants—it won't make a difference!"

"Chill, Chilly... we know you're the eldest. You make that clear on a daily basis."

Lyra pinched her younger sister's flank and felt Calypso wince. You could only push Achilles so far before he went ballistic. His jaw was already twitching, so Lyra raised a slender hand and spoke in her musical voice. "We're coming, brother. Just give us a moment to change. The Owner's Suite?"

Achilles jaw softened. "Yes. Fifteen minutes. Thank you, Lyra." He pivoted on his heel and made his way forward along the promenade.

"You really shouldn't tease him like that," Lyra chided. "You know how angry he can get."

"Probably all the steroids," Calypso remarked.

"One day, he'll hold the purse strings, Callie."

"A fact of which I am painfully aware. Come on. Let's get changed into something Father will approve of." Calypso ascended to the poolside seating area and grabbed her book, leaving her towel and drink for the food service crew to deal with.

"What are you reading?" Lyra asked, as she retrieved her sarong from her chaise.

"Something Italian… one of the guests left it." Calypso held it aloft.

Lyra nodded. Most of the family spoke multiple languages. "What happened to the cover?"

"I didn't like the artwork, so I tore it off."

Lyra laughed. "Of course you did." She wrapped the sarong around her waist and the two sisters made their way toward the accommodation decks.

About time. Nicholas Othonos looked down from the wrap-around balcony of the Owner's Suite as his sisters left the pool area. They would stop to change out of their swimsuits, of course, but he estimated the meeting would occur in fifteen minutes, as scheduled. Nicholas valued punctuality, and he had tried very hard to get that trait to rub off on his siblings.

Nicholas was third in the line of succession for the Othonos fortune, ahead of Calypso but behind Achilles and Lyra. Their father, Karras Othonos, had built a shipping empire from the ground up, beginning with a single ship and growing to a substantial fleet. The latest venture had been Nicholas's idea. Branching out from his father's flourishing business in container ships and oil tankers, the company had formed a new corporation— based in the Cayman Islands, of course—and had begun building cruise ships. But not just any cruise ships.

Rather than targeting the hoi polloi who swarmed the gigantic ships of the major cruise lines, these vessels were designed to cater to a very specific clientele: multi-millionaires who wished they were billionaires. Most cruise ships these days had more in common with a Vegas hotel than the elegant liners of yesteryear. Nicholas's idea was Olympus Cruises, a small fleet of mega-yachts and giga-yachts offering "a billionaire experience" to a select passenger list. Although they were still ironing out the exact dollar amount of assets to warrant a ticket, the demand had been sufficient to allow only eight-figure earners aboard. This worked out very well for the high-stakes gambling in the multi-room casino. In addition, investment opportunities were on offer: the Othonos family owned a Cayman bank with an offshore branch onboard each Olympus ship, and Nicholas himself had used his considerable high-tech skills to design their very own cryptocurrency.

Nicholas took a deep breath of salt-filled air as he looked down at the elegant aft promenade of the newest entry to the fleet, the *Apollo*. This was her maiden voyage, her sea trials having been completed last month. Her sister ships were off on cruises elsewhere: *Zeus* was in the Cyclades Islands in the Aegean. Nicholas checked his watch. She should be docking in Santorini shortly. The *Poseidon* was in the Pacific, bound for Bali, and *Athena* was in the Western Mediterranean, currently transiting the Strait of Gibraltar on her journey between Mallorca and the Canaries. The *Artemis* had just begun construction in the Netherlands.

One major advantage of their smaller size: many islands that didn't permit cruise ships *could* let in Olympus vessels. They were officially designated as "yachts," and even Venice had allowed the *Zeus* to include the city center on her itinerary—although that had required a little behind-the-scenes incentive.

She's magnificent! Nicholas thought as his eyes glided across the elegant lines of the *Apollo*. His gaze came to an abrupt halt as he looked to starboard at their hideous neighbor across the Puerta Maya pier. Indeed, the *Nordic Starr* was the subject of their meeting.

A rattling cough from the suite drew Nicholas back inside. Closing the enormous sliding glass doors with a tap on the control panel, he made his way to his father's side.

"I'm here, Father."

Karras Othonos was a shadow of the man he once was. While still among the wealthiest shipping magnates in the world, the one-time jetsetter and playboy was now wheelchair-bound, his body ravaged by several named illnesses, and at least one that hadn't yet received a moniker. Holding an oxygen mask in a death grip, he coughed again. When Nicholas reached out to assist, the Othonos patriarch angrily raised a hand and coughed a third time, with purpose. Satisfied that the phlegm was now better situated, he nodded with satisfaction.

"Where is your brother?" Karras rasped, before taking a brief pull off the oxygen and holstering the mask.

"He should be here any minute."

"That 'minute' is now!" a voice boomed from across the vast, open-plan suite.

"Achilles, my boy!" Karras turned his chair toward the newcomer and held his arms out, inviting a hug.

Nicholas stepped aside to allow his father to greet the eldest son. *The favorite son...* he thought bitterly.

"*Kaliméra*, Father!" Achilles gave him a spirited hug—vigorous enough to elicit a couple more coughs. But Karras recovered and gave a pair of alternating cheek-kisses to his son.

"So good to see you up and about," Achilles said. "You're looking well."

"That is what I like about you, my son... you are a terrible liar. I detest duplicity."

"Sorry we're late," Lyra said, entering the suite with Calypso, the pair of sisters dressed in demure tropical dresses.

"My girls, good to see you both." Karras beamed and greeted them as he had Achilles.

Nicholas made his way to a chair on the side of the polished mahogany dining table, wincing a bit at the pain in his hip as he sat. Achilles wheeled his father to one end that was chairless and seated himself across from the patriarch. Calypso slid into the chair across from Nicholas and Lyra came over to him and kissed him atop his head.

"How are you today, Nicholas?"

"Fair to middling."

"And the leg?"

"Fine. Thank you for asking, Lyra."

After Lyra was seated, Nicholas began. "The reason I've called you all here—"

"Wait," Achilles interrupted. "I've got some... what is it called? Old business? Stupid parliamentary rules of order..."

Nicholas sighed and sat back.

"Your cryptocurrency..." Achilles began.

"Yes, Croesus Coin. The Croesids. It's all going very w—"

"It's a stupid name."

Nicholas regarded his brother silently for a moment, and then let out a long sigh. "I thought we went over this. Given our lineage, the name is perfect. Croesus was—"

"Yeah, yeah, we all know," Achilles interrupted. "Richest man in ancient Greece, blah blah blah, rich as Croesus."

"Nice to know you were paying attention."

"And he minted the first coins in the world..."

"No, Achilles. The first *pure-gold* coins, the Croeseids... which, for the individual encrypted monetary units, I've simplified to Croesids—"

"Not simple enough. I tried to explain it to some of my mates, and... look, no one knows how to pronounce all that. Let's just call them Midas Bucks."

Nicholas felt a vein in his temple pulse, but he kept his tone level. "Midas... Bucks..."

"Yeah. Like King Midas? Guy who turned stuff to gold?"

"I know who King Midas is."

"Yeah, see? Most people do!"

Nicholas sighed. "The problem with that... we're trying to cater to the richest, most exclusive clientele. And 'Midas Bucks'... well... it sounds like toy money a hick might win at a fairground."

Achilles reddened. "Look, Nicky, you're not in charge..."

"Nor are you."

"Not y—" Achilles managed to stop himself. "Father should decide. Or we should vote!"

"Excuse me, Nicholas?" Lyra spoke up, her soothing tones gliding between the heated words. "I'm not the most tech-savvy, and I confess the business side of all of this is not something I'm comfortable with, but... well... wouldn't changing the name require a complete overhaul of the systems? Perhaps costing us a great deal of money?"

Bless you, sister. Always the peacemaker. "Yes, Lyra. A name change now would create a significant disruption. Especially since we've taken advantage of the extraordinary returns and invested a substantial amount of our company assets into our proprietary cryptocurrency."

Thankfully, Karras ended the spat. "In that case, we will keep the name. Nicholas has already explained just how lucrative this digital money is." The elder Othonos spoke with strong remnants of the Greek language tugging at his English. Lyra and Achilles retained some as well, but Nicholas had worked hard to strip it from his speech. Calypso, too, could pass for an American. Karras coughed and waved his hand. "Let's move on to the reason you called this meeting, my son. I'm getting tired."

"Of course. Well, as you know, the entire point of Olympus Cruises is that we cater to the wealthy. The crème de la crème of society." He rose from the table and walked toward the starboard side of the room. "We want the entire experience to be luxurious, so you can understand why I would prefer we not be docked across from *that*." He pointed out the wraparound window at the *Nordic Starr.*

The view that greeted the Othonos family was that of a cruise ship that had seen better days. Rust was apparent in many locations, including little streaks beneath nearly every porthole. The radar atop the bridge looked like it belonged in the previous century, and a trip in one of the launches or lifeboats that were clustered amidships would likely be a coin-flip as to whether any were seaworthy. Prominent along the flank at the stern, a long scrape indicated a failed attempt at docking at some point in her past. An attempt to cover this scar had been unsuccessful, as the coat of paint didn't quite match the surrounding hull.

"Is it one of that Icelandic company's ships?" Calypso asked. "That cheap 'no frills' cruise line?"

"Yes! Hygge Cruises," Nicholas spat the name. "A company designed from the ground up to emulate the budget airlines... but for cruises. Bargain basement prices for bargain basement people. Exactly the opposite of what *we* are... and half our passengers will have a view of *that* for the next few days. And every time they walk to shore on the pier, they'll be mingling with that ship's low-rent clientele."

"Oh, no, no, no... that won't do at all!" Karras protested, his words transitioning into a coughing fit. Lyra rose and attended to him until he recovered.

Nicholas returned to the table. "That particular vessel was involved in an incident in Saint Martin, shortly before Hurricane Irma." He flipped open a folder. "An emergency order went out for all ships to put to sea. Apparently, the captain..." He scanned a file. "Captain Olaf Björnson... failed to remove one of the lines, and the ship swung sideways, smashing into an adjacent vessel and wedging itself in. Guess who the current captain is?"

"The same man?" Calypso posited, incredulous.

"Unbelievable, isn't it? Particularly since Scandinavian crews are widely considered to be among the best in the cruise industry." Nicholas closed the file. "I wonder if the Cozumel Harbor Master is aware of the ship's history?"

Karras barked a cough-laugh. "I assume you will try to get rid of her, then?"

"As soon as possible, and I'd like to reach out to some of your shipping contacts. See if we can't jump this up the chain. With your permission, of course."

Karras waved his hand in assent.

"Excellent. I'll attend to it, then. Now, if there's nothing else…"

Achilles cleared his throat. "Actually, I've got some stuff I want to… um… shit, one sec… I have it somewhere."

Nicholas watched as his brother searched his pockets. *Probably scribbled some illegible notes on a napkin while snorting coke at that nightclub back in Tampa,* he thought with disgust. He looked at the faces of his family. His father, the mighty magnate, now a withered husk of his former self. Achilles, the favorite son, more brawn than brains, more interested in the money than the work, and with all the business acumen of a kid running a lemonade stand. Lyra, a free spirit who would be content to simply travel the globe, discovering new worlds and new loves. And Calypso. Who knew what she wanted? The youngest was an odd girl, but the few times she'd shown interest in the business, she had demonstrated promise. *But not as much promise as me,* Nicholas thought bitterly. He had read his father's will and knew that no matter what he did for the company, the future was in doubt.

As Nicholas Othonos looked around the table at his brother and sisters, a smile came to his lips. Things were about to change.

4

"Oh, oh, oh! This one! It's the best of all!"

Emily looked up to find Cecilia's eyes glued to the back of her Nikon D850 camera inside its underwater housing. The diver had been adamant about getting some great shots of the splendid toadfish, and fortunately for her, Paraiso Reef was the best place to spot them. Emily had found six for the excited photographer. They had just completed the dive, and as soon as her gear was stowed, Cecilia had grabbed her camera from the freshwater rinse tub and started advancing through the pictures. Emily was a bit of a shutterbug herself and leaned over to look. "That shot is ace!" she exclaimed. "Brilliant colors, yeah?"

The Cozumel splendid toadfish was one of the most unique-looking fish in the Caribbean, with a purple head and body decorated in vivid light and dark stripes, its fins edged in bright yellow. Protruding eyes sat atop a flat head, and barbels fringed the mouth, putting one in mind of a catfish.

Greg came to peer over Emily's shoulder. "And that fish is only found here, right?"

"Well, that's what I always thought, but an oceanographer here set me straight. Apparently, it's been seen in one spot in Belize, an offshore atoll called Glover's Reef."

Boone was nearby, and chimed in. "Em and I worked in Belize for a while, and never heard of these being down there… but we didn't get to Glover's very often. Too far south from where our dive op was." He pointed out to sea. "They've actually got some splendid toads across the channel in Playa del Carmen, too. But nowhere near as many as here."

"Too bad we didn't see any out in the open," Cecilia lamented.

"Shy little buggers, they are," Emily said. "During the day, you pretty much only see them in hidey-holes under the coral, just their heads showing. But if you like, we could bring you back here for a night dive. After dark, we see them hunting along the coral, out in the open. Sometimes we hear them grunting and croaking."

"Really?" Cecilia turned to the rest of the group. "Whattaya think, gang? Can we hold off drinking 'til tonight? Do a night dive?"

"Paraiso is the best spot in Cozumel for a night dive," Boone remarked. "Octopus, lobsters, free-swimming eels…"

"Mermaids…" Emily interjected. Boone clapped a hand over her mouth and Emily giggled into his palm.

"And if we don't see any free-swimming splendid toads, Em here will buy your drinks at No Name."

Em emitted muffled protests before slapping Boone's bare stomach with the flat of her hand.

"Ow!"

"That's what you get for muzzling my free expression. Ooh! I see a handprint! That means I get to make a wish!"

"I'll get you for that later," Boone said with a laugh.

"I *wish*... you would..." Emily said, a half-smile on her lips, dimples teasing the corners of her mouth. She plucked her sunglasses from her shirt, veiling her green eyes behind them as she headed for the flybridge ladder. Once up top, she joined Ricardo at the wheel.

"Good dive?" Ricardo asked.

"Current was a bit wonky, but we saw some nice beasties. Didn't like the look of some algae in a few spots, though."

Ricardo nodded. "*Si*, I have seen it too. This site is so close to the cruise ship piers... someone may have been dumping waste."

Emily sighed. The cruise ship industry did a lot for the island, but it also put a strain on the most valuable asset Cozumel had to offer: its reefs. Fuel, illegal dumping, sunscreens—all of it combined to make coral vulnerable to outbreaks of disease. In late 2019, Mexico had actually closed the most popular southern dive sites for several months in an effort to stem an outbreak of disease among the corals. Even now, some sites were given "rest periods," usually during coral spawning windows.

"At least we don't have much of the sargassum over here," Ricardo offered, referring to the vast swaths of yellowish seaweed that had blanketed many beaches across the Caribbean.

"True! Playa del Carmen is getting it all, poor buggers." She motioned toward the wheel. "Why don't you take us in? They're staying at Hotel Barracuda." She grabbed the radio. "Head for Dive Paradise. I'll make sure they've got room for a drop off. If not, we can go to Aqua Safari's pier."

One of the advantages of being a sub for numerous dive ops on the island was that it made it easier to "borrow some dock" from time to time for pick-ups and drop-offs. In moments, they were on their way, looping out into the channel to go north around the big cruise piers.

"What is that word?" Ricardo pointed to the side of the nearest cruise ship. The words "Hygge Cruises" were emblazoned in fading paint, along with a hazy picture of something that might have been a troll, or an elf... or a garden gnome on acid. "That word is strange. H-Y-G-G-E?"

"Oh, I read about that... it was all the rage on the internet a couple years back. It's pronounced..." Emily pursed her lips into a tiny "o" and squeezed the sound out, "'Hyooooguh.' It's a Danish word for anything cozy. You know... sitting by a roaring fire while it's snowing outside, drinking hot chocolate under a fuzzy blanket while you watch a movie with your mates...?"

Ricardo raised an eyebrow from behind his sunglasses. "You realize I'm from Cozumel, right? We don't have a lot of snowy days or roaring fires."

"Well, Bob's your uncle then, 'cause hygge can be whatever *you* find cozy. How 'bout... curling up on a beach chair with your bare feet shoved under the sand, a margarita in your hand, and your wife beside you, looking up at the Milky Way?"

"That... that I could do."

Boone joined them on the flybridge. "Kinda funny, that old dinosaur of a cruise ship being across the pier from the *Apollo*." He pointed to the *Nordic Starr* as they passed it. "And I don't speak any Viking languages, but I'm pretty sure sticking an extra 'r' on the end of 'star' doesn't make it Nordic."

"True. An extra ARRRrrrrr might make it a pirate ship, though," Emily said, lapsing into pirate-speak. "Isn't that right, Ricaaarrrrrrdo?"

Ricardo laughed. "I need to get you a parrot for your shoulder."

"I'll settle for a little yo-ho-ho and a bottle of rum."

Boone was looking up at the *Apollo* as they passed its stern.

"Thar be no black-haired siren over yonder, me matey," Emily teased.

Boone turned, a sheepish grin on his face. "Sorry. Oh, hey, Greg said they can't swing the night dive tonight—one of the other couples has reservations. Wants to know if we can take them tomorrow night."

"Fine by me. Ricardo?"

"*Si*, no problem."

"We good to go?" Greg asked, poking his head up the ladder.

"Yep," Boone said. "We'll grab you from the Dive Paradise pier at six p.m. tomorrow. One side of the dock is usually clear by then, but if they're busy, I'll message you an alternate spot."

◆ ◆ ◆

After dropping off the group of Kansans at Hotel Barracuda, Emily skippered the *Lunasea* south to the Marina Fonatur, one of three marinas on the island and the only one that Boone and Emily had been able to find a berth in. When they learned the monthly cost, Emily had joked that they might need to go find another archaeological treasure before the end of the year.

After they tied up, Boone counted out the cash from their tips, giving a third to Ricardo… and then an additional pair of twenties from his and Emily's portion.

Ricardo frowned. "What is this?"

"For Lupe. For taking care of our little buddy."

"Oh, no, no… my wife loves your dog! And our Elvis likes to have someone to play with… even if he's much, much older than Brixton." He tried to hand back the money.

Emily intervened. "Ricarrrrrrrrdo, take the doubloons or I'll make you walk the plank. Yar."

Ricardo snorted a laugh. "Very well." He pocketed one bill, then took Emily's hand and slapped the other into it. "And this is for you, for taking care of Elvis last week."

"Oooooh, you cheeky bastard."

They headed for the parking lot and soon reached a pair of cars parked side by side. Boone and Emily had arrived separately that morning, with Boone making a coffee and pastry run while Emily dropped off Brixton and picked up Ricardo.

Emily gestured grandly. "Your chariots await! The choice is yours, Ricardo. Choose wisely."

Ricardo's choices were both Volkswagen convertibles, but that was where the similarities ended. Emily's car was a Beetle, one that had come off the assembly line at the factory in Puebla, Mexico. It shone in her color of choice, a bright green, with a black fabric top that dropped down in the back and a smaller cover over the front seats that could be rolled up above the windshield. Emily had, of course, seen to it that the two straps of Velcro on that roll had a little something extra attached: a pair of large googly eyes stared ahead from it when it was rolled up. She had christened it "Señor Bug."

Boone's vehicle was far, far older, built at the same Puebla plant: a 1979 Volkswagen Thing. Bright yellow, its steel body all right angles, the boxy little automobile looked like a cross between a German military staff car and something you might take on safari back in the sixties. Devoid of any amenities, the vehicle's windows were completely removable, and the windshield itself was hinged and could be lowered down onto the hood. The canvas top folded into the back. Fortunately for Boone, this museum piece had been lovingly restored. Apparently, used Things had been quite popular on Cozumel in the eighties and nineties, and a few mechanics still had parts.

Ricardo pretended to think about it for all of two seconds before pointing at Emily's Beetle. "I choose to live."

"Excellent choice," Emily said, dropping the back cover and putting her gear bag on the back seat. Ricardo followed suit. Both cars had been covered, unpredictable pop-up showers being the norm in the tropics. "Boone, you follow in the Deathmobile."

Boone looked aghast. "Quiet! She's very sensitive."

"You don't need to tell me," Em said. "If you *look* at it wrong, the door is liable to fall off. That thing is a car crash in car form. Automotive heresy from bonnet to boot."

As Ricardo slapped Boone on the shoulder, she heard him whisper, "I like your crazy car... but Emily is more fun."

"Won't get any argument from me," Boone said with a smile.

Ricardo got in beside Emily as she started up. Beside them, Boone's Thing coughed to life, eventually stabilizing into a throaty rumble. The two cars left the marina, heading north.

"Is it strange for you to drive on the right side of the road?" Ricardo asked.

"What, 'cause I'm British? Nah, not really. When I was in London I never drove, just took the tube, taxi, or bus. I know a lot of the islands in the Caribbean drive on the left, thanks to my people colonizing the bejeezus out of everything, but oddly enough I haven't worked on any of those. I spent a fair bit of time driving in Bonaire. They're Dutch, so they're on the right, and that's what I'm used to."

"What kind of car did you have there?"

"Oh, she was a beauty! Bright green Jeep Wrangler Cabrio. Loved it. I kinda-sorta ran off with Boone and left her behind. Ended up selling her to a mate on the island. He said if I ever return to Bonaire, I could buy her back. Seems like a fair deal to me!"

"You like this car, then?"

"Oh, I'm all about my Bug, now! I suspect there may be some hippie in my ancestry."

"The Volkswagen plant on the mainland—they stopped making them, I heard."

"I know! September, 2019... sad to hear that, yeah? But there are so many of these on Coz, in every color you can imagine. Figure I'll have no problem finding spare parts. Boone, on the other hand..." She looked into her rearview mirror. "Well, whattaya know, that old banger is still behind us. I keep waiting for it to spontaneously dissolve in a cloud of rust, leaving Boone sitting in the road with a steering wheel."

"I like Boone's Thing."

Emily burst into laughter. "Oh, my... watch your phrasing there, Ricardo."

Ricardo reddened, a grin on his face. "I have to be careful what I say around you."

"No, please don't! I live to tease. Don't deprive me of my sustenance."

In minutes they were entering the Flamingos neighborhood in the south of San Miguel and Emily pulled up to a tiny yellow house with a small, gated yard that wrapped around the back. Excited barking greeted Emily's ears as she turned off the engine. The yellow Thing puttered to a stop behind her.

A brown blur whipped around the side of the house and came to the fence, the dog bouncing on his hind legs with barely contained joy.

"Brixton! Hello! Hello! Mummy's back!"

"Hey Brix, how ya doin', buddy?" Boone said as he exited his car.

The dog ratcheted up his jubilation to eleven on the dial and barked happily, tail wagging furiously, as Boone and Emily opened the fence a little, squeezing in while Ricardo ran inside to find Lupe.

Brixton was a potlicker pup Boone and Emily had rescued on the Belizean island of Caye Caulker. A short-haired brown mutt descended from many generations of strays on the island, Brixton was likely the runt of the litter, weighing in at twenty pounds. He was thought to be about two years old, but that number was a guess. His ears pointed up, but were bent over at the tips, flopping a bit when he jumped.

"Who's a good boy?" Emily piped in a falsetto pitch.

Brixton affirmed that it was in fact "he" who was the good boy by licking Emily's nose.

A muffled woof sounded from the little porch as Elvis trundled down the two steps to join them. A senior dog, Elvis still had some spunk in him, and he wagged his tail, looking for some attention from the newcomers.

"He loves Brixton so much, they play and play," Lupe said as she joined them, the newest member of the family on her hip, a bright-eyed babe named Eduardo.

"*Gracias*, Lupe," Boone said. "Hey, slugger."

The boy looked up at Boone, who towered over them, wonder in his eyes.

"Eat your mom's cooking, you'll grow up big 'n' strong!" Boone offered a fist and the boy smiled, remembering the ritual. He bumped it with a half-clenched fist.

"Would you like to have dinner with us?" Lupe asked.

"We would," Emily said, "but we promised Ricardo's uncle we'd meet him at the No Name Bar."

"And you didn't invite me," Ricardo said, stone-faced. He sighed. "You never invite me."

"Oh... sorry, Ricardo..." Em stuttered. Then she caught a little tremble at the side of his lip. "Waiiiiiit, are you having a laugh?"

Ricardo grinned. "I can tease too, *loba*."

Emily wagged a playful finger at him. "Nicely done. Wait, what did you just call me?"

Lupe laughed. "It's a good word. *'Loba'* means she-wolf, but the way Ricki used it, it means, um... 'clever girl'?"

"Oh! Like *Jurassic Park*!" Emily gushed. "The actor who said that line? Bob Peck. Y'know, he was a Brit! Used to act with the Royal Shakespeare Company. I am a fount of useless information."

"Good thing she's as good with fish identification as trivia," Boone said as he opened the gate. "Thanks again for watching Brix."

"*De nada*," Lupe said.

"Nothing on the schedule tomorrow?" Ricardo asked them.

"No, just the night dive," Emily replied. "We'll pick you up at five, yeah?"

"See you then."

Emily watched as Boone got into the Thing and opened the passenger door, smiling knowingly at her as she reached her VW Bug. "Here, Brix!" she called. "C'mere boy!"

Brixton trotted forward, tail wagging... and hopped into Boone's car. There he sat, facing Emily and panting happily.

"Would you get that for me, Em?" Boone asked, nodding to the passenger door. "Brix looks so comfortable, I don't want to reach across him."

Em held his gaze as she sauntered to the Thing and gently closed the door.

Boone shrugged. "What can I say? The pooch has great taste in classic cars."

"Good thing he loves me more, or I might be jealous. What's that, boy?" She leaned in to Brix, getting an ear-lick as she pretended to listen. "You say you're only going with Boone because you're afraid he'll cry if you go with me?" She turned to face him. "Well, that's very empathetic of you, Brixy, looking out for Boone's fragile ego like that. What a good boy!" She returned to her car. "See you back at the flat. Call if you break down."

5

The No Name Bar Beach Club was advertised as "For Crew by Crew." Long a popular hangout for crew members from the cruise ships, the bar had its share of dive op staff who frequented it. Located alongside the pool of the Hotel Barracuda, it also catered to the hotel guests. The Hotel Barracuda was popular with divers, and had been rebuilt after the original had been completely destroyed during Hurricane Wilma, an event that had required a harrowing rescue of guests by Mexican sailors from the nearby naval base.

Boone and Emily sat beside the pool, finishing the last of their dinners. Across from them, Santiago Pérez, Ricardo's uncle, set his knife and fork on the plate.

"*Delicioso!* Who would have suspected this place would have Turkish food? I've never had it before. Very good!"

"They've got dishes from all over," Emily said. And indeed, the crew bar's eclectic menu was decorated with a border of national flags, the menu items themselves playfully named for the many different job titles found aboard cruise ships. Em took a final bite of her chef's salad. "Mm, mm, that is one tasty Safety Officer! How's your Chief Purser, Boone?"

Boone chuckled around a mouthful of cheeseburger. "Juicy."

Santiago finished his cerveza. "Thank you for inviting me—this has been a good meeting. We would certainly welcome your dive operation's assistance in a weekly cleanup. And I will put in for a license for you to charter lionfish cull dives."

Ricardo's uncle worked for Cozumel's Marine Park and was heavily involved in the island's efforts to walk back some of the damage that had been done to the reef by the explosion in cruise ship traffic. Boone and Emily had asked him there to learn how they could help. As the waiter cleared the dishes, Santiago stood to shake their hands. The divemasters now had tentative plans to schedule weekly cleanup dives, and offer lionfish hunts to divers with the proper training—training that Bubble Chasers could provide. Just like everywhere else in the Caribbean, the highly invasive species needed to be controlled.

"You sure you can't stay for afters?" Emily asked.

Boone chuckled when Santiago cocked his head. "She means dessert."

"*Gracias*, but no… my wife has made a pineapple cake and it is my favorite! Besides, you were already generous enough to buy my dinner."

"Our pleasure," Boone said.

After he left, Emily dropped back down into her chair. "Well, I for one am going to finish my mango-rita and order some baklava!"

Just then Emily's smartphone rang, the old-style telephone sound indicating the call was coming in on the business line. Boone had suggested Emily add the second line for Bubble Chasers on her phone, since she was by far the better salesperson. Em's South London accent didn't hurt, either. Provided the callers could understand her, they frequently found it charming.

"Bit late for a business call," Boone remarked. "You can let it go to voicemail if you like."

"As the holder of the business mobile, I say we answer." She tapped the screen, her face lighting up as if the caller could see her. "Bubble Chasers Diving—we make your underwater dreams come true. This is Emily." Em listened for a moment, her brow knitting ever so slightly as she lowered the phone and handed it to Boone. "It's for you."

Boone took the phone. "This is Boone Fischer."

"Hello, Mr. Fischer. I have been looking at your website. You are the owner of Bubble Chasers Diving, yes?" The voice had a light accent that Boone was unable to place.

"Umm... co-owner... you were just talking to my partner."

"Oh, well, since I have you... I was wondering if we might charter a dive with you tomorrow."

Boone looked up at Emily. "Tomorrow? It's a bit short notice..."

Emily shrugged, noisily sucking up the last of her mango margarita through a straw.

The voice continued. "Of course, and please forgive my rudeness, calling so late and so last minute. We just arrived this afternoon and we're only here for a few days. I've read your Tripadvisor reviews and you are highly recommended."

"Well, we aim to please, Miss...?"

"My name is Lyra. Please, I simply must dive tomorrow. I can pay double your rate for the inconvenience."

Boone's eyebrows shot up and Emily leaned in, her expression saying, "What?"

Boone rubbed his fingers and thumb together, signaling money. "That's very generous, thank you… and I believe we can accommodate you. How many are you?"

"Just two. My sister and I."

"Only two? We usually charter for a minimum of four divers…"

"Oh… well then, how about we pay as if we are twelve. Would that be acceptable?"

Boone briefly thought of protesting that was too much, but he sensed this person would never miss it. "That's very generous, thank you. I'm assuming you've dived before?"

"Yes. We are SSI certified."

"Scuba Schools International, good. I'll need you to bring your logbooks and certification cards. Do you need to rent any equipment?"

"No thank you, we have everything we need."

"Where are you staying?"

The voice on the phone hesitated. "We… we are staying near the southern cruise ship piers. But we can come to you. We have access to a car. Where is your boat?"

"It's actually in a marina just south of there. Marina Fonatur." Boone spelled the name out for her. "There's parking just beyond the traffic circle. We're on Pier 4, down at the end. Boat's name is the *Lunasea*."

Their new client laughed—a very appealing sound, almost melodious. "I like that name."

"We're quite fond of it too. We like to leave early. Would you be able to get there at eight?"

"Uhm… one moment." Boone could hear her speaking to someone else, and a groan and a sigh were quite audible. Lyra came back on the line. "Yes, we will be there at eight," she said with finality.

"Great! We'll see you then."

"You will be diving with us, yes? You're not one of those owners who sits behind a desk?"

Boone smiled. "Uh… no, I'm not much of a desk type. If the boat's out, I'm on it. I don't always dive every dive. We switch off—"

"But you will dive the dives with us tomorrow." It was said politely but it wasn't a question.

"Sure. You're paying well. I'll dive all the dives."

"Wonderful! Until tomorrow, Boone."

Emily had been watching him intently during the conversation and now she tilted her head to the side. "Well…?"

Boone handed her the phone back. "I think tomorrow's going to be an interesting day."

———◆·◆———

"I could get used to this," Stallion sighed from the hot tub out on the balcony.

Angler looked over at the man. Stallion was immersed nearly to his chin, his prominent Adam's apple bobbing on the surface of the water like a mooring ball. Angler chuckled inwardly. *Nah, not a mooring ball… a golf ball. Looks like he swallowed one but wasn't entirely successful.* Still, Stallion was an expert marksman and Angler was glad to have him on the team. *Maybe it's those bug-eyes of his that makes him such a crack shot.* If it weren't for the man's epilepsy, Stallion would likely have been a top sniper in any one of the armed services. That being said, Angler had kept a close eye on him when they rappelled down to the ship. That flashing IR strobe their contact had left to mark the entry point could have triggered an episode.

"*Bozhe moi*, this vodka is to kill for," Tolstoy said, smacking his lips. The Russian had made short work of the lock on the minibar and was currently testing a bottle of Chopin Potato Vodka.

"The phrase is 'to die for,' Russkie," Potluck said from the open door to the balcony. "Oh, jeez, how long do we have to stay cooped up here, eh? I wish we could go out and get some great Mexican food. Bet they do great tacos." Potluck's rural Wisconsin accent turned the word into "tack-os."

Angler shifted in his seat in the common area. "Our credentials will hold up to a cursory examination, but we have to keep a low profile until we sail again. Our employer was clear about that."

"That's not for three days!"

"What, you don't like the service of room?" Tolstoy teased. "You could have made me fool… you order half of menu already."

"I'm not the one with the belly, Boris. I exercise." Potluck turned and flexed. Her tank top did nothing to hide the impressive musculature that leaped to the fore. "Boss, why did we bring this commie?"

Angler shrugged. "Because he's good." And the ex-merc from the Russian military contractor, the Wagner Group, was extremely skilled at hacking and lockpicking—what he jokingly called "digital lockpicking and analog hacking." A clever turn of phrase, considering how atrocious the man was at English idioms.

"*Nyet*, I am not good, I am best. If you need break in to ship systems… or the cabinet of liquor," he added, waggling the bottle of vodka, "I am the king of the pile."

"Yeah, you Russkies are good at hacking," Stallion said. "Too bad you ain't as good at fighting."

"Pfeh… ask Germans at Stalingrad if we no good at fighting."

"Oh, sure, maybe *then*... but weren't you in that Russian mercenary group in Syria? Kinda like our Blackwater or KBR... the one our boys blew the crap out of when you came at us? What was it...?"

"Wag-nur," Potluck supplied.

"Vahg-nur," Tolstoy corrected. "Like German opera composer."

"Why is a Russian company named after a German?" Potluck mused.

"Is long story, not important. But yes, I was there at battle of Kasham." Tolstoy topped off his shot glass. "We support Syrian Army Unit going after ISIL fighters but we get too close to United States Special Forces. They call in artillery and airstrikes. But there not be so many casualties as corrupt American media say. And if two minutes more, I be able take control of American Predator drone. Then things be very different."

"What happened?" Stallion asked from the hot tub, blinking his bulbous eyes with what appeared to be genuine interest.

"My transmitter truck destroyed. I am told American AC-130 gunship was vectored onto my signal. I survive, but my leader not want to take blame, so he throw me under the train. Tell superiors we lose because of me." Tolstoy stared into the shot glass. "Fuck it. My skills wasted in Syria." He drained the glass. "This job... much better. After this, I will retire."

"Same here," Stallion said. "Hey boss, any idea yet who exactly is paying for this?"

"I don't know, and I don't need to know," Angler said. "The digital currency is real enough and I was able to access the down payment portion of it with no difficulty. Already shifted it to my Swiss account."

"*Da*, I as well," Tolstoy said with a yawn. "And I did a little snooping in the code..."

Angler shot up from the plush chair. "Don't! He made it very clear that—"

"Keep your clothing on," Tolstoy said, raising a calming hand. "I was very careful, and I was only making sure remainder of currency was legitimate. It is."

Angler ground his teeth. "Our employer said that any attempt to discover his identity would make the contract null and void. And there was certainly an implication that further bad things would happen."

"I know, I know… I did not dig further. The encryption was top notch, anyway."

"Goddammit, Tolstoy, don't screw this up!" Potluck shouted. "I'm planning to retire after this, too!"

"Take a pill to chill! Is okay. I cover digital footsteps."

"But this room is probably bugged!"

"Oh, it is." Tolstoy rose to his feet and walked over to a lamp. "Here…" He moved over to a table. "…and under here. And one in bathroom and one in each bedroom. I redirected their signal to a looping file of room tone. It will sound like we don't enjoy talk much."

Stallion cleared his throat, his Adam's apple snapping up and back. "Won't messing with those bugs piss off our employer?"

"I asked him to do it," Angler said. "Nothing in our agreement said anything about bugs. We need some control here. Once we put to sea again, we set things in motion and there'll be no going back. If things go south and the mission's looking like a soup sandwich, I wanna be able to talk freely about what we're gonna do about it."

Stallion relaxed. "All right. I trust you, boss." He settled back into the hot, jetting water. "Hey, can we order massages? I think I may have turned my ankle a bit during the insertion."

Angler snorted. "Nice try. You've been walking fine."

"Seems kinda stupid we came in that way. Couldn't we have just posed as passengers or crew?"

"Do you have any idea the level of security even a run-of-the-mill cruise ship has? And this one, with its uber-rich clientele… even more so. But now that we're aboard, Palantir can provide us IDs that can piggyback onto existing crew and passengers, once he's established their routines and patterns. Until then… we stay put."

6

"You get the Mexican Coke?" Emily called out to Boone from aboard the *Lunasea*.

Ricardo gave a laugh from the stern. "You know... here, it's just Coke."

"You know what I meant. The one in the glass bottle, with sugar instead of corn syrup."

"Well, whatever you call it, I got it," Boone said as he carried the cooler along the pier to their berth. "I also got that apple soda you like, Ricardo. Plus a few other extras. Figure they're paying us a pretty penny, might as well have something beyond oranges and soda."

"Nothing wrong with a sugary soda and some fruit after a long dive!" Emily remarked.

"True." Boone stepped across from the pier, carrying the heavy cooler with ease.

"What sort of nosh ya get?" Em asked, opening up the cooler to see for herself.

"Usual apples and oranges, but also some sandwiches, couple salads…"

"Oh my… Pineapple empanadas for afters! And what's this, San Pellegrino? You went all out."

"For the amount they're paying, we can splurge. Whatever's left, Ricardo can give to Lupe."

"What an excellent plan," Ricardo offered. "I approve."

Emily went up to the flybridge to check the gauges while Boone remained below to run through their checklist. He started up the ladder, popping his head above the top rung. "Hey Em, do we have any—?"

"Oh, you have got to be kidding," she interrupted.

"What?"

Em looked down at him, her face a mix of amusement and bewilderment. "Our charter guests have arrived."

Boone came up the rest of the way and joined her at the wheel. Strolling down the pier were two figures that were immediately familiar to him. One was tall, dressed in a flowing beach kimono decorated in cherry blossoms, her jet-black hair stark against the sheer, white silk. She walked with grace, despite the sizeable gear bag slung over one shoulder. A coral-colored bikini and lightly tanned flesh made occasional forays into the sunlight as she walked. Beside her, in a simple beach tunic and floppy hat, was the other woman from yesterday's sighting aboard the *Apollo*. She carried a gear bag as well, and walked with a plodding determination. She was shorter than the other woman, though nowhere near as altitude-challenged as Emily.

"Well, Booney, you were right." Em looked up at him with a smirk tickling the corners of her mouth, dimpling one cheek. "This *will* be an interesting day." One eyebrow rose above her big green sunglasses.

Boone looked down at her. "Uh…" Nothing else came out. The sounds of the marina filled the silence: the creaking of lines, the jingling of fasteners, and the thumps of fenders and hulls near constant in the morning air.

Em laughed. "Better let me do the dive orientation, if that's the maximum level of conversation you're able to muster."

Boone recovered and stepped to the portside rail of the flybridge, overlooking the pier.

The raven-haired woman spotted him and her face lit up. She waved with her free hand. "Ahoy, the boat!" she called out, a delicate accent rising on the sea breezes.

"Ahoy, the shore!" Boone called back. "You've got some nautical lingo, I see!"

"I should hope so—our family is in the maritime business." She reached the *Lunasea* and set down her bag. "Mr. Fischer… I hope it is all right that we are a little ahead of schedule. You said you liked to leave early, and my sister managed to arise on time, for once."

"And I've had my coffee and a bowel movement, too," the sister said, deadpan. "I'm batting a thousand." The woman didn't have the lilting accent of her taller sister—in fact, she sounded a bit like a petulant American teen, although her age was difficult to determine.

Em pushed in alongside Boone. "Hi, I'm Emily Durand, co-owner of Bubble Chasers."

"Hello, Emily. My name is Lyra Othonos, and this is Calypso."

"Callie's fine," the sister mumbled.

"One sec," Boone said, scrambling down the ladder before crossing to the gunwale. "Can I take your gear?" he asked, stepping across to the pier.

"No, not yet," Lyra said rather abruptly. She looked back up the pier. "Where is he?" she muttered.

Callie half-turned, her quiet voice now ramping up to a bellow. "Nicholas!"

Just ashore from the pier, a young man in slacks and a powder blue shirt looked up from a cell phone. Boone had just assumed he was a boat owner. The man raised a finger, continuing his call.

Callie turned all the way around to face shore. "Whoever that is can wait. Get your butt over here if you want to interrogate our charter! We're not going to wait all day!"

"I apologize for this," Lyra said. "Our brother is rather protective, and he wanted to meet you before we boarded."

"Oh, that's all tickety-boo," Em said from the portside rail of the flybridge. "I'm all in favor of protective siblings."

Callie gave her a look, but went back to gesturing at Nicholas, who had finally stowed his phone and now headed toward them.

Boone thought there was something odd about the man's gait. "Your brother not interested in diving?" he asked.

"Oh, he enjoys diving and I'm sure he would like to," Lyra said, "but he said his leg was bothering him today. He had an accident, I'm afraid."

It's a prosthesis, Boone thought. Still, Nicholas seemed to be walking with confidence, and soon reached them.

"I'm sorry, business call. Dealing with an issue at the pier." He held out his hand and Boone took it. "I'm Nicholas Othonos. You're Mr. Fischer?"

"Yes. Boone. How d'ya do?"

"Fine, thank you. Sorry for the formality, but it's something I need to do."

Callie snorted a disgusted laugh. "My brother lives for this sort of thing."

"Callie..." Lyra warned. "He's just being careful."

Nicholas seemed unfazed by the exchange. "It's required for insurance purposes and board oversight, as my sisters and I are all chief operating officers of Olympus Cruises. I researched your operation, and it appears you are quite popular. No record of any accidents." He fished his phone back out of his pocket and tapped the screen. "Just a few quick questions..."

He proceeded to run down a list, asking about medical training, oxygen on board, their radio, and access to hyperbaric chambers. Boone answered each in turn. Nicholas seemed satisfied and replaced the phone. "Our vessel has a helicopter, in the event there is an accident. Lyra and Callie both know how to call for it..."

"What if we *both* drown?" Callie said, smiling at Nicholas.

Nicholas sighed, looking away from her. "May I meet the rest of your crew?"

Boone gestured to Ricardo, who stepped across to the pier to shake hands with Nicholas. "This is Ricardo Pérez, dive instructor and co-owner of Bubble Chasers. He's been diving in Cozumel since he was a teen. And Emily is..." He turned back to the boat. "She was right here. Em?"

Emily came into view, coming up from the head. "Sorry, was in the loo." She hopped across and stuck out her hand, a shining smile on her face.

Nicholas seemed momentarily thrown. Boone recognized the look—he'd seen it on plenty of men when they got a glimpse of Emily Durand. It was probably plastered on his own face, two or three times a day. Probably this morning back at the condo, come to think of it... when Emily had stepped out of the bathroom sporting a new green-and-white striped tank top and white shorts, her hair done up in side braids that merged at the back.

Emily continued to smile at Nicholas and reoffered her hand. "I did wash it," she teased.

He blinked, interrupting the stare that was threatening to take over, and reached to take her hand. "Forgive me. Nicholas Othonos."

"Emily Durand. So, you three came from that gorgeous ship the *Apollo*, yeah? Spiffy yacht, that!"

Nicholas was back on his game. "Thank you. I had a lot of input on her design. The ships of the Pantheon line are based on a lengthening of a mega-yacht built for a sheikh in the United Arab Emirates."

"A shipshape ship for a sheikh," Em blurted. Nicholas blinked and Emily smiled, removing her large sunglasses. "Sorry, Nicholas, but you set me up so brilliantly. But in all seriousness, that is probably the most beautiful ship I've ever laid eyes on."

"Thank you. I'd be happy to offer you a tour…"

Calypso hefted her bag and offered it to Boone. "Okay, let's get this show on the road. You need to see our dive cards and logs, right?"

"Yes," Boone said, taking the bag and stepping over with it, turning back to offer his hand. After he helped her across, he did the same for Lyra.

"Thank you, Boone," she said, holding on to his hand a bit longer than was strictly necessary before releasing it and taking her gear to a bench. Boone glanced back to the pier to find Emily looking at him. She gave him a wink and turned back to Nicholas.

"A tour would be lovely, thank you Nicholas."

"Wonderful," he said, taking out a sleek card case and extracting a business card. "Feel free to call me when you return, and we'll set it up. We're only here two more days before we head out on the second leg for Grand Cayman."

Emily slipped the card into a front pocket of her white shorts. "Will do!"

As Em popped her ever-present sunglasses onto her face and boarded the *Lunasea*, Nicholas turned for shore, retrieving his phone once more.

"So, you have any specific requests as far as dive sites?" Boone asked. Emily began to cast off and Ricardo pulsed the engine, in preparation to navigate their way out of the marina.

"Yes!" Lyra said. "I want to dive The Devil's Throat!"

"Uh…" Boone hesitated. Both Lyra and Callie had advanced certification, but their dive logs made it clear they were intermittent divers at best, and the dive she had requested was not for the faint of heart… or the claustrophobic.

Devil's Throat was a bucket-list dive for many, much like the Great Blue Hole in Belize—and like the Blue Hole, it was a deep dive that required pushing the recreational depth limits. The "throat" was a steeply descending swim-through, the entrance of which was located at an already-deep 83 feet. Swimming down into darkness, the divers would eventually emerge at 135 feet, the wall dropping off into the abyss, with no bottom in sight.

"We'd never take a client there on our first day with them," Emily said. "It's a very advanced dive."

Lyra looked like she was about to protest, but Boone held up a hand. "We'd need to do a couple dives with you first. We could take you there tomorrow morning, if the current is cooperative."

Lyra shrugged. "I was planning on asking to dive with you again tomorrow anyway, so this is acceptable."

"How about we take you to Palancar Caves?" Boone suggested. "There are a lotta swim-throughs and mini-caverns there… maybe whet your appetite for Devil's Throat. Then we can hit Chankanbaab or Tormentos for the shallower dive."

"I leave myself in your capable hands," Lyra said, which elicited a derisive snort from Callie.

Emily grabbed the double-sided whiteboard to apply her artistic talents in her favorite medium —multi-colored markers— while Boone climbed up to the flybridge to give Ricardo their destination.

Lyra followed Boone up and sat on the starboard bench. "We are going to one of the southern dive sites, yes? We have some time?"

"Uh, yeah, probably twenty minutes."

"Good," Lyra said, slipping out of the kimono to reveal the coral-colored bikini. "I would like to feel a little sun and spray." She held the folded garment, looking around as if some place to put it would magically appear.

"Here," Boone offered, taking the silk wrapping. "Looks pretty lightweight and we'll be going at a fair clip." He gave it a quick fold and placed it in one of the glove boxes alongside the wheel as Ricardo exited the marina and turned to port.

Lyra tilted back her head and smiled up at the blue sky, her sunglasses already receiving droplets as the *Lunasea* picked up speed. Her black hair fluttering and shining in the sunlight, she sighed with pleasure. "This is not something one can feel on the big ships."

"Once the *Apollo* gets up to speed, I imagine it's quite nice out on those balconies I saw."

"Oh, you've had a look at our ship?" Lyra asked, all innocence.

"You know I have," Boone replied with a friendly smile.

Lyra laughed. "Yes, I suppose I do." She lapsed into silence for a moment, basking in the sun. "Your boat's name, *Lunasea*... I like that. You are very clever."

"I've never been accused of being clever," Boone said, eyes on the horizon. "But I'll let Emily know. That name was hers. Though I did talk her out of the first one she came up with."

"Which was?"

"*Quit Looking At My Stern*."

Lyra laughed.

"Yeah, I kinda liked it but didn't relish painting that many words. Or explaining it to anyone who didn't get it."

"On your site, it says this is a fast-boat? But it doesn't look like most of the ones on Cozumel that say that."

Boone didn't want to go into detail about why the *Lunasea* was fast, so he simply said, "The previous owners made some modifications, and she can pour it on when she needs to. How fast can *your* ship go?"

Lyra shrugged a tanned shoulder, biting her lip in embarrassment. "I really should know things like that. That's the sort of thing Nicholas could tell you. Oh, and I must apologize for my brother. He has always been a bit awkward around people. The way he was staring at your partner... your business partner, I mean..."

"Oh, I didn't mind." Emily's voice came from below as she ascended the ladder. "Bit of a boffin, in't he?"

Lyra tilted her head. "I don't know that word."

"Oh, you know...nerd, brain box... bit of an egghead, yeah? I mean that in the best possible way. Smart guys are sexy, right Boone?"

"Don't ask me, I'm just a good ol' boy deck monkey."

"Opposable thumbs, too!" Emily came over to him and rose up on her toes to plant a playful kiss on his cheek before turning back to Lyra. "I'm looking forward to my tour of your ship! It really has a helicopter?"

"Yes."

"Where do you keep it?" Emily asked. "I didn't see it when your ship passed by."

"Oh, it probably came in early to the airport. Nicholas likes to send a party in ahead of the ship. There is a landing pad aft of the bridge and a hangar they can store it in." Lyra pointed up into the sky. "Maybe Nicholas can take you for a ride."

When Boone bit his lip, Emily swatted him on the stomach without even looking. She turned back to him. "I want to get started drawing the other dive site on the board. Are you leaning toward one or the other?"

Boone chewed his lip, looking south. "I'd say Tormentos, if it's clear. We can keep Chankanaab in the back pocket."

"What, you don't want to go diving with the submarine?" Emily teased.

"I've had my fill of submarines… let's shoot for Tormentos."

"Right-o." Em disappeared down the ladder.

Lyra watched her go, then removed her sunglasses. "Submarine?"

"Cozumel has an Atlantis tourist sub that dives Chankanaab in the mornings." Boone thought back to the first time the submersible had come up alongside them, triggering memories of the narco sub they'd encountered in Bonaire.

"Ah, yes… they have one in Barbados," Lyra said. "One of our other ships visited there and I took a ride on it."

"We've come across her a few times—kinda fun to wave at the people in the windows." He barked a laugh and shook his head.

Lyra raised an eyebrow. "Yes…?"

"Emily… she keeps threatening to put on a Bigfoot costume under her scuba gear and lie in wait for it."

Lyra smiled thoughtfully, then swung her long legs up onto the bench and draped an arm over the starboard rail. "So, Boone… tell me something about yourself."

Boone pondered the question. The events of the past few years could fill a novel. Maybe two or three. He decided for the simple route. "Not much to tell. I'm from the States. Moved to Curaçao and started divemastering there. Moved to Bonaire, met Emily… then we hit a few other islands and started our own business."

"You enjoy travel, then. As do I."

"Where all have you been?"

Lyra laughed. "You said it would only take twenty minutes to get to this dive, so I will just say many, many places. I have been all over the United States, too. Where are you from?"

"Tennessee."

"Ah, Nashville country music… Dolly Parton." She squinted at him. "You don't sound like you are from there."

"Stick a few beers in me and I do, but my dad was Dutch. I think his accent hit my mom's and sorta smashed it flat."

Lyra gave a radiant smile. "That is a clever way of putting it. You are not just a… what did you say? Deck monkey?"

Boone shrugged. "I've been known to enjoy a banana now and then. How 'bout you? Where you from? I've been trying to place the accent."

"I grew up in Greece along with my elder brother. We lived outside Athens until I was ten. Then my father remarried and moved to America, where my other brother Nicholas was born. My sister Callie was born the following year."

"Ah… that explains why Callie and Nicholas don't sound like you do."

"They have spent most of their lives in the United States, although Nicholas was schooled in England, and often travels to Europe to meet with naval architects and visit the shipyards." Lyra shifted on the bench. "My accent is not so strong, is it?"

"No, no, I didn't mean to suggest…" Boone smiled. "I like the way you speak. It's very musical."

Lyra opened her mouth to say something, blushed, then stood. "I suppose I should put on my wetsuit."

"Yeah, we'll be there before you know it. Trust me, you're gonna love this dive!"

◆ ◆ ◆

Finishing her safety stop at the end of the dive, Emily floated just below the surface, watching as Lyra's long legs mounted the ladder at the swim platform, the shorty wetsuit clinging to her every curve. Boone would be waiting above to assist. Em turned around in the water column to spot her remaining charge and found Callie observing her, bobbing up and down in her safety stop.

Emily raised an "OK" sign in question. Callie looked at her computer, then responded in kind before tossing off a perfunctory thumbs-up, indicating she was going to surface. She kicked for the ladder and Emily followed.

"How was it for you?" Boone asked as he took Emily's fins.

"Turtle city!"

"Yeah. I counted thirteen."

They had just completed their second dive at Tormentos. The first dive at Palancar Caves had been rife with turtles as well, and an enormous school of horse-eye jacks had been waiting for them in one of the first sand-bottomed canyons. A pair of eagle rays, three nurse sharks, and a free-swimming green moray as long as Boone was tall had made for a spectacular dive.

Emily boarded the boat and tucked her gear under the nearest bench. *Chartering for just two divers sure cuts back on the clutter,* she thought. "Where's Lyra?"

"She already went up top." Boone started stripping off his wetsuit. "You want to take us back in?"

"Nah, Ric's got it." Emily unzipped the top of her wetsuit and went to the Igloo to grab a soda. Calypso was rummaging through the rapidly melting ice. They'd eaten lunch during the surface interval between dives, but neither sister appeared to be big eaters. *More for Ricardo and family,* Em thought.

"You sure got a lot of food. Bit of an overkill for just Lyra and me," Calypso remarked. She raised a dripping bottle of tan liquid. "What's this 'Lift' drink?"

"Oh, Manzana Lift. It's apple soda, made by Coca-Cola. Never had it 'til I came here. Pretty scrummy!"

"I'm guessing 'scrummy' is 'yummy' with other letters," Calypso remarked as she returned the bottle to the ice, coming back up with a bottle of San Pellegrino. "So... tell me about this 'Devil's Throat.' Is it dangerous?"

"Well... it's a very deep dive and the swim-through can be quite claustrophobic. We just need to be sure we don't have any nervous nellie newbies when we try it, yeah?"

Callie looked at her a moment, taking a sip of the sparkling water. "Do you really talk like that, or do you put it on a bit?"

Emily blinked. "How'd'ya mean?"

"Your accent, for one."

"Oh. I'm from South London, and we—"

"I've met plenty of people from London, but your accent is pretty strong," Calypso interrupted. "And you seem so cheery and clever all the time. Your entire dive briefing was like a stand-up routine. Makes me curious if you're compensating for something." She held Emily's eyes, waiting for a response.

What is her deal? Is she goading me? Em tamped down her annoyance. "I... it's just how I talk... I don't 'switch it on' or anything, if that's what you're asking." Then she lifted her chin. "Are you taking the piss?"

Calypso suddenly smiled. "Yes, just kidding. I'm sorry. My father always says I'm a bit of an instigator."

"Oh... okay."

"And your dive briefing was very amusing. I liked the funny pictures. The little turtles were particularly nice."

"Um... thank you."

"Yes, it brought back memories. I used to draw pictures like that when I was a child."

"Hey, Callie?" Boone called from up top. "Lyra would like to join the night dive tonight. You interested?"

Calypso turned her head partway toward Boone, still looking at Emily. "I'll pass. I've got plans this evening. Thanks for asking, though." She tossed her half-finished Pellegrino into the cooler and went up the ladder, leaving Emily alone on the deck below.

"Bit of a twat, that one..." she muttered to herself.

7

An hour before sunset, the Kansas group was loading their gear aboard the *Lunasea* at the Dive Paradise pier, alongside the Hotel Barracuda. Two of their number had bowed out after going overboard on the margaritas at La Mission the night before. Greg and Cecilia were near the stern and the other couple, Bill and Cindy, sat across.

"Whoa..." Greg murmured under his breath.

Boone raised his head and followed Greg's goggle-eyed gaze toward shore, expecting to see Lyra. He did. But she wasn't alone.

"I hope you don't mind if I join you," Nicholas said as he reached the *Lunasea*, carrying a gear bag and a small, black hard case. "Callie suggested I should take a break from work." Nicholas was already in his wetsuit, the shorty cut revealing the prosthesis.

"Not a problem, welcome aboard." Boone took the brother and sister's gear and then reached out to help them across. Nicholas ignored his hand, grabbing a rung and stepping across with his good leg, swinging the prosthetic one after. Boone couldn't help notice a slight wince.

"I know what you're thinking, with my leg..." Nicholas began. "But I have the same advanced certification as Lyra, and probably more dives than her under my belt."

"No worries. We've had a group called SUDS charter dives with us several times. They help disabled veterans experience scuba diving—or *re*experience in many cases, since a lot of vets were divers before their injuries. Besides, this being a night dive, we'll be going at a leisurely pace."

Nicholas smiled and sat on the nearest bench. "Well, on this dive... *you* may have to try and keep up with *me*." He patted the hard case. "I've been meaning to try this out." He popped the latches and swung the lid open.

Inside was a black object that looked a bit like a drone. Nicholas lifted it out and pivoted a couple appendages into place. A pair of housed propellers were on the underbelly, one on either side. Two grips were set into the top, and Boone could see thumb-activated controls on each.

"Whoa, what is that space-agey thingie?" Emily asked, joining them.

"It's some kind of scooter," Boone surmised.

Nicholas gave a dismissive laugh. "That rather minimizes its capabilities. But yes... a scooter of sorts. I call it the Underwater Personal Conveyor, or UPC. I designed it myself. It's constructed of lightweight composites so it floats, but there's a trigger here that can flood an interior chamber with water to bring it closer to neutral buoyancy, depending on the depth. It can be purged at the surface to return to flotation." He turned the leading edge to face them. "It has a high-def underwater camera with low-light settings, high intensity underwater light..." He turned it around. "In the back I've got a variable intensity strobe and an integrated distress beacon. A rigid antenna can be extended three feet for surface operation, and I've got a sixty-foot antenna on a spool for subsurface signal. I wanted it longer but there was only so much I could cram in and still keep it compact."

"How fast can it go?" Boone asked.

"The two propellers provide enough thrust to achieve four and a half knots on the turbo setting, although that would drain the battery very quickly. At two knots, a full charge can provide nearly two hours of operation." He held the grips and used the thumb controls to pivot the ring-shaped housings right and left, pulsing the propellers a few times for effect.

"That's incredible!" Emily said. "I'm guessing that viewscreen is for the camera, yeah? But what goes in there?" She tapped the top, where there was a clear, watertight compartment alongside the viewscreen.

"Ah, I planned to allow for a cellphone to be put in there, but I haven't gotten around to integrating that port with the underwater antenna. If you had a full-face mask, you would be able to make and receive calls. I've designed software to facilitate hands-free activation of various apps as well."

Emily smacked Boone in the arm. "Told you he looked smart."

Lyra put a hand on Nicholas's back. "Nicky is the clever one in our family."

It was a simple, sweet compliment, but Boone saw something dark cross Nicholas's face. *And did he tense when she touched him?*

"Thank you, Lyra. I'm glad *somebody* thinks so."

"What's that?" Greg asked. The Kansans had gathered to admire the tech and Greg was pointing into the hard case. A foam-lined compartment to the side held a small device. "Looks like a remote control for a drone."

"That's exactly what it is. The *Apollo* has several quadcopters with excellent optics that we use to shoot promotional footage for the cruise line. I've just taken one of their spare controllers and adapted it to use with the UPC. This viewscreen here is tied to the camera in front. I can use it as a remote submersible."

Boone looked up. The sun was nearing the end of its journey toward the horizon and a fiery orange glow was spreading out across the sky. "We'd better get going."

"On it!" Emily scrambled to the bow line, calling up to the flybridge. "Ricardo! Start 'er up!"

Boone went to the stern line, reaching across to free it from the piling. "All right, folks! We're going to Paraiso, also known as Paradise." He nodded toward the Kansans. "Some of you have been there before, but let's see if we can find you some free-swimming splendid toads!"

In minutes, the *Lunasea* was on station above the dive site. Just to the north, the Hygge Cruises *Nordic Starr* was still docked at the southern flank of Puerta Maya, backlit by the bright lights of the cruise ship pier.

While Emily gave a dive briefing, Boone checked the current. Typically, this site had very little, but as it was tucked in near the massive piers, every once in a while, the flow of the water could surprise you. Tonight, no surprises. He could see Em looking over at him as she spoke, no doubt waiting for his go-ahead. He raised his fingers in an "OK" sign and chopped his flattened palm toward the north.

"Right-o, we've got minimal current running south to north, so we can take it nice 'n' easy. Be on the lookout for free-swimming morays, lobsters, crabs, and maybe an octopus or two. Keep your eyes peeled for splendid toads; they start croaking a lot at night and we may catch one on the hunt. And don't forget to check the water column for my personal favorite, Caribbean reef squid! If you're lucky, a few of them might come and have a chat with your dive light!"

"Everyone's got a good dive light, right?" Boone asked. "And if you need a secondary backup light, we've got some extras on board."

"And just a reminder," Emily added. "I started the briefing with this night dive etiquette and I'm gonna end with it: don't shine your light directly at another diver's face... annnnnnd... Cecilia?"

"Don't shine it on the fish... shine it near them or on the coral."

"Because... Gregory?"

"It'll blind them, and spotlight them for predator fish that might dash in and eat them."

"Excellent! Gold stars all around."

"All right, folks, let's get wet!" Boone called out. "Em's in the lead and I'll be bringing up the rear. We'll have little green strobes hooked to our vests if you need to find us. Pool's open!"

"Nicholas, do you need some help?" Lyra asked her brother.

"No, I'm fine," he replied.

Boone watched as the young man detached his prosthetic leg—the stump extended just past the short pantleg of the wetsuit. His eyes caught Boone's.

"Do you have somewhere to store this where it won't roll around?"

"Uh, sure. I can secure it below."

Nicholas handed the leg to him. "They make fins for amputees, and there are even prosthetics designed for diving, but I want to test a single fin with this, see if it streamlines my steering."

"Is this the first time you've used the scooter?"

Nicholas sighed. "The UPC? In open water, yes, but I tested it extensively onboard the *Apollo* in the ship's pool."

"Uh…"

"It's a substantial pool," Nicholas said, strapping a sizeable swim fin onto his booted foot.

Boone shrugged. This dive site had a maximum depth of fifty feet and Nicholas seemed competent. Emily was already in the water with the Kansas divers hot on her fins. Boone went down to the forepeak and placed the prosthesis into a storage compartment alongside the head. Returning, he found Nicholas seated on the swim platform, Lyra alongside him.

"Look at that sunset," she breathed. "Magnificent." She looked back over the shoulder of her sleeveless wetsuit. "Are you coming, Boone?"

"Right behind you," he said, quickly slipping into his gear. He reached back to give the little plastic strobe a twist and the light began to flash in two-second intervals. Off the stern, he could see Emily's greenish strobe pulsing below the surface. The lights of the other divers swept to and fro.

Nicholas slid over to the edge and grabbed hold of the ladder. Waving off Lyra's offer to assist, he lowered himself into the water. "Mr. Fischer, would you hand the UPC down to me?"

"Sure."

Boone picked up the device; it wasn't exactly light but not overly heavy, either. He handed it down to Nicholas, who popped his regulator into his mouth before taking the UPC from him.

"See you below," Lyra said, slipping beneath the darkening waves.

Boone watched as Nicholas set the device in the water and flipped a few switches as it bobbed on the surface. A bright dive light came on and a cascade of bubbles streamed from the side. *Must be that buoyancy trick he was talking about.* Finally, a strobe similar to but brighter than Boone's own winked on and Nicholas angled the UPC down and dove toward the bottom. After a moment, the strobe dimmed as Nicholas dialed down the luminosity.

"You good, Ricardo?" Boone called up to the flybridge. When he heard an affirmative shout from above, Boone took a giant stride and joined the dive. It wasn't full dark yet, so he could see all the divers and he did a quick head count. Four Kansans, Lyra and Nicholas, and Emily strobing away in the distance. All good. He switched on his dive light, a SEAC R30, and adjusted it to the lower setting.

Ahead, Nicholas was engrossed in the controls for his device and Boone decided he'd better stick close. As he approached, he observed how the man had braced his leg over the stump, creating a central fin. Nicholas raised his head, spotted Boone, and flashed an "OK" sign, then gave a little wave and throttled up. The propellers spun in their housings and he shot forward, reducing speed as he neared the other divers.

Lyra gave Boone a wave and kicked hard to follow her brother. In short order, the divers were spread out, shining their lights in various nooks and crannies. Boone spotted an octopus pulling itself along the flank of a coral head and gently circled his light around it to draw attention to the creature. Lyra moved in closer and the octopus came to a halt, its brownish coloration suddenly flashing to a powder blue. Boone could hear Lyra's delighted exclamation through the water. Greg and Cecilia came over to view the creature and Boone looked around for Nicholas.

Spotting him, he swam over in his direction. He was stationary, pivoting the UPC in an arc, its light illuminating a free-swimming spotted moray that was on the hunt at the edge of the corals. Eyes on the viewscreen atop the scooter, he was clearly filming.

Boone glanced to the north and spotted Emily's strobe, her dive light tracing a circle in the coral. He waited for Nicholas to finish filming, then caught his eye and pointed north. He nodded and they headed toward a cluster of divers who were looking for whatever Emily had spotted. To his right, Lyra moved toward him, and he indicated Emily's circling light to her as well.

In moments, Boone knew what she'd found. A guttural croak-ing sound was easily audible in the water, short bursts of grunts in clusters of four to seven croaks, the odd noises sounding very similar to a cellphone on vibrate if it had been left on the table. A splendid toadfish singing his throaty song. Boone could make out answering grunts from nearby, likely from other splendids in their lairs, calling out to potential mates or warning away rivals. Emily's circle had moved as she tracked something, so he guessed she'd spotted one out-and-about.

Sure enough, as he reached her, a good-sized specimen was making its way across the coral, its purple hues and yellow fins vibrant in the dive lights. He was pleased to see no one was spending too much time with their lights shining directly on it.

Boone caught Emily's eye and pumped an "OK" sign three times at her. *Nicely done.* She mimed a curtsy. A gentle thrum-ming sound came from behind Boone as Nicholas maneuvered his conveyor closer to get some footage. He lined up the nose with the toadfish and looked down at the viewscreen.

And that's when something went wrong.

All of a sudden, the bright light on the nose of the UPC winked off. The gentle hum of its propulsion suddenly crescendoed to a whine and Boone watched as the device and its rider spun hard to the left and accelerated sharply. He could see from Nicholas's body language that this was not something he had initiated, and the man was frantically punching controls. Boone reached out a long arm and made a frantic grab for Nicholas's fin as he flashed by, winding up with a fistful of bubbles.

Boone began finning after Nicholas, twisting around as he did so to quickly signal to Emily. He tapped the sides of his index fingers together, then pointed his palms at her, then pointed down at the bottom: *Buddy up. Stop and stay here.*

Turning fully to face his quarry, Boone poured on the speed. The strobe on the back of the UPC was visible in the distance. *It's heading straight out into the channel,* Boone thought frantically. The Cozumel Channel plunged to a depth of a quarter mile and the current there could sweep a diver up into the Gulf of Mexico.

Swimming perpendicular into the northward current, he could feel himself being nudged to his right. He remembered Nicholas saying the device could reach four and a half knots, which was just over five miles per hour. *I'll never catch him,* he thought. The Olympic swimmer, Michael Phelps, had a top speed of six miles per hour. Boone was an exceptional swimmer, and with his long legs and arms, lanky frame, and sporting a pair of fins, he could match that. *But not while wearing scuba gear and tank,* he thought. *Come on, Nicholas, just let go!*

Boone had seen divers so intent on saving an expensive underwater camera that they'd nearly drowned themselves. If Boone were any judge of character, Nicholas was a stubborn, confident young man; he'd likely believe he could fix the problem and wouldn't want to lose his toy. *Won't do you much good if you get swept into the Gulf. Although he did say it had an emergency beacon.* Though the sun had set some time ago, there was sufficient moon and starlight to make out his target, so Boone tucked his dive light into his vest—keeping it in hand would be an unnecessary drag on his speed.

Boone's great stamina had its limits, and he could feel his sprint losing steam. *And yet... I'm gaining on him. Gaining quickly.* As he drew nearer, Boone could see why: Nicholas had fanned his single fin down to create drag and act as a brake. *At least he's maintained depth—*

As if it heard his thoughts, the UPC's housings suddenly pivoted up, propelling the device down as it reached the drop-off. They'd been at a relatively shallow depth, but Nicholas descended to nearly seventy feet before he hauled up on the handles, forcing the nose up, struggling to maintain depth, still intent on saving the device, his fingers locked onto the control handles in a death-grip. Their overall speed faltered.

Now or never. Boone dug deep and found a final burst of momentum, purging air from his lungs to boost the speed of his descent. He came down atop Nicholas, grabbing one of the man's hands and tearing it from the scooter's grip. Just before Boone could pull him completely free, Nicholas frantically stabbed at a switch near the back of the unit. The flashing strobe at the UPC's rear illuminated a long, thin tendril that unspooled from the back. In the gloom, Boone could just make out a float on the tip, pulling the antenna up toward the surface.

Both men sagged in unison, their muscles exhausted as the UPC shot away from them. As Boone guided Nicholas toward a shallower depth, he glanced back over his shoulder. The strobing light abruptly turned ninety degrees, heading north.

8

Emily did her best to remain calm. She and Boone had had more than their share of brushes with danger, and in the grand scheme of things, this situation didn't hold a candle to many of them.

When Boone shot after Nicholas, Em had quickly gathered the divers together, signaling them to stay and flashing plenty of "OK" signs all around, before moving alongside Lyra. She had placed a gentle hand on her bare arm and given a squeeze—partly to reassure her, and partly to have a grip on her if the woman decided to go after her brother.

In the distance, she had watched the two strobing lights—one at the trailing edge of Boone's vest, the other on the UPC. They'd winked on and off in the darkness, heading out to sea. Emily was well aware that to the west lay the channel and a precipitous drop-off. The lights had grown fainter and fainter before disappearing from sight—whether due to distance, or from being obscured by the edge of the drop-off, Emily couldn't be sure.

Boone had been gone for several minutes now. Emily checked her gauges, glowing green in the shadows. This being a shallow dive with minimal current, they still had plenty of air. In the water around them, she could hear the gentle thrum of the *Lunasea*'s engines as Ricardo held position above and behind the divers. He would be keeping an eye on their lights, and probably wondering why most of them were stationary. He might have seen Boone's dive light, partially obscured and tucked into his vest, as it headed west. If so, he might have radioed for help.

Another minute passed, and as Emily reached out to reassure Lyra once more, the woman looked at her, fear in the eyes behind her dive mask. Abruptly, she turned and started kicking toward the channel and Emily quickly overtook her with powerful kicks of her own. With her tiny stature, she didn't have the reach that Boone's physique gave him, but she was no slouch when it came to speed. Her legs, well-sculpted with muscle, pumped like pistons. She put a hand on Lyra's shoulder, arresting her advance.

Lyra looked at her in a panic, started to move around her.

Em reached out with a fingernail and gave Lyra's mask two sharp taps. Lyra blinked. Emily held up a hand, palm facing Lyra, then pointed two fingers at her own mask before tapping herself on the chest.

Stop. Look at me.

When she had Lyra's attention, she held up her gauge, indicating the psi in the tanks, which was still above 2,000, plenty of air for their shallow depth. She pointed out to sea, then back at her gauge, then pumped an "OK" sign.

Plenty of air. Them too. It's okay.

Lyra seemed to calm ever so slightly, then suddenly her eyes grew wide and she pointed westward.

Emily turned. A dive light. And from the brightness of the beam, she knew it was Boone's, switched to its higher setting. A smaller light winked on beside it, likely Nicholas's secondary light. Both lights were aimed her way. Relief washed over Emily, and she felt almost giddy as the tightly coiled tension left her body. She signaled Lyra to wait there, then kicked a few fin strokes back toward the group.

Emily knew they had plenty of air to continue the dive, but who knew what condition Boone and Nicholas would be in? Best to abort and issue a refund. She shined a light on her fist, pulsed a thumbs-up, then aimed her dive light skyward and traced circles on the surface of the water, reminding them to do that as they ascended so that Ricardo would know where they were coming up. He would maneuver around the circling lights, putting the boat on the down-current side of the group, so no one would have to fight the current getting to the ladder.

As they drew nearer, Emily could see that the malfunctioning scooter was gone. Nicholas was moving at a good clip, pumping his single fin with strong strokes. Lyra kicked forward and Emily let her go. She went to Nicholas, reaching out to him, but her brother shook her off, looking at the ascending Kansas divers and angling toward them, heading for the surface.

Emily flashed a questioning "OK" sign to Boone and he replied with the same signal, then followed it up with an unofficial hand gesture, miming the wiping of sweat from his forehead. Emily laughed into her regulator, then flicked her fins in a double kick to close with Boone, clamping her arms around the young man in a relieved hug. He returned her embrace.

Em broke free and jerked a thumb up. The pair rose to join the others, floating at fifteen feet below the surface. After three minutes, Emily went to the swim ladder to assist with the loading of the divers. Reaching the well-lit ladder, she noticed Lyra was climbing up it and Nicholas was no longer in the water. Swimming around the Kansans who were lining up to board, Emily grabbed hold of the swim platform and shrugged out of her vest and tank. Pushing her gear onto the platform, she pulled herself up after it, looking for Nicholas. She spotted him right away, seated on the starboard bench and frantically digging the remote control out of the hard case that sat beside him. Lyra stood close by, looking on with concern. Emily could just make out her words.

"Calm, brother… it's just a toy."

Nicholas shot her a furious look, then raised the controller and powered it on.

Emily assisted Cecilia out of the water, then spotted Boone coming up. "Boone, can you take over here?"

"No worries," he called out.

Em slid her tank into a slot behind the portside bench and approached the Othonos siblings. "Are you all right?" she asked Nicholas. Her words were directed at him, but her eyes asked the same question of Lyra.

Nicholas replied first. "I *will* be if I get my prototype back!" He looked at the screen on the top of the controller. Emily could see the feed was blank. "I don't understand. I activated the beacon and I know it's in range… especially since I unspooled the underwater antenna."

"Where is it?" Emily asked.

Nicholas tapped the touchscreen on the device. "Just under five hundred yards…"—he turned sidesaddle on the bench, pivoting the controller to and fro before pointing—"…that way."

Emily looked where he was indicating. "The Puerta Maya Pier. That's where your ship is docked."

Nicholas looked up. "And that blasted *Nordic Starr* rust bucket," he muttered, before looking toward the stern. "Is everyone aboard? Would it be possible to move your boat closer to the pier to improve my signal?"

Emily did a quick head count, then again for good measure. "Boone, can you ask Ricardo to bring us north, closer to the pier?"

"We're going that way anyway. Why?"

Lyra spoke up. "My brother is trying to retrieve his device."

Boone nodded, heading up to the flybridge.

Nicholas looked down at the controller. "I don't understand... we should be close enough. This appears to be working but it's almost as if..." He inverted the controller and opened a back panel. After digging a finger inside, he flipped it right-side up again.

Emily saw the viewscreen flicker before filling with a gloomy image of the sea bottom. Some external light source was suffusing the water with a greenish glow.

"There! That's got it." Nicholas pressed a control on the side and the sand and sea lit up in the viewscreen. A pair of butterfly fish flashed past. "Something was interfering with the signal. I switched the band and was able to take control again."

Emily sat beside him on the bench, peering at the screen. "Looks like it's sitting on the bottom," she observed.

"Yes. Let's see..." He laid his thumb tips on the little joysticks, pressing forward on the right one and tapping the left one back several times. The view was obscured by a cloud of sand as the UPC rose from the bottom. He glanced at Emily. "Right stick controls the attitude of the propellers. Left stick is thrust. I've pointed them up and pulsed the propellers in reverse a few times to pull it up slightly."

"Ah, 'cause you'd kick up a cloud of sand if you pointed 'em down and went forward."

"Precisely."

"What was that green glow we saw?" Emily asked.

"I suspect that's the nighttime underwater lights on the *Apollo*." He worked the controls and brought the nose up. The hull of a ship filled the screen, green lights shining from the sides.

"Your scooter went straight to your ship?" Emily said. "And then just sat on the bottom right under it? That's a bit weird, innit?"

Nicholas frowned. "I did give the UPC the ability to return to a preprogrammed GPS location, in the event that control was lost."

"Well, that explains it," Lyra said.

"Not really," Nicholas replied. "I never activated that feature. I was still ironing out some bugs." He returned to the controls, bringing the UPC level. The viewscreen now showed the flank of the massive concrete pier. "At least I can test out the controls. I'll bring it around to this side of the pier." He tapped a control. "I know I asked you to move the boat closer, but could we hold station here?"

"I'll ask Boone!" Lyra volunteered, making her way to the flybridge ladder.

Emily watched the visual as the underwater drone skirted the length of the pier, then reached open water. After a moment, Nicholas spun the UPC about and pitched the nose up, bringing it to the surface. The view screen went white at the sudden change in light before adjusting to show the scene: on the left, the brilliant lights and colors of the *Apollo*, the waterline glowing green. In the center, the bright, orangish lights of the pier. And on the right, the *Nordic Starr* was haphazardly illuminated by an asymmetrical pattern of white lights—no doubt many bulbs were burned out. The water's surface was at the bottom of the image and slowly rose to obscure the view.

"Is it sinking?"

"Yes, I don't want to purge the seawater yet. I just popped up to get my bearings." He pushed both joysticks forward, heading back to the pier, then pivoted right. "Fighting the current a bit..." he noted.

The camera image moved along the end of the pier, then passed the stern of the *Nordic Starr*.

"Wait! What was that? Go back!" Emily reached for the controller, her fingertips brushing the backs of Nicholas's hands. He tensed and she pulled back. "I'm sorry, I just... I saw something. May I?" She held her hands out.

Nicholas turned to look at her. "I... yes, of course." He handed her the controller. "Now, to rotate, you'll want to—"

"Like this?" Emily interrupted, effortlessly pivoting the UPC and sending it back toward the *Nordic Starr*. She slowed as the hull of the ship came into view.

As we passed that Hygge Cruises ship, I saw a shimmer... like a thermocline... but more than that, it seemed like... there!

"What is that?" Nicholas asked.

"That... is something they shouldn't be doing."

Emily maneuvered closer and pivoted so she had a view down the length of the hull. The water was distorting in a cloud, emanating from a bilge port. "Looks like they're dumping gray water. That's when—"

"I build ships—I know what it is. It's the non-sewage water from sinks, showers, laundry... but it can still contain pathogens and harmful chemicals. At present, there are no international regulations for that."

"At least it's not *black* water... oh, wait..." Emily trailed off as a second jet from a port further down began, and this was noticeably hazier than the first. "Sodding hell, even *treated* sewage can't be released within three miles of land."

"Correct. And the MARPOL convention requires a ship be *twelve* miles offshore if it's untreated... and what are the odds that this ship has a decent sewage treatment system." Nicholas reached over and toggled a switch. "I've started the video camera. Can you bring it closer to the black water discharge?"

"Easy peasy. One closeup of liquified shite, coming right up." Em gently nudged the left joystick and the view moved closer to the new emission.

"Hold there."

Emily did so. "Those wankers... we already have enough damage happening to the reef when cruise ships *follow* the damn rules."

"Where's the scoot....er... the drone thing?" Boone asked, coming down the ladder with Lyra close behind.

"Right next to that Hygge Cruises ship," Em said, pushing a stereotypical Scandinavian sound onto the name.

Boone leaned in. "Is that...?"

"Hygge poo."

"Those sons of bitches," Boone muttered.

Em delicately manipulated the joysticks and adjusted the angle of the shot. "I have to say, Nicholas... toy or no, your gadget is brill!" When Nicholas looked at her quizzically, she finished out the slang: "...liant. Brilliant." Emily found herself remembering Calypso, winding her up about her accent. "Sorry. I have a way of speaking that can sometimes..."

"I love the way you speak," Nicholas said matter-of-factly.

The jet abruptly stopped, and Emily backed away to find the gray water dump had ceased as well. "Looks like they finished."

"Too late for them," Nicholas said with a sneer. "I've got everything I need. That ship is a thorn in my side, and this will be reported. I want to thank you for spotting that, Miss Durand."

"Miss Durand is so formal, considering we just filmed high-def sewage porn together. Call me Emily."

"As you wish. Thank you, Emily."

"And now for the cherry on top," Em said, spinning the UPC sharply to the left and making for open water. "Where's the button that purges the water when you're ready for flotation?"

"It's this one here. Why, what are you doing?"

"Our movie needs end credits." She spun the vehicle around and pitched the nose up, breaching astern of the Hygge Cruises ship. Activating the purge control, the distant UPC sucked in surface air and flushed the ballast. "Tada!"

Filling the viewscreen was the stern, the faded paint of the lettering clearly visible in the bright light on the nose of the scooter: *Nordic Starr.* And the home port: Reykjavik, Iceland.

◆ ◆ ◆

"Here you go," Boone said, setting the UPC on the bench alongside Nicholas. After retrieving the man's prosthesis, he had jumped in to bring the scooter aboard.

Nicholas finished attaching the socket of the artificial leg and looked up. "Thank you, Mr. Fischer. Would you give it a quick dip in the freshwater rinse?"

"Sure." Boone brought the device over to the tub they used for divers to clean their underwater cameras. It was too large to immerse, but by dipping and rotating it a few times, he was able to remove the corrosive saltwater. He brought it back to Nicholas. "Here you go."

Nicholas pointed under the opposite bench where Lyra was sitting, still clad in her shorty wetsuit, its zipper partway open, revealing the top of a white bikini. "Could you bring me the case, please?" he asked.

"Sure." *Of course, it had to be behind her legs,* he thought. Boone squatted and reached under the bench. Lyra nudged the side of his face with her thigh and leaned in.

"Thank you for saving my brother," she said in a soft voice.

Boone blushed and quickly slid the black case out, losing his balance and flopping onto his butt on the deck. Lyra giggled and looked wistfully up at the starlit sky. Boone spotted Emily coming down the ladder. *Man, I hope she didn't see that.*

"I saw that," Em whispered with a smile, as she passed him on her way to the swim platform to secure the stern ladder.

Boone regained his feet and brought the hard case to Nicholas. "So, you gonna send that video to the Marine Park? We know several of the staff, if you'd like us to handle it. Ricardo, our skipper, has an uncle over there."

"Thank you, but I'll contact them directly. Since the footage is on my equipment. Chain of evidence, and all that."

Boone shrugged. "Okay."

Nicholas snapped open the case and tucked the controller into its slot in the bottom before lifting the UPC.

Emily came alongside Boone and hip-checked him playfully. "So, Nick, once you've got that thingamajig on the market, let me know, yeah? That was a right bit o' fun!"

"You're an excellent pilot," Nicholas noted.

"So I've been told," Emily said, looking at Boone.

"She likes to be flattered," he said.

"It's not flattery if it's fact," Em replied, stripping off her wetsuit as the lights of San Miguel came into view.

9

With the *Lunasea* nestled against the dock at Dive Paradise, Boone and Emily helped the divers disembark. The Kansas gang insisted they didn't need a refund, but Boone insisted right back that he and Emily would take them out for a fun shore excursion to make up for it. No one in their group was interested in doing Devil's Throat—especially since they were flying out the following day—so Boone suggested they meet at their hotel at two in the afternoon.

"Sounds good!" Greg said, gathering his and Cecilia's gear and heading toward the hotel.

Boone reached over to take Lyra's gear bag before helping her across. As she alighted on the pier, she stumbled into him and he steadied her as her thick, raven locks cascaded over his face. He was ninety percent confident it wasn't a real stumble.

"Thank you," she said with a smile.

"Part of the job. No customer shall faceplant upon arrival."

"A very exciting evening, Boone. I imagine Calypso will be sorry she missed it."

Boone chuckled. "Depends on how into peril your sister is." He turned away from Lyra to assist Nicholas with his equipment but found Emily had already done so and was currently offering him a hand across. Nicholas hesitated, but then took it and stepped to the pier.

"If you'd like the tour of the *Apollo* now, I believe it's the least I can do. I have a car waiting..."

"Oh, Nick, thanks ever so much, but Boone and I have to get up at stupid o'clock to prepare for the Throat dive. How much longer are you in Coz?"

Nicholas's face betrayed a trace of disappointment, but he smiled and picked up his hard case and gear bag. "Some of our guests are traveling to Chichén Itzá tomorrow but we will be departing the following morning."

"Oh, bugger... and Boone here just committed us to an excursion tomorrow after the dives..."

Boone shrugged. "We could reschedule," he suggested.

"No, no, it's the last day for the Kansas gang," Emily said quickly. "And we really did cheat them out of half the night dive. But maybe a rain check? I imagine you and your fleet of fancy ships will come to Cozumel again, yeah?"

Nicholas hesitated. "Of course. Next time. Good night."

Boone saw something pass over the man's face as he turned away and headed up the pier.

"And Callie and I will see you tomorrow morning," Lyra said, leaning in and placing a kiss on each of Boone's cheeks. She lifted her gear and followed her brother. Boone made a concerted effort not to watch her departure.

"Ooh la la, a European double-smooch, very fancy," Emily teased.

"I was ambushed," Boone said sheepishly. "Sorry 'bout that, I—"

"Oh, please, I'm a big girl. Besides, you did yeoman's work not watching her arse as she walked away." Emily leaned to the side to look around Boone. "She has a little runway-model thing going. Kinda hot." Emily swiveled her head back toward the boat. "Right, Ricardo?"

Ricardo jerked, caught staring. He shook his head with a half-smile. "Do you need me to help bring the boat back?"

"No, we got it," Boone replied. "I saw your bike down in the hold. You heading out from here?"

"*Si*, I am meeting Lupe for dinner. My uncle is watching Eduardo and Elvis for us."

"Is it your uncle who works for the Marine Park?" Emily asked.

"Santiago, *si*."

"Well, when you get back from dinner, be sure to tell him to be on the lookout for a video of the *Nordic Starr* being naughty below the waterline. Oh, bugger, that came out sleazy."

Ricardo laughed. "You have a way with words, Emilita. You and Boone are welcome to join us for dinner."

"Nah, we aren't about to mess up your date night," Boone said. "Besides, we need to get back and walk Brix." Boone didn't like to leave the dog alone for too long; they usually arranged a dog sitter for the two-tank morning dives, but for a night dive, the pooch was fine.

"Where are you dining?" Em asked.

"La Choza."

"Love that place," Boone said. And he did; situated a couple blocks back from the main drag, the restaurant was somewhat protected from the hordes of cruise passengers. The kitchen churned out regional favorites, and locals and expats kept it supplied with a brisk business.

"Be sure to get the avocado pie!" Emily gushed. "When I first saw that on the menu, I thought, 'oh my, no.' But I went from yuck to yum in one bite."

"I know it well," Ricardo said, ducking down the interior steps to retrieve his bicycle. "I'll see you both at the Marina at sunrise, yes?"

"Easy on the margaritas," Boone warned, as he helped the Cozumeleño with the bike.

◆ • ◆

After securing the *Lunasea* at the marina, Boone and Emily took Em's Bug south on the main highway that looped around the southern half of Cozumel.

"Everything went pear-shaped so fast," Em said. "I can't believe you caught up with Nicholas. It looked like that thingie was going flat-out."

"I almost *didn't* catch him," Boone admitted. "He used his fin as a brake and managed to slow himself enough that I was just able to reach him. Of course, he could've just let go of the damn thing. It malfunctioned, I guess."

"Maybe. But weird it wound up right under their boat, yeah?"

"I suppose. Maybe it was stuck in a clockwise circle when I yanked him off of it. From where we were, it would make sense." He watched Em chew that over for a bit. "Sorry you missed your five-star tour," he said.

"Oh, that... I'll survive. Luxury breeds envy, yeah? Personally, I'm quite happy with our new digs."

Just then, they reached their current accommodations, the Residencias Reef condos. Situated five miles south of the marina and under seven from town, it was far from the bustle of the cruise ship crowds. They had managed to find a reasonably priced rental condo there shortly after they arrived. Owned by an author of thrillers, it seemed somewhat appropriate, given what they'd been through the last few years. Though in the past, Boone and Em had been quite frugal in their choice of lodgings, they'd decided to kick it up a notch after their windfall from Belize. The oceanside balcony was ideal for unwinding at sunset, and the fact that the resort allowed dogs was an added bonus.

As Boone reached the condo, he heard a flurry of sniffing behind the door. "No sneaking up on you, huh, Brix?" He opened the door and the potlicker dog nearly bowled him over with frantic affection, but quickly redirected his attentions to Emily.

"Ohhhhh, I *know*, Brixton… we've been gone for *years*! You wanna go walkies?"

Brixton froze, ears flopping with the sudden cessation of movement. Then he took off like a shot and retrieved his harness and attached leash, dragging them to the door.

"Good boy, Brix!" Boone took the items and affixed the vest to the pooch. "Okay, let's go see what we can see. Or sniff. But no chasing those coatis, okay, buddy?"

"Listen to Boone, Brixton. One of those little buggers bit me, remember?"

Boone laughed. "When they say, 'don't feed the wildlife'…"

"I know, I know."

"Especially if you don't bring enough for everybody…"

"You are never gonna let me live that down, are you?"

"Hey, I have so few victories in this relationship, you gotta give me that one."

The Cozumel coati was a species of small mammal that may have been introduced to the island by the Mayans. Looking like a cross between a long-nosed raccoon and a cat, the animals lived in family groups and were known to hang around some of the southern resorts, looking for handouts. Shortly after they arrived on-island, Emily had made the mistake of offering her last bite of a banana... and when the other seven didn't get anything, one decided to vigorously demonstrate his displeasure. A trip to the clinic had capped off the event.

Boone let Brixton drag them down a path, the tropical foliage illuminated by a mixture of solar lights, some staked in the ground, others strapped to trees. A hermit crab slowly made its way in front of them and they paused to allow Brixton an exploratory sniff.

"Better just eat a quick dinner and hit the hay," Boone suggested. "Early day tomorrow."

"Yeah, you're gonna want some extra time in the morning to spruce up. Need to look your best for the reincarnation of Aphrodite."

"You're the only goddess I see on this island."

"Ooh, nice save. Point to Mr. Fischer."

"Are we doing a tennis thing now? I can never tell."

"Hey," Em said, changing the subject abruptly. "What do you think of Calypso?"

"Callie? I dunno. Sulky teen."

"Boone, she's in her twenties."

"You know what I mean. She's the youngest in the family. Probably got a chip on her shoulder."

"I don't think she likes me."

"Why do you say that?"

"She said some stuff... I dunno."

Brixton spotted a neighbor's dog and strained against the leash. Boone waved and let the potlicker advance for a friendly greeting.

"What did she say?"

"Oh, nothing... just winding me up. You need to bone up on Devil's Throat? Last time you dropped us in a hundred yards away from the entry."

"We didn't have Ricardo with us that day," Boone said, glancing at his smartphone and tapping an icon. "He'll put us right on target. Here, take Brix a sec."

Emily took the leash from Boone, its length pulled taught as the dog greeted the neighbor's Shih Tzu. "What are you looking at?"

"Just checking the weather. Heard there was a system coming in, but I think it's angling up into the Yucatán below us." He pulled up the radar. "Yeah, it's gonna soak the mainland, but we should be fine. Minimal wind. Devil's Throat, here we come."

❖ • ❖

"Here we go," Stallion said, as Angler wheeled the room service cart that had been left outside the door into the suite. "My steak better be rare this time, or me 'n' the chef are gonna have words."

Tolstoy rose from his chair, tossing aside the room service menu he'd been perusing long after they'd ordered. "I cannot believe there is no Caspian caviar. This is a cruise for the most rich, yes? And they do not have best? It is inconsolable!"

"Inconceivable," Potluck said, lifting one silver lid after another, inspecting the meals.

"*Chto?*"

"The word you were trying to dredge up from your third-grade English classes is 'inconceivable.'"

Tolstoy wrinkled his brow. "*Nyet.* I do not think that means what you think it means."

Angler chuckled as he came in from the balcony. The way these two went at each other, he figured they'd have sex sooner or later. He was pretty sure they hadn't yet; the suite was large but not very soundproofed. Stallion's snoring was proof enough of that. He reached across Potluck and snagged the grilled snapper he'd ordered. Smothered in peppers and onions, the head was still on it, just the way he liked it.

Stallion grabbed a knife and cut into his steak while the plate was still on the tray. "Dammit. Medium. I'm making them take this back." He strode to the retro phone beside the bar but only raised the receiver an inch before Angler pressed it back into the cradle.

"No, you're not. Eat the damn steak. You got one more dinner after this, then we're going to sea and we'll do our job, and then you can go buy your own damn steakhouse."

Stallion's look of annoyance transitioned to one of contemplation. "Maybe I will..."

Tolstoy took a sizeable bite from the hamburger he'd ordered. Thus far, hamburgers had been the *only* thing the Russian had ordered.

"Angler, this is Palantir, do you copy?"

Angler reached to his earpiece and triggered it, the action activating the wireless lavalier microphone clipped to his shirt. The others followed suit, so the message would go out to all four members of the team. "This is Angler. Dinner is served."

"Uh..." The electronically modulated voice hesitated. *"Dinner is served'? I don't see that on the list of code phrases I sent you..."*

Unseen to the speaker, Angler rolled his eyes. "Negative, Palantir. That's just basic English. Our room service arrived and we're eating it."

"Ah. I trust everything is to your satisfaction?"

Tolstoy and Stallion both opened their mouths, but Angler shot them a look.

"Food's great. But I'm guessing you didn't call to check on our dinner."

"Correct. The helicopter crew have finished their maintenance checks and the hangar is locked for the night. Tolstoy, I want you to go up via the crew stairs that are situated four doors down the corridor on your right. Familiarize yourself with the controls. You did read over the manuals for the ACH160, I trust?"

Tolstoy rapidly chewed and swallowed the bite of hamburger in his mouth. *"Da.* Is piece of pie. I have flown the 145. Controls are similar."

"Good, but I still want you to go up and spend two hours in the cockpit. There is a keyboard lock on the hangar. The code is 1-2-3-5."

Tolstoy blew a raspberry. *"Tupoy,"* he muttered.

"Say again, Tolstoy."

"He's on the job, Palantir," Angler butted in. "Anything else?"

"That's all for now. Palantir out."

"Pass code is like for children," Tolstoy said after the members of the team killed their mics. "Oh well, at least I get to leave room."

"Again," Angler said.

"Chto?"

"You get to leave the room… again. You snuck out last night for seventeen minutes."

Tolstoy's look of innocence dissolved into an impish grin. "You are soft sleeper."

"Potluck, go with him. Make sure he doesn't get lost on the way to or from the bird."

"Can I finish my pasta?" she asked.

Minutes later, the Russian and the Wisconsinite slipped out of the suite, situated at the end of a passageway on the port side of the ship. Dressed in the expensive casual wear their employer had provided them, the pair went straight to the fourth door on their right, on the interior side of the corridor. Moving quickly, they climbed the single flight of stairs, which ended at a pair of doors. The door labeled "Bridge" was situated on the left. The "Hangar" door was to the right, on the stern side.

Tolstoy stood before the keypad and sneered at the red light at the top. He affected a look of sheer stupidity on his face and punched each number slowly, speaking each one as he did so. "One... two... three... and now I will be so clever and skip to... five." The light switched to green and a metallic click sounded.

Potluck suppressed a smile and pulled the door open. "Come on, Ivan."

Potluck entered the hangar with Tolstoy on her heels. Once inside, the Russian paused and took a black case from the inner pocket of his blazer.

"Lockpicks?" Potluck asked. "I doubt they lock the helo if they lock the hangar."

Tolstoy smiled, opening the case, which was actually a flat box. Shiny gold paper caught the light and it was clear the box was some sort of cigarette pack. He extracted one and popped it in his mouth. The cigarette itself was black and the filter was wrapped in more gold paper.

"What the holy hell is that?"

"A Black Russian. You want?" Tolstoy handed her the box while he fished a lighter from his pocket.

106

Potluck examined the black box, its edges gilded with gold. "Black Russian. It says London. These aren't Russian."

"I know, but who cares?" He lit the cigarette and admired it. "It look cool, *da*?"

"Where the hell did you get these?" she asked, handing the pack back to him.

"Duty Free shop on main level. They had good vodka too." He took a puff, then walked around the helicopter. "Airbus ACH160. Corporate model. Is not on market yet and standard H160 not have folding rotor blades, so the ship owners must have influence. Or maybe is prototype."

"Pretty enough," Potluck noted. "So, *did* you read the stats our employer sent us?"

Tolstoy smiled, taking another drag of the cigarette before speaking.

"Composite airframe, strong but light. Twin Turbomeca Arrano turboshafts and the tail rotor is shrouded for to be silent. Blue Edge rotor blades cut noise up to fifty percent from conventional rotor shape. Can hold twelve passengers, but with VIP seating is more often five to eight. Cruising speed is just over 150 knots, maximum speed 175. Range is…" He thought for a moment. "At cruising speed, range is 530 miles. Less with full load."

"Wow, you actually read it."

Tolstoy grinned, the gold filter pinched in his teeth. The ebony cigarette waggled as he spoke. "Nothing else to read but shitty menu with no decent caviar." He bypassed the cockpit door and moved closer to Potluck, reaching around her to slide open the passenger door. "You know… helicopter is very roomy. We have two hours. For to learn controls… I only need thirty minutes."

10

A faint glimmer of pink suffused the eastern sky as Boone's yellow Thing puttered to a stop in the marina parking lot beside Emily's Bug. Ricardo stepped out unsteadily and Emily burst into laughter as she exited her vehicle.

"Another successful transit from Point A to Point B, with no loss of life or limb! How's the tailbone, Ricardo?"

"It's still there, I think."

"Har dee har har," Boone muttered amiably. "Did you get the tanks?"

"Yes indeed. Already wheeled them down to the boat. Brixton settled in?"

"Elvis was still asleep," Boone said, "so we snuck Brix into the guest room."

Ricardo yawned. "Coffee?" he asked hopefully.

"Boone and I tanked up at our flat but there's a thermos up top with your name on it."

"*Gracias!*"

"*De nada.* Y'know, I realize we get up at the arse-crack of dawn a lot, but there's something magical about it, yeah? Well... provided you get enough caffeine into you so your brain can properly enjoy it." She thrust out her arms in a Y and took a lung-filling breath, tilting her head back, breathing in the pre-dawn air with a smile on her lips.

Watching her, Boone felt his own breath taken away. He'd known Em for a few years now, but there were still times when her beauty walloped him anew. Em wasn't wearing anything particularly alluring, having selected an oversized Baja hoodie to keep out the early morning chill. The shorts she wore were faded from sun and salt and below them, the lightly tanned skin of her legs picked up the soft glow of the impending sunrise. She had braided her hair into two cords that twined together into a short length of ponytail at the back, the better to avoid tangling her copious hair in her mask.

Em abruptly dropped her arms and retrieved her green sunglasses from the neckline of her hoodie. "Here comes the day," she said, looking east over the interior of the island: an expanse of squat, tropical trees and low scrub for the most part. As pinks shifted to oranges, she slid her sunglasses atop her nose and headed down the pier. "C'mon, Booney. Time to make the crumpets."

Boone grabbed two bags of gear from the Thing and hustled after her.

"We have company," Ricardo called out from the flybridge, coffee thermos in hand.

A black SUV from a motor pool in San Miguel drove into the marina parking lot. The windows were rolled down and Boone could make out the Othonos sisters in the rear seats.

"They're early," Em said.

"Fine by me." Boone walked back up the pier, leaving Emily to arrange their gear. As he neared the shore, he watched the driver—a local clad in a white dress shirt and black slacks—open the hatchback and extract four tanks, two with BCDs and regulators already attached. *That's odd.* It was unusual for divers to provide their own tanks, particularly ones who hadn't brought their own for the last three dives. No yellow and green markings, though, so not labeled as Nitrox. Frowning, Boone joined the sisters at the lot.

"You brought tanks? We've got plenty. Just air, though. Devil's Throat is too deep for Nitrox."

"Oh, these are air," Calypso said. "We have a full dive shop and compressor on board the *Apollo*."

Lyra laid a hand on Boone's forearm. "I hope it is all right. Callie told me that Nicholas insisted we have our own tanks and gear for such a dangerous dive."

"Dangerous is a bit harsh. Challenging, yes. But look, I can assure you, all of our gear is carefully maintained. We use the most reliable fill station on-island and—"

"I'm sure your gear is fine," Calypso interrupted. "My brother's a paranoid… 'wanker'? Is that the word your girlfriend would use?"

"Callie, be nice," Lyra chided.

Boone shrugged. "Hey, s'okay… the customer is always right." *Except when they're not,* his brain added. He reached down and snagged the two outfitted tanks. The driver grabbed the other two as Lyra and Callie retrieved their gear bags. Together, the group made their way to the end of the pier, Boone well in the lead.

"What's with the tanks?" Emily asked.

"Tell ya later," Boone said quietly, lifting one across to her.

Once aboard with their gear arranged, Boone went to Callie and Lyra's stations and checked their rigs. Both women had integrated dive computers. While some recreational divers used simple dive computers on their wrists, many opted for one that replaced the pressure gauge on the first stage of the regulator. The advantage was that all of the data you'd need was in one place: current depth, time at depth, ascent/descent rates, and air in the tank. "Wristies" would have to look at two different readouts.

Em slipped over beside Boone as he opened the valve on one of the tanks and checked the pressure. Seeing what he was up to, she opened the valve on the other. Some fill ops might give you a tank with a stingy 2800 psi. For most divers and dives, that would be fine, but an air hog might burn through that too quickly. And for Devil's Throat, Boone liked to make sure each tank was topped off at 3200; the ones he and Emily had on board were already verified to be at that pressure.

"I've got thirty-three," Boone said.

"Same here." Em shut the valve to conserve the air.

"They *are* good tanks."

"Ours are fine," Emily muttered.

"Callie said their brother insisted," Boone explained. "No biggie. *Oye*, Ricardo! Let's head out!"

◆ ◆ ◆

Em watched as Boone pulled himself up onto the swim platform, his long arms cording with muscle for the brief moment of exertion. Her lanky fella had just free-dived down a short distance to confirm the current. Dripping saltwater, he flashed her a quick thumbs-up. Emily smiled back as the young man toweled off.

"All right, ladies… Em has asked me to handle the briefing…" Boone looked back at her to confirm.

Because Little Miss Sunshine Floppy Hat doesn't like my style, Em thought. *Know your audience.* But she just smiled and waved him on, focused on finishing up the white board drawing of the dive profile.

The *Lunasea* floated near the southernmost tip of Cozumel, above a dive site known as Punta Sur (Southern Point). Once they were finished with the briefing, Em would head up to the fly-bridge to take the wheel from Ricardo, while he headed down to the bow to eyeball the drop point. Lyra and Calypso had donned their wetsuits, and the younger sister had taken her floppy sun hat off. During their southward passage, Em had been silently willing the breeze to whip that thing off, sending it sailing into the ocean to join the schools of flying fish.

"You are about to experience *El Garganto del Diablo,* The Devil's Throat." Boone gestured to the water around them. "Because of the depth of this dive, we don't want to burn too many bubbles finding the entrance to the swim-through, so we'll locate the exact entry point when we're geared up and ready to jump in."

Lyra smiled and sat forward on the bench in front of her tank and BCD. "I'm a little nervous," she admitted.

"No need to be," Boone said. He nodded to Calypso as well. "You both have plenty of dives under your belts and the current is being surprisingly cooperative today."

"Plus, there's only two of you to wrangle, so we'll have a close eye on you both at all times," Emily chimed in. "And thanks to our arse-crack-of-dawn departure, looks like we have the place all to ourselves!"

"Always a plus," Boone acknowledged. "So, Ricardo will get us above the entrance, and we'll drop to the sand. You'll see a number of coral heads there and I'll guide you to the first opening to the swim-through, situated at about eighty-three feet. Watch your entry and don't kick the sponge that's growing in front of it—just drop down into the first chamber. It's a large, sandy-bottomed cavern called The Foyer."

Boone turned back to Emily, who stood and secured the whiteboard to the back of the flybridge ladder, facing the little audience of two. The map of the site was surprisingly by-the-book, and without the usual riot of color from multiple dry-erase markers. Boone raised an eyebrow at her. Em pretended not to see it and he shrugged and tapped a space near the top of the dive plan.

"From Foyer, we'll proceed to the main opening of The Devil's Throat. It might take me a moment to find it; sometimes the sand gets shifted up against the walls and can obscure the little entrance. Unlike the famous Cathedral chamber to the south, the Throat is pretty cozy, so watch your buoyancy. We don't want you doing a steel drum solo with your tanks on the ceiling... well, aluminum drum solo, I guess it would be. And careful you don't kick up sand from the bottom. It's dark enough down there without blasting the person behind you with a sandstorm."

"How dark is it?" Lyra asked.

"Plenty dark once we've gone a ways into it. You'll want your dive light on when we enter. And you both have spares?"

Lyra nodded. "Yes."

"I'm surprised Nicholas didn't insist on spares for the spares," Calypso muttered.

"It's not pitch black, though," Emily interjected. "There are a few mini swim-throughs here and there that let in light from the outside. Still... it *is* kinda spooky, yeah?"

Calypso threw her a glance, then returned her gaze to Boone as he continued.

"Since it's just the four of us, let's keep it simple. I'll lead, Lyra you're next, then Callie. Emily will bring up the rear."

"Insert buttocks joke here," Em deadpanned. *Yep... there's the eyeroll from Callie, right on cue,* she thought.

"The Throat itself is a sixty-foot-long tunnel, pitched down at a forty-five-degree angle. You'll be falling into the darkness much of the time. When we get to the bottom, you'll see open water. The exit is at 135 feet and you'll pop out of the wall at a sheer drop off, so deep you won't see the bottom."

Lyra squealed and clapped her hands together, a mix of fear and delight.

"You got that right," Em said with enthusiasm. "That view is Dench!"

Lyra looked confused. "What is that word?"

"More colorful slang," Calypso muttered.

Boone laughed. "She means like the actress Judi Dench. You know... something badass."

"Oh, I like her," Lyra said. Calypso sighed and checked her dive watch.

"Okay, once you exit the cave, don't go swimming into the blue. The currents around Punta Sur can be very strong, so while it's calm up here, no telling what it'll be down there. The channel can produce strong upwelling or downwelling currents, so hug the wall and I'll assess the current and how much air you both have. If conditions are good, I will take us south, to the left, and we'll come back shallow through the Cathedral. If you've heard about a cool-looking cross in there, sorry, but Hurricane Wilma took it out long ago. But it's a beautiful swim-through, much less claustrophobic than Devil's Throat."

"And if we are low on air, or the current is too strong?" Lyra asked.

115

"Then I'll take us north instead and we'll make our way up to about eighty feet. You're both excellent with your air consumption, so the current would most likely be the reason we have to go that way. We'll then enjoy the scenery as we make our way along the top of the wall toward Colombia Deep. I'll send up the safety sausage and Ricardo will stand by to pick us up. We'll drift at a five-minute safety stop if air allows. The Throat exit is technically below recreational depth limits, so a little extra beyond the usual three minutes is a good idea. Questions?"

Calypso raised her hand.

"Yes, Callie?"

She pointed at the whiteboard. "I don't see any scribbles of mermaids or sea unicorns. I feel cheated. Surprised you didn't draw a little devil on there for us, Emily... given the name of the dive and all."

Emily had counted on this exchange and she smiled sweetly. "Oh, sorry." She unclipped the whiteboard from the ladder, flipped it, and reattached it.

Lyra burst into laughter. On the whiteboard was a surprisingly passable likeness of Calypso in full scuba gear, blowing bubbles... but with her sun hat on. Its broad brim was extended to near-comical proportions, flapping in the water, and from the school of eagle rays around her it was clear what Emily was going for. The rays had their wings in similar motion to that of the hat's brim.

Emily tapped the Callie-Ray with the dry-erase marker in her hand. "Yeah, so... Lyra... you may see one of these on the way up, but they can be quite standoffish, so don't approach too closely." She bounced the marker against her lower lip, then uncapped it and added angry eyebrows. Lyra laughed harder.

Emily wasn't sure what reaction she would get from the younger sister, and frankly she didn't care. But Callie surprised her. The sullen sister's face cracked a smile that looked somewhat authentic.

"Nice one," she offered. Her smile faded to her default expression, but she added, "You're all right."

"Oh, far from it," Em said, capping the pen. "I'm positively barmy. Was nicknamed Emiloony in middle school. Surprised no one's locked me up, yet."

"Lucky for me, the men in the white coats haven't caught up with you," Boone said. "If you can keep the madness at bay, head up top and take over the wheel and send Ricardo to the bow."

"You're not the boss of me!" Em sang, scrambling up the ladder. "Ricardo, you're up!"

———◆◆———

Boone nodded to Ricardo as the Cozumeleño passed by him, stepping up on the gunwale and making his way forward. Boone gathered the upper part of his wetsuit that dangled from his waist and slid into it with practiced ease. "Lyra, Callie… gear up while we put the *Lunasea* above the Throat."

Callie stood in front of her gear and turned on her air. Boone saw that Lyra had already Velcro'd herself into her BC harness and was reaching back over her shoulder, trying to find her valve. Boone leaned over and twisted it on.

"Thank you, Boone." Lyra raised the integrated computer on its hose and looked at the screen. "It says I have 3200 psi… wait… 3100…" She held it out to him.

Boone took the computer. The readout was at 3100 but after a second it flickered back to 3200. "Tanks sometimes lose some pressure during the boat ride. I'm betting you're right on the line of about 3150 and it's just bouncing around. You've got plenty. You're very good with your breathing."

"You've been watching me," she stated, a curl at the corner of her full lips.

"I wouldn't be a good divemaster if I didn't."

She grabbed his arm. "You will protect me down there?"

Boone didn't think the question had any true anxiety in it, and this was probably more of her flirtation. But that line of thinking wasn't professional; claustrophobia could take hold of some people on this dive. He placed his hand on hers. "You'll do great. I'll be right in front of you, guiding the group. You need me, tug my fin. But ya know what?"

"What?"

"You won't need to do that... 'cause you'll be too busy experiencing a once-in-a-lifetime dive. Breathe easy, gentle kicks. The angle of the tunnel will practically let you fall. You'll just be gliding through a coral tunnel. Sit back and enjoy the ride."

"Yes..."

Boone suddenly realized he was circling the pad of his thumb on the back of her hand. It was something he sometimes did when talking someone down from a panic attack or a bout of seasickness—he must have unconsciously started the motion. He quickly withdrew his hand.

Lyra blinked, then smiled, pearly whites flashing. "Thank you."

"Uh... sure... no prob." Boone scrambled for the flybridge ladder. "Em? How we doing?"

"Ricardo's on the scent!"

Boone joined her at the wheel and looked over the dash at the bow. Ricardo was crouching on the starboard side as they moved slowly south. After a moment, he chopped his hand to starboard and Em turned the wheel, stopping when Ricardo held his palm up. He stood, pointing just off the starboard bow.

"Right down there!" He scrambled around the side to head up and take the wheel.

Boone descended to the deck. "All right! Here we go!"

11

Emily descended last, dropping toward the sandy bottom above and behind Calypso. Far below, she could make out Boone near the coral outcrops that framed the entrance to The Foyer. Lyra was nearly to the bottom herself, angling toward him. Emily gently emptied her lungs to speed her descent, pausing to pinch her nose and equalize her ears. Boone was able to effortlessly equalize with just a movement of his jaw, a skill Em was envious of. She *could* do it with some difficulty, but the nose pinch was far easier for her.

Boone raised his mask to her and lifted his hand in an interrogative "OK" sign. She flashed the gesture back to him, and he switched his attention to Lyra and Calypso in turn. When everyone was gathered around him, he turned and finned toward the coral. Finding the entrance to The Foyer, he dropped inside. Lyra followed. Calypso hesitated, looking back at Emily. Em raised her fingers to flash a signal to Callie, but the young woman had already turned away and was following Lyra into the opening.

Emily gently kicked and angled herself down the swim-through into the sandy chamber. A vast school of big-eyed, silvery fish flashed in the dappled light. *Glassy sweepers,* Em noted. The Devil's Throat dive wasn't about spotting marine life, but this gathering was impressive. The scintillating school parted for the divers and re-formed in a far corner of The Foyer.

Boone was near the back wall, his dive light in hand, scanning the edge of the chamber. Turning back, he gestured to the group, then circled the beam of his light on a chute in the sand that dropped into darkness. A final "OK" sign was offered up and everyone responded in the affirmative. Reaching down to the sand, he took a small handful and tossed it into a little cloud, then waggled his finger: *No, no.* He then brought up his index and middle fingers and wiggled them up and down aggressively, miming someone kicking too hard. He shook his head. Then he "kicked" his fingers gently and nodded in the affirmative.

Lyra smiled around her regulator, nodding back before taking her dive light from a pocket and turning it on. Callie took hers out too. Boone turned, rose slightly, then tilted his body forward and dropped into the hole. After a moment, Lyra followed.

Em watched Lyra's long legs drop from sight and moved toward the entry point, preparing to follow Calypso. It was then that the younger sister turned, scribbling on an underwater slate that was clipped to her BCD. Emily floated closer as Calypso held it up to face her.

I changed my mind. Sorry. Let's go over the top and wait for them.

Em stared at her. *You have got to be... no, no... if she's scared, she's scared.* A sudden onset of fear or anxiety... no one was immune. Emily herself had been struggling with occasional bouts ever since her harrowing ordeal on the slopes of Saba's Mount Scenery during Hurricane Irma. And Boone, too, had had a panic attack last year that might have been tied to an underwater incident he'd experienced. Emily had been taking weekly online therapy sessions with a woman she had been fortunate to find during her time in Belize and it had helped immensely.

Although Callie didn't strike me as the wilting flower type. But maybe her ill-mannered demeanor is all an act. All things considered, though, it sure would've been nice if she had gotten cold feet *before* Boone and Lyra had dropped down the Throat. Signaling them to come back was an option, but they'd have the difficult task of turning around in there, which was a surefire way to end up with a whiteout of sand. The actual transit of Devil's Throat didn't take all that long. Better to swing up and over. She could follow his bubbles and find one of the smaller tunnels and tubes that cut into the Throat in a few places, then flash her light down there to let him know she and Callie were outside and okay. And worst case, she could signal Boone as he came out.

Em held up an "OK" sign and gestured for Callie to follow as she finned back toward The Foyer's skylight.

———◆•◆———

Despite having dived Devil's Throat numerous times, Boone felt a surge of adrenaline as he dropped into the inky gloom. He had turned his dive light down to its lower setting, so Lyra and Callie could enjoy the atmosphere of the swim-through, which was much of the reason this experience was so memorable. He glanced back and saw Lyra's light sweeping around, throwing shadows as its beam came into contact with uneven surfaces inside the tunnel. Along the roof of the swim-through, a glittering trail of bubbles led back the way they'd come. Callie must've gotten a slow start, as he couldn't make out a light further back. *Em will have her well in hand,* he thought. He looked forward again, taking a moment to cover the beam of his light with his palm. A dim glow came down from above and to the right, one of several smaller openings that pierced the Throat in places. Ahead and far below... dark as pitch.

Boone allowed himself to fall into the shadows, a touch of negative buoyancy allowing him to move down the sloping tunnel with only an occasional kick. The walls were close and the sound of his breathing—both the intake through the regulator and the expelled bubbles—seemed amplified in the closeness. The rhythmic sounds were interrupted by a dull, metallic clang from behind and above. *Lyra probably hit her tank against the roof. Happens to the best of us.* Reaching out to gently apply a two-finger hold to a nearby ridge of dead coral, he came to a halt and twisted his torso in the claustrophobic passageway to look back up the way he'd come. There was a slight bend in the tunnel as it angled toward him and he could just see the beam of Lyra's dive light—but there was something off about it. It was illuminating the ceiling of the Throat, the circle of light moving slightly side-to-side. *But it's not getting any closer.*

Boone quickly turned his dive light to its higher setting and contorted himself around in the Throat, careful not to kick up too much sand. He finned back up in three carefully controlled kicks. As he reached the bend, the first thing he spotted was the tip of Lyra's fin. Kicking harder, he ascended into line with her and his heart rose into his throat.

Lyra was lying motionless against the side of The Devil's Throat. Her dive light floated in the water column, attached to her wrist by its lanyard, spotlighting the ceiling above the opposite wall. Her raven hair, tied back in a ponytail, fanned out above her, black tendrils moving in the water like a gorgonian. Her mask lay facedown in the light sand of the tunnel floor. *Fainted? Or something worse?* Boone settled beside her as best he could—the tunnel was probably no more than four feet across at that point. He could see that the mouthpiece of the second stage of her regulator, the primary breathing apparatus, was in her mouth. *Good.* Boone let go of his dive light, letting it float on its own lanyard as he reached a hand behind her head and tipped her chin up, using his other hand to ensure her mouthpiece stayed in place. Her eyes were closed. He gently shook her. No response. It was at that moment that Boone noticed something else. *No bubbles!* Lyra's integrated computer lay on the bottom beside her and he clawed for it, scanning the readout. *2200 psi? That's better than what I have in my own tank! Unless...* He tilted her to the side and grabbed the manual inflator for the air bladder in her BCD. Buoyancy control devices were basically a human version of a fish's swim bladder. Connected to the tank along with the primary and secondary stages of the regulator, you could add air to the BCD to add buoyancy. Boone thumbed the inflator. Nothing happened. The tank was empty.

In a rush, Boone yanked the yellow-hosed octopus loose from where it was attached at his side and brought it to her face. The octo, or second stage regulator, was a backup air source, feeding off of the same tank. Taking a calming breath of his own, he positioned the octopus as close to her mouth as possible, then pulled her regulator free and inserted the mouthpiece between her lips, praying she didn't take in much water. Rolling her slightly to the side, he tilted her head back to open the airway.

Come on, come on... Blackouts in the water could lead to laryngospasm, an automatic response where the body closed the airway to keep water out. He was fairly sure that the tank had only just run dry. The sound of the tank banging the ceiling might have been the moment she realized she wasn't drawing any breath from the reg. Again, he gently shook her. If she didn't breathe in the next five seconds, he'd focus on surfacing. Fortunately, as his mental count reached three, he heard a slight intake of breath, followed by a weak cough. Boone watched a welcome cluster of bubbles leave the octopus and flutter to the roof of the swim-through.

Okay… we're probably two-thirds of the way through the tunnel, but taking her down to 135 is not a good idea. Ditto trying to get her out through one of the side tunnels. I've done that before, but it's tricky enough without carrying an unconscious diver with you. Nope, back the way we came. This strategizing occurred in less than three seconds, and Boone was about to begin the process of turning her around when a new thought entered his mind.

Where are Emily and Calypso?

◆ ◆ ◆

Emily had reached the top of the coral head that encapsulated The Devil's Throat and she and Calypso had coasted along, watching the twin streams of bubbles rising from the landscape below. The Throat was not a solid tunnel, and the escaping air from Boone and Lyra found many places to make its way toward the surface.

Em glanced back at Calypso. The woman was glancing to and fro, looking at the fish, any sign of the earlier claustrophobia now absent. Callie looked at her dive watch, then checked her integrated computer. Looking up, she saw Emily watching her and flashed an "OK" sign.

Em returned it, then looked back down. *Boone and Lyra should be about two-thirds done… huh. That's odd.* Emily could only see a single stream of bubbles now. *One of them is probably in a solid stretch of tunnel*, she thought, continuing to make her way to the drop-off to greet Boone when he came out. A moment later, the bubbles seemed to halt... then started to move back the way they had come.

Em kicked hard and descended to the roof of the Throat. The bubbles were now stationary. Did Boone and Lyra cluster together? Perhaps Lyra got cold feet too, and Boone was taking her back?

Em looked up at Calypso and raised a flattened palm to her. *Stop*. She swam to the point where the bubbles were rising from. *Damn, just a little crack*. She began to scan the outcrop, searching for a penetration point.

◆ ◆ ◆

Boone had briefly considered removing Lyra's vest and tank completely. This went against everything he'd learned in rescue classes, but the tank was empty and she was breathing his air. Plus, turning her around in the narrow tunnel and maneuvering her out of the Throat would be easier without the extra bulk. But these thoughts had quickly been cancelled out by the knowledge that removing her rig would take precious time, and keeping the octopus in her mouth during the procedure would be tricky. Also, some residual air might actually remain, and as he reached the lower pressure of shallower water, he might be able to inflate her BCD, which would make things easier when they hit the surface.

He managed to turn her around in the swim-through, the action kicking up a lot of sand that nearly created a white-out as the dive lights reflected off of the clouds of particles. Fortunately,

Boone had a clear mental picture of the immediate surroundings and aimed himself up the forty-five-degree angle of the tunnel, starting to kick. Lyra appeared to be in a state of semi-consciousness, and Boone was okay with that at the moment. If she suddenly came fully awake and went into panic mode, this rescue could end very, *very* quickly. Grasping her firmly with one arm behind her lower back under her tank, he pressed her against him, using his other hand to keep the spare air source tightly in her mouth.

Metallic bongs of tank on tunnel echoed around them as Boone finned with bold strokes, the confines of the Throat making it inevitable that they periodically collided with the sides. Lyra's tank was empty, and Boone's was half-full; their impacts rang with different tones, like two distinct musical instruments, playing a haphazard duet.

A shaft of light shone in the tunnel ahead, moving to and fro. *Emily?* Nearing the beam, Boone noticed that it was coming from outside the swim-through. He made his way into the light and looked up, the light illuminating his mask. The beam abruptly switched to the bearer, as Emily shone the dive light on herself, then returned it to Boone. The white spot of the light moved slightly to the side, and he could see she was spotlighting Lyra.

Quickly, Boone fired off a rush of signals. He slashed his hand across his throat, then tapped the flat of his palm against his regulator, then pumped a flattened hand in the direction of The Foyer, and finally jerked a thumb up. Without waiting for recognition, Boone resecured his grip on Lyra and kicked hard for the entrance.

Out of air. Sharing air. Heading to Foyer entry. Ascending.

Emily understood each of the signals and what was meant by them, given the context. Lyra had run out of air, was on Boone's octo, and he was taking her to the shallow end for an emergency surface.

Quickly, she signaled to Calypso with a thumbs-up, ordering her to ascend. The woman shrugged, holding her arms out, palms up. Not an official dive signal, but Emily took it to mean *What's going on?*

Emily began to ascend, quickly pointing at the bubbles and signaling "out of air," before repeating the thumbs-up signal. For most people, a "thumbs-up" meant things were good, but this was certainly not the case today.

She checked her gauge, making sure not to rush her ascent, and ensuring Calypso was doing likewise. Boone might be in danger of getting the bends this day. No sense in everyone risking decompression sickness.

12

In a situation where a diver was unconscious—or, in Lyra's case, borderline unresponsive—the cardinal rule was to get the distressed diver to the surface and get them medical help as quickly as possible. While the temptation might be strong to ascend quickly, the problem with a rapid ascent was the risk of decompression sickness.

Through the course of a dive, as greater depths exert increasing pressure, nitrogen from the air a diver is breathing is absorbed into the tissues at a higher rate than at sea level. When a diver ascended too rapidly, the sudden drop in pressure could cause the nitrogen to be released into the body at a dangerous rate, the bubbles blocking blood flow to crucial organs, including the brain and heart.

While the classic term "the bends" referred to the pain occurring in joints or extremities, the bubbles could cause far more serious damage, affecting the nervous system, and in some cases causing sudden death.

As Boone finally exited the tiny entrance to The Devil's Throat and rose into The Foyer, he took a moment to assess Lyra's breathing. She seemed to be taking in air from the octo, and bubbles continued to be expelled. Behind the lens of her mask, her eyelids were fluttering.

I'll try to rouse her again once I get us outside.

No longer in the cramped confines of the Throat proper, Boone was able to ramp up the speed. In moments, he reached The Foyer's exit and threaded Lyra through it, angling up into sunlit water. As soon as he had room to maneuver, he shifted his grip to the bottom of the octopus, letting part of his hand cup her chin, tilting her head back to maximize the breathing passage.

Out in the open, Boone breathed a little easier. Since Lyra was taking in air, he decided against a rapid ascent. Because she was not fully conscious—and thus not in full control of her breathing—there was a risk of an overpressure injury in her lungs. If she wasn't exhaling naturally during a fast ascent, the abrupt drop in the surrounding water pressure could cause a pocket of air to expand suddenly and cause a rupture. However, if she didn't come to her senses before they reached the shallows, he would skip the safety stop.

Before beginning the ascent, Boone thought about the orange surface marker buoy, or "safety sausage," at his side. The device was a simple inflatable tube, connected to a line and reel. This was ordinarily filled with air from the secondary regulator and sent to the surface for the dive boat to spot. *But my octo is otherwise occupied,* he thought. *And one of my hands is occupied, too.* Boone realized that unrolling the SMB and inflating it from his primary regulator while maintaining the octopus in Lyra's mouth would be a tall order. Fortunately, he wouldn't have to.

Emily was kicking down toward them, and Boone could see she had just deployed her orange float; far above, the inflated tube shot toward the surface. Calypso floated about twenty feet above Emily, looking down at them, her form silhouetted by the sun's glow. Boone reclipped his buoy and signaled to Emily with his free hand. He tapped his backup regulator and signaled "OK," which wasn't strictly accurate, but he wanted Emily to know Lyra was breathing. He pointed at Emily and then Calypso, then waggled a horizontal hand and flashed a three. *You two, level off and take a safety stop.*

Emily flashed a "three" and an "OK" sign back at him, indicating she understood. Slowly she ascended, continuing to face him, the eyes behind her mask full of concern.

Boone moved behind Lyra, triggering the inflator on his BCD to give the pair of them some positive buoyancy before gripping the valve of her tank in his free hand and beginning to kick for the surface. Twin sets of beeps emanated from their dive computers as he pushed the ascent a little too much at times, but in general he kept it slow and steady. Normally, he hated hearing those beeps, but since his hands were full, it was a good way to control their ascent without looking at the gauge. At about fifty feet, he leaned forward and shouted through his mouthpiece in the vicinity of her ear, giving her tank a little shake. One of her hands came up and weakly pawed at the water before floating limp again.

Boone spotted Emily above, his eyes following the line rising from her, locating the surface marker buoy. Hopefully, Ricardo would be homing in on it. Boone continued his ascent, only slowing when the twin computers scolded him. The distinct rumble of a marine engine sounded in the water around him and Boone scanned the surface. *There!* The underside of the *Lunasea* approached from the west; Ricardo had likely been keeping station over the exit to Devil's Throat, waiting to see if they went left or right.

Boone passed Emily, who was at about thirty feet. She flashed him an "OK" sign and he nodded back, maintaining his grip on Lyra. A final decision to forgo his own safety stop was made, and he broke the surface.

The dive boat's stern was within fifty feet of the safety sausage and Boone inflated his vest fully and tilted Lyra back, kicking hard for the stern ladder. Ricardo, seeing the situation, made a last course correction and left the wheel, practically sliding down the flybridge ladder and dashing aft.

Boone filled his lungs and shouted as loudly as he could. "Oxygen!"

Ricardo abruptly halted his charge and changed direction, moving to where they kept the emergency supplemental oxygen.

Boone brought Lyra to the edge of the transom and was debating removing her vest and tank when the young Mexican reached down and took over the grip on Lyra's tank valve, beginning to haul her out of the water. With help from Boone, they managed to bring her up onto the swim platform, the octopus pulling free from her mouth.

Boone stripped off his fins, hurling them past Ricardo, who was attending to Lyra, removing her BCD. On the deck beside her, the green hard case with the oxygen lay open. As Boone scaled the ladder, he spotted a dive boat slowing off the port side. Marino Mundo's *Barco Rápido*! He could make out Jorge at the wheel.

"What happened?" Ricardo asked frantically.

"Out of air." Boone pointed to the approaching dive boat. "Ricardo, get us underway and radio Jorge. Have him pick up Em and Callie beside the marker buoy."

Ricardo was already climbing the ladder. "We're not going to wait?"

Boone dropped to the deck beside Lyra. "No time. We need to get her to San Miguel. Em and Calypso still need to do a safety stop. Currents are good, they'll be fine." He looked down at Lyra. She looked pale, and if she was breathing it was shallow. Boone shouted up to Ricardo, who was halfway up the ladder, "Wait! Make sure Jorge sees the surface buoy. Once they confirm they've got eyes on, floor it!"

"You got it!"

Boone leaned over and placed his ear above Lyra's mouth. *Might need to clear the airway before grabbing the oxygen,* he thought, sparing a brief second to listen. *Good, I can hear—whoa!*

A warm splatter of bile and saltwater shot straight into his ear as Lyra spat up and began coughing. Boone quickly tilted her onto her side and reached into the case to retrieve the O_2 wrench, turning the oxygen valve into the open position and grabbing the mask.

"Lyra! Can you hear me?"

She continued to cough violently, but managed a nod.

"Good! I want to put this oxygen mask on you... can you give me a few more coughs first? Make sure you're cleared out?"

Lyra didn't need any encouragement, but she did seem to imbue the next few coughs with added purpose. Boone lowered the mask and she took it with a trembling hand, holding it over her mouth and nose. The deck under Boone's knees rumbled with vibration as the *Lunasea* leaped forward from her idle. Ricardo angled the boat toward the ocean, no doubt intending to increase to full speed once outside of the reef. Boone raised himself up and looked to starboard. Jorge was waving back at him, then pointing into the water ahead of his own bow. Like most skippers out here, he was a diver as well, and flashed two fingers to his eyes, then pointed into the water ahead of his bow and signaled "OK." Boone understood his message: *I see the buoy. All's well.*

Boone let out a breath. Leaving Emily behind was a tough choice, but under the circumstances it seemed the right thing to do. He knew her skill level, he knew Marino Mundo was a top-notch dive op, and the current was minimal. Lyra had to get to medical attention as quickly as possible. He was fairly sure Emily would have done the same, if their places were reversed. Still, he felt rather sick about it.

——◆·◆——

"That's not our boat." Calypso was floating alongside Emily, looking around, trying to find the *Lunasea*.

Minutes ago, as they neared the safety stop, Emily had watched the underside of her dive boat race away as another one approached. She knew immediately what was in Boone's head. He'd seen the arriving boat—another charter for Devil's Throat, no doubt—and had opted to get Lyra ashore for medical attention immediately. *It's what I would've done,* Em thought. During the eternity of the three minutes as she floated at fifteen feet, she'd spied a trail line being deployed, the fifty-foot rope and buoy slapping into the water behind the new arrival's stern. When the three minutes were up, she had ascended toward it, signaling Callie to join her.

Now at the surface, she grabbed hold of the trail line and tossed a loop of it over to Calypso. "It's okay. It's the *Barco Rápido* from Marino Mundo. I know them. Boone must've decided he couldn't wait."

Calypso grabbed the line and started hauling herself toward the boat. "So, he just *left* us?"

"If you mean, 'He left us to be picked up by a buddy from a capable dive op so he could save your sister's life,' then yeah, he left us." Em realized her words had come out a little heated. "Let's get aboard."

"*Hola*, Emily!" Jorge called down to her from the swim platform.

"Jorge! Thanks for the save! I'm gonna owe you a brill bit o' dance for this one, yeah?"

"I'm thinking next Friday night at Tiki Tok and we will be even," Jorge said with a laugh, reaching past Emily to take Calypso's fins as she reached the ladder.

"It's a deal!" Emily tossed her own fins onto the platform, shrugging out of her BCD as Calypso climbed out of the water. "Did Boone say where they were going?"

"Not yet, but I'll call them in a moment." He took Emily's tank as she scaled the ladder.

"There are four hyperbaric chambers in the city, but I don't know what our diver's condition is. Can you take us to the Iberostar?" Emily asked, referring to the resort nearest Punta Sur. "Have them arrange a taxi? I'm so sorry if we delayed your dive…"

"*No es nada.*" Jorge waved his hand dismissively, as he turned back to the group. "Nobody minds if we do a good deed before we dive, no?"

Emily grinned broadly as the six divers aboard all made it clear they could delay their gratification for half an hour. She waved to the water behind the stern as the *Barco Rápido* rose up on plane and headed northwest for the shore. "Just so you know, the current is ace, so you'll have a grand time of it!" She walked forward, joining Jorge at the wheel.

"What happened?" he asked.

"Diver ran out of air in the Throat," Em explained. "Exactly what happened, I don't know. Oh, hey... next Friday? Drinks are on me."

"Oh, no, no... I always buy, *pollito*."

"Not this time... 'cause I need to borrow cab fare. All our stuff is on the *Lunasea*."

Sitting on the deck with Lyra's head on his lap and his cell in his hand, Boone ended the call he'd just made and rang up Ricardo. The man answered quickly.

"I don't think I've ever had someone phone me from a few meters away," Ricardo began.

"I didn't want to leave Lyra lying on the deck to come up to you."

The *Lunasea*'s hull form didn't offer the smoothest ride when she reached top speed. Lying flat on the deck would've been a recipe for a bruising transit with a side order of seasickness, so Boone did his best to protect her head from the jarring bounces. He'd made sure to stuff his wetsuit and a balled-up tarp under her knees, doing his best to keep her legs elevated. Furthermore, Lyra was swathed in every dry towel Boone had been able to scrounge. She was still a little pale but seemed to be breathing easily now.

"So, where to?" Ricardo prompted.

"Head for the Aqua Safari pier. We're taking her to the International Hospital up the street. I called ahead."

"*Si, claro.*"

Boone hung up and slipped the phone back into his drybag. He glanced to starboard as they passed by the southern cruise ship piers, the sterns of the *Nordic Starr* and the *Apollo* receding as they raced north.

Lyra couldn't see the piers from her position, but she'd clearly heard his end of the phone call. "Wait... aren't you taking me back to my ship?" she asked, her voice muffled by the oxygen mask. "We have a doctor on board."

"And I'm sure he's very good, but here in Coz we've got specialists for diving accidents. I'm taking you to the Cozumel International Hospital. They're not far from a pier we can use, and they've got a hyperbaric chamber."

During his time in Belize, Boone had heard good things about Subaquatic Safety Services, which had a location on Ambergris Caye. A call to the SSS facility in San Miguel had confirmed their chamber was free, and a UHMS accredited physician was currently available and on site.

And their chamber there has room for four.... Having skipped the safety stop, I might need to make use of it.

Boone hadn't felt any symptoms of DCS, though, and his rapid ascent hadn't pushed the deco limits too far, so all might be well. Lyra on the other hand...

"How are you feeling?" he asked.

Lyra held up a hand and waggled her fingers. "My fingertips are tingling."

That's a symptom of DCS. "Any pain?"

"My elbow hurts... maybe I banged it in the tunnel?"

Or maybe nitrogen bubbles are clustered there. "Any pain in your other elbow or your knees? Headache?"

Lyra thought for a moment. "I don't think so."

"Okay... good." He took her outstretched hand and gripped it. "You're going to be all right."

She adjusted her head in Boone's lap and looked up at him, her face upside down from his vantage point. Her large eyes, a deep brown, shone with moisture. After a moment, she removed the oxygen mask with the hand Boone wasn't currently holding.

"No, let's keep the mask in pl—"

"I will put it back." She reached up with her free hand and stroked his cheek. "You saved me."

Boone smiled. "Maybe a little."

"Thank you, Boone."

"*De nada.*"

The corner of her mouth quirked into a smile, dimpling one cheek. "Did you give me mouth to mouth?"

"Uh... no."

"Good. I would have hated to have missed that..." She stroked his face, and her fingertips brushed his lips.

Boone reddened and retrieved the oxygen mask. "Well, if it makes you feel any better, you *did* throw up in my ear." He freed his hand from hers and pressed the mask into her palm before guiding it back to her face. "Let's keep the mask on, okay? I need to call Emily and let her know where we're headed."

Boone stretched his arm out for his drybag, the rough transit having rolled it under the portside bench. Dragging it closer, he located his phone and made the call... and Emily's drybag rang from its place in the corner of the cockpit. *Oh... right... I left her in the water.* He began scrolling through his contacts to find Jorge, but his phone suddenly rang with an unidentified number. He tapped the phone and answered. "Hello?"

13

"Boone!"

"Em, thank God!"

Emily was overjoyed to hear Boone's voice… and from the relief she heard in it, he was happy to hear hers too.

"Where are you? I'm so sorry I left you, but—"

"Shut your gob, it was the right move. And Jorge plucked us out, no worries. I even got a date out of it." When Boone laughed, Emily plowed ahead. "Listen, we left Iberostar in a taxi about five minutes ago and the cabbie was good enough to loan me his mobile. Where are you? How is Lyra?"

"She's fine." Boone mentioned some of the symptoms to Emily, but stressed that she was breathing well and didn't seem to be suffering from anything serious, all things considered. He explained where they were taking her.

Em turned to Calypso and repeated what she'd been told. Callie nodded, seeming to mull something over. "So she's going to be okay?"

"Yes." Em returned to the call. "What about you? Any symptoms?"

"No. Once I had her breathing, we made a fast ascent, but not crazy-fast. Still, I'll let the doc at the facility decide if I need to spend any time in the chamber."

"Boone, what happened down there?"

"I don't know. Her integrated showed 2200 psi, but that tank was bone dry. I didn't see any leaks... did you see any sudden eruption of bubbles coming up from the swim-through?"

"No, everything looked normal from above."

"I just can't explain it. Hey, we're about to reach the Aqua Safari pier in midtown. I gotta go. Get to the boat and get your phone. I'll be at the hospital on 5th Street South."

"Okay, see you soon. Love you." She hung up, then laughed.

"What?" Calypso asked.

"Oh, nothing... Boone and I just have a habit of meeting at hospitals."

Calypso gave her a quizzical look, then stared out the window for a moment. "What did he say happened?"

"He isn't sure. The computer said she had plenty of air, but she didn't."

"Nicholas said he watched them fill the tanks himself," Callie said. "Well, I'll need to get my belongings anyway, so I'll take her gear back to the *Apollo* and have it inspected."

"After you see your sister," Em prompted.

Callie shrugged. "You said she was fine. I'd only be in the way."

"Well... there's a good chance Lyra's gear will go to the SSS facility. A diving accident like this, they may check things out."

"Oh. In that case..." She leaned forward in her seat. "Driver, drop me at the Puerta Maya pier."

"Wait, what? What about your personal belongings… and your… hat?"

"I'll send someone for them."

The taxi was nearing the cruise ship terminal and turned off the highway, coming to a stop outside the Puerta Maya Shopping Mall.

"Here's fine," Calypso said. "Pop the trunk, please?" She opened her door and exited, going around back to retrieve her tank, vest, and regulator. Emily had left her rig to pick up from Jorge later, but Calypso had insisted on bringing hers. She came back around to the side of the cab. "Thank you for the dive, Emily. I'm sorry if I've been mean to you." She started to go, but turned back. "Oh… and thank Boone for saving my sister's life." With that, she closed the door and trudged toward the piers.

Emily watched her go as the cab pulled away, heading back to the highway. *I can't decide if she's a nutter, or just an arsehole,* she thought.

"*Señorita?* To San Miguel now, *si?*"

"*Si.* Aqua Safari pier, *por favor.*"

<hr />

Dr. Aguilar, the attending physician at the SSS Hyperbaric Facility, ushered Lyra up the steps into the spherical chamber, painted white with red and blue stripes. "You will need to remove your jewelry," he said, gesturing to a necklace she wore. "Earrings as well."

Lyra began removing the necklace, a small bow and arrow dangling from a thin chain of platinum. She had stripped out of her wetsuit and now wore a thin blue hospital gown a nurse had provided. "My dive watch, too?"

"Yes. Anything metal. Oxygen levels in the chamber will be maintained at normal levels and you will be given on-demand oxygen via masks, so there isn't the same risk of a spark that you would find with hyperbaric oxygen therapy. That being said, this is a prudent precaution."

Boone had already communicated everything he could about the accident during his call from the *Lunasea*, and it had been decided that Lyra would need to receive treatment immediately. Boone and Ricardo had brought her to the facility by taxi as soon as they had tied up at the pier.

"You are welcome to receive treatment as well, Mr. Fischer," Dr. Aguilar offered.

"I think I'm fine. I'm not showing any symptoms..."

"As I'm sure you are aware, symptoms can arise later; twenty-four to forty-eight hours sometimes."

Boone hesitated, looking toward the chamber. Inside, he could see two beds. "I'm not sure it's necessary..."

Lyra beckoned with a finger. "Don't be silly. I promise I won't bite."

"No, it's not that... I can't bring a phone in, right?"

The doctor shook his head. "No."

"Well, I'm thinking I may need to talk to Emily... and the boat is sitting unattended at the pier."

"That is not a concern," Ricardo said. "I will go back now and move the boat if needed."

Boone turned to Dr. Aguilar. "Well, doc... if you were me?"

"I would take the treatment. It's better safe than sorry and it will be in use anyway. It's a multi-place, double-lock chamber, so we can bring you out early if Ms. Othonos requires further time inside. And you can communicate with me, if you need to speak with your crew mates."

"All right." Boone removed his dive watch and sport sandals, then took his phone from a pocket of his cargo shorts and handed it to the doctor.

"Your necklace, too."

Boone reached up to the hollow of his throat. "This? It's glass on a leather thong, no metal. A Statian Blue Bead. I can take it off, though..."

"No, glass is fine."

Boone stepped up to the chamber. "Ricardo, head back to the boat and meet up with Emily. Oh! And tell her to gather Lyra's gear and bring it here." He ducked inside. The entrance wasn't overly small, but Boone's great height required him to bend over to avoid banging his head.

"It's very cozy," Lyra said, standing near the back of the chamber. "Would you prefer one bed or the other?"

"Lady's choice," Boone said, shuffling his bare feet.

Lyra sat on the bed nearest to her and then reclined on her side, tossing her hair dramatically. She laughed, smiling brightly. "You must admit, Boone... there is something romantic about this."

"Oh, I don't know about that," a voice said from the door. A portly woman in scrubs turned her back on them and closed the inner door, rotating a latch into place, sealing herself in with them. "Not unless you are into threesomes."

Boone grinned and sat on the other bed. "I'm guessing you're in here to check our vitals?"

"Correct. I am Nurse Vargas, and I will be your 'tender.' Now, if you'll both lie down, please, I'll fit you with the on-demand oxygen masks."

145

After a few minutes, the intercom crackled. "Can everyone hear me?" Dr. Aguilar's voice came from a speaker overhead. "I will begin increasing pressure in three... two..."

———◆·◆———

"One moment..." Emily said, digging through her pockets for the wad of pesos Jorge had given her. While the U.S. dollar was very welcome in Cozumel, one could get better value with the local currency. Emily found the money Jorge had loaned her and gave the taxi driver the fare and a generous tip.

"*Gracias!*"

"And thank *you* for getting me here so fast, and in one piece!" Emily hopped out next to the venerable Aqua Safari dive shop. When she and Boone had first arrived in Coz, they'd actually rented a room above the shop until they'd found a place. Racing across the grassy median that divided the main drag, she ran onto the short pier toward the *Lunasea*, tied up on the south side. She stumbled to a halt, well short of the dive boat.

"What... the bloody hell... is that?"

Hovering above the water alongside the *Lunasea* was a small quadcopter drone. Emily could just make out a camera on the underside. The drone pivoted slightly, examining the length of the boat. After a moment, it rose, moved over the boat, rotated, then began to descend toward the deck alongside the dive benches.

Emily began moving again, reaching the bow of the *Lunasea* in moments. She paused to retrieve a gaff hook pole they kept clipped alongside the cabin near the bow, handy for hooking mooring lines. Then she stepped across onto the gunwale and moved around the side of the cockpit, gaff hook at the ready.

Reaching the end of the cockpit, she jumped down to the deck, braced herself, and swung.

Her sudden movement must have been spotted by what might have been a wide-angle lens. The drone abruptly pitched back, rising several feet in an instant. Emily's swing went wide and she stumbled. The quadcopter spun 180 degrees and the lens of the camera pointed right at her. She raised the pole and advanced, but it simply backed up over the water, its "eye" still on her. After a moment, it pivoted to focus on the dive bench, then rapidly rose into the air and raced to the south.

"What was that?" Ricardo, out of breath, ran up to the boat.

"A drone."

"Who's driving it?"

"I dunno... some tourist on one of the cruise ships, maybe."

"Why were you trying to hit it?"

Emily looked at the pole in her hand, then burst into laughter. "You know... I have no idea. Just seemed like the thing to do! Maybe I thought it was full of sweets."

"Where is the sister... the sullen one? Callisto?"

"Calypso. She wanted to get off at her ship."

"Really? And not see Lyra? I swear... rich people." He climbed across to join Emily.

"How are they? Boone and Lyra?"

"They are fine. They are both in the chamber."

"He's in there with her?" Em snorted a laugh. "Oh, I'm going to have a field day with that. Lemme get my mobile and give him a bell."

"He can't have his phone inside the chamber, but he wants Lyra's gear brought over."

"Right! We need to figure out what went wrong." Em went to the portside bench and found Lyra's rig. She swiftly detached the regulator from the tank and twisted the valve open and closed. "Boone was right. Bone dry."

Ricardo looked at it closely. "I don't see anything wrong. O-ring is in place, no signs of damage." He slid it from the rack and hefted it across to the pier.

Emily detached the inflator hose from Lyra's BCD and picked up the vest and regulator. As she crossed the deck to hand them to Ricardo, her eyes strayed to a Bubble Chasers tank. "Wait a tick..." Setting down the BCD, she attached Lyra's regulator to one of their fresh tanks.

"What are you thinking?" Ricardo asked, reboarding the dive boat.

"Just spitballing," Em said, opening the valve. "We know our tanks have 3200 psi. If there's nothing wonky about Lyra's *tank*, then..." Her eyes went wide. "Blimey... have a gander at this." She held up the integrated computer and turned it toward Ricardo.

"5400 psi?! Impossible, the tank would explode."

"Boone said this read 2200 when she ran out of air in the Devil's Throat."

"3200 plus 2200 is..."

"Exactly. This computer showed a full tank before we dived. I know. I checked it."

"So... a computer malfunction?"

Emily shook her head. "That would only half explain things... and I don't like what the other half is. They said they got these from *Apollo*'s shipboard dive shop. Well, whoever filled Lyra's tank... *didn't* fill it."

14

"Wait. You are saying… what are you saying?"

Lyra looked confused as Emily finished laying out her hypothesis over the chamber intercom.

"I think she's saying the accident might not have *been* an accident." Boone said.

"So… someone was trying to kill me?"

"Or Calypso." Emily mused from the speaker. "It was a coin flip which of you got the dud tank."

"Except… that computer would have to be matched to the tank," Boone pointed out.

"True… and they were," Emily said. "The driver, when he took their tanks out of the boot… two of them were already rigged up."

Boone looked over at Lyra lying on the bed across the chamber, the hospital gown doing a poor job of covering her long legs. "I wonder…"

She looked back at him. "What?"

"Your BCDs and regulators… are they your personal gear?" Boone asked Lyra.

"No, we just use what the shop gives us."

"You wear different sizes?"

"No… we both wear a small. We each just picked one when we were on the boat."

Boone couldn't see Emily, but he knew she would be viewing them from a screen at the control station in the adjoining room. Looking up, he found the camera for it. "Dr. Aguilar, are you there?"

"Yes, Mr. Fischer."

"Do you have someone on staff who can examine the computer? Run a diagnostic or something?"

"I know a specialist who repairs dive computers for the shops. I will call him in."

"Great. And I think I'm good with the treatment. Okay for me to step out?"

"Well… if you'll bear with us for another thirty minutes, we can call it two hours and Nurse Vargas can check your vitals again."

"What about me?" Lyra asked.

"With you, Miss Othonos, I wish to continue the treatment for the recommended five hours. Given your out-of-air situation, it would be highly advisable, especially considering that you displayed symptoms of DCS, according to Mr. Fischer."

Lyra sighed and lay back on the bed. "I don't want to be alone."

Boone looked up at the camera. "Em, you told Callie where we'd be?"

"Of course."

Boone sat on the edge of the bed. "I'm sure your family will be here any minute."

"Angler, this is Palantir."

"Go ahead, Palantir."

"I have an assignment. Time sensitive. I'm going to allow one of your team to break curfew for this. Have them take a taxi to the Aqua Safari pier in San Miguel. It's a concrete pier across from the intersection of the main oceanside street and 5th Street South. There will be a dive boat there, the Lunasea. *Board the boat and retrieve a tank, regulator, and buoyancy vest located on the bench on the port side. They will be marked 'Olympus Cruises.' Are my instructions clear?"*

Angler didn't like the sound of this. Everything had been carefully planned, and this was not a part of any of it. "I'm assuming we want a low profile on this?"

"If possible, but speed is of the essence. Whoever you choose, have them wear the crew clothing I provided. If anyone asks about why they're taking the tank, they're retrieving it for Olympus Cruises. Now get moving! No telling how long the boat will remain. Palantir out."

"Tolstoy… since you've been sneaking out anyway… you hear all that?"

"*Da.* I get to stretch my feet?"

"And your legs. And Potluck? You're going too. Keep Tolstoy from wandering into Cuban cigar stores and tequila shops. Get changed and be out the door in three minutes."

Tolstoy and Potluck scrambled for their suitcases as Angler sat down heavily in a plush chair.

This sounds like a screwup. And we're pulling cleanup duty.

Boone and Emily entered the main lobby of the hospital, heading for the sunlit street outside the tinted glass doors.

"You two seemed very cozy in there," Em said.

"Lemme guess… you spied on me for a while before you turned on the intercom."

"And that hospital gown she had on didn't leave a lot to the imagination."

Boone cracked a half-smile. "Nurse Vargas kept me from throwing myself at her." He reached down and took Em's hand. "But it's a good thing you came when you did… I think my will-power was starting to waver."

"How are you feeling?" Em asked. "I mean, apart from the sexual frustration."

Boone laughed and squeezed her hand. "I feel good. I really did control the ascent, so I'm not too worried. But I'll keep an eye out for any symptoms." He pushed open the door into the bright noonday sun.

Emily hissed and popped her green sunglasses onto her face. Boone opened his drybag, looking for his aviators. A man in a white shirt and slacks exited a town car parked against the curb and walked with purpose toward the hospital.

Boone found his shades and slid them on. "The *Lunasea* still at the pier?"

"No, Ricardo took the boat back to the marina. He's bringing my car up for us."

"What, he didn't want to drive mine?"

"Where would he find enough coal to power it?"

"No need… he can put his feet through the floor and pull a Fred Flintstone."

Emily snorted a laugh. "Nice one, Boone."

"Boone…? Boone *Fischer*?"

Boone turned. The man from the town car had just passed him on his way to the hospital doors, but now stood facing him. Boone gave a brief nod. "Yes, I'm Boone Fischer."

Without another word, the man swung a roundhouse punch.

Boone had made several observations when the man walked purposefully by him: here was someone who knew his way around a weight room… and he was angry. By the man's tone of voice when he said Boone's name, the divemaster had a feeling something like this was coming. He simply stepped back and the looping punch missed.

"Hey!" Emily shouted.

The man recovered his balance and advanced again. "You hurt my sister!"

Boone recognized the man's accent; it was similar to Lyra's. The man swung again and Boone sidestepped it. "You must be Lyra's brother! Listen, she's fine."

"She could have been killed!" He charged and Boone executed a quick capoeira tumble to the side. The man lumbered past, like a bull who'd missed his matador, and came face to face with Emily.

"Stop!"

The man came up short, stumbling to avoid crashing into the petite blonde who had planted herself before him, four feet eleven inches of defiance.

"You're Lyra's eldest brother?"

Nostrils flaring, the man nodded.

"What's your name?"

The man straightened and pronounced, with almost comical levels of pride, "*I*… am Achilles."

"Really? Badass name. But *he*… is not Hector!"

The man blinked, the *Iliad* reference throwing him off his game.

"Boone saved your sister's life. The problem was with your ship's gear. She ran out of air a hundred feet down and Boone brought her up out of a dark tunnel, sharing his air... he could have died saving her. And you want to punch him?" She poked his chest, right below a pair of gold chains that hung above several opened buttons. "You want to take a shot at Boone, you'll have to go through me." Emily held the defiant look for a brief moment, then suddenly withdrew her poking finger and offered her hand, flashing a brilliant smile. "Nice muscle tone on those pecs. I'm Emily, by the way."

All of the rage drained out of Achilles as his aggressive expression slid into one of confusion. A smile broke through and he took her hand. "I am very pleased to meet you." He turned to Boone and offered his hand to him as well. "Please forgive my behavior. My sister is the world to me. I thought, perhaps..."

"It's okay... no harm done." Boone clasped his hand and gave him a firm shake. Not surprisingly, Achilles was a knuckle-crusher, but Boone held his own. "Where's the rest of your family?"

Achilles's jaw tightened as he released Boone's hand. "My little brother will be along shortly. Said he had to finish a meeting. Calypso told me about the accident, then went to change her clothes." He shook his head in disgust. "I came immediately. My father wanted to come, but he is not well enough." Achilles looked toward the glass doors. "I should go to her."

"Lyra will be fine," Boone assured him. "The doctor said he's not seeing anything serious, but they're keeping her in the hyperbaric chamber for a few more hours."

Achilles nodded. "Thank you." He turned to Emily. "And you..." His eyes looked her up and down. "Thanks for stopping me from beating him up."

Em smiled patiently. "Don't mention it."

Achilles entered the lobby and went toward reception.

Emily turned back to Boone. "He's lucky you didn't use your cappuccino on him."

"*Capoeira.*"

"Are you sure that's what it's called? Whatever. Your Brazilian dance karate."

"There was no need. I knew you had my back. Where's Ricardo meeting us?"

"Right here, but actually, y'know what... I'm a tad peckish. Let's pop over to Colores y Sabores and grab some grub to go. If Ricardo shows up, we'll see Señor Bug when he turns the corner."

"Sounds like a plan." Boone started toward the water. The little restaurant was just a few doors down from the hospital and had excellent street tacos.

"Well smack me bum and call me Susan..."

Boone glanced down at Em. "Um... what?"

Emily suddenly released his hand and crossed the street to the north side, staring intently, even going so far as to lower her sunglasses—a rare daytime display. Boone joined her. On this side of the street, they could see the Aqua Safari pier.

"It's back," Em said.

"What is?"

She pointed. "I completely forgot to tell you about it... that thing was checking out our boat when the taxi dropped me off."

Boone sighted down her arm. "A drone?"

"Yeah... with four little whirly-thingies... I took a swing at it."

Boone laughed. "Why?"

"I don't know!" Em blurted. "Ricardo asked me that too."

Boone started toward the main road. "Maybe it's one of those tourism or real estate drones, taking shots for a website or something."

The drone hovered about fifty yards out from the pier, which was currently devoid of any boats. Two people stood on the pier, a man and woman wearing white slacks and matching royal blue polo shirts with some sort of gold writing on the breast. They were speaking together, and at one point they both seemed to be looking at the drone. As Boone and Emily crossed Rafael E. Melgar Avenue, the pair walked back up the pier to the street and turned right, the woman stretching out a hand to hail a southbound taxi. She was thwarted when the man suddenly bolted across the street to a liquor store advertising free tequila shots. Cursing a blue streak, she crossed to join him.

Eyes back on the drone, Boone grabbed the smartphone from his pocket and raised it, tapping the icon to bring up the camera. As he reached the pier and started down it, the drone abruptly rose into the air before pitching forward and racing out to sea.

"Weird, yeah?"

"Yeah..."

"You get a photo?"

"Maybe. Pretty far away, though. Lemme see..." Boone was opening the photo when his phone buzzed with a text. "It's Greg from the Kansas crew."

"Oh, right! We were going to take them out for a jolly after we finished with the morning dives."

"Yeah, we were supposed to meet them. It's their last day."

A single toot from a horn sounded and Boone turned to see Ricardo waving from Emily's Beetle. Boone pointed at 5th Street South and the car turned and pulled over to the side.

"Y'know... we were about to eat anyway..." Boone said, crossing back to the hospital's street. "Maybe we should combine our need for food with an excursion."

Em grinned. "Take them to Coconuts?"

"Read my mind."

"Angler... Palantir."

"Angler here."

"We have a problem," the electronically modulated voice said.

Angler ground his teeth. "Go ahead."

"The boat is gone and the gear has likely been removed from the dive boat and turned over to the authorities. This is a serious issue for our employer. We can't wait for the rest of your team, so I need you and Stallion to deal with the situation. I have been authorized to offer you both an additional twenty percent bonus if you can perform this service within the next thirty minutes."

"Twenty per... holy shit," Stallion blurted. "That's—"

Angler drew his finger across his throat, silencing the mercenary. He hesitated. They were already being paid very handsomely for this job—he had a suspicion that this "service" was likely some wet work. Angler didn't have a problem with killing for money, but it wasn't something he relished.

"Angler, do you read?"

"What do you need us to do?"

The voice told them.

"Driver, please to be turning left at the park."

"Wait, what are you playing at, Tolstoy? The ship is south." Potluck watched as the taxi driver turned onto a two-way road heading east. A dirt median ran down its length, dotted with red flamboyant trees. "Angler will have your ass. We need to get back and report."

"What is to report? Boat not there. Drone see this, so nerd in earpiece know this. We deserve little fun." Rubbing his hands together with glee, Tolstoy plunged his hand into a plastic bag from the souvenir shop next to the liquor store. He pulled out a horrendous Hawaiian shirt covered in Day of the Dead sugar skulls and yanked the tag off of it. "Don't worry, I not forget you. I get you sexy T-shirt."

Potluck smiled despite herself—the Russian merc had a strangely boyish quality, though she guessed his age at forty or so. She sighed with amused resignation. "Where are we going?"

Tolstoy grinned and dug a wad of brochures from his pocket. He selected the topmost and thrust it at her.

"Coconuts?"

"*Da!* Is bar on top of cliff over ocean. It has zoo, and good drinks and food and… other things."

The driver laughed. "You heard about the picture albums." Like many Cozumeleños, he spoke excellent English. "We live in different times. They don't put those out anymore."

Tolstoy looked crestfallen. "*Der'mo!* I have missed the bus."

The driver looked back at him in the mirror. "Oh, they still have them! You just have to ask the bartender."

The Russian clapped his hands together. "Is good!"

Potluck leaned forward between the seats. "What photo albums?"

15

"My beloved daughter!" Tears in his eyes, Karras Othonos stretched out his arms, leaning so far forward Nicholas feared he might upend his wheelchair.

Lyra came to him and they hugged, her father clutching her with surprising strength considering his condition. "I'm fine, Father. The doctor said I am in excellent health."

"Calypso told me what happened. You could have died!"

"But I did not. Thanks to Boone Fischer."

"This 'Fischer,' he owns the company that took you on the dive? Is the business legitimate?"

"The dive operation has an excellent track record," Nicholas interjected. "They are fairly new on Cozumel, but both Mr. Fischer and his co-owners struck me as highly competent. Wouldn't you agree, Calypso?"

Calypso shrugged. "They seemed to know what they're doing."

"They saved my life!" Lyra blurted. "My equipment... something went wrong."

"It's more than that," Achilles said. "It was sabotaged."

"Now wait, we don't know that…" Lyra said uncertainly. "The technician at the hyperbaric facility wasn't sure if it had been tampered with or if it was a software glitch."

Nicholas frowned. "What do you mean?"

"The guy said the computer was showing the tank was full when it wasn't!" Achilles ground his teeth, beginning to pace.

Karras coughed violently, reddening. "Someone tried to kill you, Lyra?" he managed to gasp.

"I don't know! It may have just been an accident." Lyra looked to Calypso. "It could have been *you* that picked that tank, Callie."

Callie gave a rare show of emotion. "My God. But who…? Wait… we picked those tanks up directly from the ship's dive shop. And they keep everything locked up in there, right?" She stood and advanced on Nicholas. "Who is the man that runs it? He's Greek-American, in his forties."

Nicholas grabbed his phone, triggering speed dial. "Security, this is Nicholas Othonos. Go to the dive shop and bring me Matthaíos Boston." He thought for a moment. "He may resist, so be prepared."

"I don't understand," Karras said. "Matthaíos is a good man, I know his mother. He would have no reason to harm you two."

"We don't know that he did anything wrong," Nicholas said. "But it's best we question him directly. And I'll have security check the camera feeds." He steepled his fingers over his nose for a brief moment before straightening in his chair. "In any event, I believe we should delay our departure for Grand Cayman by a day at least."

"You don't get to decide that!" Achilles barked.

Nicholas sighed. "Of course not. Father?"

"I have no objection."

"Good!" Lyra said. "Then we can properly thank Boone and Emily for saving me. Let's invite them to the ship."

Nicholas nodded. "I *did* promise Emily a tour of the *Apollo*."

"Fine with me," Achilles said. "That is one sexy girl." He crossed to the windows overlooking the Puerta Maya Pier, the Hygge Cruises vessel filling the view. "Hey, Nicky... I thought you were going to get rid of that thing."

Nicholas smiled. "I've made a few calls. We'll soon have an unobstructed view to the south."

"Nicholas," Calypso began. "Lyra told me about the malfunction with your little scooter thing..."

Nicholas sighed. "Underwater Personal Conveyor. UPC."

"Whatever. So... did you ever find out what went wrong with it?"

"No. It seemed like it was getting an input from elsewhere, but that would be impossible... it's a prototype."

Calypso nodded, deep in thought. "And where were you storing it before the night dive?"

"With the rest of my gear in the ship's dive sh—" Nicholas stopped talking and grabbed his phone, tapping the screen to redial the last number he'd called. "Security... have you got him? Put Matthaíos on the phone!"

"Uh... we were just about to call you, sir. He isn't here. And it looks like he left in a hurry."

———— ◆ ◆ ————

"Welcome to the wild side!" Emily announced as she pulled into the sandy parking lot of the Coconuts Bar and Grill, located on the east coast of the island. The coastal road bordering the rougher "ocean side" of the island had only a few buildings along its twelve-mile length. Ahead of Em's Beetle, palms and other tropical trees rose up along a set of ascending stairs. Though the hill was hardly more than a bump in the terrain for most places, on Cozumel it was the highest point on the island, rising to just under fifty feet. Greg and Cecilia hopped out along with two more of the Kansas crew, pausing to look at the ocean waves that crashed against the lower terrain just to the south.

"Is Ricardo joining us?" Cecilia asked.

"No, he and his family are planning on taking a trip to the mainland tomorrow." Em had invited Ricardo on the drive back to the marina, but he'd declined and offered to watch Brix while he and Lupe packed. When they arrived at the *Lunasea*, they'd discovered that Calypso hadn't yet retrieved her bag and sunhat, so he'd offered to run those over to the *Apollo* on his way back home.

"Looks like we're gonna get some rain," Greg noted, as a few drops fell from the tropical skies, speckling the sand of the parking lot.

"No worries," Em said. "It's a fast mover. And they've got plenty of umbrellas at the tables and a thatched roof over the bar."

"I never mind a little rain," Cecilia remarked.

"Let's wait for Boone and company to get here before we head up," Emily said. "Oh, that reminds me! Need to get something out of the boot." Em stepped to the rear of the Volkswagen and popped the latch. Unlike the original Beetle, the newer models had a "normal" layout, with the trunk in the back and the engine in the front, under the hood—or "bonnet," as Emily thought of it. She grabbed an item from the boot before closing up.

"What's that for?" Greg asked.

"Oh, this?" Emily held up a muffler. "Just something I picked up from the side of the road. Feel like giving me an assist with a little prank-a-roo?"

Greg laughed. "Uh… sure."

"Good, 'cause I'm on the petite side and I think you can hide it behind your back better."

"I want to help!" Cecilia exclaimed.

"Excellent. Stand over here near the edge of the lot. Here's what I need you two to do…"

Minutes later, a low rumble heralded the arrival of Boone's Thing. Its top down, the yellow museum piece shuddered as Boone shifted gears and crunched into the hard-packed lot. Emily had scrounged a couple palm fronds and directed him into the space beside her bug, engaging in a pantomime that was somewhere between an airport taxiway marshaller guiding a plane and a burlesque fan dancer. Not surprisingly, Boone's polarized sunglasses were glued to her the whole way. *Not that I blame him,* Em thought, ending her display by demurely hiding her tank top and shorts behind the fronds.

Bill and Cindy, the remaining Kansas couple with Boone, burst into applause. Boone nodded his head in appreciation. Meanwhile, Greg and Cecilia approached Boone's car, and Emily was pleased to see Greg briefly crouch near the back before opening the rear door to usher Cindy out.

Boone unfolded his long legs from the yellow car and stepped onto the packed sand. "If we're getting a performance like that *before* you've had a few drinks… we might want to make sure the bartender locks those photo albums away."

Emily laughed, tossing the fronds aside. "My exhibitionism has its limits. Glad you made it! We're starving!" She gestured to the group. "C'mon, gang!"

The group followed but Cecilia lingered. "Excuse me? But…" She stepped back from the Thing and looked underneath. "I think something fell out of your car."

"Y'know, I *thought* I heard something go clunk when you pulled in," Greg added, piling on.

Boone frowned, retracing his steps. Crouching, he reached under the rust-rimmed bottom of the car, coming up with the muffler. He looked at it for only an instant before raising his sunglasses to peer at Emily.

Bill broke the silence. "That's funny. From the sound of it, I didn't think you *had* a muffler."

Emily and the Kansans burst into laughter. Boone smiled, going to the trunk—on his ancient Volkswagen, it was on the front of the car. He put the muffler inside.

"I can help you reattach it, Boone," Emily offered.

Boone closed the trunk and turned to her, looking down at her face. "I don't think a muffler with 'Honda' stamped on it is likely to fit."

Emily smiled serenely, eyes hidden behind her green shades.

Boone put his arm around her shoulders and addressed the group. "Hey, y'all! Welcome to Coconuts! Did you know they have a pet crocodile named Wilma?" Suddenly, he scooped up Emily and tossed her over his shoulder. "Sometimes, they let ya feed her."

Emily squealed with laughter as Boone trudged up the steps that led to the bar and grill. With Boone's great height, she had quite a view. The tropical shower increased in tempo and everyone moved under the cover of the trees that lined the stairs.

"You okay up there, Em?" Greg called out from several steps down.

"Oh, yeah, peachy keen," she said, propping her elbows against Boone's back and cupping her chin in her hands. "Actually, this is a much safer mode of transport than his car."

The group laughed and took in the sights, the steps sporting a variety of amusing signs sprinkled here and there. Greg paused and pointed at a sign beside a gumbo-limbo tree. "Ha! 'The Gringo Tree! Always Red and Peeling!'" He stopped to take a photo and the rest of the group joined him.

Emily smiled, enjoying the moment as Boone ascended the steps. She took it all in: the swaying trees, the sound of the rain drumming on the leaves, the sight of the stone steps beneath as she was carried up the mountain, the feel of a man's powerful grip, holding her tightly over his shoulder—

"*Stop-stop-stop-put-me-down-put-me-down-put-me-down!*" The frenzied whisper burst from her lips as her heart suddenly pounded in her ears.

Boone stiffened, the alarm in her hissed words freezing him in his tracks. He set her down immediately.

"Em, what's wrong? I'm sorry—did I hurt you?"

Emily shushed him, not wanting the Kansas group below to hear. "No, it's… oh bugger me, it's…" She gestured helplessly at the terraced terrain around them, then emitted a short laugh that was tinged with a sob. "Although this is only fifty bleeding feet, not three thousand…and a tinkle of a shower instead of a storm."

Boone's face went pale. "Oh, Jesus, Em… Mount Scenery… I…"

"S'okay!" Em blurted, her eyes darting down to the group, who had finished their photo session. She pushed away from Boone. "Meet you at the top!" she called out with forced gaiety. "Need to hit the loo!" With that, she turned and rushed up the steps.

As Boone watched Emily dash up the hill, he gave himself a vicious mental kick. *Stupid, stupid, stupid.* The decision to carry her had been a spur-of-the-moment bit of flirtation, and he'd completely forgotten the connection it might have held for her. Back on Saba, as the outermost bands of Hurricane Irma had begun to lash the island, Emily had been carried up 1,064 steps to the island's highest peak by a homicidal lunatic, slung over his shoulder like a sack of potatoes, eyes watching the steps receding beneath her as they ascended into the steadily thickening clouds surrounding Mount Scenery. *I must've triggered a panic attack.* Swallowing hard, Boone glanced down at the approaching Kansans and forced a smile on his face—a difficult feat, with the thought swimming in his head that his seemingly innocent action had hurt the one he loved.

"Is there *really* a crocodile up there?" Cindy asked.

"Yep. And Chimichanga the cockatoo, a blue macaw named Tequila, some other birds… a few cats and a couple dogs. Sometimes we bring our pooch here… but figured our cars were packed enough today. Ricardo's taking care of him."

Greg reached his step. "Hey, umm… Boone, down below you said something about 'photo albums.' Are these the ones with the… umm…"

"Topless women, Greg," Cecilia said, smacking his arm. "I saw your guidebook. And you aren't going to see them."

Boone started up the stairs. "Yeah, it's a bit of a tradition, but they've kinda toned it down. I actually haven't seen them myself."

"But… they do exist, right?" Greg asked, earning himself a second arm-punch.

The steps ended and a sandy path leveled off and led through the palms, ending at a huge thatched roof covering a circular bar. Beyond, a seating area with plastic tables and blue umbrellas rimmed the cliff's edge, overlooking the crashing waves of the eastern coastline.

"Check it out!" Cindy pointed excitedly to an area alongside the bar. A white umbrella cockatoo was gripping a rope perch strung between posts, spinning on it like a gymnast on an uneven bar.

"That's Chimichanga," Boone said, approaching the bird and addressing it. *"Hola."*

"Hola!" the bird croaked.

Cindy laughed and reached toward the bird, but Boone held up a hand in warning.

"Not a good idea. He's a biter."

"Hola!" Chimichanga affirmed.

"Whoa, check out all the T-shirts!" Greg was under the thatched roof, looking up at the ceiling. Every inch of the circular space was plastered with T-shirts from all over the world. Countless license plates decorated the support beams, and numerous humorous signs—most extolling the virtues of beer or sex—lined the walls. Greg dropped his eyes and focused on a large, brown book that was placed on the edge of the bar. He looked back at Cecilia, then nonchalantly approached the bar and raised a hand toward the book.

"Wait..." Boone said in a low voice, halting Cecilia before she could stop her husband. "Let him. Trust me."

Eager for titillation, Greg opened the book... and was greeted with a spring-loaded rubber cobra that popped out and bounced off his wrist. Greg yelped and stumbled back to gales of laughter from his friends.

A Mexican man wearing glasses and sporting a green parrot on his shoulder was wiping down some menus at the edge of the bar. "Señor Hiss strikes again. *Hola,* Boone. You need a table for your guests?"

"Yeah, thanks Cuco. One by the view if we could."

"Pick a good one," the man said, handing Boone a pile of menus. "The conch ceviche is on special." He made a show of looking around Boone. "Where is your lovely señorita?"

Boone felt a lump rise in his throat but he swallowed it down. "She'll be along."

◆ ◆ ◆

"I thought I was on the mend!" Emily said into her mobile. The tears from several minutes ago had evaporated and her voice carried more frustration than anxiety.

"You are. You've made tremendous strides, Emily. You know that, don't you?"

Emily sighed and nodded. The face on her smartphone's screen smiled.

Emily had bypassed the restrooms and instead gone to the north side of the Coconuts property, managing to snag the Wi-Fi from the lobby of the little hotel next door. After firing up WhatsApp, she'd placed a video call to her therapist, who'd picked up on the second ring. Christine Dale was an American expat based in Costa Rica that Emily had been fortunate enough to find when she'd arrived in Belize and suffered her first panic attack. Christine was an unconventional therapist, but her advice had done wonders thus far.

"From what you described, Emily... the sensory stimuli—the stone stairs, the trees, the rain, and being carried over the shoulder—it's not at all surprising that triggered an episode."

"But I haven't had a—"

"Wait, let me finish... give me three long breaths while I make this point. The situation was pitch perfect to trigger a panic attack. *But...* when it did... you came down from it very quickly, did you not?"

Emily breathed out a long, slow breath. "Yes. My heart was hammering when Boone put me down, I was hyperventilating a bit, and I was still pretty amped when I got to the bar—partly because I ran up the steps, I s'pose. But yeah, by the time I had my mobile out, I was close to normal."

"You were upset when you called me, but what I saw and heard was a young woman who was angry with herself. And instead... you should be proud of yourself."

Emily smiled. "You're right." She blew out a final, cleansing whoosh of breath. "Say, Christine, how's the diving in Costa Rica?"

"Come here and find out." She turned to listen to someone off-camera before returning to the video call. "I have to go and lead a group session. *Namaste*, Emily. And be proud."

"Thank you, Christine." Emily ended the call and slid the phone into her shorts pocket. The rain stopped, brushed aside by a late afternoon sun.

16

"Here she comes!" Cecilia called out, her voice colored by the half a margarita she'd consumed. "Emily, you missed the mariachi band!"

Boone looked up from his cerveza as Emily approached. *She looks good,* he thought with some relief. He started to rise but she pressed a hand on his shoulder and pushed him back down into the molded plastic chair. He wasn't surprised to feel her fingertips dig in meaningfully, a message to "drop it and move on."

"Sorry, lads 'n' lasses, I had a call to make." Emily plopped down beside Boone.

"Call go okay?" he asked.

"Oh, yes. Her royal majesty is in fine health and inquired about my own well-being. So seldom do you see such attention to the peasantry from a monarch."

Boone started to speak again but Emily gave him a look, and then changed the subject with a visual display, producing a little green object and setting it down with a flourish.

"What's that?" Greg asked.

"It's a grasshopper, silly," Cecilia said.

"I know that. It's just that it looks really cool and I want one."

Emily laughed. "Well, keep your eyes peeled for a guy in a hat made of woven palm leaves. He makes these from palm and grasses and straw. I caught him on a break on my way over."

"Another critter for your menagerie?" Boone asked. He addressed the table. "Emily has some carved wooden animals from Belize and a buncha little ones that she got from a bar in Bonaire."

"That *you* got me from a bar in Bonaire. Well... except one."

"You still haven't told me who gave that flamingo to you," Boone prodded. He'd been trying to learn the identity of that mystery date ever since she'd hinted at it back in Belize.

Emily responded by making the grasshopper hop across the table to Cecilia's frozen margarita. Held lightly in Em's fingertips, the woven insect slowly turned to look at Boone, then quickly looked back at the perspiring glass. Then back at Boone.

He laughed and rose from the table. "All right, all right... it'll be quicker if I grab it from the bar. Rocks? Salt?"

"Salt, yes... but I'll go frozen this time. Cecilia's looks gooooood. What's left of it."

"Back in a jiff."

Boone ducked under the thatched roof and made his way to the bar. The crowd was starting to grow, and he had to wait a moment to catch the bartender's eye. He ordered Emily a margarita and kept his eyes peeled for their waiter, a colorful character in a fancy apron, figuring he'd send the young man over to the table to take Em's food order. Looking around for the server, his eyes passed over the crowd before returning to the bartender as Emily's drink was presented. After thanking the man, he handed over some pesos and turned to leave, but stopped two steps from the bar. *What did I see?*

Boone looked beyond the bartender to the far side of the circular bar. A man in a flamboyant shirt covered in colorful skulls was hunched over an open photo album, pointing at a page and laughing uproariously, coughing out a cloud of cigarette smoke. Beside him, a thick-set woman in a tight T-shirt rolled her eyes, but there was the ghost of a smile on her lips. *They look very familiar.*

"Earth to Boone. You get lost? My grasshopper thirsts."

Boone blinked and looked down at Emily, who had sidled up beside him. "The couple from the Aqua Safari pier," he said, nodding his head toward the pair. "The ones we saw when the drone was there."

"Who? The bloke looking at the Big Book o' Boobs? I don't recognize... wait a tick. They had on some kind of boating polos, didn't they?"

"Guess they're off duty," Boone said.

"Check out the weird fag."

"Emily!" Boone rasped, mortified.

Emily laughed, "Oh for shite's sake, Boone, learn my lingo. The *cigarette*, you berk."

Boone shook his head, then glanced across. "It's black."

"Yeah, I recognize it from my youth. A Black Russian... or as I call it, a Poseur Puffer... all the Goth kids smoked 'em. It's a Brit cig, comes in a fancy black box with gold foil."

"You ever smoke?"

Emily smiled, looking into the middle distance. "Not cigarettes."

Boone nudged her. "C'mon. Let's take a leisurely stroll to the other side of the bar. Here's your marg."

"Thanks much." She sipped and followed Boone as he made his way around the bar. "Mmm, good that!"

Boone nodded, half-listening to Em, the other part of his attention drifting toward the couple. The man was a loud talker and
he seemed to be several drinks into his evening. From the sound
of it, he was Eastern European—maybe Russian. The woman
sounded like a refugee from the movie *Fargo*.

"*Kiska*, come on," the man begged. "You get free shot if you
do this!"

"Oh, no, not happening. Come on, let's settle up. We've been
gone long enough. The boss is going to be pissed."

Boone led Emily to a spot just behind the pair and squared off
with her. "This seems like a good spot for us to enjoy your drink."

Emily smiled, licking the salt rim and taking a sip, glancing furtively around Boone's biceps. "He's moved on to another
booby book."

"*Bozhe moi*, look at the *siski* on this one!"

"I'm going down to call a cab. You pay the bill." The woman
got up and left.

"Oh, don't like that be!" he cried, tracking her as she left. As
his eyes swept back, he spotted Emily, giving her a fairly thor-
ough once-over as he tucked a fresh cigarette into the corner of
his mouth. "How about you, little one? You want free shot, yes?"

Boone stepped forward but Emily stopped him.

"Oh, you want to see these?" Emily gave her breasts a quick
cup through the tank top. "No, alas, they don't let me do that
anymore. I cost them too many shots. I mean, one time, I got
so plastered, I was..." she trailed off, as if remembering something fondly.

The man's cigarette fell from his mouth. "*Da?* I mean... yes?"

"Oh, I was way too hammered to remember anything... but
it's all there in that brown book on the other end of the bar. Half
the content is me, I think."

Boone stifled a laugh as he and Emily made their way back to the table. "Señor Hiss will eat well today."

"Depends on if he's a picky eater," Em said. "Russian macker might not be on the menu."

"And 'macker' is…?"

"Oh, did you not absorb that one yet, either? It's a man who hits on women. Womanizer. A player. That older Othonos brother, Achilles? That's a macker."

They reached the table and joined the Kansas gang just as the food arrived.

After their dinner, Boone and Emily chauffeured the group back to the Hotel Barracuda, parking their cars in the lot across the street.

"We had such a great time!" Cecilia said. "Thank you so much for the diving and the outing."

"You heading back to the States, then?" Emily asked.

"Yep. Off to Houston in the morning, then on to Wichita," Greg said. "Back to the grind."

"Let's grab one more drink by the pool," Cecilia insisted. "Boone, Emily, will you join us? Our treat!"

Boone looked at his watch. "We gotta go pick up our dog, but it's still early. Em?"

"Fine by me. We have some driving to do, so maybe just a couple Cokes."

They went into the No Name Bar and found a few chairs alongside the pool. It was fairly busy, and the only spot available was next to a speaker that was pounding out "Despacito." As they sat down, Em's cell jangled with her old-timey ring. She answered, "Bubble Chasers Diving. We make your underwater dreams come true. This is Emily." She listened, then spoke loudly to compete with the music, looking at Boone as she replied. "Oh, hi Nicholas! What's up? How's Lyra doing?" She plugged one ear with a finger, then rose and cocked her head, motioning for Boone to join her farther from the music.

"Be right back," Boone said, leaving the table to follow her.

"Uh, yeah, he's here... just a tick, let me put you on speaker." Em retreated to a far corner of the seawall-enclosed dining area and tapped the speaker icon. "Okay, we're here."

"Mr. Fischer, this is Nicholas Othonos. Lyra owes her life to you, and my father would like to thank you personally. And Miss Durand... Emily... I believe I still owe you a tour of the *Apollo*. If you are free tomorrow, would you care to join us for an early brunch?"

Em tapped the icon to switch the speaker off and held the phone against her chest, looking at Boone. "No dives tomorrow, posh yacht, grateful billionaires..."

Boone grinned and gently took her wrist, lowering the phone and tapping the speaker icon. "Hey, this is Boone. I thought you were leaving tomorrow."

"Our itinerary had to be adjusted after the accident. And this morning's trip to Chichén Itzá was cancelled due to rain, so we've rescheduled that for tomorrow as well."

"Well, in that case, we'd love to join you. What time and where?"

"The 'where' is simple—just meet me at the pier alongside the *Apollo*. Shall we say 9:30 a.m.?"

"We get to sleep in?" Emily gushed. "Count me in!"

"Yeah, sounds good," Boone said.

"Excellent. I'll text you a QR code that will allow you access to the terminal. And if you would be so kind as to bring your passports? Given our clientele, our security procedures are fairly strict."

"No problem. We'll be there."

"Until tomorrow, then."

"Thank you, Nicholas! See you at the *Apollo* at half nine!" Em tapped the hang-up icon.

"Nicholas? On the *fokking* Olympus *fokking* Cruises' *Apollo*?" a heavily accented—and heavily drunk—voice asked, practically spitting the question.

Boone turned to the outdoor table nearest them. A man across it was rising unsteadily to his feet. He wore a white shirt with gold-striped epaulettes on his shoulders. Upside down on the table—alongside an expanse of beer bottles—lay a captain's hat. On the nearer side of the table, another crewman was hunched over with his back to Boone, head in his hands. He also wore a white shirt, with fewer stripes on his shoulder boards.

The standing man forcibly blinked his eyes, bringing Boone into focus. "Nicholas *fokking* Othonos, *já*?"

"Yes…?" Boone realized that the song had ended for the latter part of the speakerphone conversation. The No Name Bar was a crew bar… and from the look of this man's uniform and the Scandinavian sound of his accent, Boone had a hunch. "Are you with the *Nordic Starr*?"

"*Já*. For now. Tomorrow… who knows?" He tossed down a wad of pesos and turned from the table, paused, then reached back and grabbed a nearly empty Corona. Noticing he'd left his captain's hat, he swept it up as well, slapping it on his head as he stood swaying. "Nicholas Othonos…" He spit into the sand. "May his urine burn." He staggered away toward the lobby. "Gunnar! Come!"

177

The figure on the near side of the table pounded a fist into the plastic surface, causing all of the bottles to jump in a multi-layered chorus of clinks. His dejected posture from before abruptly faded as he straightened in his chair. He planted his hands on the table and began to rise, his white shirt's short sleeves ending in shockingly hairy forearms.

Holy... I'm tall, but this guy is huge. Boone stepped back and moved Emily behind him.

Still facing the table of empty beer bottles, his massive back to them, the giant boomed in a sing-song accent, "You know this... Nicholas?"

"We've met..."

The man turned, revealing a florid face, Neanderthal brow, and epic beard. He towered over Boone, his barrel chest straining the top buttons of his crisp uniform shirt. Over the left breast, a golden nametag read, "Gunnar Thorsson."

Boone's brain screamed *Viking warrior!* He let out a breath, shifting his weight, beginning a gentle capoeira bounce. *Here we go...*

Gunnar's reddened face quivered and the huge man dissolved into blubbering tears. "Why did he do that? This job is my life..."

Still alert, Boone allowed himself to relax ever so slightly. "Do what?"

Gunnar shook his head, his tears increasing. "We have to leave. We cannot come back to Cozumel. It is one of our main ports of call."

"You dumped shite and worse into the water, and you're surprised you're getting kicked out?" Emily blurted. "You break the rules, you suffer the consequences. If the Marine Park bans you, then—"

"The Marine Park didn't ban us—that *fokking* Othonos *rassgat* did! Said if we didn't leave, he would release underwater footage of our dumping and have our registry revoked!" The mountainous man turned and lurched after his captain. "I don't want to go back to Iceland," he sobbed, staggering away.

———◆·◆———

"Now who is one sneaking out?" Tolstoy inquired as Angler and Stallion entered the suite. He was sprawled on the loveseat in the communal area, and Potluck was just settling into a nearby chair.

"Something came up," Angler growled. He made his way toward his bedroom to change but halted, looking from the Russian to the Wisconsinite. "What are you two grinning at?"

Potluck waved the question away. "Nothing. Hey, you said something came up. Like what?"

"Something you idiots would've handled if you didn't dawdle coming back from the boat."

Stallion uttered one of his odd, braying laughs before speaking. "But Angler 'n' me handled it all right." He grabbed the room service menu. "Man, I worked up an appetite."

"Get changed first." Angler stripped off the Olympus Cruises polo shirt and tossed it into his room. His body bore several old battle scars, and while there was nothing sculpted about his musculature, it was clear to anyone looking that what was there was hard as granite.

"Is that blood on your slacks?" Tolstoy asked.

Angler and Stallion both looked down, but it was the team leader that the Russian had been addressing. Angler licked a thumb and rubbed at the droplets. *Damn. Getting sloppy.* He went into his room and closed the door. The drive out to the island's interior had gone well enough, but the shipboard dive shop operator had put up quite a fight when he realized what was about to happen to him. Angler took off the white slacks and went to the sink to run water over the bloodstain. He quickly gave up and keyed his mic. "Palantir, Angler. If you're listening, I'll need another pair of crew pants. Size thirty-four." Signing off, he stared at his weathered face in the mirror for a moment. "What are you looking at?" he snarled. "An extra twenty percent... just means you can quit this line of work that much sooner."

17

The following morning, Boone and Emily took Brixton on an early morning walk, the potlicker dog dragging them from scent to scent. The walk would end at one of the last condos in the complex, where they'd arranged for a fellow dog owner to watch Brix for the day.

"Y'know, we should invite Ricardo, too," Boone said, handing Emily the leash and taking out his phone. "After all, he was right on top of us when we came up. Just as important in the rescue."

"Good point," Em said. "But I think he and Lupe had something planned, yeah?"

"Oh, right… they're heading over to Playa for the day. Still… they might prefer some yacht time." He tapped Ricardo's contact.

"*Buenos días*, Boone."

"Back at ya, Ricardo. Hey, where you at?"

"On the ferry, heading to the mainland. Why?"

"Oh, nothing… Wait! Your uncle Santiago with the Marine Park—when you spoke with him, you mentioned the dumping that the *Nordic Starr* was doing during the night dive, right?"

"Yes. And to be on the lookout for a video of it. I haven't spoken to him, though."

"Can you check with him? See if he ever heard anything about it?"

"I'll ask, but it probably doesn't matter now."

"Why?"

"Because the *Nordic Starr* left port this morning. We watched it sailing off to the north while we were boarding the early morning ferry."

Boone and Emily arrived at the Puerta Maya cruise ship terminal at a quarter past nine, having parked Emily's car in the lot beside the shops that ringed the terminal like a walled fortress of consumerism. Passing under a thatched-roof entryway, Emily held up her phone to a bored security guard at the end. He scanned the QR code Nicholas had sent them and waved them in. As they made their way through the shops, they could see the pier ahead, the leftmost, southern side empty. The *Nordic Starr* had indeed departed. On the north side of the pier, the swept bow of the *Apollo* rose above the shops.

Boone chortled, pointing. Affixed to the bow was a golden statue of the Greek god Apollo, clutching a lyre, his head wreathed by a halo of what looked to be sunbeams. "It's got a figurehead! I don't know how I missed that when she was coming in."

"Perhaps you were ogling another figure at the time," Emily replied. "Cor, that's a bit much, though, innit?"

They reached the edge of the pier, where a young man in a royal blue polo shirt stood, holding a sign reading "Emily Durand and Boone Fischer."

Boone approached. "Hey. I'm Boone, this is Emily."

The man seemed startled, checking the front of the sign, before lighting up with a smile. "Welcome to the *Apollo*. Nicholas Othonos sends his apologies for not being here to greet you. I'm to take you to the brunch. Follow me, please?"

"It would be our pleasure," Emily said, peeking at the young man's name tag. "Keith, is it?" When he nodded, she plowed ahead. "Lead on, good sir!"

"Right this way." He turned and headed up the pier toward the ship.

"Nicholas mentioned this was a maiden voyage for the *Apollo*," Boone remarked. "This your first cruise?"

"Oh, no, I've worked on a number of cruise lines, but this is my first cruise aboard a luxury mega-yacht."

"What a coinky-dink, it's my first too!" Em took the young man's arm and leaned in conspiratorially. "So, what's it like, working for them?"

"Well... I just started... so... I don't know." He leaned down and whispered, "The passengers are really, *really* rich... so it can be hard to please some of them."

"Well, you're doing a bang-up job for us," Boone said, "so we'll be sure to let Nicholas know."

Keith beamed. "Thank you! Although, I haven't done very much."

"But that 'not-much' that you *did* do, was done with a smile," Emily noted, with a bright smile of her own.

Keith stepped beside a tower on wheels that was snugged up against the ship, with a security officer standing alongside. "Here we are."

Boone looked around. "What, no gangway ramp?"

"We can deploy one when needed, but we have our own elevator. Although there is a little gangway when we reach the top."

Emily whistled. "That's flash."

Keith nodded to the man beside the elevator, then turned back to Boone and Emily. "Did you bring your passports?"

They handed them over and the security officer swiped the bar code of each through a reader before handing them back. "Miss Durand, Mr. Fischer, you're good to go." He pressed a button on the side of the tower and the doors opened.

After they stepped inside, Emily looked around at the interior. "Where on earth do you keep this?"

"It accordions down somewhat," Keith said, as he swiped an ID card on a lanyard across a panel and the doors closed. "The ship has a crane that lowers it into place once the ship is docked."

The elevator rose swiftly, and the opposite door opened into a short, enclosed gangway that led to the ship. Keith led them down a passageway covered in artwork and recessed lighting. He ascended a short flight of stairs to a door, where he again swiped his card. With a click, the door opened onto the end of a balcony that wrapped around the upper superstructure.

"Just how big is this ship?" Boone asked.

"The *Apollo* is 542 feet long, with a gross tonnage of 19,000 tons. A bit smaller than the *Zeus* and *Poseidon*, but larger than the *Athena*."

"Well, that's sexist," Emily muttered good-naturedly. "I don't see all that many passengers."

"Olympus likes to keep the guest list on the low end, usually no more than 120 passengers, with roughly two and a half crew to every guest. And this being a special shakedown cruise, we're only two-thirds booked."

Heading aft, the trio reached a broad expanse of polished teak decking under a retractable awning. A square, finely appointed table was set near the end, the white tablecloth gleaming in the mid-morning sun.

"Boone!"

Her face beaming, Lyra Othonos approached from the far end of the balcony, pausing to hand off a half-finished mimosa to a member of the waitstaff. Lyra's black hair shone, her lithe figure draped in a diaphanous aqua caftan that fluttered gently in the tropical breeze.

"Annnnnnd just like that, I'm underdressed," Emily muttered.

Boone glanced down at her, the lime green sundress fitting Em perfectly, its needle-thin straps accentuating her beautiful shoulders. "Not in my eyes."

"That's 'cause your eyes don't know a Versace when they see one." Emily gazed up at him. "But thank you. And aren't you now glad I talked you into shoes and socks?"

Lyra reached them and delivered a pair of kisses to each of the divemasters. "Thank you so much for coming. Please, come meet my father."

"Lead the way," Boone said.

They followed Lyra to a sliding glass door that opened at their approach. Inside was a beautifully decorated room that looked to be an open-plan living space. The left side of the room was dominated by a long dinner table. Instead of place settings of dishes and cutlery, its polished mahogany surface held a number of leather binders and Montblanc pens atop leather desk blotters.

A cough drew Boone's attention to a corner of the room. In a wheelchair sat an elderly man with a luxurious mop of snow-white hair, attended by a nurse. The man brusquely waved away a proffered oxygen mask and manipulated a joystick on his armrest, nearly running over the nurse's foot.

"Welcome aboard. You must be the young divemasters who saved my daughter's life."

Lyra kissed the man's cheek. "Boone Fischer... Emily Durand... this is my father, Karras Othonos."

"Very pleased to meet you, sir," Emily said, dipping a curtsy.

"Oh, no need for that!" Karras said through a coughing laugh. "I'm not royalty. Descended from peasant stock and proud of it."

"Father was a truck driver and fisherman who built his business up from nothing," Lyra added.

"Well... not nothing," Karras corrected. "My uncle had a few U.S. surplus Liberty Ships. After hauling fish from the docks for a few years, I wanted to join him, so I decided to enroll in the Merchant Marine Academy in Hydra."

"Such a lovely little island," Lyra gushed. "It's in the Aegean south of Athens. There are hardly any cars on the island... only donkeys."

"Sounds a bit like the way Grand Turk used to be," Boone said.

"That is in Turks and Caicos, yes?" Lyra asked. "I hear the diving there is very good. Have you worked there?"

Boone smiled. "Not yet."

"Mr. Othonos, you went to an academy on this Isle of Donkeys...?" Emily prompted.

"Yes. One of the oldest maritime colleges in the world. It's been around since 1749."

"When it was named Saint Nikolaos," a voice added. "Apparently I was named for it."

Nicholas Othonos spoke from the far end of the stately suite. Dressed in a lightweight, navy-blue blazer atop white slacks, he crossed the room to them. "Forgive my tardiness. I had some business to attend to."

"Your business is still in your ear," Emily said with a wink.

"What?" Nicholas reached up and touched an earpiece. "Oh. Thank you." He plucked it from his ear and pocketed it. "I am sorry I couldn't personally meet you at the pier."

"Oh, yeah, before I forget," Boone said, "the fella who guided us up here was very polite... good at his job."

"Young and eager go-getter," Emily added. "Keith, his name was."

Nicholas gave a perfunctory nod and gestured toward the balcony. "I hope you two are hungry."

"Positively ravenous," Em said. "We usually eat breakfast around sun-up."

Karras grunted with approval. "Everyone should start work with the sunrise." He placed a hand on the controls atop his armrest and began a leisurely roll toward the opening. "I wish I could convince my eldest of that. Achilles has a tendency to stay up late and rise later."

"Speak of the devil," Nicholas muttered.

Achilles arrived from the side of the balcony, dressed casually in silk slacks and a pale-yellow shirt open nearly to the sternum. He sported a pair of sunglasses and a single gold chain with some sort of medallion on it. Fighting back a yawn, he made his way toward the brunch table.

"Hung over, I expect." Nicholas said.

"Nicholas!" Karras spat with surprising vigor. "You will respect your elder brother, especially in front of guests." His speech dissolved into a fit of coughing and Lyra leaned down to retrieve the oxygen mask.

Nicholas sighed and gestured to Boone and Emily to follow him to the table. "He will be fine in a moment. Please, be seated."

The square table was arranged with two place settings on three of the sides, and a single setting on the nearest end, this one with no chair.

"Boone... I know my sister would appreciate it if you sat beside her, here..." Nicholas tapped the back of a chair to starboard, then moved toward the portside of the table. "And Emily, I hope you'll join—"

"Emily! From the hospital!" Achilles strutted over to her and pulled out a chair next to the far, aft side of the table. "Come sit beside me."

As Emily shrugged and sat in the proffered chair, Boone watched a darkness pass over Nicholas's face. Just as quickly, he dredged up a smile and moved across to his seat. After Achilles had seated Em, the older brother struck a lounging pose in his own chair at the far end of the table and Boone turned to watch Lyra approach. He stood to pull out the chair beside him.

Karras rolled into his place at the table. "Where is Calypso?" When his query was greeted with shrugs and "I-don't-knows," he shook his head, muttering "No punctuality in this family." He placed his palms on the white tablecloth. "I will say grace."

Boone bowed his head and listened to the family patriarch speak the blessing in his mother tongue. *Beautiful language... no idea what he's saying.* He snuck a peek during the prayer and noticed all were looking down except Nicholas, who was glowering side-eyed at his brother.

"And now... a prayer for *agapiménos mou...*" He bowed his snow-white head and prayed silently.

Lyra leaned in to Boone, close enough that her lips brushed his ear as she whispered. *"Agapiménos* means beloved. My father's second wife passed suddenly a few months ago."

"Efcharistoúme," Karras concluded, then picked up a bell that sat beside his place setting and gave it a gentle, tinkling ring.

Boone thought for a moment that perhaps this was part of a Greek prayer ritual, but then felt silly as he realized Karras was merely signaling the waitstaff to begin the meal service. As a battalion of trays and tureens descended on the table, Boone took his napkin and dropped it in his lap. Turning to speak to Lyra, he found the young woman smiling at him.

"Uh… how are you feeling?" Boone asked.

"I feel wonderful… full of life! Thanks to you."

"Good. But listen… I was just doing my job."

"You are very modest."

"Sir?" A voice came from over his shoulder.

"Yes?" He turned to find a blonde woman in a white polo and skirt holding a tray.

"Mimosa, Bellini, or Bloody Mary?"

"Oh, uh… maybe just some OJ?"

She signaled another waitress who could have been her twin, this one bearing a tray of fruit juices. Across the table, a waiter with a silver coffee service atop a cart was making the rounds. A familiar floppy sunhat came into view as Calypso helped herself to the coffee pot, bringing it over to the empty seat beside Nicholas. She tossed down a battered, coverless paperback book and poured herself a steaming cup. From the look on the coffee server's face, Boone figured this was a colossal breach of etiquette. Calypso handed it to the waiter and he winced as he took the scalding silver sides in his hands before placing it back on his cart.

"Where have you been?" Karras asked, not quite raising his voice.

Calypso held up a finger as she drained the cup and set it down. "Sorry, Father. I lost track of the time." She snagged a Bloody Mary from the cocktail tray as it approached. "Good to see our saviors made it." She took a noisy crunch of celery as she sat.

Boone glanced over at Emily, who was doing her best to seem interested in whatever Achilles was speaking about to her. The elder brother leaned over to say something in low tones and Emily forced a laugh, shedding her sunglasses and looking over to Boone with a widening of the eyes that signaled, "help me." Fortunately, the arrival of the main dishes offered Em a distraction.

"That looks absolutely scrummy," she gushed, as bowls of yogurt and baskets of breads were set down and lids were lifted from trays of egg dishes, breakfast meats, and arrangements of tropical fruits.

"I prefer my meals out here to be family style," Karras said. "It reminds me of home. I hope you don't mind. You can place an order for anything you'd like, if you prefer."

"Not on my account," Emily said. "And Boone will eat anything you put in front of him... so keep your hands clear of his plate, Lyra."

The meal took nearly an hour, with Karras telling tales of his hard-working youth, Lyra fawning over Boone, Achilles fawning over himself to impress Emily, Calypso tossing well-aimed barbs of snark, and Nicholas quietly interjecting from time to time. Boone took it all in, and was beginning to think that this family, for all its wealth, wasn't particularly happy.

As the servers began removing plates, Boone felt a buzz from his pocket. Though his Southern mama would've whacked him upside the head for looking at his phone during such a fine meal, he slid the cell out enough to read the text notification. It was from Ricardo.

My uncle says no one reported anything to the Marine Park about the illegal dumping.

Boone slid his cell back into his pocket as an assortment of tropical fruit sorbets made the rounds. *And yet, that gargantuan Viking of a crewman said the Hygge Cruises crew had been told to leave.* He made a show of looking off to the south. "I see the *Nordic Starr* is gone," he said, addressing Nicholas. "Well done. I'm guessing you reported everything to the Marine Park. What did they say?"

"Oh... they were *very* interested in the video. Revoked their port privileges."

"Yes, thank you for doing that, my son." Karras said, selecting a stemmed, crystal parfait dish of mango sorbet. "That *thing* was offensive to look at and I'm sure our guests prefer the current view."

"So... after you sent them the video, the Marine Park banned them from Cozumel and forced them to leave?" Boone prodded.

Nicholas shrugged. "I think the Harbor Master likely made the call."

"You're still planning to depart tomorrow?"

"Yes. We have a private tour out at Chichén Itzá at the moment, but once they're back aboard, we'll prepare for departure."

"Where is your next port of call?" Em asked.

"Grand Cayman."

"Yes, about that," Lyra said, rising from the table. "Father... given that we decided to combine our maiden voyage with a shakedown cruise, I believe we have several unoccupied suites. Isn't that right, Nicholas?"

"Yes... but why—"

"In light of their saving my life, I would like to invite Boone and Emily to join us on the next leg of our cruise."

"Oh... I don't know..." Nicholas began.

"Excellent idea!" Karras said. "Please... it is the least we can do."

Boone watched Nicholas's face as the man made several failed attempts at starting a sentence, but finally he smiled. "I suppose we can make that happen."

Calypso squirmed in her seat. "I'm sure they have dive charters to fulfill. This is so last minute..."

"Actually..." Em retrieved her phone and looked. "Nope. All clear next couple days. Our 'first mate,' Ricardo, wanted some time with his family, so we're taking a breather."

"You'll love it!" Achilles said. "I promise you, you've never experienced this level of voyage. The finest food, the finest wines, entertainment, gambling, the spa." He leaned toward her. "Hot tubs. Massage."

Em scooted ever so slightly away from him. "I admit, I could go for some pampering. Boone?"

"Well... what about Brix?"

"Brix?" Lyra asked.

"Brixton. Our dog. Ricardo's wife usually looks after him but they're over on the mainland for a few days."

Lyra beamed. "Oh, we allow dogs aboard!"

Karras nodded as vigorously as his aged neck would allow. "Yes, we find that many of the wealthier families prefer to travel with their pets. We have a groomer and a full-time dog walker on staff. I myself have a dog aboard. A kokoni named Cerberus." He laughed. "He's only ten pounds, so not exactly a hound of hell."

"So, it's settled!" Lyra pronounced. "Be back here at..." She trailed off. "When are we leaving?"

"Tomorrow morning at nine," Nicholas said. He rose from the table. "Emily, after you finish your sorbet, I believe I still owe you a tour of the ship?"

"Oh, please… she'll have a whole cruise to tour the ship now, Nicky," Achilles said. "Besides, I've already invited her on a helicopter ride."

"What?" both Nicholas and Boone said at once.

"Yeah. Perfect weather for it. We're going whale shark spotting up by Isla Mujeres."

"My son is an excellent pilot!" Karras said with pride.

"You're invited too," Achilles said to Boone.

"What a marvelous idea," Lyra said. "I will go as well."

Boone looked to Emily, who bit her lip and shrugged her bare shoulders.

"Well… okay."

"Wonderful!" Lyra exclaimed. "I will need to change."

Achilles rose. "I need half an hour for pre-flight. Nicholas, can you show them how to get to the helipad?"

Nicholas tossed his napkin beside his plate and stood with a wince. "I'm sorry, but there is too much to do."

"You just offered to give Emily a tour," Calypso said with a sly smile, "so how busy can you be?"

Nicholas ignored her and addressed Boone and Emily. "Enjoy the flight. Callie will show you to the helicopter." He walked stiffly away.

18

"Nicholas doesn't seem to like his older brother all that much," Boone observed, as Calypso led them up two decks to the helipad.

Callie scoffed. "Achilles is just an asshole. And Nicholas has always had a stick up his butt, but after the accident he's gotten a little dark."

"The accident... where he lost his leg?" Emily prompted.

"I certainly didn't mean the time he fell off his tricycle," Calypso replied. "It happened nearly a year ago at a shipyard in the Netherlands. A naval architect was giving him a sneak peek at a ship being built for a rival company and a catwalk gave way."

"He's lucky to be alive," Emily said.

Callie shrugged. "That's what Lyra's always telling him. But if he felt underappreciated before, it's even worse now. If anything, he's been working twice as hard to impress our father. Feels the universe owes him something. As if he's the only one in this family with skills." She unlocked a door with a keycard and pushed it open. "Well, here you are. I'll see you around. I've got stuff to do."

Boone and Emily stepped through and Callie pulled the door shut behind them.

"Bright 'n' sunny disposition, that one," Emily said, as the pair of them followed the wraparound of the upper-deck promenade to the side of the helipad.

"So… when exactly did Achilles ask you out on this airborne date?" Boone inquired, as they watched the flight crew attend to the helicopter that sat atop the pad.

Em tapped a finger on her lower lip. "Hmm… after I took a piece of *spanakopita* and before the yogurt and honey."

"Surprised you said yes to him, given the looks you were throwing my way."

"Umm… helicopter ride? I don't know about you, but I've never been on one! Besides, I insisted you go along. I know his type. Achilles is a heel."

Boone chuckled. "I see what you did there."

"Just a little mythological wit to brighten your day."

Achilles strode from the helicopter, wearing a flight suit and carrying a helmet under his arm. "Okay! We're ready to go!"

"Still waiting on Lyra," Boone said.

"My sister changes outfits so often, it's a wonder she has time for eating and sleeping," Achilles scoffed. "Come! I'll show you the helicopter while we wait."

They didn't have to wait long. Just as Achilles was completing his tour of the interior, Lyra approached the edge of the helipad wearing a sundress that was strikingly similar to the one Emily wore, though powder blue in color. She climbed aboard the helicopter, and a waiting crewman slid the door closed behind her.

The cabin was laid out with seven leather seats: three in the back, one on either side in the middle, and two just behind the cockpit facing aft. While Achilles went outside to enter the cockpit, Boone and Emily each took a middle seat. Lyra selected the rear-facing seat across from Boone.

"All right, everyone strap in!" Achilles began flipping switches. "The co-pilot up here is Stavros. He'll be hands-off, but my father insists on having him with me. If you look inside your armrests, you'll find some wireless headsets with microphones. They'll patch into the inflight intercom. Put those on so we can talk without yelling."

Boone found the headset and put it on. On the side of the earpiece, he found a switch and toggled it on, immediately hearing the co-pilot's voice.

"I was entering the coordinates from the shark spotter and came across this navigation entry for a point in Grand Cayman. No idea where it came from."

"What's so strange about that?" Achilles replied. "We're going to Grand Cayman next, after all."

"Yes, but… when we use a heliport, we rent time at the one on North Church… near the Burger King. This navigation point is inland… not even near the airport."

"Must have been the main pilot, then." Achilles replied. "What's his name… Jackson?"

"Jason. But he always has me handle navigation entry, and I'm telling you, I didn't set that waypoint."

"Well… leave it in there. Doesn't affect us. Spooling up!"

In moments, the whine of the engines rose to a roar, and as the blades bit into the humid air, the ACH160 rose from the deck and headed out to sea.

Eyes on his laptop screen, Nicholas Othonos watched the helicopter angling toward the north, eventually leaving the field of view of the cameras atop the bridge. He leaned back in his suite's desk chair, staring at the screen. Once more, his elder brother had stepped in and taken something from him. But if he was honest with himself, Emily was a distraction. *Admittedly, a very beautiful distraction.* Still, she and Boone were clearly in love; giving her a tour would have been a waste of his very valuable time. And the events at The Devil's Throat and the subsequent delay of the *Apollo's* departure had altered his carefully structured plans.

The accident last year at the Dutch shipyard had robbed him of his leg, true enough—but it had also served as an epiphany. Life was short. And he had already spent far too much of it trying to impress upon his father his rightful place in the organization. *Karras may have built the business into a powerhouse,* Nicholas thought. *But I'm the one that turned it into so much more.*

Tapping the keys on the laptop, he switched the camera feed to the corridor outside his door before reaching into a desk drawer and retrieving a second laptop. With practiced fingers, he brought up the program. Eyes scanning the layered code, he adjusted some of the dates and times. Satisfied, he retrieved a wireless earpiece from his pocket and made a call.

"Have you ever seen a whale shark?" Lyra asked Boone.

Boone nodded. "Yeah, once. Off Glover's Reef in Belize."

"And of course, I was up top, skippering that day," Emily said. "And it was at depth, so I didn't get to see it."

"Well, you'll be seeing one today!" Achilles said over the headsets. "We pay a few locals to give us a heads-up. There is a pair off Isla Mujeres, but they are already swarmed by cattle boats so we're going to skip Mujeres and head further north to Isla Contoy, where a fisherman spotted one."

Boone looked out the windows on the left as the white sand beaches of Cancún's Hotel Zone came into view. Across the lagoon, the city itself was visible. The "Fort Lauderdale of Mexico," Cancún was known as a mecca for spring break partiers, and Boone was smugly proud that he and Emily had never actually visited. They preferred the quieter coastal towns of the Riviera Maya to the south.

"Aren't we outside the season for whale shark spotting?" Em asked.

"We're right on the front end of it," Achilles replied. "A few months from now, there will be a lot more. I spotted twelve when we were down here aboard the *Athena* last year."

"How many ships does your family own?" Em asked.

Achilles laughed. "A lot. Who knows?"

"Nicholas does," Lyra said.

Achilles turned around to glare at her over the back of her seat. Boone noticed the co-pilot reaching for his set of controls, just in case. "I don't *need* to know the size of our fleet. Nicky can tell me how many ships we have... when he's working for *me*." He turned back around. "I've got it, Stavros."

"According to Father's will, as the eldest, Achilles will take over the business when he passes," Lyra explained. "My father is somewhat old-fashioned in that regard."

"It's the way it should be," Achilles said.

"Your father…" Boone began, thinking of the wheelchair, the nurse, the oxygen. "Is he… um…"

"He is not well," Lyra said sadly. "The doctors gave him six months a year ago. But then his second wife—Nicky and Callie's mother—suddenly died, and—"

"Lyra!" Achilles barked, "this is not a subject for people outside the family."

Below, Isla Mujeres passed by. Five miles long and half-a-mile wide, the low-lying Mexican island reminded Boone a little of the Belizean one he and Emily had last lived on, Caye Caulker. *Well… except for the beaches and the mega-resorts and the larger population*, he thought. *If anything, it's like Ambergris Caye was crammed into Caulker.*

"Hey, Lyra," Em began. "Did you swing by your ship's dive shop? Ask about the computer malfunction and the half-empty tank?"

"Oh… well… no…" Lyra said, looking uncomfortable. "I still think it must have been an accident…"

"The guy who runs the dive shop ran off!" Achilles interjected over the intercom. "Nicky sent security to question him, but he was gone. Wiped all of the security camera footage, too! He probably realized he'd given them a malfunctioning computer. If I ever get my hands on that guy, I'll—"

"Sir," Stavros interrupted, "spotter plane at two o'clock high."

"I see him. Looks like he's inbound." Achilles banked the helicopter to the east before resuming his northward track. "Ah, there's a few shark-watching boats out there. No one is supposed to swim with the whale sharks until next month, but they do it anyway."

"How far to the one you're looking for?" Em asked.

"The fisherman gave us a set of GPS coordinates just south of Isla Contoy... should be there in ten minutes."

Nine minutes later, the co-pilot raised a pair of binoculars and sat up in his seat to look over the cockpit controls, glassing the seas ahead. Very quickly, he lowered them and pointed.

Achilles made a small adjustment and began to descend. "Looks like two of them! Lyra, in the console next to your seat are several pairs of binoculars. We can't get too close or the sound of the engines and the rotor wash will spook them. Learned that the hard way, last time."

Achilles descended to one hundred feet and hovered, rotating ninety degrees. Lyra handed binoculars to Boone and Emily and soon the passengers were all pressed against the windows on the right-hand side of the cabin, Emily going so far as to leave her seat and kneel in the space between rows.

"Thar she blows!" she crowed in her atrocious pirate voice.

"Whale sharks aren't whales, Em," Boone teased.

"Don't patronize me, ye scallywag," Emily growled, then dropped the voice. "Actually, I was reading about why they often spend time at the surface like whales. Not to breathe... but to warm up between deep water feedings."

Boone focused on each massive animal in turn. If he had to guess, one was over thirty feet in length, the other one significantly smaller. "One full grown one... and the other looks like a young adult."

"Maybe it's a baby?" Lyra suggested.

Emily turned on her instructor voice. "Although whale sharks birth live young, a foot or two in length, the juveniles leave the mother in short order."

"They give birth like a mammal?" Lyra asked.

"No… they hatch from eggs that mummy dearest carries around inside her."

"Beautiful *and* smart," Achilles said, turning and leaning over the back of Lyra's seat to look at Emily. Boone looked up from the binoculars to spot the co-pilot grabbing for the controls again. "Definitely looking forward to having you on my ship."

Emily stayed glued to her binoculars. "I'm sure Boone and I will see you around. Wait… looks like the big one's diving… and there goes the other one."

Achilles returned to his controls and after a moment, pulled up on the collective and banked sharply away to the south, gaining altitude. Emily flopped onto her butt at the change in direction.

"Hey," Boone warned, "we need to strap in."

"No worries," Em said, crab-walking across the carpeted cabin to her seat. "All good."

Lyra mouthed, "Sorry," and stuck her head into the cockpit, spitting something out in Greek.

Achilles ignored her. "Hey, we could land in Mujeres… grab some lunch."

"I don't know about Boone, but I'm still stuffed from brunch," Emily said. "Plus, I need some time to pack. I've never dressed for a luxury yacht cruise before. And what Boone's wearing right now is pretty much the best thing he owns."

"Well, tomorrow night is my birthday dinner," Achilles said. "Father always invites the passengers to attend, so you'll need something for that. We've got a tailor aboard and a few shops. I'll set you up, no charge. Oh, and… the *Apollo* has an amazing pool, so *you…*" He threw Emily a leer. "Bring a bikini or two."

◆ ◦ ◆

Since they'd only used a fraction of their fuel, Achilles pushed past cruising speed and had them back aboard in just over twenty minutes. As the helicopter's blades wound down, Boone took off his wireless headset, toggled it off, and turned to open up the arm rest. As he was tucking the headset away, his eyes registered something out of place in the immaculate interior—something that seemed familiar. While the side door was sliding open, Boone unfastened his seatbelt and stepped toward the rear of the cabin.

"Why thank you, good sir," Emily said to the crewman outside, when he offered her a hand.

"Boone? Are you coming?" Lyra asked.

"Right behind you."

Crouching beside the triple row of plush leather seats at the back, he reached his long fingers into the gap between them and the left side of the aft bulkhead to retrieve the object. He exited the helicopter in time to see Achilles stepping down and tossing his helmet to the waiting crewman before swaggering up to Emily.

"Thank you so much for the ride, Achilles," she said. "One more thing I can check off my list of stuff-I've-never-done."

"I'll give you a ride anytime. Hey, I'm planning on going clubbing tonight, if you're interested…"

"Oh, Achilles, you're so sweet to ask… but remember that thing about me needing to pack? Yeah, still need to pack. And walk the dog. And get a good night's sleep."

Achilles waved it off. "Your loss. Anyway, I'll be looking forward to seeing you tomorrow." He turned to Boone. "And you, too. Not as much as her, of course."

Boone shrugged. "Can't blame you. Thanks for the flight."

When the young man who had brought Boone and Emily aboard ship arrived at the edge of the helipad, Achilles jerked a thumb toward him. "That guy will guide you back to the pier... uhhh... can't remember his name... Mark, I think."

"Keith," Boone supplied.

Achilles looked Boone up and down. "Yeah, you'll definitely want to visit the tailor. Have...um..." He snapped his fingers a few times. "Keith! Have Keith run you by on your way out, let them get your measurements." Achilles strutted away, taking a smartphone out of his pocket and placing a call as he headed for an access door.

"What did you pick up from the floor?" Lyra asked.

"Oh... nothing... just a cigarette butt. Everything looked so nice in there, I couldn't leave it."

"He's always picking up trash he finds when diving," Emily said.

"Why am I not surprised?" Lyra leaned forward to give Boone a pair of cheek kisses. "See you tomorrow, Boone." With that, she turned and left.

"Lookee there, she ambushed your cheeks again. And... you're blushing! Hard to do with that tan of yours, but you're managing it."

Boone shook his head, smiling. "Well, I think you've got an admirer of your own."

"Yeah, about that... if you leave me alone with Achilles, I'll feed you to the whale sharks." She held up a finger when Boone started to reply. "And yes... I am well aware that whale sharks are filter feeders... so first I'll have to dice you into a fine mince."

Boone laughed, then waved toward the waiting youth. "Hey, good to see you again, Keith. Lead the way."

Emily took Boone's arm. "We're popping by the tailor, if that's no trouble?"

Thirty minutes later they stepped from the elevator tower onto the pier and made their way to Em's Beetle.

"All right, spill it," Emily said. "What's this about you picking up a cigarette butt?"

"Well, as you said, I'm very eco-conscious."

"Yeah, yeah… underwater, maybe. But picking up rubbish from a billionaire's private helicopter isn't exactly saving the planet. What were you up to?"

"Just what I said. Picked up this. Look familiar?" He produced the butt on his palm, showing off its gold filter and a few millimeters of unburnt black paper. "Remember that Russian guy at Coconuts?"

"Cor, it's one of those Goth sticks, yeah?"

"Looks like the same cigarette to me," Boone said. "I've never seen one before yesterday… you said these are British?"

"Yeah, couple mates in college went through a phase and smoked them for a month or two," Emily said as they reached the car. "But I haven't seen one in years. Weird, yeah?"

Boone took hold of the fastener for the canvas roof. "Top down?"

"Rain check…" Em said, looking up. "Yep, let 'er breathe."

"Let's swing by the marina and secure everything on the *Lunasea*," Boone said. "Then we can see if Brix feels like taking a cruise."

19

"Brixton! Missed you, boy!" Emily gushed, crouching beside the ecstatic dog when they entered the condo. The neighbor who'd been looking after the potlicker had dinner plans and had used a spare key to leave the dog inside.

"Let's get you some food, buddy," Boone said, going to the pantry. "Hey Em, you want to give Ricardo a call? Let him know we'll be away for a couple days? Sailing in the lap of luxury."

"Hobnobbing with high society," Em warbled in an aristocratic dowager's voice. She snickered. "Hobnobbing. Funny word that. Kinda like 'hobgoblin.' Hobnobbing with hobgoblins. Say that three times fast."

"Did you just have an episode?" Boone asked, laughing as he filled Brixton's bowl.

"Sorry… vocab tangent. I'm better now." She called Ricardo. It went to voicemail so she hung up and sent a text, detailing their plans. Finishing that, she made her way to the bedroom and opened their closet. *Not exactly the wardrobe selection for a luxury cruise,* she thought.

Em's taste in clothing leaned heavily toward comfort: tanks, tees, shorts, and the occasional sundress. Nevertheless, she had a few stylish options and quickly laid them out on the bed. She glanced over at Boone's side of the closet. *Oh, lord no, this won't do. And it won't have to,* she thought with a smile. While Boone was being measured, Em had surreptitiously examined the shop's stock and handed the proprietor a note on the way out. She headed back to the main room. Boone was playing tug-of-war with Brixton, who had his teeth locked onto a knotted piece of rope.

Emily crouched to dog-level once more. "Hey Brix! Wanna go walkies? Well... drive-ies, then walkies."

The dog released the rope, his tail a blur of wags.

"I thought you needed to pack." Boone said.

"Oh, I can do that in thirty minutes. I just didn't want to spend the whole day with Achilles and his testosterone. And you... you can pack in thirty *seconds*. But not to worry, we'll be getting you something proper. I can't have you dragging me down with your boat bum couture."

Boone shrugged. "You're the boss."

"Damn straight. Now let's go somewhere where Brix can get a walk and we can get a bite on the beach."

Ten minutes south of the condo complex, Boone and Emily came to a decorative sailboat alongside the road and the thatch-topped sign for the Playa Palancar Beach Club. Far from the cruise ship crowds, the little private beach club was situated in an undeveloped spot on the coast, over half a mile from the next nearest property. In addition to a bar, it had a simple seaside restaurant that specialized in fresh seafood.

Boone turned off the coastal highway onto the crushed limestone road that threaded through the dense tropical foliage on either side. With its top down, the boxy VW Thing crunched along at a cautious pace. Strapped into the back seat, Brix had his paws up on the top of the rear door behind Emily, enjoying the breeze and sniffing the air.

"You're awfully quiet," Em said. "Well... I take that back. You are *frequently* quiet. I mean, you seem to be deep in contemplation."

"Mm."

"Cogitation... rumination..."

Boone smiled. "You having another episode?"

"What are you thinking about, you berk?"

"The *Nordic Starr.*"

"What about it?"

"Oh, shoot... sorry, I completely forgot to tell you. In the middle of brunch, Ricardo texted me. His uncle told him that no one reported anything to the Marine Park about the illegal dumping."

"What? But Nicholas said... oh, so *that's* why you were asking him about it in that weird way."

"I wasn't being weird."

"I could tell something was up, the way you looked at him... but I was too busy keeping Achilles's hand off my knee."

"What?" Boone turned to her, a rare flash of anger on his face.

"Eyes on the road," Em said, turning his head face-forward with a fingertip on his chin. "Only happened once. And he apologized when I explained what would happen to his fingers. But we're getting off the subject. Those Scandinavian guys seemed pretty pissed at Nicholas. You think he, what...? Blackmailed them to bugger off?"

"Something like that. I suppose if he'd gone through proper channels there'd have been an investigation. The ship might have been stuck there."

"An eyesore for daddy dearest," Em said. "So just threaten them to make them leave right away."

"And they'll probably go on dumping illegally in other ports."

Boone turned into a little parking area in front of the sandy entrance to the club. While Boone led Brix to the beach, Emily visited the bar for a couple bottles of Pacifico to take on the stroll, letting a hostess know they'd be back for dinner shortly.

"Nothing but beach either way, so... north or south?" Em asked when she joined Boone near the shore and handed him a cerveza.

"Brix seems to have a northward urge," Boone said, letting the potlicker pull him along by the leash. As Boone gave ground, Brix picked up his pace.

Emily laughed, jogging to keep up. *Some days, you walk him... other days he walks you.*

Once they were a hundred yards or so from the beach club, Boone crouched and unclipped the leash from Brixton's harness. The dog was off like a shot, running through the surf's edge with wild abandon.

"Don't know how much exercise he'll get aboard ship," Boone explained. He raised his beer bottle. "To unexpected cruises."

Em clinked. "To weird billionaire families. And you getting some new threads."

After a vigorous walk, paired with a game of fetch with drift-wood, Boone and Emily headed back to the beach club, seating themselves at a table in the sand. The sun was low in the sky, the tops of the gentle waves sparkling. They ordered a grilled seafood platter to split and asked for a bowl of water for Brix.

"Sandals off, toes in sand," Emily announced.

"Way ahead of ya," Boone replied. He rapped the molded plastic tabletop. "A far cry from white linen tablecloths and fine china."

Em held up the knife and fork wrapped in a paper napkin. "And I have a sneaking suspicion this silverware isn't silver."

"Never understood the need for all that," Boone said. "If the food's good, I'm happy."

"Your mum didn't have some special dishes to bring out for holidays?"

Boone shrugged. "I guess. We had some antique red glass plates we used for Christmas dinner."

"How is she doing, by the way? Have you spoken to her lately?"

"She's good. She keeps saying she wants to come visit, but... well, she was saying that back when I was in Curaçao."

"She a diver?"

"Nah. Loves the beach, hates the ocean."

Emily laughed. "Really? Where on earth did *you* come from?"

"My dad. He got me into snorkeling while mom enjoyed the beach."

"Oh, right, the Dutch Navy guy she met in Aruba. Y'know, we should go there sometime. I've only done the 'BC' of the ABC," Emily said, referring to the ABC Islands of Aruba, Bonaire, and Curaçao. "You talk to your father at all?"

"Nope."

Em waited for Boone to say more, but he just took a swig of his Pacifico and reached down to scratch Brixton behind the ears.

Emily knew the divorce had been a trying time for his mother and a young Boone, who was only twelve at the time. She had tried to tease out additional information, but it was a subject he never seemed eager to discuss.

"How 'bout *your* folks, they doing good?" Boone asked. "I feel like I kinda know them, with all the FaceTime calls you rope me into."

"My family's good. And I don't *rope* you into those! You look over my shoulder and get sucked in."

"That's 'cause you chase me around with your phone, shouting 'Say hi, Boone!'"

"That doesn't sound like me," Em said innocently.

"How's married life treating your sister? I remember you got back from her wedding, right before we… uh…"

"Right before we chased down a terrorist submarine and then bonked in a hammock?"

Boone laughed. "I guess it all boils down to that, doesn't it?"

"I'd like to think we've got a bit more going on than terrible hammock sex and exploding submarines. Though, when I say that out loud… blimey, that'd make some great punk rock band names. 'Live at Dingwalls, it's… Hammock Sex! With opening act, Exploding Submarine!'"

Boone executed a sincere spit take, sending Mexican lager into the sand. "You're a goober," he managed to cough. "Certifiable… in a good way."

"Yeah, me mum always said I was a few bites short of a biscuit."

"And I love you for it."

"Aw, you'll make me blush, Beanpole. You, I just keep around to get bits and bobs from the top shelf of the cupboard."

"It's nice to feel useful. Just hope you don't leave me for a stepladder."

The food arrived, a tantalizing spread of grilled seafood, mostly shrimp and snapper. Lobster was out, it being the protected breeding season, but they'd doubled down on the shrimp to compensate.

"Tuck in!" Em snagged several shrimp. "So, this Othonos family... they strike you as... I dunno..."

"There's stuff going on under the surface," Boone said, levering a fish filet onto his plate. "I'm gonna go out on a limb here, but... I'm thinking Nicholas is the only one who does any work."

"Apart from the father... Karras," Em said. "Though I'm guessing there's going to be a passing of the baton at some point, yeah?"

"Might explain some of the vibe I was picking up from the table," Boone said.

"What vibe?"

"Resentment." Boone lifted his cerveza to his lips but didn't take a sip. Lowering it back to the table, he was silent for a moment, looking out at the water.

Emily helped herself to some fish, eyes on Boone. *He's mulling something over... best to sit back and let the gears grind.* The fish was good, almost certainly that day's catch.

Finally, Boone lifted his bottle again and took a drink. "It's funny..."

Emily waited, but finally prodded him. "Well?"

"The accident at Devil's Throat... and the malfunction of Nicholas's underwater scooter. What if they're connected? And what if they weren't accidents?"

"Possible, I suppose."

"But that just confuses me even more."

"How so?"

"It's just... well, here we have a super-rich family where one family member stands to inherit the whole business..."

213

"Yes?"

"And the 'accidents,' if that's what they were... they were directed at the ones who are getting screwed in the will?"

"Fair point," Em mused. "I suppose Achilles would be the one you'd expect to find facedown in the conservatory with a candlestick beside him and Colonel Mustard sneaking out the window."

Boone laughed. "I woulda gone for Miss Scarlet."

"Of course you would. Careful, you'll make Lyra jealous."

"Yeah, I don't know what to say about that."

"Between her and Achilles pining for us, I'm just assuming we're giving off sexy pheromones or something."

Boone leaned across the table. "Then we should go back to the condo and do something to work up a sweat. Flush it out of our systems."

Em gave Boone a lascivious smile. "I don't think that's how it works, but I'm up for it. You know... for science."

"Wait... where are we going?" Matthaíos Boston asked from the back seat, the first note of concern rising in his voice. Outside the windows of the rental car, the low buildings of the outskirts of San Miguel had given way to tropical scrub and trees.

"We're taking the scenic route," Stallion said from the rear, where he sat beside the Greek dive shop owner. He wore a blue polo with the Olympus Cruises logo on the breast. "Hey, what kind of Greek name is 'Boston?'"

"I am Greek American," Matthaíos said distantly, sounding distracted.

"Oh, well... maybe shoulda gone with 'Matthew,' then, fella."

Angler glanced into the rearview mirror. Matthaíos was looking back over his shoulder, toward the receding town. Stallion stared straight ahead, giving the team leader a wink. Angler had an odd sensation of repetition—not exactly déjà vu, but something akin to it.

"We were just supposed to pick up new tanks, yes?" Matthaíos suddenly turned back around and looked straight into the mirror, his face taking on an expression of serenity as he stared into Angler's eyes. "Why did you kill me?" he asked in a hollow voice.

What the...? Oh, Goddammit! Not another one of these! Angler tried to wake up, but the dream held him in a tight embrace. *Okay, fine.* He tried to turn the steering wheel and pull over, but the car continued inexorably forward. He was just along for the ride—in more ways than one. *Screw it,* he thought. *Let's get this over with.*

Matthaíos was back to his squirming. "The dive gear wholesale shop is in the middle of town. Turn around, we have to go back!"

"Juice him," Angler heard himself say.

Stallion twisted in his seat and applied a handheld stun gun to the side of their passenger's neck. Matthaíos screamed, his body contorting grotesquely. Unlike the non-lethal weapons of Hollywood that magically induced unconsciousness, a real-world stun gun inflicted a great deal of pain, immobilizing the target with an assault on the muscles and nervous system.

Matthaíos wept. "Wh... why are you doing this?" When Stallion zapped him again, he shrieked and blubbered even louder, tears running in rivers down his cheeks.

Angler felt his insides curdle. *God, I hate it when they cry...* He had killed a lot of men in his time, often with little more thought than flipping off a light switch. *But when they cried...* Again, he tried to force himself awake. Again, the effort was futile.

The Dream Angler turned off the road, rolling up to a low wall with a gate. Integrated into the bars of the gate, metal letters proclaimed "CAPA", an acronym for *Comisión de Agua y Alcatarillado*, the agency in charge of sewage and potable water on the island. To the right of the gate, letters painted on the wall warned *"Prohibido el Paso."*

"Time to pass-o the gate-o," Stallion proclaimed, pocketing the stun gun. "Pop the trunk, Chief." Exiting the car, he headed back to the trunk. Angler found the release for it, then looked at the dive shop owner, curled up against the door, his whimpers soft now. The trunk slammed shut, rocking the car gently. *Lot of detail in this one,* Angler thought. *Frikkin' subconscious is going for an Oscar in cinematography.*

Glancing across the hood, he watched Stallion approach a padlock on the gate, an L-shaped tire iron held loosely in his fingers. Looking back toward the road, craning his long neck both ways, the lanky mercenary checked for any of the infrequent cross-island traffic before returning his bug-eyed gaze to the lock. Raising the tire iron in both hands, he brought the wedge-end down sharply on the top of the padlock. The second time was the charm: the lock popped open. He swung the two sections of gate aside.

Angler rolled the car forward onto the rough road that ran straight to the south, disappearing into the low tropical trees. Palantir had suggested this location, one of three such gated roads, each one cross-hatched with numerous short, dead-end roads that contained a total of 220 freshwater wells that supplied the drinking water for the island.

Stallion closed the gate behind them and returned to the car. "Tolstoy and his lockpicks would still be at it," Stallion snorted.

Angler proceeded slowly down the road, bumping over areas where it was broken in places, clumps of tropical grass poking up through the cracks. A pipe ran along the ground at the side of the road, its rusted metal exterior held in place by evenly spaced braces of concrete.

"How are you going to do it?" Matthaíos asked from the front passenger seat.

Angler looked into the mirror and saw that their victim also sat in back, head against the glass. *Well, that's a new one,* he thought with irritation. The dreams had started a few years ago, and were one of the reasons he was hoping to hang it all up after this job. At first, he'd found them disturbing, but now they were just annoying as hell.

"Put your seat belt on," he forced his dream self to tell the second Matthaíos. "Safety first."

Sarcastic irony was lost on the dream, and the man simply turned in his seat to face Angler. "How many more will you kill?"

Probably a few, Angler thought as the car was suddenly at a complete stop, the scene having shifted to a well at the dead end of one of the many side roads. Angler's front seat visitor was gone.

"Please, I have a wife and children!" Backseat Matthaíos pleaded.

"And I've got a mortgage," Stallion replied, pressing the stun gun to the man again. The snapping pops sounded, but less frequently, and at a noticeably lower volume.

Matthaíos winced but appeared unhurt. Eyes widening with hope and determination, he tore open the door. Stallion grabbed at him, but the dive shop owner managed to pull free.

"You idiot, didn't you charge it fully?" Angler shouted, already out of the car, moving to intercept their quarry.

Matthaíos stumbled, the muscles in his legs still jelly from the earlier shocks. Angler caught up with him just as the man grabbed a chunk of limestone and swung it. Angler caught the arm, twisting and upending it, breaking the elbow with a gruesome crunch. Matthaíos cried out, dropping the rock. Angler spotted movement from the corner of his eye, as Stallion arrived and swung the tire iron against the man's temple. Matthaíos crumpled, his face smashing to the ground right beside the cuff of Angler's slacks, spattering the material with droplets of blood.

So that's where that came from... Angler crouched, looking at the man's face. Eyes that saw nothing stared at the mercenary's shoe. Angler fished Matthaíos's wallet out of his pocket. He would throw it far into the brush on their way back. "Pick him up," he said, grabbing the man's arms. Stallion grabbed his legs.

Together the two mercenaries lugged Matthaíos to the nearby well. They started a gentle rocking motion and on the third swing released him, arcing the body over the well where it collided with the opposite lip, rebounding to fall into the pit. A splash.

"We done here?" Stallion asked.

"One sec." Angler went to the well, intending to check and make sure their victim had landed facedown, in case he'd been playing possum. He looked over the edge.

A familiar face looked up at him from the surface of the water. Angler saw himself.

Oh, fuck this. With a supreme effort, he wrenched himself out of the dream, sitting bolt upright in the bed. As his heart rate and breathing returned to normal, Angler became aware of sounds in the darkened suite. From the living area, the hellacious snores of Stallion, asleep on the couch. And through the wall, the muffled grunts and cries of Potluck and Tolstoy, rutting away in the adjoining bedroom.

Angler looked at the bedside clock: 4:32 a.m. Grabbing one of the excessive number of pillows, he lay on his side and crammed it over his head. Today was going to be a long day, and dammit to hell, he was going to get *some* sleep.

20

The next morning, as Brixton scrambled to keep up with the flood of new sensory information that was assaulting his nose, Boone and Emily headed through the terminal to the Puerta Maya pier, threading their way through strangers of every stripe. Emily held Brixton's leash, Boone following, rolling a pair of suitcases. One of them struck a raised cobblestone with a sharp thump and Brix jumped at the sudden noise.

"Oh, sorry about that, buddy!" Boone said.

Brixton chuffed an annoyed sneeze, probably to tell Boone he'd prefer if that sound was not repeated.

"Bad Boone! Don't scare our pooch! And don't bollocks up my suitcase—that's a Tumi!" Emily gave Brixton a vigorous rub. "If he does that again, Brix, you can bite 'im on the bum."

"Is that positive reinforcement for him, or negative reinforcement for me?" Boone asked.

"Why can't it be both?" Em started forward again, Brixton trotting along happily, uttering a short bark as they reached the pier.

"You excited, buddy?" Boone asked. He spotted a familiar crewman waiting near the elevator.

"Boone Fischer and Emily Durand. Good to see you again! And you've brought your friend."

"Keith, how you doing?" Boone asked.

"Very well, thank you. I'm to show you to your suite. Oh, and thanks for putting in a good word."

"Oh… yeah…" Boone said. "We mentioned you to Nicholas Othonos. And… uh…"

"And he probably didn't know who I was," the young man finished, laughing. "But the head steward overheard it, and that's all that matters. This way!"

Emily dropped down to Brix's level. "Oh, Brixy, this is your first time on an elevator, yeah? S'okay, wittle shmoogee, we're going to go up, up, up!"

Brix wagged his tail. Whatever was happening, Emily sounded excited about it, so it seemed that was good enough for him.

"Will we be seeing you around the ship, Keith?" Boone asked.

"Sure. I've got a lot of duties. If you're lucky, you'll catch me playing piano in The Muse Lounge. I'm in the musical theater biz back in New York, so I sing a lot of Broadway standards… and I take requests. I'll be playing for Achilles Othonos's dinner tonight, too."

"Cor, that's impressive," Emily said. "Hidden talents, Keith!"

"Everyone onboard has more than one job. I'm banking some bucks before I head back to New York and start auditioning again."

"You know any Billy Joel?" Boone asked.

Keith laughed. "I saw him at the Garden! Not exactly musical theater, but drop by The Muse and I'll play you a few of his hits."

The elevator doors opened, and Keith led them aft.

"You two must have made an impression. You've got a great suite on the port side." He opened an interior door. "We'll take this passthrough..."

Brix snuffled under doors as the quartet made their way across the ship to a corridor on the opposite side.

"And here we are!" Keith announced. "Your quarters. Let me give you your keycards."

While Keith dug through his pockets, Boone looked down at Brixton. The dog turned his head to the left and sniffed the air. Stiffened. Sniffed again. At the end of the corridor stood a door, identical to the one they were currently in front of. The dog stared in that direction and strained against the leash.

"No, Brixton, this is our room here," Em said, taking in the slack on the dog's leash as Keith opened the door and led them inside.

"Whoa." Boone stared goggle-eyed at the suite. They had just stepped inside and the living area alone took his breath away. Hardwood floors were topped with expensive-looking rugs and chic furniture. The marble countertop of a wet bar in the corner shone in the glow of the track lighting overhead. Spotless glass doors to the balcony stood open, and Boone could see a Jacuzzi out there, off to one side.

"Oh my God, this is..." Emily took a few steps into the room. "Smack my gob, I am gobsmacked."

Keith laughed. "Yeah, it's not your run-of-the-mill cruise ship, is it?"

"I wouldn't know, but color me impressed! Boone, pay the man!"

Boone found a twenty and handed it to Keith. "Hey... I got measured at the tailor's yesterday, and ..." He gestured at his current ensemble, the exact same slacks and shirt he'd worn to brunch.

Keith gestured to a touchscreen just inside the door. "You can pull up a schematic for the ship right here." He tapped the screen to bring it to life and brought up a layered map of the ship. Tapping a microphone icon, he said, "Tailor." The layers shuffled themselves to the correct deck and a green circle appeared over a location.

"Fancy," Boone said.

"You can load a temporary ship's concierge app onto your phone that will sync with it and allow you to access directions that will lead you right to the men's clothing store. This panel can also order room service, schedule spa treatments, and notify you of entertainment options."

Keith showed Boone and Emily how to access various functions, then gave them a quick tour of the two bedrooms with an opulent bathroom bridging them.

"Oh Brix, look! They put food and water bowls out for you!" Em pointed alongside the bar.

"We can provide you with a dog bed, too, if you need it."

"Thanks. Uh… where do we go if Brixton needs to…?" Boone trailed off.

Keith went to the touchscreen and brought up the schematic, tapping the mic icon again. "Dog park." The uppermost deck appeared and a crescent-shaped area glowed green. "There's a nice little section of grass and fencing just aft of the pool. Currently, the only other dog aboard belongs to Mr. Othonos, so you'll probably have it all to yourself. And if you like, you can access the dog walker and groomer in the Services section of the touchscreen. Oh, and that reminds me…" Keith went to the bar, retrieved a folded leather sleeve that lay there, and handed it to Boone.

When he opened it, he found a pocket on either side containing a black credit card, embossed with the Olympus Cruises logo. "What're these?"

"On rare occasions, special guests are given these cards. Karras Othonos insisted you not pay for anything while aboard ship." He leaned in conspiratorially. "And between you and me, *everything* here is designed to extract very large amounts of money from our guests... all of whom can easily afford it." He tapped one of the cards. "Use those at the tailor, the groomer, restaurants, bars, the spa. Anywhere! Well, except for the casino. The company discovered that allowing a guest to gamble with company money wasn't good business practice. There is a cap on the amount available, but you won't come anywhere near it, and they will cease functioning upon arrival in Grand Cayman."

"Yoink!" Emily snatched one of the cards from the folder.

Keith glanced at his watch. "The ship will depart at ten, which is in twenty minutes. I have to run. If you need anything, don't hesitate to call."

After Keith departed, Boone tucked the remaining card into his wallet and strolled out to the balcony, noting the sturdy glass barrier. "Seems safe for Brix to hang out on the balcony with us." He looked to the northeast along the Cozumel coast, though much of that view was obscured by an enormous ship from one of the main cruise lines. He glanced astern, noting the wraparound edge of a balcony that likely belonged to the neighboring suite at the end of the corridor. A small table and two chairs sat there, similar to the ones on their own balcony.

Boone glanced back into their cabin, watching as Emily rooted around the outer pocket of her suitcase. She was wearing a lightweight, white summer dress. *Not sure I've ever seen that one,* he thought. It was surprisingly fetching, even with her crouching to retrieve a Ziploc of Brixton's food from her luggage. And while he wasn't sure he'd seen that dress on her before, he was absolutely certain he'd *never* seen the pair of pearlescent white sunglasses she'd worn aboard. Stepping back inside, he picked them up from the bar, holding them between thumb and forefinger until she looked up at him. He raised an eyebrow.

Smirking, Em rose and snatched them from his hand. "You got something to say?"

"For all the time I've known you... your shades have always been ... *always*... green."

"How one-dimensional do you think I am?" she huffed, tucking the sunglasses into the neckline of her dress. "I have layers upon layers, like an onion. A sexy, sexy onion. And like an onion... I will make you cry, if you dis my fashion."

Boone laughed, surrendering the round. "So, what should we do first?" he asked.

"Let's head up top and watch the departure," Em suggested, pouring some dog food into a bowl. "Maybe we can wave at some dive boat buddies and fill them with jealousy. Yell 'I'm king of the world' and all that."

"Lead the way. Though *Titanic* references probably aren't the way to go on a ship like this. On the other hand..." He stepped back into the suite and gave her a half smile. "Do I get to draw you later?"

Em scoffed. "Who's the artist here?"

Their suite had been impressive; the rest of the ship equally so. The attention to detail was astonishing and every surface gleamed.

Bet they spend half the day scrubbing, Emily thought, as they made their way to a viewing deck near the bow. She gripped a rail on the port side, sucking in a lungful of salty air before sighing it back out.

"You can say that again." Boone rested his forearms on the rail and leaned atop them, bringing his face down to her level. "Beautiful day for a voyage, wouldn't you say Ms. Durand?"

"Indubitably, Mr. Fischer."

Boone laid a finger under her chin and brought her in for a brief kiss. When their lips parted, Emily cleared her throat.

"That's all I get? Stingy bugger."

Boone smiled and moved in for a more passionate kiss—one that was unfortunately timed, as the *Apollo* engaged its thrusters, and the abrupt lurch banged their lips and teeth together.

Emily dissolved into muffled fits of laughter, holding her battered upper lip. Boone, too, held his mouth, amusement in his eyes.

Emily lowered her hand. "Oh, we're a pair of smooth operators, aren't we?" she said, stifling further giggles.

"If this was a Hollywood moment, that woulda ended up on the cutting room floor," Boone said.

"Hoowee, here we go!" a boisterous voice rang out from nearby. A neighboring couple stood at the railing a few feet away. The owner of that voice was a rotund man in a tan suit and bolo tie, sporting a ten-gallon hat. "Yeehaw!"

"A real, live cowboy," Em said loud enough for Boone to hear. "I've never seen one in the wild."

"Oil-boy, more likely," Boone said, as the *Apollo* backed away from the pier into the channel. Aided by maneuvering thrusters, the massive yacht soon had her bow aimed to the northeast.

Emily pointed to a dive boat further out in the channel, on its way south as it skirted around the *Apollo*. "There's one of Cozumel

Marine World's boats!" She waved and the skipper in the fly-bridge waved back.

"Looks like the *Manati*," Boone remarked, raising a hand in greeting. Below them, the bow wave of the *Apollo* intensified as she rapidly picked up speed. Boone looked up, craning his neck to try to see the bridge that towered over them. "Bet you'd love to drive this baby, huh?"

Em shrugged. "I like to feel the water under me when I skipper," she said. "But I wouldn't mind getting a look at the bridge."

"I'm sure Nicholas can make that happen," Boone said.

Em nodded, frowning. "I'm not happy about him lying to our faces about contacting the Marine Park. Bit dodgy, that. He and I might need to have a little chinwag." She looked at Boone. "But maybe *after* we use one of those magic cards and score some fancy duds."

21

As Boone and Emily opened the door to the suite, Brixton was there in an instant, nearly bowling them over.

"Oh, I missed you too!" Emily cooed, sweeping a garment bag away from the dog's onslaught of devotion, like a matador swishing a cape. "Give us a tick to unpack, and then we'll go for a stroll, yeah?"

"Whattaya think, Brix?" Boone asked, stepping inside the door. He held out his arms and turned in a circle.

Brixton sniffed at the fabric of the eye-poppingly expensive suit, then wagged his tail, preparing to greet Boone with a sloppy kiss.

Emily set aside her garment bag and intercepted the pooch. "No licking the suit, Brixy!" She crouched, half-petting the dog, half-holding him in place. "Isn't Boone dashing, though? Can you saaaaayyy.... Saville Row?"

Brix knew this game, and barked a short "woof," eliciting laughter and affection.

Boone crossed the room and slid open the glass doors to the balcony. "Get yourself some fresh air, boy! We'll go up top for a walk in a moment."

Brixton didn't need any encouragement, the salty, briny smells in the air drawing him outside.

Boone turned from the balcony and stepped inside the nearest bedroom, examining his suit in a full-length mirror. Apparently, Emily had picked it out yesterday while he was being measured, selecting a lightweight Gieves and Hawkes suit with a shark-skin weave. Boone had protested that he had imagined something white and tropical, but Emily had muttered something about *Miami Vice* and insisted the light charcoal she'd chosen would be more versatile. She'd managed to arrange an incredibly comfortable pair of dress shoes for him, too.

Emily's reflection appeared next to his. "Well?"

"I gotta say, Em… I kinda feel like James Bond in this thing. And I mean that in a good way."

"You look amazing, Boone," Em said, clearly meaning it from the tone in her voice. Then her face scrunched up. "But who taught you to tie a tie?"

"Well… no one."

"Here, face me…" Reaching up, she swiftly unraveled the hangman's noose of a knot he'd constructed and started afresh, biting her lower lip in concentration.

Boone looked down at her, breathing in the scent of her shampoo. "So… when do I get to see what you picked out for yourself?"

Her teeth released their grip on her lip as she broke into a smile, but stayed focused on his tie, not looking up. "You get to see that dress when it's time for the big dinner… and not before."

"That hardly seems fair. Why do I have to wear the monkey suit 'til then?"

"Because I came aboard looking presentable," Em said, stepping back to admire her handiwork. "There!" She rotated Boone to face the mirror. "Now check your pockets—I think you've got a tie clip."

A sudden flurry of barks sounded from the balcony. Boone frowned. "Those aren't happy barks," he said, as he left the mirror and headed toward the balcony, Emily close behind.

"What's up, Brix?" he called before stepping outside. The dog stood rigidly, hackles raised. While his barks diminished to a growl, he didn't turn his head at Boone's voice, which was unusual. Boone followed his gaze.

On the stern suite's corner balcony stood a tall, lanky man, his frame not unlike Boone's. The first thing that caught Boone's eye was the man's throat—an impressive Adam's apple dominated the space under his stubbled chin. He had unusually large eyes, squinting from the tropical sun's glare off the surrounding water. The man was about three-quarters of the way into a cigarette, his exhales blown into the *Apollo's* wake by the ship's forward motion.

"Cute dog," the man said, a touch of rural American twang in his voice. "I don't think he likes me, though."

"Sorry 'bout that," Boone said, reaching down to give the still-growling Brix a reassuring neck scratch. "He's usually pretty chill."

"No skin off my nose," the man said, taking a puff. "Nice suit. Y'all move cabins or something? Didn't think we had any neighbors."

"We just came aboard," Boone said, as Emily joined him.

The man's bulbous eyes swiveled in their sockets to take in Emily. "Howdy, ma'am."

"Stallion, who are you talking to?" a gravelly voice asked from around the corner of the aft balcony. A craggy face beneath a close-cropped haircut appeared, flinty eyes quickly focusing on Boone's. Brix's growl increased. The head vanished out of sight. "Get the hell back in here," the voice hissed.

The lanky man rolled his eyes and sauntered back around the corner, tipping a nonexistent hat to the divemaster couple.

Brix continued to growl.

Emily crouched. "Easy, boy. Just a goofy guy. Everything's okay. C'mon, let's get your harness on, yeah? Go check out the dog park?"

As Emily took Brixton back inside, Boone remained. *Who the heck names themselves Stallion?* he wondered, looking at the table on the adjacent balcony. A highball glass sat empty and alongside it, an ashtray. The tray contained quite a few butts, most of them white, but several others caught Boone's eye. They were gold.

———◆ ◆ ◆———

"What were you thinking?" Angler growled after he sealed the door to the balcony.

"I didn't know anyone was over there," Stallion protested. "Tolstoy 'n' me have been hanging out on that corner for days, not a soul in sight next door. Besides, it's not my fault Little Miss Cheesehead won't let us smoke inside."

"It's a stinky habit, you frog-faced hick," Potluck snarled.

"Hick? You're the one who was prob'ly birthed in a dairy barn."

"Stallion, you will show this woman respect," Tolstoy said from across the room.

"Hey, just 'cause you two are bumping uglies—"

"Shut the fuck up, all of you!" Angler roared. "We have a job to do, and that job is going down in less than eight hours! Enough of this petty bullshit." He pointed at Stallion. "You. Stay off the balcony. Your mission is a bit trickier than ours, so keep your head down until go time. You need to smoke, do it in here." When Potluck started to protest, Angler silenced her with a look.

"Can *I* smoke outside, then?" Tolstoy asked.

"No! And no more sneaking out for duty-free crap. The helicopter... we good to go?"

"They fly it yesterday but I check systems late last night. It has been refueled."

"All right. I'm going to duck out and pay a visit to our secondary evac option. We'll be getting the final set of instructions in a few hours. Until then, check your gear, go over the plan, eat some food, get some rest. By nine a.m. tomorrow we'll all be multi-millionaires."

"How much money do you think that one has?" Boone asked. He and Emily stood on a small hillock within the park, the little fenced-in area having been tastefully landscaped.

"Which one?" Em asked, looking around the pool area that was in view from the fenced-in dog run.

"The young guy with the weird hair and the nice clothes."

"Ah, now *that* is a hairpiece... and not a good one," Em observed. "And those clothes are expensive, but not properly fitted. So, I'm gonna say... software geek. Probably worth one hundred mill."

Boone whistled appreciatively. Brix looked up, saw the sound wasn't meant for him, and went back to work, sniffing every patch of ground in the little enclosure.

"Okay, my turn," Em said. "Umm... that one. The old bloke sitting with his daughter."

"Uh... I don't think that's his daughter."

"What? Oh. Ew."

"Old money... betcha he's got a good broker. I'll go as high as...a quarter billion."

"You win. Hey, Brixton, you done? How about we take you to the groomer, huh? Maybe schedule a dog sitter?" She clipped the leash back onto the dog's harness. "And we can grab an early lunch, and check out some of the other shops down there... maybe a trip to the spa."

"Sounds like a plan."

Using the ship assistant app on his phone, Boone led them down to the commerce concourse of the *Apollo*, pausing to drop Brix off at the groomer, located in a short alcove at the periphery of the inner mall. At the end of the alcove was a simple bistro with an outdoor balcony, and they spent a half hour enjoying a light lunch. Returning to the interior of the ship, they came upon a shopping concourse surrounding a vast atrium, the focal point of which was a fountain, with statues of Greek gods standing in a circle at its center. The figures were depicted in the style of classical Greek sculpture, coated in a garish gold patina.

"Very tasteful," Boone deadpanned.

"Oh, yes. Nothing gaudy there," Em replied.

Ringing the atrium and extending into the distance stood a small number of gleaming storefronts, offering clothing, handbags, shoes, jewelry, liquor, cigars...

"Wait one sec," Boone said, stopping at the cigar store.

"What, you thinking of chomping on a Cuban during the trip?" Emily asked, following him inside.

"Nope." He paused near the entrance, letting his eyes take in the whole shop. Immediately, black and gold leaped out at him.

"Welcome to my store, *señor* and *señorita*," the proprietor said. He sounded Cuban, which Boone figured was useful when selling high-end cigars. "May I help you find something?"

"Yeah," Boone replied. He stepped to the shelf that had drawn his eye and picked up a box of Black Russian cigarettes. "These are unusual. Are they popular?"

The man shrugged. "This is our maiden voyage, but our shops on the other ships usually sell some on every cruise."

"How about this trip? Anyone buying these?"

The man laughed. "Since you ask, there is a man who has come in twice. Bought half of my stock. And the funny thing is…"

"He's Russian?" Boone asked, tapping his finger on the word on the box.

"*Sí!* He thought it was very amusing to buy these. I explained they were actually British cigarettes, but he didn't care. Very thick accent, hard to understand. You know him?"

Boone smiled. "I've run into him a few times." He set the box down by the register and slid his black card alongside it. The proprietor raised an eyebrow and smiled knowingly as he rang the order up.

"Boone, you don't smoke," Em protested as they exited the store.

"I don't wear suits, either," Boone remarked. "Figured it'd be rude to interrogate and run. We can gift it to someone on Coz." He tore into the wrapping around the black box and opened it up.

"That's them!" Em said. "Same as the one you found in the helicopter, same as the ones the Russian guy had."

"And same as the ones in the ashtray on our neighbor's balcony," Boone said, tucking the box into an inner coat pocket.

"What, the weird guy with the big eyes? He wasn't smoking one of those."

"No, but someone was. Saw some butts in the ashtray."

"Well, he wasn't Russian, that's for sure. So, where to next? Hermès? Louis Vuitton? Tiffany? Dior?"

"I'm guessing those are stores," Boone surmised with a chuckle. "Y'know, just 'cause we have a card that can buy a ton of stuff doesn't mean we should go nuts."

"Noted. Though I do need shoes to go with my new dress."

"What's wrong with those?" Boone asked, indicating the pair she'd worn aboard. They had a short heel and seemed fine to him.

Em rolled her eyes. "Oh, Boone... your tenuous grasp of fashion is endearing. These are for comfort."

Boone lifted a foot, waggling the dress shoe Emily had arranged for him. "What kind are these, by the way?"

"No idea. They were the only size thirteens he could find." Em looked around. "Bingo! There's a Manolo Blahnik next to the bank!"

"Pantheon Bank... whattaya bet the Othonos family owns it?"

"No bet. C'mon! Shoes."

◆ ◆ ◆

"We don't usually do these updates during business hours, Mr. Othonos," the branch manager of the shipboard Pantheon Bank protested.

"Business hours are meaningless when dealing with crypto-currency," Nicholas said, brushing past the bank manager and approaching the server room door next to the vault. He applied his thumbprint to the touchpad and the door clicked. "I designed the Croesus Coin, and it is incumbent on me that it remains the most secure option in cryptocurrency on the market."

"It already is, is it not?"

Nicholas opened the door. A whir of cooling fans from the racks of servers filled the air, and winking green pinpoints of light greeted his eyes before the motion-activated overheads snapped on. He turned, leaning his head toward the branch manager and lowering his voice. "William... I just discovered a minor vulnerability. A potential exploit. Now, I won't bore you with technical details, and the odds that anyone else will have spotted it are virtually nil. That being said, I want to patch it immediately." He stepped through the door, shrugging his laptop bag off of his shoulder.

"But shouldn't your father be involved?" the manager asked.

"No. My father is not technologically inclined."

William stepped forward. "Well, perhaps I should—"

"You *should* leave this to me," Nicholas said as he blocked the door, preventing the manager from joining him. "Reason One, this error was in my own coding, and I am not about to distress my ailing father with such a minor issue. And Reason Two... William... I consider you as much of a security liability as anyone else. I am the only one to handle the cryptocurrency security— is that understood?"

William hesitated. "Your brother, then? Isn't he senior to...?"

"Achilles wouldn't know a line of code if it gave him a blowjob," Nicholas snapped in a sudden burst of anger. He took a breath. "I apologize. That was crass. Look, William, you've been an exemplary employee. And I expect you'll continue to be one. The fix will be in place very quickly, but if word of this gets out in the next twenty-four hours—to *anyone*—I will hold you personally and financially responsible in the event someone overhears you talking about it and exploits the vulnerability."

The manager paled. "Understood, sir. I'll leave you to it."

"Thank you." Nicholas closed the door and extracted his laptop from its bag. Setting it down at a small workstation, he booted it up. As the machine whirred to life, he pulled a USB cable from a pocket in the bag and attached the laptop to one of the servers. A few keystrokes later, he detached the cable, packed up, and left the room. Nodding to the bank manager, he headed for the exit.

———————◆◆◆———————

"I didn't know shoes could cost that much," Boone said, holding open the door for Emily.

"And that was the least expensive pair... hey, look!" Bright yellow Manolo Blahnik bag in hand as she exited the shoe store, Emily spotted the youngest Othonos son exiting the Pantheon Bank, a laptop bag over his shoulder. "Oy, Nicholas!"

The young man appeared startled, looking back at the bank before turning and spotting Emily. He fired up a smile. "Oh... Emily... so good to see you. And Boone, you look very sharp."

"Thanks. I owe it to your money and Em's taste." Boone nodded toward the bank. "No rest for the wicked, huh?"

Nicholas's smile faltered. "How do you mean?"

"Well... I'm guessing this bank is part of your family business... and here you are having to work, while folks like us are enjoying a luxury cruise."

"Oh... yes," Nicholas said, glancing furtively at an expensive-looking watch.

"Say, Nick," Em began, "you still owe me a tour. I'd *love* to see the bridge if you—"

"I am terribly sorry, but I have rather a lot to do..."

Emily nodded in understanding. "Gotta prepare for the birthday bash for Achilles, yeah?"

Nicholas's lip twitched and Boone thought a snarl was pushing at the corners of his smile—a smile that seemed more forced the longer the man kept it on. "Yes. My father always throws impressive parties for him."

"I bet! That's why I dressed up raggedy Boone, here." She lifted the yellow shopping bag. "And I'm all set."

"Yes, well... I'm sure you will look stunning," he said.

"Well, you'll see for yourself, won't you?" Em said brightly.

Nicholas nodded, laughing. "Of course, of course. Forgive me, but I really must be going. Enjoy the cruise!" With that, he turned his back on them and headed for a bank of elevators.

Boone watched the man go. *He's been talking about giving Em a tour for days, and now...*

Emily stepped into his field of view. "Bit out of sorts, that one."

"Yeah..."

"Well, c'mon! Let's check in on Brix. Then to the spa—that has *got* to happen," Em started toward an alcove with a pair of restaurants. "Oh! And we should play one round of blackjack or roulette or something..."

Boone remained rooted in place, watching Nicholas ascend toward the upper decks as the glass elevator rose above the shopping atrium before vanishing into the ceiling.

22

Boone and Emily were thrilled with the dog sitter the ship employed and Brixton took to the woman immediately. Lucinda was from Grenada, and Boone wondered if her sing-song speech pattern reminded the potlicker dog of some of the Garifuna voices he'd grown up with on Caye Caulker. Leaving the dog in the sitter's care back at their room, they headed down to the inner concourse.

"Glad that worked out," Em said. "We've got a lot to do before the big dinner... and I think we'll be in Grand Cayman by tomorrow morning, so best get cracking!"

"Didn't realize just how close Cozumel is to the Caymans," Boone remarked.

They continued walking for a moment before Emily stopped. "When you say something like that... you realize I'm waiting for you to fill in some numbers, yeah? And I saw you tapping away at that in-room touchscreen, looking at maps, so..."

Boone laughed. "You know me too well. Cozumel to Grand Cayman... 324 nautical miles."

"Okay... and what's the top speed on the *Apollo*?" Em crossed her arms. "I saw you looking at schematics too, Booney. Make with the stats—I know you're dying to tell me."

"Top speed is twenty-seven knots. But the cruising speed they've chosen for the passage was showing eighteen knots. Guess what 324 nautical miles divided by eighteen is? Ms. Durand to the chalkboard... we'll be there in how many hours?"

"You know how much I hate maths."

"Eighteen hours! Cool, huh? We'll hit Grand Cayman at four in the morning."

"You coulda just said that up front. Okay, now where is the spa...?"

Boone fired up the Olympus app and led the way. "Should be right down... there it is!" He pointed.

"Mud bath, here I come!"

Boone gave her a look. "*That's* what you're going for? How about a massage?"

Emily snorted. "I can get those from you. You have a supply of hot mud back at the condo? You holding out on me?"

Boone came up short, backtracking to a storefront they'd passed. "Hold up. I bet this is the onboard dive shop the faulty gear came from." He tried the door. "Locked." Peering inside, he could make out dive gear on the walls and racks of wetsuits and rash guards.

"Didn't Achilles say the owner ran off?"

"Yeah." Boone stepped back, scanning the signs in the window. "Guess he's still on Cozumel."

"Or maybe... he's still hiding aboard," Emily said, affecting a spooky voice. "Stalking the bowels of the ship like the Phantom of the Opera... except, well... except that he's a dive shop owner. So... probably not as good with a pipe organ."

"Uh-huh..."

"Oh, come on, Boone, that was gold!"

Boone blinked, then smiled. "Sorry." He tapped the window where a sign was taped to the glass inside, showing two boats. "The *Apollo* has its own dive boat aboard."

"Well, yeah, all cruise ships have lifeboats and expedition launches..."

"True, but look at these! The *Castor* and *Pollux*."

"Wacky names."

"More Greek mythology, I'm guessing... but check them out. They're not little dinghies. The *Castor's* a 'scout boat,' outfitted for diving and fishing... and the *Pollux* is a 'limo tender.'"

"A tender that tends to limousines?"

"A tender that *is* a limousine," Boone corrected with a laugh.

"That's nice. Do they have mud baths?"

Boone smiled, pulling up the *Apollo's* schematic on the ship's app. "Looks like they store them in a bay in the stern. Tell ya what, you go on ahead and pamper yourself. I want to check these out."

Em shrugged. "Fine by me. Let's meet up in two hours." She looked around and pointed back toward the central atrium. "Hey, there's The Muse, that bar Keith said he plays piano at." She rose up on her toes and gave Boone a peck on the cheek. "See you there at two."

Boone watched her go, then followed the map on his phone, heading back through the concourse and passing by a casino that dominated the area aft of the glass elevators. Taking the nearer portside passageway toward the stern, he found a stairwell that would take him down to the ship's boats. Making his way down two flights, he approached a door to the launch bay.

Locked. Taking out his room keycard, he swiped it in the keypad but received an unhappy beep and a red light in return. Boone peered inside the window in the door, but then turned at the sound of footsteps coming down the stairwell.

"Oh, hey… sorry," a man in mechanic's coveralls said as he reached the last flight of stairs. "Usually it's unlocked when we're in there. We get a lot of guests wanting to look at the boats, so we try to keep the bay staffed." He opened the door with a card. "You looking for a tour?"

"Sure!" Boone followed him inside. "Whoa…"

The internal boat launch spanned the width of the *Apollo*, with the limousine tender just to Boone's right on the port side. Across the enormous room, the scout boat *Castor* sat opposite from the *Pollux*. Each boat was locked into its own track beside huge doors set into the hull on either side. Further amidships, jet skis and other smaller recreational equipment were stored alongside several orange, fully enclosed lifeboats.

"Are you the only one who works down here?" Boone asked, looking around the expansive chamber and not seeing another soul.

"No, no, there's usually a staff of eight, but we got a call asking everyone to pop upstairs for a meeting. Kinda weird. No one was in the meeting room. Anyways, I just let the boys stay up top and grab some lunch."

Boone looked from one end of the bay to the other. "This is impressive."

"You should see the *Zeus*! They have a small submersible on that one. We've got a number of smaller vessels—lifeboats, jet skis, couple Zodiacs—but the main attractions are our two primary tenders," the man said. A patch on his coveralls read "Rudy." He swept a hand toward the two boats. "They're stored as you see them, locked into these lifts, called 'davits,' that have rails that run up to the edge, where we lower them into the sea through those watertight doors."

"I'm guessing you can't do that while underway," Boone remarked, noting that the doors seemed to go down to the waterline.

"In practice, we usually wait until we're at anchor, or at very low speed in shallow water. There are drainage grates all along the interior of the doors that feed water overboard, so it's possible to release them during transit, but the sea state has to be pretty calm for that."

Boone observed that the rails ran all the way across from port to starboard. "And if you're at a pier... you can send both boats out the same side, if the other door is blocked?"

Rudy nodded. "Yessir. Each davit can shift forward and back as well, if we need one out of the way." He stepped up to the nearest vessel. "So, this shiny blue beauty next to us is the *Pollux*. She's a thirty-three-foot limousine tender, full of luxury amenities. Here, step inside."

Boone looked around at the white leather seats and gleaming wooden railings. The rear interior was set lower, with a small, circular bar in one corner. Opposite the bar, an entryway led to an open area of seating at the stern. As one moved toward the cockpit, a single step led to a raised area beneath a two-piece retractable moonroof.

"The *Pollux* is built for speed. Can hit up to forty-eight knots. And if we keep her down to about twenty, she's got an impressive range."

"May I...?" Boone asked, pointing at the cockpit.

"Sure, just don't touch anything. I've got it open to the sky at the moment, but there is a roof that retracts."

Boone stepped into the open-air section around the wheel, looking at the high-tech instrumentation. As he turned to rejoin Rudy, movement caught his eye. "Hey, I thought you said you were the only one here."

"Yeah?"

"There's someone over on the other boat."

"Really? Maybe one of the fellas came back down." Rudy exited the *Pollux* and Boone followed him across to the other boat. "This is the *Castor*. She's for diving and fishing expeditions. Not quite as fast as the *Pollux*, but she's got a better range and a more stable ride."

As they neared the midpoint of the bay, a burly man exited the cockpit of the *Castor*, making his way down a ladder that rose from a side of the lift to the nearside gunwale. He wore a blue polo, white slacks, and carried a small cooler.

"One of your guys?" Boone asked.

"No. But he's wearing hospitality clothing."

The man held the cooler aloft, saying simply, "Restocking," in a gravelly voice before turning and walking away, head down. He went to a stairwell door on the opposite side from where Boone had entered. As he stepped through the door, he threw a single glance Boone's way before vanishing outside.

Boone had seen those eyes before, for just a brief moment. And he recognized the rumbly voice, too. It was the hard-eyed man from the balcony, the one who had appeared at the corner to berate the goofy-looking guy with the bug eyes.

"You want to see the *Castor*?" Rudy asked.

"No, I better get back. Thank you so much for taking the time, Rudy. Say, can I get back upstairs that way?" he asked, pointing to the door the man from the balcony had just exited through.

"Sure thing. It's pretty much a mirror to the one you came down."

Boone walked as fast as he could without appearing unnatural, then picked up his pace when he reached the stairs. The man had been dressed in an outfit similar to the one Keith wore, but he hadn't been wearing it on the balcony. *And he didn't exactly give off a hospitality vibe,* Boone thought, as his long legs took the steps two at a time. Two flights up, at what he knew to be the main concourse level, he paused, listening for feet on the stairs above him. Glancing at a decal at the side of the door, he could see there were three more flights leading up. *He had too much of a head start.* Boone sighed, and headed out the door.

Probably being paranoid, he thought. *Just some guy delivering mini-bottles of champagne to a boat so rich folks could get drunk while catching wahoo off Grand Cayman.* Boone relaxed a bit, strolling down the side passageway, looking at the smaller shops, but his mind kept returning to the man's eyes. And Brix... Brix did not like that guy's buddy.

Emily had often remarked on Boone's uncanny instincts for picking up on things that others missed. But not long ago, in Belize, Boone had disregarded several warning bells from his intuition, and nearly gotten the both of them killed. He'd vowed he wouldn't be so quick to dismiss such feelings in the future.

Reaching the atrium, he spied The Muse across the way. He still had an hour before he was supposed to meet Emily, but he decided he'd head over now. *Maybe Keith will be there, playing the piano,* Boone thought. *And if so, maybe he knows this guy.*

———◆•◆———

Emily sighed and felt her entire body relax, letting the thick mud support her weight. She could almost picture the toxins being sucked out of her naked body by the mineral-rich clay. The sound of ocean waves susurrated from a noise machine in the corner, and the soft glow of the room lighting barely penetrated the slices of cucumber over her eyes.

"Nice, huh?" a female voice asked from the adjoining alcove, the words echoing in the enclosed space.

"Legendary," Em moaned. "My fella don't know what he's missing. You floating in hot goo, too?"

"You know it. You got cucumber slices on your eyes?"

"I do indeed. Was feeling a bit peckish… wondering if I should eat one."

Emily's neighbor laughed. "Getting it into your mouth with muddy fingers might be tricky. I'm Chloe, by the way."

"Pleased to meetcha, mud buddy. I'm Emily."

The two floated in contented silence for a while before Emily spoke again.

"So, Chloe… what brings you aboard this nautical palace?"

"Just a little R&R," Chloe responded. "I'm here with my partner."

Em waited a moment before prodding for more. "Business partner, or…"

Chloe laughed. "No, no… Lisa's my special gal. I sold my business. I used to design security software and my little company was snapped up by a bigger company. So now I get to float in mud and travel the world. How about you?"

"I'm a stowaway."

Chloe laughed again. "I'll never tell."

"I'm a divemaster from Cozumel. My boyfriend and I…" Em was about to mention saving Lyra, but trailed off and course-corrected. "We took some of the owners diving. They had a jolly good time… and they had an empty cabin… bing bang boom."

"Wow, congratulations! Enjoy the cruise! Just don't fall for the cryptocurrency pitch."

"The whoozawhat now?"

"The Othonos family has their own line of digital currency. Croesus Coin. Croesids, they call them. Terrible name. 'Rich as Croesus,' I think is what they were going for. Anyway, they have people approaching guests during the cruise to offer special rates on initial investments." Chloe laughed, the sound not as playful as before. "Everything is so high-end here, but the whole thing struck me as one of those low-class timeshare pitches."

"Did you buy any?"

"I did. Just a few units. Like I said, I design security software… and I was curious. I did a little digital snooping. I'll admit, their system is well-designed, but…"

Emily waited before blurting, "Don't leave me hanging, sister of the clay!"

"Well, uh… this part of the spa is a bit of an echo chamber. And it's kind of sensitive. I'd come over there and whisper it to you, but I'm waaaaaay too comfortable."

"Same here. Well, that… and also I'm completely starkers. Tell ya what, after I hit the showers, I'm heading over to The Muse to meet my fellow stowaway at two, if you'd care to do your whispering there over a beverage."

"Sounds like fun," Chloe said.

"We can be all secret-agenty and talk in code, yeah?"

"Don't tell a programmer to talk in code, unless you want an earful of C++ and SQL."

"No, I was thinking more like…" Emily put on an atrocious Russian accent, "The little cucumber enjoys the mud at midnight."

Chloe laughed. "See you at two."

23

"Sorry, Keith doesn't play until the evening," the bartender said. "Usually around eight."

"Okay, thanks." Boone sat on a chrome stool at the polished bar at the back of The Muse. "I'm meeting someone here at two," he said.

"No problem. Can I offer you something to drink?"

Boone didn't like to drink alone, so he figured he'd wait for Emily before getting a beer. "You got any Ting?"

"Anything?" the man said, sounding confused before suddenly laughing. "Oh, any *Ting*! Yes, I do indeed," the man said, retrieving a green bottle of the Jamaican grapefruit soda from an underbar fridge.

"Bottle's fine," Boone said, when the bartender reached for some glassware.

"Here you go, then," he said, laying down a cocktail napkin and setting the bottle down atop it. "On the house."

"Thanks." Boone placed his smartphone on the bar and brought up the ship's app. Tapping into the "About" section, he found a crew manifest, complete with smiling headshots and short bios that reminded him of theatrical playbills. Sipping his Ting, he went through them all. Went through them again. No sign of the man he'd seen. And certainly no sign of the weird-eyed, lanky fellow—a photo of *that* guy would've leaped out of the phone.

"Another Ting?"

Boone looked up. "Nah, I'm good. She'll be here any minute and I'll order something more fun. Hey, question for you…" He held up the phone. "Is this crew list complete?"

"Well… I've been on a few of the Olympus ships, and they update it before every voyage. But this is the maiden voyage for the *Apollo*, so they might not have everyone there. Why?"

"Nothing, just curious." He thought for a moment, noting the bartender's white polo shirt with a gold Olympus logo over the breast. "The royal blue crew shirts… who wears those?"

"Those are for entertainment, hospitality, concierge services… basically anyone who interacts with guests. Well, except food services." He tugged his white shirt. "Bartenders, waitstaff… we all wear white."

Boone nodded, leaning his elbow on the bar, thinking. *That guy was wearing blue… but wasn't there someone else…?* He sat up straight. *Right after we left the hyperbaric chamber…the Aqua Safari pier, with the drone overhead… the man and woman on the pier were wearing the same outfits. Then showed up at Coconuts wearing tourist clothes, the man smoking those black and gold cigarettes.*

Boone refreshed the crew list and went through it again, looking for the couple that had been at the clifftop bar. No sign of either of them. "One last question… sorry… in the crew… is there a Russian? Real thick accent, smokes a lot."

The bartender shrugged. "Could be. This is our first trip out, so I haven't had a chance to meet everyone." He looked from Boone as someone approached.

"Metaxa, one rock."

Boone turned to see he'd been joined by a man who looked a little familiar. After a moment, he remembered the face. Or rather, the bottom half of the face. It was Stavros, the helicopter co-pilot from the whale shark expedition. The man had been wearing a helmet.

Stavros raised his tumbler of golden-brown liquor to Boone, then took a sip, nodding with appreciation. "Good. You ever try this?"

"Can't say I have."

"It's a brandy and wine blend from Greece. Very, very good. Not like that wretched ouzo. On behalf of my people, I apologize for that."

Boone laughed. "Hi, Stavros. I was on board the helicopter flight up to Mujeres."

"Ah, I thought you looked familiar." He waggled his tumbler, the ice clinking against the glass. "In case you think I'm one of those pilots who day drinks and climbs into the cockpit, no. The helicopter is down for maintenance, I am told. Normally, I am always on standby, so this is a rare opportunity for me." He took another sip, clearly relishing every bit of it.

"Is Achilles a good pilot?" Boone asked.

Stavros rocked his head back and forth, considering. "Yes. When he is paying attention, very good. When there is a pretty lady... not so much." He looked toward the entrance of the bar and laughed. "And here she is, the reason I had to grab the controls."

Boone looked back over his shoulder to see Emily entering, hair damp and with a serene smile on her face, the Manolo shopping bag swinging lazily from her fingertips. Boone rose from his bar stool as she approached.

"Looks like you had a relaxing time."

"That was... amazing." Emily oozed onto a stool. "My skin is still vibrating."

Stavros laughed. "Someone has been to the spa."

"Em, you remember our helicopter co-pilot, Stavros?"

"Mm-hmm... hi."

"Can I get you something to drink, Miss?" the bartender interjected.

"Something fruity with dark rum in it. Other than that, I leave it to you."

"A Tecate, if you've got it," Boone requested, when the bartender looked his way. "Well, Em... Stavros here was just telling me that during the chopper flight, your beauty nearly killed us all."

The pilot laughed. "A bit of an exaggeration... but yes, you were a bit distracting for Achilles. But I am being unfair to the man. He really is quite good. Although Nicholas is proving an excellent student. He may turn out to be an even better pilot than his brother, I think."

"Really? How long has he been taking lessons?" Em asked.

"He came to me about two months ago, while the *Apollo* was in the last stages of completion."

Boone had a thought. "Hey... when we were putting on our headsets, you were saying something to Achilles about a strange navigation waypoint?"

Stavros nodded, sipping his Metaxa. "Yes. The other pilot and I like to keep the waypoint inventory minimal, so we can toggle through them quickly. But since it was on Grand Cayman and that was our next port of call, I didn't want to delete it, in case it was there for a reason."

"Whereabouts was it?" Boone asked. He didn't know Grand Cayman well, so he brought up a map of the island on his smartphone, toggling the satellite view on and setting the phone on the bar top.

"May I?" Stavros asked, turning the phone to face him. "I remember it was south of the airport." He zoomed in, then moved the map around for a little while. "Ah, yes... here." He pressed and held a fingertip on the map and a marker popped up. "It was at the end of this road of condominiums, just to the west of this reservoir or cistern or whatever it is." He slid the phone back.

Boone examined the spot. "Weird. In the middle of nowhere. Looks like half these condos haven't even been built."

Stavros shrugged. "Not my concern. As I said, whoever put that location into the system, it wasn't me."

"Do you smoke?" Boone said abruptly, reaching into his suit coat pocket.

The bartender overheard. "Sorry, but smoking isn't allowed in The Muse."

"No worries, wasn't planning on it," Boone said, setting the pack of Black Russians down on the bar and opening it up. "Just a little show 'n' tell."

"I don't smoke," Stavros said, looking at the cigarettes. "Those are unusual."

"I found one of these in the passenger compartment of the helicopter," Boone said.

Stavros frowned. "I thought I smelled cigarette smoke in there! We don't allow smoking on the helicopter, no matter how rich you are."

"Emily?" A redheaded woman with a pixie cut approached the bar.

"Chloe, I presume?"

"I realized I never actually *saw* you," the woman said, laughing. "But somehow, you look as I would have pictured." Chloe caught the bartender's eye, pointing at a large glass jar full of white wine and fruit, a spigot affixed at its base. "Could I get some of that mango sangria?" She looked around. "And Emily, should we grab a table?"

"I'll bring you your drink," Boone offered. "Stavros, good to see you again."

"You as well." The co-pilot finished his Metaxa and rose. "And now, if you'll excuse me, I'm going to go do something I rarely get to do. Take a mid-afternoon nap."

After spotting Em and Chloe in the corner, Boone brought the beverages over and introductions were made. They enjoyed their drinks for a time before Emily leaned in conspiratorially. "The thirsty mermaid enjoys hockey."

Without missing a beat, Chloe responded, "The water is warm in the devil's bathtub."

Both women burst into gales of laughter. Boone sat back with a bemused look on his face, waiting for an explanation.

"So, Boone… Chloe here has some juicy gossip that she didn't want to reveal in the spa."

"Juicy is probably the wrong word," Chloe said with a laugh. "Dry, technical, and boring would be a better way to describe it. Here, give me your cocktail napkins." Chloe then extracted a pen from her purse and proceeded to explain the nature of the Croesus cryptocurrency and the exploit she'd discovered.

"I won't pretend to have understood more than a third of that," Boone said. "Are you going to let them know?"

"It's a pretty minor bit of script that's the culprit, not a gaping hole, so it's not exactly pressing. And besides…" Chloe cleared her throat. "The way I found out involved a little 'intrusion' that wasn't strictly legal."

"You're a hacker?" Boone asked.

"I don't like that term… I'm a digital security expert."

"So… you *didn't* hack their systems?"

"Oh, I did. But it was just a little 'white hat' hacking. Actually, that's how I first got interested in my line of work. I hacked my college's computer lab servers." She laughed. "They caught me, but after I showed them the vulnerabilities I'd used, they put me in charge of the lab. Anyway, I'll let Olympus and the Pantheon Bank know what I found. But *after* the cruise. And anonymously."

◆ ◆

"Do we have time for a few quick hands of blackjack before we get dressed for the dinner?" Emily asked, after they'd parted ways with Chloe and exited the piano bar.

"You tell me." Boone indicated his suit. "I'm all set."

Em grabbed Boone's wrist and looked at his watch. "Seating is at six… yeah, we can do it." She laughed. "You know, that old dive watch doesn't exactly go with the suit."

Boone laughed. "I am *not* using the little black card to go buy myself a… um… what's an expensive watch?"

Emily shook her head. "You are hopeless."

"Rolex! That's a good brand, right?" Boone said with a grin, opening the tinted glass door of the casino.

Inside, the lighting was set to a lower level than the surrounding atrium and the chatter of patrons and electronic noises from slot machines was muted somewhat by the pristine red carpeting. A frieze of stylized artwork depicting scenes from Greek mythology decorated the upper band of the walls above mahogany cornice. The style of the images put Boone in mind of what he'd seen on Greek urns.

The flashy slot machines were largely sequestered in an area in one corner, with table games dominating the remainder of the casino. A pair of bars were at the left and right, and the house bank was located at the far end.

"Cor, this is quite a bit larger than the casino at the Divi in Bonaire, innit?"

Boone nodded, remembering with fondness the cozy little casino at the south end of Kralendijk. "Yeah, that place was cool. I only gambled there a couple times: once I doubled my money, the other time I lost every bet I made."

"You gotta have a system," Em said. "Bas taught me a few tricks. It took me a while, but I won more than I lost by a fair bit."

Boone tilted his head at her. "How many times did you go there? And who's Bas?"

Em smiled, playing with Boone's tie, pretending to straighten it. "You do realize I had my own life on Bonaire, Booney?" She released the tie with a playful flick. "Anyway, let's see what our options are, yeah? Hold my shoes."

Boone followed, carrying her shopping bag and watching as Emily strode away, scanning the table games. He smiled, remembering the times she'd beaten him soundly at poker night with the other divemasters on Bonaire. Until Emily had arrived on island, Boone had usually walked away with the biggest haul every night. The owner of Rock Beauty Divers, "Frenchy the Belgian," had practically accused Boone of witchcraft.

"I swear, Boone Fischer... you must consort with dark powers. I have never seen you fall for a bluff, not once."

And it was true. Boone's instincts usually told him when someone was bluffing or holding a high hand. But when Emily came along, she'd run rings around him. He couldn't read her like he could the others, at least at the poker table.

She came back. "Okay, we've got roulette... house always has the edge there, so no thank you. Baccarat... no idea how to play that. Poker... kinda want to do that, so I can beat the house *and* you, but we don't have the time. So that leaves blackjack. Let me look at the tables."

Emily sidled over to the nearest blackjack table and Boone watched her eyes follow the play. After a moment she shook her head and moved to the next one. As she approached, a familiar ten-gallon hat with a red-cheeked oilman underneath pivoted from its spot at the table.

"Oh, good! Waitress... I'm runnin' low, can you get me another Pappy Van Winkle, neat?"

Emily blinked, momentarily thrown. Boone stifled a laugh and was about to step in, but Emily forced a smile on her face.

"Right away, sir!" She stalked over to the bar, Boone on her heels.

"Well... you *are* wearing food-service white," Boone said, nodding at a cocktail waitress they passed, wearing a short white dress that looked like it was hinting at a classical toga.

"My dress looks nothing like that," Em muttered as they reached the bar. She slapped down the magic black card and the bartender perked up, no doubt anticipating a top shelf order. "Give me two fingers of your cheapest, your absolute *worst* bourbon."

The bartender opened his mouth. Closed it. Tried for speech again and succeeded. "Uhh... worst? Ma'am?"

"There's a nice tip in it for you if you give me a glass of the cheap stuff," Em said sweetly.

"Well... I've got something we use for mixed drinks for the crew..."

"Perfect. Just slop it in a glass."

Looking baffled, the man dredged a nondescript bottle from below, pouring two fingers and sliding it to Emily.

"Thank you... give yourself fifty percent, yeah?" After the card was retrieved, Emily picked up the tumbler and marched back toward the blackjack table.

Boone knew a little about bourbon—most folks who lived in the Caribbean had an above-average knowledge of booze. Pappy was one of the finest bourbons out there. "You're not going to pass that off as Pappy Van Winkle bourbon, are you?"

Em reached the table. "Here you are, sir. Love the hat, by the way."

"Thank ya, little lady." The man sipped. "Mm, mm!" He raised the glass to Emily. "This is the best of the best, by the way."

"Is it?" Em asked, all innocence.

The man sipped again. "Delicious."

The oilman returned to his game, promptly losing a hand. Boone noted with satisfaction that his supply of chips was on the low end, compared to the other players.

Em led Boone away from the table. "Well, I can't play at that table," she said with a laugh.

"He didn't seem to notice what you gave him."

"Guys like that... he just got it because it was expensive, not because he's got taste."

Boone smiled. "You may be right about that."

"I know I'm right. And when have you ever *actually* seen a Texan with a bolo tie and a hat like that?"

Boone smiled. "Never. And there's a ton of Texans visiting Coz. We've gone out to dinner with quite a few."

Emily sidled up to a third table.

"What's the buy-in?" Boone asked an older woman who had just won a hand.

She looked back at Boone, giving him—and the suit—an appreciative once-over. "A thousand."

As one, Boone and Emily turned on their heels and headed for the exit.

"Sod that," Em muttered.

24

"*A*ngler, *this is Palantir.*"

Angler ceased his pacing. "Go ahead, Palantir."

"*Everything is a go. The helicopter is fueled and ready. All you'll need to do is bring it out of the hangar and extend the rotor blades.*"

Tolstoy nodded, speaking into his mic. "We can do this in under fifteen minutes. Is no problem."

"So, where exactly are we going to land, eh?" Potluck asked.

"*I will transmit the coordinates when you are well on your way, once I have intel on whether anyone has been alerted. In fact—and this is important—you will not be hearing from me again until then.*"

Angler watched as the members of the team looked to him, confusion on their faces. "Palantir, may I ask why? I was counting on you being our 'eyes' for the op."

"*I will have my hands full, accomplishing my own objectives. Neutralizing security cameras and cutting off communications is paramount.*"

Angler nodded, a motion that Palantir couldn't see. *Unless, of course, he's got other bugs or cameras in here that Tolstoy didn't find.* "Understood, Palantir. We will be on our own until airborne."

"In the instant I trigger the power failure, I will be 'tricking' the ship into believing it is simultaneously on fire and sinking, causing fire doors and watertight doors to seal. In addition, all keycard locks will be reset and reprogrammed to only respond to the cards I've given you. If you follow the route through the crew corridors I've suggested, you will likely avoid any encounters—though with the fire and flooding alarms going off, and no communications to the bridge, most of the crew will be too busy to give you any problems."

"Sounds good to me," Stallion said.

"And Stallion. Your evac with your hostage will occur via the Castor, *the sport fisher tender. She has been fueled and I will remotely release the boat once I see you are aboard."*

"Yeah, about that," Stallion said. "I still don't get why your boss wants to separate us..."

"I understand. I'm sure he has his reasons. But I thought the same thing, and when I pointed out the additional risk to you, he agreed to increase your personal payout by an additional half-million."

"Consider my objection withdrawn."

"Remember, the signal to act will be the toast. Achilles will bang on a glass with a piece of silverware. The people in the room will shift their attention to the captain's table. That will be my cue to cut the ship off from the outside world, and your cue to move in."

"If it is *his* birthday," Tolstoy wondered aloud, "is not the custom that someone else call for toast?"

"Uh, yeah..." Stallion chimed in. "And what if he doesn't hit a glass..."

"He will. He loves to be the center of attention. He always does it. One year, he broke the glass with a butter knife."

"How do you know that?" Potluck asked.

There was a pause before the modulated voice spoke again. *"Because I do my research. Look… you all know your jobs. If everyone does their part, by tomorrow morning we will all be rich. When Achilles calls for the toast, take out security and secure the Othonos children."*

———◆·◆———

"Brixy!! How are you? Did you have a good time with Lucinda?"

The potlicker jumped up and put his paws on Emily's waist, tail whipping back and forth.

"Brixton was a very good boy. We had a wonderful time, didn't we?" Lucinda began gathering up dog toys that were strewn all over the suite.

"Oh, you can leave those," Em said. "S'okay if we hire you for dinner time, too?"

Lucinda crouched beside the dog. "Would that be okay wit' you, Brixton? You want to lime some more wit' Lucinda? We can play some more wit' Marlin!" She waggled a plush clownfish and Brixton took it into his mouth, squeaking it repeatedly. "He has tried out all of my toys, and dat one is his favorite, I t'ink."

Boone and Emily had hired Lucinda with the Olympus black card, but Boone fished a couple twenties out of his wallet. "Thanks for making our little fella so happy… can you come back at…" He turned to Emily.

"Half five."

"Five-thirty?" Boone translated.

"Of course!"

"And order whatever you want from room service for your own dinner," Emily said. "Seems only fair."

Lucinda laughed. "I will do dat. Ah gone, see you again soon."

The door to the suite clicked shut and Em slipped out of her clothes. "I think I've still got some mud in a few nooks and crannies. Shower time."

"Need any help in there?"

"Aww, very sweet of you to ask. But we don't have the time. And I'm not about to retie that tie. You look perfect." She paused at the door to the master suite, looking back at him. "But after dinner… ask me again."

Boone blew out a breath as her bare body vanished from sight. "Well, Brix… I don't know about you, but I could use a little fresh air." He opened the glass doors and stepped out on the balcony, head swiveling to the left. The ashtray had been removed and the little corner table stood bare. Boone looked down at Brix. "Looks like we've got the balcony to ourselves this time, buddy."

The dog went to the stern side of their balcony, sniffing the air. He let out a chuffing breath, then turned to look at Boone.

"C'mon, Brix… let's check out those toys Miss Lucinda left with you."

Forty minutes later, Emily stepped from the master bedroom and Boone's jaw hit the floor.

"Holy… Em, you're…"

Emily Durand's knee-length dress was basic black, but there was nothing "basic" about the overall effect. Off-the-shoulder, the dress bared a fair amount of her upper back, and dipped down in front just enough to remain tasteful. The material was lightweight, and lifted from her legs when she pivoted back and forth to show it off, a slit at one side showing a little leg. And however much those shoes had cost, Boone couldn't deny just how good they looked on her. Em had put her hair up, simple silver earrings dangling above her lightly tanned shoulders.

"What do you think?" she asked, amusement in her voice. "Assuming you *are* still thinking?"

Boone cleared his throat. "I mean… you're gorgeous every day of every week, but… wow."

"That sounds like a thumbs-up to me." She winked. "Maybe more than a thumb." Em suddenly laughed. "I'm sorry, that was naughty of me. What can I say? Little black dress! Brings out the temptress." She held out a thin, silver necklace. "Here. I did your tie, you do this. Teamwork, yeah?"

Emily turned and Boone stood behind her, bringing the necklace up to her throat. He held the two ends near each other, but then paused.

"It's a basic clasp, Boone…"

Boone dipped his head and brushed a soft kiss on the back of her neck, eliciting a shiver as a burst of goosebumps arose from her flawless skin.

"Boone!"

"What can I say?" he whispered into her ear. "Little black dress."

Boone fastened the necklace, then spun her around and pressed a passionate kiss to her lips. Having planned a simple hit-and-run kiss, he started to withdraw but Emily grabbed his tie and prevented his retreat. Passions intensified, and then…

Squeak. Squeak. Squeak-a-squeak-a-squeak-a-squeak.

The kiss dissolved into laughter as they turned to find Brix sitting on the floor looking at them, an orange mouthful of fishy squeak-toy in his jaws.

Squeak.

Boone grinned. "Canine-us interruptus."

Emily composed herself, then said firmly, "Brixton, I know you like to sleep with mummy and daddy, but guess what? You get your own room tonight!"

◆ • ◆

The grand dining hall of the *Apollo* was situated amidships on a middle deck. Boone and Emily arrived just before six, pausing before the entrance to have their room cards scanned and identification checked by a burly security officer in a red polo shirt and white slacks.

Inside, the dining room was laid out in tiers, with the bulk of the tables spread across a central area, three broad steps down from the entry foyer. White tablecloths, fine china, and polished silverware gleamed in the light of massive crystal chandeliers. On either side, raised mezzanine platforms held smaller tables, with a galley access situated to port, and a mirror-backed bar at starboard.

"There's Keith!" Emily said. On the portside mezzanine level, beyond the serving doors, stood a baby grand piano. Keith had traded his blue polo for a tuxedo, and he was currently playing some non-intrusive classical music.

At the far end of the hall, a dais rose above the rest of the room. The Othonos family was seated along the back wall, looking down on their guests. Karras and Achilles wore tuxedos, while Nicholas had opted for a stylish black suit. Calypso wore a red dress, looking more comfortable than fashionable, while Lyra shone in an elegant white dress that could have graced any red carpet.

"Lyra's dress is astonishing," Emily breathed.

"I like yours better," Boone replied. "But then, I don't know a cufflink from a tie clip."

"Here's a hint: you're wearing both. But you'll have to figure out which is which. I'm guessing that's the captain, yeah?"

"Looks like it," Boone said. At one end of the table sat a bearded gentleman in a crisp white uniform adorned with black-and-gold shoulder boards. Boone glanced around the room. Numerous servers in white moved about the room, the more casual polos now gone, replaced with white jackets, bowties, and gloves. Two security men stood against the walls, one on the dais and another near the bar. Unlike the security officer outside, these men wore black suits and red ties.

A tuxedo-clad maître d' noticed them standing in the foyer and approached. "Welcome. Whom do I have the pleasure of seating?"

Boone looked around, just to be sure he was the one being addressed. "Uh... Boone Fischer and Emily Durand."

"Boonemily, collectively," Em added with a playful curtsy.

"Ah, yes, you are on the port mezzanine level, near the Othonos table..."

"And near the piano?" Emily asked.

"Why, yes."

"Ace!"

"This way, please."

Boone and Emily followed the maître d' up a short flight of carpeted stairs, passing by the galley access and reaching a table midway between the serving doors and the piano. The tables here were smaller than the ones below, designed for parties of two. The maître d' removed the tented place card with their names printed on it in a calligraphic font, and it was almost immediately replaced by a small plate of hors d'oeuvres. Boone pulled out Emily's chair and was about to seat himself when he noticed Lyra rising from the head table, smiling brightly and beckoning him with a wave.

"I think Lyra wants us to go over to them," Boone said.

"And I just got comfy," Emily said, standing back up. As they made their way past the piano, Em gave a discreet wave. Keith, who was in the midst of a complicated chord progression, limited himself to a smile and a nod of acknowledgment.

"It's so good to see you," Lyra said. "You both look..." She heaved out an appreciative breath. "...*fantastic*. Truly."

"Yeah, we can clean up nice when we have to," Boone said amiably. "Though having those magic black credit cards certainly helped. Thanks for that."

"It was our pleasure." She gestured to the uniformed man beside her, who rose from the table. "Boone... Emily... this is the captain of the *Apollo*, Captain Xiphias. He has been with Olympus Cruises since its early years, most recently commanding the *Athena*."

"I am privileged to make your acquaintances," the man said.

Boone shook the man's hand, and Emily gave it a brief squeeze.

"Welcome, friends," a pale Karras said from the center of the table, flanked by Nicholas and Calypso.

He doesn't look well, Boone thought. "Thank you again for inviting us, sir. And Nicholas... Callie... good to see you."

Nicholas nodded, appearing distracted. "I hope you enjoy my brother's dinner."

Callie gave a small smile just on the border of a smirk, taking in Boone's suit. Then she looked over at Emily. "I see you've been visiting our shops," she said.

Boone was about to reply when a boisterous shout rose from the far end of the table.

"Hey, there they are!" Achilles stood and squeezed past the others. It appeared he might have begun the festivities a bit early, an empty scotch glass sitting at his place.

"Oh, goody," Em muttered, moving around Boone so Achilles would have to encounter him first. Fortunately, the waitstaff suddenly appeared with the soup course and Karras waved Achilles back to his seat.

Boone took Emily's hand and they returned to their table, passing Keith just as he completed his current piece.

"I'm guessing Billy Joel is not on the music-menu for this kind of shindig?" Boone asked.

Keith laughed. "I might be able to sneak something in during the dessert course, but for now it's going to be Brahms."

"Looking forward to it!" Emily said. "And looking forward to sitting again. It's been ages since I rocked a pair of high heels."

Boone and Em reached their table just as the soup arrived, a rich, green soup the waiter referred to as *Caldo Verde*, a Portuguese Kale Soup. This was quickly followed by the appetizer course, and a delicate salad.

"I'm thinking we need more balsamic vinegar in our lives," Emily remarked through a mouthful of greens.

Boone nodded, distracted by some activity at the dais. Nicholas had just risen and headed for the starboard door at the back of the raised area, a phone held to his ear. That wasn't anything unusual—the young man seemed to run half the operation around here. No... it was Calypso's reaction. She rose from her seat, looking after Nicholas, opening her mouth to say something. When the door swung shut behind her brother, she sat back down, glancing over to the portside door beside the captain's table before smiling over at Karras and saying something, eliciting a laugh from the old man.

"What's up, Boone?" Emily asked, setting down her fork.

"More weird family dynamics," he said. "Nicholas just ducked out."

"Poor bugger's probably got some mega-corporation duties to attend to. Hope he got a few bites of this salad—it's quite good." She looked back at the dais. "What's with Calypso?"

"Dunno. She almost looked like she wanted to stop Nicholas from leaving."

"She didn't strike me as the type to care about fine-dining etiquette," Emily noted. "I mean, look... she's using her smartphone at the table."

Boone watched the youngest Othonos holding her phone below the edge of the table, tapping the screen. *Well, I peeked at mine at brunch*, he thought. *Don't go casting stones.*

"Oh yeah, 'ere we go!" Emily said as the main course arrived, rubbing her hands together with such eagerness, Boone could imagine smoke rising from them.

The waitstaff set down the plates and removed the lids, revealing lobster and steak with mashed potatoes and asparagus. Boone suddenly realized there had been a pop-up on the ship's app asking for his preferences, but he'd forgotten to answer. Watching Emily tear into her plate, he decided he needn't mention his lapse.

"Cor, the garlic mash is delish," Em moaned.

Boone grabbed hold of a silver-plated shellfish cracker, chuckling as he examined the burly red claws of the lobster on his plate. "Can't remember the last time I had a Maine lobster." In the Caribbean—and in much of Florida, for that matter—the lobster you got on the menu was the spiny Caribbean lobster, devoid of claws, with a pair of impressive armored antennae instead.

"How is it?" Emily asked, after Boone had cracked into a claw and taken a bite.

"Softer. Sweeter."

"So, our lobsters are in better shape, is that what you're saying? Maine lobsters just sit on the couch, eating bonbons, getting all soft 'n' sweet?"

Boone laughed, taking another bite. "They're both delicious. Just different."

While Emily attacked her Black Angus ribeye steak with animalistic fury, Boone leaned back and glanced around the hall, wondering just how much money there was in here, if you added up the assets of all of the guests. Most of the men were in tuxedos, but a few were in simple black suits. He spotted the Texas oilman on the opposite mezzanine—he'd left the giant hat behind, and was sporting a bow tie with his tux. Women in the hall offered the most splashes of color, with dresses in gold, red, and blue breaking the sea of black and white. Well, that and the red ties of the two security men. And the blue polo over by the bar...

Boone sat up straight. The flash of color had drawn his eye, and there—over by the bar—a familiar face. The Russian from Coconuts. Mr. Black-and-Gold Cigarettes. He was dressed as Keith had been when they'd first come aboard—a blue polo and white slacks. The man had just entered from the door beside the bar, carrying a cooler. Not unlike the one the man he'd seen down below had had, in the tender bay.

The man went to the edge of the bar, setting the cooler down. The bartender, wearing a vest, bowtie, and arm garters, came over and asked the newcomer a question. The Russian spoke animatedly, appearing to make a joke. The barman smiled, looking equal parts amused and confused.

Something's... off. Boone looked over at the security officer who stood beside the bar door near the Russian. *Guard doesn't seem concerned.* Boone examined the door the Russian had come in from, then found himself scanning the hall, noting the other exits. He retrieved his phone, tapping on the ship's concierge app.

"Peasant," Emily mumbled around a bite of steak.

Boone smiled. "Just want to check something." He frowned. "Huh. No Wi-Fi."

"What, you brick your mobile again? Here, gimme mine."

Boone fished her phone from a pocket and handed it over. They didn't get dressed up often, but he'd soon learned Emily hated carrying around a purse, so he became the keeper of her phone when they went out on the town.

"Weird." She checked her settings. "Yeah, you're right... Wi-Fi is down."

Boone nodded, pocketing his phone and glancing back at the bar area. The Russian was speaking... but not to the bartender.

⬥ ◆ ◆

"They are starting to clear main course plates," Tolstoy said.

"*Understood,*" Angler's voice came over the Russian's earpiece. "*Everyone move into position. Potluck, make sure to lock that galley exit with the code you were given. Once Palantir triggers his take-over, everything should lock anyway, but I want to be sure, in case there is a delay. Tolstoy, any problem with yours?*"

"*Nyet.* The code worked. Bar area exit is secure."

"*Good. Let's do this and get rich. See you all inside.*"

⬥ ◆ ◆

He's got an earpiece, Boone thought, as he watched the Russian speaking quietly to no one. *There.* A flesh-colored wire running up from his collar.

"Boone, what is up with you?"

"Our Russian friend with the funky cigarettes is here."

Emily looked toward the bar. "So? We figured he worked for the ship, right? Although… he's a bit underdressed, I must say."

The man opened the cooler, retrieving a bag of ice to hand the bartender. Busy mixing drinks, the barman waved at him to put it down behind the bar. There was something odd about the way he removed the ice, barely lifting the lid to slide the bag out.

"Come on," Boone said abruptly.

"Boone, what? He's dropping off ice."

"No… I don't think so," he said, helping Emily up. He looked to the back of the hall, eyes sweeping across the table atop the dais: Lyra was chatting amiably with the ship's captain, and Achilles was speaking to his father across Calypso, who was tapping the screen of her smartphone.

Em stood, grabbing her own phone, but didn't yet follow. Behind them, the doors to the galley swung open and the dessert course made its entrance. "Boone…"

"Emily, I ignored my instincts back in Belize and nearly got you killed. I'd rather make an ass of myself than risk doing that again."

Atop the dais, Achilles rose. Lifted a stemmed glass and a dessert spoon.

"What are you going to do?"

Boone moved toward the front. "Talk to the captain, or maybe the security guard near the main table—"

Achilles struck the glass to call for a toast… and the room went dark.

25

Everything happened in less than a second. As the last ringing tone of silverware on crystal hung in the air, pale emergency lights came on and guest voices rose in alarm. The distant blare of claxons clashed with what sounded like the ringing of an old-timey school bell. The doors on either side of the dais crashed open, black-clad figures in combat armor bursting into the room. To port, closest to Boone and Emily, a feminine figure raised a stubby submachine gun and double-tapped the security officer beside the door. Across the table, a lanky man aimed his weapon at the Othonos family. Boone immediately recognized him as the bug-eyed man from the neighboring balcony. Head pivoting, even as he began shoving Emily toward the galley, Boone saw the Russian on the opposite mezzanine lifting a silenced pistol from the cooler, dropping the guard there with a pair of clacking puffs.

"Go! Go! The galley!" Boone pushed Em ahead, trying to keep his body between her and the figure nearest them, whom he recognized as the woman who had been with the Russian at Coconuts.

Emily needed no encouragement, staggering for the doors with all the speed her dressy shoes would allow. Boone began to follow, but a burst of fire from an unsilenced weapon came from the front of the hall, followed by a gravelly-voiced shout.

"Everybody, freeze!"

There, by the main entrance, was the other man from the neighboring balcony, the one Boone had seen in the tender bay wearing a blue crew shirt. Now, he was dressed like the two on the dais. At his feet, the security guard from outside the main entrance was dropping to his knees, hands clasped behind his head. As Emily pushed through the galley access doors, the mercenary lifted his weapon and fired off a burst, shattering one of the small windows set into the doors and pockmarking the wood. His weapon swung to Boone, who halted in his tracks, raising his arms.

"Goddammit, nobody move! No one else has to die today, if you all follow our instructions."

A shout drew Boone's attention back to the rear of the hall. Achilles had grabbed a steak knife and taken a drunken stab at Bug-eye, who actually laughed as he stepped back from the swing and calmly kicked the eldest Othonos sibling squarely in the balls. Achilles crumpled out of sight behind the table, the sounds of retching just audible over the panicked screams from the guests.

Another burst of unsilenced automatic weapons fire from the man at the front, firing into the ceiling. "Listen up! Othonos family... stay put! Everybody else—and I mean *everyone*—get your asses down to the central dining area now!" When people began to move, the man called out to the female merc. "Potluck! Go get that girl who ran into the galley."

Emily ran frantically toward the back of the galley, her eyes drawn to a single door, its exit sign still lit by the auxiliary power. The eerie emergency lights cast a dim glow over the room. Several members of the galley staff were at the door, pulling at it, pounding on it.

"*Está cerrada!*" a man in a chef's hat shouted. Emily knew basic Spanish, but context was the best translator: *It's locked!*

Emily rushed to help, nearly turning her ankle. Still holding her mobile, she savagely tore off her high-heeled shoes as she reached the door, peering at the keypad beside it. A red light glowed back at her. She looked at her beautiful, expensive shoes... then aimed the heel of one of them at the keypad and bashed it repeatedly. Her fruitless exercise was interrupted by a shout from the door to the dining hall. She hoped it was Boone. It wasn't.

"All right, everybody, hands up and get yer butts out to the dining room!"

Emily dropped her shoes and crouched, putting a stainless-steel shelf of pots and pans between herself and the voice, with its extreme Midwestern accent.

"The door is locked. Yer not gonna get ote that way! Nobody is gonna get hurt—we just need you all to come sit in the middle of the hall for a couple hours, okay?"

The galley staff raised their hands and made their way toward the door. One of the busboys looked down at Emily as he went around the shelves of pans.

"Somebody else back there?"

Frantic, Em crouch-walked around the shelving as the sound of boots came from the other side.

"Looks like someone lost a fancy pair of shoes. We all saw you run in here, blondie." The boots began to turn the corner around the pots and pans.

Shitshitshitshit. Emily mirrored the move around the other side, her eyes looking frantically for a weapon. Instead they found... linens. A laundry cart half-full of tablecloths. And beside it...

The boots began to turn the corner. "Olly, olly, oxen free..."

Emily lunged from her crouch and plunged down the laundry chute, a burst of gunfire roaring from above.

◆ • ◆

"You... get down there." The gravelly-voiced mercenary gestured to Boone as he reached him.

Boone had been staying near the galley door, looking for an opportunity to follow Emily, but the female mercenary had gone in moments ago. Furthermore, the leader—Boone felt certain the man who'd come in the main entrance was in charge—had kept a close eye on Boone as he herded guests and staff down to the well of larger dining tables in the center of the hall.

"You look familiar..." the mercenary leader said. He squinted. "Oh, yeah... you were getting a tour of the boats... the guy with the mutt next door. Well, behave... and you and your pooch can live happily ever after."

Automatic weapons fire sounded from the galley, drawing the man's attention. Boone spun around and took two steps, intending to rush in, but the doors burst open, the female merc coming out, looking pissed.

"Bitch jumped down the laundry chute." She raised her gun, aiming it at Boone. "Who's this beanpole?"

"The boyfriend, would be my guess."

"What do we do about the girl?"

"Ignore her. All Wi-Fi is down, ship's coms are down, and the ship is halfway between Cozumel and Cayman. No one's getting a cell call in or out. Get this jackass down there with the others."

"Let's go, handsome." The woman twitched the barrel of her submachine gun at him and Boone complied. Hands raised, he made his way around the piano. "You too, Piano Man," the female mercenary said, addressing Keith.

Boone looked at Keith as the actor-turned-crewman rose and joined him. *He's scared, but he's still in the game,* Boone thought. Together, they moved near the captain's table and headed down the stairs beside it to the bottom level. Boone's eyes caught Lyra's, shining with a patina of tears and fear. "It's okay," he said, loud enough for her to hear.

"Listen up, everyone!" the leader of the mercs shouted. "We are not here to kill you... we are not even here to rob you. We are here... for *them.*" He pointed toward the Othonos family. "Provided you sit your asses down and wait for two hours, all the rest of you will make it out of here alive."

The captain was stepping down from the dais, about to go down the steps as instructed, when he turned back to the head mercenary. "But... the alarms... the siren is a fire alarm! And the bells... the watertight doors are sealing!" As if the system heard him, the ringing suddenly stopped, though the fire alarms continued. "The watertight doors are sealed now! Is there flooding? Did you set off an explosion or something?"

"Ignore the alarms!" the mercenary replied, loud enough for the room to hear. "We are simulating a couple disasters to seal off compartments and keep the crew busy."

A shriek from the dais. "Father!" Lyra was clutching at Karras's shoulder.

The leader looked toward the main table, frowning. "What's wrong?"

The lanky, weird-eyed merc shrugged. "I dunno, I ain't no doc."

"Please!" Lyra cried out. "He's having a heart attack!"

"Goddammit, just what we need…"

Stallion shifted his feet. "Uh… if he dies before…"

"I know I know!" The mercenary leader looked down at the guests clustered below. "Can't believe I'm saying this, but… is there a doctor in the house? Or… ship?"

A middle-aged guest raised her hand. "Yes. And I'm a cardiologist."

"Well, that's handy." He pointed at two of the busboys who had just reached the bottom of the stairs. "You two, come back up. Bring him down there to the doc." He strode toward the dais, stopping abruptly. "Wait. Where's the other one? Nicholas Othonos." He turned toward the people below. "Nicholas Othonos, if you are in here, get up here right the hell now!"

"He left," Calypso said.

"What? When?"

The youngest Othonos shrugged. "Maybe fifteen… twenty minutes ago." She pointed to the starboard dais exit. "He went out that door."

"Dammit… Stallion, that was your station, you didn't see anyone?"

"Don't blame me," the lanky man protested. "Fifteen minutes ago, we weren't in position yet."

The leader fumed for a moment, then filed the problem away. "We go with what we got."

Achilles got a hand up onto the table, trying to rise. "You... you can't do this..."

"Stallion... zip-tie that idiot before he gets himself killed," the leader said. "Potluck, gather their phones."

The female mercenary moved toward the table, weapon at the ready. "What about the old man's phone?"

"We ain't taking him, so we don't need his. We only need phones from... Lyra, Calypso, and Achilles." He pointed at each in turn. "And Nicholas, if we can find him."

Boone studied the Othonos siblings. Achilles still appeared nauseous, his arms behind his back. Calypso looked scared, but there was something odd about her fear. *There's something else,* Boone thought. But he filed that away when Lyra's tear-filled eyes locked onto his own. He held up a hand, keeping it low, and mouthed, "It will be okay."

Beside her, the mercenary leader checked his watch. "Let's get this show on the road. Attention, everyone! As you may have noticed—and I'm sure you have, because I can see some of you trying to call or text—there is no Wi-Fi, there is no cell signal. So, save your batteries... or play solitaire or something. Furthermore, all doors with keypads or card swipes have been reset and locked. At the moment, half of the complement of the ship should be in here. Crew elsewhere are no doubt discovering everything is powered down, and many of them are locked into whatever rooms or areas they were in. All of you in here will be quite safe as long as you stay inside this hall."

The leader paced, his eyes scanning the crowd. "In a few minutes, I and my three scary friends will be leaving you. And some of you might take it upon yourselves to try to break through the locked doors. I would advise against that." He ceased his pacing and yelled across the hall, "Tolstoy! Let them know what prize they'll win if they try to open a door."

"H'okay, please to be listening!" the Russian called from the opposite mezzanine, where he had been covering the guests below with his pistol. Boone noted the man now had a small backpack slung over one shoulder. Tolstoy opened the cooler and retrieved a boxy contraption with several straps hanging from it. "This… is bomb."

Screams and commotion rose from below. Tolstoy raised a hand for silence. When that didn't work, the mercenary leader fired off another burst into the ceiling. This did little to quell the fear in the room, but it did restore a measure of quiet.

"No one is going to be hurt, if no one is going out doors," Tolstoy said. He gestured behind him, then across to the galley. "Both side exits already wired with one of these." He placed the device back in the cooler and began circling the room, heading for the front of the hall. "I will now attach one to main entrance. When we leave, we will attach two more to two doors behind our hosts. If you open a door, seal will be broken and… boom."

Anxiety rose again, but Tolstoy waved an arm and headed it off.

"No, is good! You all watch American movies, yes? You know bombs with timer, yes? These have *good* timer. In two hours, bombs will deactivate. You understand? When bomb active, you will see blinking red light. But in two hours, light turn off. You will be safe to go." He began to attach a device across the double doors.

Boone was just close enough to the dais to overhear the female mercenary, the one the leader had called Potluck, speak to her boss. "Angler, what about the laundry chute?"

Angler, Potluck, Stallion, Tolstoy. Code names, Boone thought.

"Nobody's gonna use that…" Angler muttered.

"Lover boy down there might," Potluck suggested, looking down at Boone. "He was there when I mentioned it."

Angler chewed his lip. "Fuck it." He aimed his gun down at Boone. "You. Get up here. Gimme your phone."

Boone made his way up the stairs just as Tolstoy reached them. The Russian peered at him.

"You… you look familiar…"

"I get that a lot," Boone said sullenly, watching Tolstoy extract another device and attach it to the portside door.

"Turn around, hands behind your back," Angler barked, grabbing Boone's phone. "Potluck, do the honors. We'll lock him in a closet somewhere."

"Why not just shoot him?" she asked, as she zip-tied Boone's wrists together.

"Guy's a dog owner. Can't do that to the dog."

Potluck guffawed. "The security guys mighta had dogs."

"They were armed, he ain't. Besides, I didn't kill mine. The two you took out, you get their sidearms?"

Potluck and Tolstoy answered in the affirmative and Angler shoved Boone over to where the Othonos family stood clustered together, Lyra holding up a pale Achilles.

"All right, this has taken too long already," Angler rumbled. "You three… you're coming with us. Everybody plays nice, everybody lives. Stallion, get the door."

The merc with the bulging eyes fished a card from a pocket in the vest of his body armor and tapped it to the panel beside the door. It beep-clicked and the red light beside it went green. He held the door open and the other mercenaries ushered the trio of Othonos siblings through. Boone followed, but Angler stopped him.

"What's your name?"

"Boone."

"Nice suit, Boone. Don't give me a reason to mess it up. Blood stains are murder to get out." Pushing him into the passageway, he raised his voice. "Tolstoy, you got the last bomb?"

"*Da!*" The Russian held it up for the room to see and raised his voice. "This one go on the outside! Remember... try to leave... and you *will* leave. This earth!" He burst into laughter at his own joke and followed Boone and Angler into the passageway. As the door clicked closed, Tolstoy lifted a card on an ID lanyard and touched it to the keypad. The light went red.

Angler took charge. "Stallion, in the lead with Calypso. Keep an eye out for Nicholas Othonos. Potluck, you take Lyra." Angler grabbed hold of Achilles. "I've got this one. Tolstoy, take our temporary guest. We'll lock him in the maintenance locker in the hangar."

"Is good plan," Tolstoy said, tossing the remaining bomb onto the floor without attaching it. When Boone looked quizzically at it, Tolstoy laughed. "They fake! Just a little something to make everyone think twice. Go."

Quickly leaving the wider guest passageway, the group opened a door and entered one of the narrower crew corridors. The sounds of ringing bells and blaring claxons was louder here. As they proceeded, Tolstoy laughed again. "I remember you now! You were at the bar with the book of breasts! Hey! That sexy little blonde you were with... where is she?"

◆ ◆ ◆

"Oooohhh..." Emily came to in a heap of linens, her head throbbing. Pushing aside the piles of tablecloths and napkins, she realized she was in the laundry bin, lying on its side—no doubt knocked over when she plunged into it. A flash of lime green caught her eye in the sea of white. *My mobile!* Boone always teased her about the garishly colored protective case, but the bright hue certainly came in handy now. Her fingers closed around it. *Still no signal... no Wi-Fi.* Warbling sirens filled the air. *Fire alarms?* Em mused, her thoughts still fuzzy.

Rising unsteadily to her bare feet, she gently touched her forehead, wincing when her fingers found a little lump. "Blimey, they make that look so easy in Hollywood." She looked back at the mouth of the chute. A metal flap hung partway down, and Emily now had a vague memory of a metallic clanging sound right out of a Warner Brothers cartoon. *Musta banged my noggin on that. Now, what was I...?*

Suddenly it all came back, and Emily ran through the laundry room to a stairwell door. This being an internal crew stairway, there was no keypad on it. *Need to get to the bridge!* She pulled open the door and rushed in. Bare feet slapping on the steps, Emily launched herself up the stairs, heading for the bridge.

26

"What do you want with us?" Lyra asked, her voice trembling.

"What do you think?" Stallion responded, following up with a braying laugh. "Money, of course."

"Shut up, Stallion," Angler admonished. "Let's keep the questions to a minimum, okay? You all do as you're told, you come out of this healthy, we come out wealthy. Simple as that." He looked back at Boone. "What do *you* do, Mr. Fancy Suit? You some software developer or something? Or you just sucking at the teat of mommy and daddy's trust fund?"

"I'm a divemaster."

Angler raised an eyebrow before turning away, eyes on the stairs as they ascended one level. "Divemaster? How'd you end up here in those fancy duds?"

"Walked down the pier. Took the elevator."

Angler chuckled. "Smartass, huh? Cool customer, too. If you're a divemaster, I'm guessing that means you know how to drive a dive boat?"

"Yeah."

"Good to know..."

Stallion appeared at the top of the stairs, Calypso in tow. "Angler, no sign of that other Othonos brother," he called down. "You still want me up at the bridge?"

"Yeah, take your hostage and secure it. Don't want them fixing what Palantir did to their systems before we're away." Angler reached the top of the stairs. "The ship's largely automated and with the big dinner, probably a skeleton crew in there. Shoot to kill only if you have to."

"Roger."

"Wait. Here." Angler handed Boone's phone to Stallion. "Add it to the rest. Ditch them in the bridge when you're done there. Don't want anyone using those to trace us."

Stallion and Calypso separated from the others and headed down a passage, pausing at a stairwell door. "How come there's no lock on this one?"

"Fire safety codes," Calypso said quietly. "Most of the stairwells don't have locks."

"Well, all right then. In we go." He turned back to the rest of the team. "See y'all later!" With that, he and Calypso passed through the door.

The remaining group continued aft until they reached another passthrough.

Potluck swept her barrel around the corner, then relaxed her stance. "Clear."

"Good," Angler said. "Stairs to the helipad are right over there."

Potluck, in the lead, abruptly halted. Cocked her head. "Hey... you hear that?"

◆ ◆ ◆

Emily had always been blessed with a keen sense of direction, and soon reached an external gangway that led to the bridge. She yanked on the door handle and the little keypad emitted an annoyed buzz, a little red light staring at her disapprovingly. "Shite!" Em looked at the barrier, deciding brute force wasn't going to cut it. *That looks right sturdy. Probably reinforced to resist piracy,* she thought.

A catwalk extended around the bridge and she ran to the side, looking through the huge, canted windows to the interior, lit by emergency lights. Two white-uniformed figures, a man and woman, were inside; the crewman frantically pushing buttons, the crewwoman absorbed with a ship's intercom. Emily pounded on the windows, gaining their attention before pointing back toward the door. The crewman shook his head, grabbing a pad of paper and pen from a workstation. He angrily scrawled on the pad and held it up to the window.

Doors locked. Power is down.

Emily thought hard. Realizing she still had her mobile, she brought up its Notepad app and typed quickly, then boosted the font size and held the screen against the window. The crewman with the pad moved closer, squinting at what she'd typed.

Terrorists with guns. Hostages in dining hall.

The man's eyes widened, and he yelled something to his mate. Emily could hear the muffled shouts through the glass but couldn't make out any words. More animated silent discussion. The crewwoman's face suddenly lit up. She pointed at Emily, then held up both hands, palms facing her.

Guess she wants me to wait, Em thought.

The woman went to the back of the bridge, where a vented panel was set into a corner. Flipping several catches, she removed the panel and set it aside. Cables of various colors filled the alcove behind the opening. The crewwoman pushed aside the cables, then turned sideways and slid through them. Emily waited, but an escalating whine followed by a thrumming sound vibrated against her ears. She headed aft toward the noise. The bridge had wings that extended out for better visibility when docking, but here on the outside gangway they actually blocked her view of what was making the sound. But she didn't need to see it to know what it was. *That's a helicopter starting up!*

Emily took the catwalk around the portside wing and her suspicions were confirmed as the ship's helicopter rose from the pad below, coming to a hover across from Emily. As it began to rotate, she was able to make out the face of the single pilot within, his features lit by the glow of instrument panels.

Nicholas Othonos.

The young man didn't seem to notice her, standing there in the dim illumination of the emergency lighting. The chopper rotated to starboard, then pitched its nose down and accelerated away.

A metallic clank from high above her head drew Emily's attention, followed by a shout. "Hey! You down there?" a woman's voice called out.

"Yeah!" Em looked up, spotting the face of the crewwoman looking down at her from the roof of the bridge.

"Did I hear a helicopter?"

"Yeah. Just took off."

"Listen, I'm new, but I remembered one of the engineers going up onto the roof to work on one of the radars. There's a ladder at the back of a cable closet that leads up here. I'll leave the hatch open for you. Come back around the bridge. You should see a set of rungs to let you climb up."

"I see them..."

"Good! The hatch is at the base of the largest radar pillar. Careful coming down, there are a lot of cables in the shaft. But get in here and tell us what's happening! I think we've almost got the power thing worked out, so I need to get back. We have to get the communications back online!"

Clamping her mobile in her teeth, Emily set her bare feet onto the rungs, noting they were somewhat slippery from the humid, tropical air. She found herself laughing on the way up, as she imagined the sight she made, a barefoot woman in a cocktail dress with a mouthful of green smartphone, scaling the side of the bridge.

In minutes, she found the hatch and lowered herself into the shaft, where another set of rungs awaited her. Hugging the wall, with cables brushing her back, she started down, sparing a couple fingers to loosely grip her mobile. The chute was quite dark, but light spilled in from an opening below. As she neared the bottom, she could hear the two crew members talking, but then another sound. A staccato series of clinks, like a small metallic object was skittering across the floor below. The crewwoman spoke.

"What the hell is th—"

A deafening BANG punched Emily's eardrums, just as blinding white light flashed from the opening to the chute.

———◆·◆———

"Move it, people!" Angler shouted, as they raced up the last flight of stairs.

Potluck reached the door to the helipad level, retrieving one of their special cards and swiping it against the keypad. The keypad squawked at her and the door remained locked. "What the hell?"

"Let me try," Tolstoy said, pushing past and lifting his own card from a lanyard.

Boone had noticed the other two carried their keycards in their vests. Tolstoy, still dressed as a crewmember, kept his around his neck, along with an ID card—no doubt a false one.

"Is no good," he said when his card failed as well.

"Told you we might need this," Angler said, unslinging a stubby Mossberg Compact Cruiser shotgun from his back and extending a short handle near the barrel's tip. "Stand aside." Tilting it down at a forty-five-degree angle, he aimed it at the lock plate and pulled the trigger. A dull, thudding boom echoed in the stairwell as the dense, 12-gauge breaching slug blasted the lock mechanism.

Boone watched as Angler kicked the door open and Potluck swept through the opening, SP5 submachine gun leveled. Tolstoy remained behind, covering the hostages. Boone recognized this door from the morning before, when Callie had led them up here for their whale shark tour. The helipad would be just around the corner. From outside came Potluck's shout.

"Boss, we got a problem! The helicopter's gone!"

—————◆◆◆—————

Clinging to the ladder rungs, Emily waited for the ringing in her ears to subside. *Must've been one of those stun grenades law enforcement uses,* she thought, thankful she'd been far enough away from the opening to the access shaft when it went off. Still, the effect had been jarring enough that she had dropped her mobile down the chute.

Footsteps. A voice with a Southern twang. "You… sit down in that chair. Our employer said not to tie you up… guess you've got issues. But he ain't here right now, so don't give me a reason. Sit still. Need to secure these two before the flashbang wears off."

Emily carefully crept down the last few rungs. The cables leading up to the various radars and radio masts were plentiful enough that she should be able to remain out of sight, her black dress giving an assist in that regard, blending with the shadows in the unlit chute. Finding a gap in the cables, she looked out into the bridge. She could see a man dressed in black tactical gear, zip-tying the wrists and ankles of one of the crewmembers. The other one was already immobilized.

Movement to the left. Emily found another gap to peer through and spotted Calypso, sitting in a swivel chair at a bridge workstation. The mercenary came into view, addressing his hostage.

"And now we wait. Then you 'n' me are going on a boat ride. Wait… why did you switch chairs? I told you not to goddamn move!"

"Please don't hurt me!" Calypso cried, her voice shaking, appearing on the verge of tears.

"Calm down, you'll be…" He trailed off, listening to something. He stiffened. "What do you mean, the helicopter's gone? Gone where?"

As he turned away, listening to the reply, Emily watched Callie's look of fear melt away, replaced by an expressionless mask. The young woman reached beneath the tabletop of the workstation she sat at.

"No, I didn't see it leave," the mercenary shouted. "I came into the bridge by the internal entrance, the way we planned!"

Callie twisted a bit in her chair, retrieving something.

"Dammit," Stallion muttered, then listened. "Okay... understood. Radio back in five." He turned back to his hostage. "All right, change of plans..."

"Correct," Calypso said, raising a pistol and shooting Stallion in the face. The mercenary's bulbous eyes bulged even more in disbelief before the light went out of them. The shell casing pinged against the floor as the lifeless body of the merc crumpled with a thud.

Shocked, Emily watched as the youngest Othonos retrieved the mercenary's submachine gun, then turned toward the bridge crew. Em began to part the cables to go assist the young woman in freeing them, but froze when Calypso raised the weapon and fired a burst into each of the prone crew members.

A scream threatened to claw its way up Emily's throat, but she managed to choke it down, remaining silent as she released the cables and retreated into the shadows. Tears flooded her eyes, but through the moisture she watched Calypso toss the merc's weapon beside his body, then return to the workstation where the gun had been stashed. Moving with cold efficiency, the young woman removed a bulky briefcase—nearly the size of a small carry-on—and laid it on a nearby tabletop, hopping into a swiveling crew chair in front of it. Popping the latches, she opened it, revealing a computer screen set into the lid. In the lower half, Emily could make out a keyboard and numerous switches and exposed circuit boards. Calypso powered everything up, flipped a number of switches, then peered at a readout in the corner of the screen.

"Dammit. It's out of range." Calmly, she retrieved a headset and mic from inside, settling it on her head. She opened her mouth to speak but snapped it shut. "Almost forgot," she muttered to herself, just loud enough for Emily to hear. "Need to butch it up." She tapped her keyboard, then cleared her throat and spoke. "Palantir to Angler, do you read?"

———◆·◆———

"This is Angler, I read you Palantir," the mercenary leader replied to the synthesized voice. The distortion seemed a little different than before, perhaps another setting on whatever voice-changer Palantir was using. "We weren't expecting you so soon, but it's a good thing, because—"

"Someone took the helicopter, yes, I know. Listen carefully, because our timetable has changed. First... did you deliver the package to the Castor*?"*

"The drone? Yeah, it's aboard."

"Good. We'll need that, so keep it safe. Now, get down to the tender bay. Board the Castor *and I will selectively restore power so you can use the davit to send it out. The* Apollo *is at a standstill, so you should have no problems with entry."*

"Understood. Stallion is supposed to use the *Castor*, too... should we coordinate with him?"

"Stallion is dead."

Angler, Tolstoy, and Potluck all stiffened. "Say again, Palantir?" Angler rumbled.

"One of the bridge crew was armed. I watched it happen on a video feed. There was nothing I could do. I'm sorry."

Angler gave a mop bucket a vicious kick, sending the wheeled object crashing into a workbench in the close confines of the empty hangar bay, where it careened off and skidded out onto the empty helipad. Taking a deep breath, he composed himself. "So we're down another hostage?"

There was a long pause.

"Palantir, do you read?"

"Still here, Angler. I'm working on it. Get to the boat."

The mercenary leader motioned to his team. "You heard the man, we're getting wet. Potluck, take point. Tolstoy, bring up the rear. And you..." He pointed at Boone. "Think we'll keep you around a little longer to skipper the boat."

"Gonna be hard to steer like this," the tall divemaster said, shrugging his shoulders, his arms zip-tied behind his back.

"Nice try. We'll cut those once we're aboard. All right people, move out."

———— ✦ • ✦ ————

While scanning the interior of the hangar, noting several items of interest, Boone had only heard one side of the radio communication. Even so, it had been enough to tell him that things were not going as planned. He was fairly sure that this was a kidnapping. Achilles and Lyra would likely be safe, of no value to these people if they perished. *Although... why did they send Calypso off separately?* That didn't make much sense to him. But one thing seemed clear. If he boarded the boat with these people, he wouldn't be coming back. *And Emily is still out there!*

The group crossed the helipad and made their way to the door Angler had breached.

"Bozhe moi, I could use a cigarette," Tolstoy groaned, as he entered the stairwell. "I smoke all I had."

"I can help you with that," Boone said.

"Chto?" The Russian halted at the top of the stairs, his pistol pointed at Boone.

"Cigarettes. Left suit coat pocket. Help yourself."

Tolstoy reached inside Boone's pocket and came out with the black-and-gold box of Black Russians. His face lit up. "I love these!"

"Me too! Lighter in my right suit pocket," Boone lied.

Transferring the box of cigarettes into his gun hand, Tolstoy reached into Boone's empty pocket.

And Boone headbutted him. Hard. Slamming the crown of his head into the man's nose, the young divemaster felt bone and cartilage shift with the impact. Boone had another card to play if the blow resulted in a dropped pistol. It did. As Tolstoy rocked back, gun and cigarettes falling from his fingers, Boone darted his head forward like a striking fer de lance, snagging the man's lanyard in his teeth. Wrenching it free, he stepped back and delivered a powerful *benção*, a capoeira kick intended to force separation. In this case, that "separation" sent Tolstoy tumbling down the stairs, colliding with Angler, who was already turning at the sound of Tolstoy's agonized grunt. The mercenary leader and Achilles were both bowled over and fell into Potluck, sending them all crashing into a heap. Lyra flattened herself against the railing, managing to stay upright, Boone was pleased to see. She looked up at him, hope in her eyes.

Turning, he rushed back through the ruined door and ran around the outer wall of the hangar, ducking into the workshop. Spinning around against the workbench, he managed to snag a pair of wire cutter pliers he'd spotted there earlier. Tolstoy's lanyard dangling from his teeth and the pliers clutched behind his back in his bound hands, Boone ran out of the workshop, heading around the other side of the hangar on the port side of the ship. Pausing for a moment, he carefully maneuvered the head of the wire cutters back to the zip-tie restraint as he listened for the sounds of pursuit, eyes raising toward the glass windows of the ship's bridge ahead.

———◆•◆———

"*Chyort!* I will kill him!" Tolstoy shrieked in a nasal voice, his ruined nose gushing blood.

"Let him go!" Angler shouted as he rose to his feet. "There's no time! We've got to get to the boat!"

27

Emily watched as Calypso removed the headset and set it into the case. Tapping the keys inside the container, she brought up a new window on the screen. With a deliberate, clacking keystroke, Emily saw a single red word appear, all caps and large enough for her eyes to make out: ARMED.

Calypso sat back. "Well... two out of three will have to do until I find you, Nicky..."

A beep and a click sounded from out of sight to Emily's right. The outer door she'd first encountered—someone was unlocking it. Startled, Calypso looked toward the entrance.

"Callie! Are you all right?"

Boone! Emily's eyes locked onto the pistol that lay beside the case. From where Boone stood, the bulky briefcase would block it from his view. Emily tensed, but Calypso made no move to grab it. Instead, she summoned up another expression of fear and hysteria.

"Oh, thank God!" she cried. "Boone!"

"Listen, the terrorists may be following me, so we should…"
His voice trailed off. "What happened here?" Boone was out
of sight of the cable closet opening and it sounded like he was
remaining close to the outer bridge exit.

"It was terrible! He killed the crew, but then I remembered
the captain kept a gun—you know, for piracy?"

Emily looked through the cables at the fallen mercenary,
gauging the distance to the dead man's submachine gun. *Too
far,* she thought.

"Better him than you," Boone said. "Look, I managed to get
one of their keycards. We need to get you back to the dining hall.
The bombs on the doors are fakes. We've got to get the crew to
restore power and communications. Hey, what's that? Looks like
it's powered up."

"Oh, this, yes… I found it over there. It's battery-operated and
might have a satellite hook-up. I was trying to figure out how to
use it… maybe call for help?"

Emily watched as Calypso tapped a couple keys, closing the
window that said ARMED.

"Damn, I think I messed something up. Can you take a look?"
Calypso swiveled away from Boone. As she rose from the chair,
Emily watched her slide the gun off the edge, palming it against
her thigh as she moved aside.

Heart hammering, Emily mentally raced through her options,
realizing none of them were good. Fate chose her course of action.
As Boone came into view and bent over the case, Calypso raised
the gun. Emily burst through the cables.

"WAIT! I-know-where-Nicholas-is!" she screamed in a jumbled
rush.

———————◆•◆———————

Boone and Calypso both jumped at Emily's shout and sudden appearance. Boone had known something was fishy, but was surprised when he saw the gun pointed at him. Time seemed to slow as the barrel of the gun wavered between the two divemasters. At the speed of thought, pieces of the puzzle began to snap into place.

"And I know what he's up to," Boone blurted, raising his hands. "And what *you*... were planning."

Calypso's eyes went from one to the other, madness dancing behind them. "What was I planning?"

"You were controlling those mercenaries, using that thing-amajig," Emily said.

Calypso smiled. "Only when the power was out. Usually, my phone sufficed. Speaking of which, fetch my phone from the belt pouch on Stallion."

"Did you give them those names, or did they pick them?" Boone asked, crouching by the dead merc, eyes flicking to the man's weapon.

"Don't even think of touching that gun. I'm an excellent shot, I assure you. My phone is the one with the black case. Good. Set it on the table next to the briefcase. Leave the keycard, too. Step over there beside your girlfriend."

As Boone set the phone down, he suddenly remembered something he'd filed away at the time. "You were messing with your phone a lot just before the lights went off. *You* triggered the lockdown just as Achilles called for a toast."

Calypso raised an eyebrow. "You're good. Anything else?" She twitched the gun at Boone, directing him to get closer to Emily.

"There never was a kidnapping," Emily said quickly. "The helicopter! Your brothers and sister and the mercenaries... they were all supposed to be on the helicopter..."

"You were going to blow it up, weren't you?" Boone deduced. "Remove everyone else in the line of succession in your father's patriarchal will, leaving you to inherit everything. That's why you had the 'kidnappers' send you off separately."

"And Lyra's faulty dive computer," Emily added. "And Nicholas's scooter malfunction..."

Calypso smiled at Emily. "You come across as a bit of a ditz, but you're not, are you?" She shrugged. "You ever read Machiavelli? One of our guests had a copy of *The Prince*; I swiped it and tore off the cover. I've been reading it—in the original Italian, of course. *Dividere e Conquistare.* 'Divide and conquer.' When the opportunity arose to take a few chess pieces off the board early, I figured, what the hell?"

"So, when you said Nicholas had insisted on you and Lyra using the ship's dive gear..."

"A lie, of course. I arranged the gear. Altering the computer readout wasn't too difficult." She gestured to her case. "Not for someone with my skills. Still, Lyra was a bit tricky. Had to make sure I got in front of the good rig first, so she'd take the one I'd sabotaged." Her face darkened. "Shame my little signal-hijacking trick didn't work with Nicholas... then I wouldn't be scrambling to salvage this scheme." She sighed. "I'll just kill Lyra and Achilles now and take care of Nicky later." She raised the gun.

"He isn't coming back." Emily said quickly. When Calypso hesitated, Em plunged ahead. "The helicopter... Nicholas was piloting it."

"He was?" Boone asked. Then a lightbulb went off. "Wait. I know where he's headed."

"You do?" Emily asked. "Oh! The navigation point that Stavros was on about?"

"Yeah… and he told me where it was."

Calypso appeared flustered, muttering, "What the hell is he up to…?"

"I think I know that too," Boone said distantly, remembering Nicholas's odd behavior outside of the Pantheon Bank branch in the shopping atrium, the laptop over his shoulder. His resentment of his older brother, who stood to inherit everything. And he recalled their conversation with the software security developer, Chloe, and her discovery of a vulnerability in the company's cryptocurrency.

"Spit it out!" Calypso yelled.

Boone blinked, coming back to the present. "Callie, your plan was clever. A botched kidnapping gone horribly wrong with you as the sole survivor, set to inherit everything… but the problem here is, you'll inherit *nothing*."

"Go on…" Callie said, her voice half-menacing, half-intrigued.

"You weren't the only Othonos who wanted it all. And Nicholas, considering all the work he's put into the business, felt he'd earned a right to more than your father's will gave him. So he's going to take it. What's that cryptocurrency Nicholas designed? The Croesids?"

"God, I hate that name," Calypso hissed. "What of it?"

"How much of your family fortune is invested in those units, would you say?"

Callie grew pale. "Most of it."

"And he's going to steal it all," Emily said. "And we know how."

Boone glanced down at her. *But… we* don't *know exactly how*, he thought. He looked at her expression. There it was, the poker face. But this time, he was able to read her. *This is the only lever-*

age we have, and she knows it. The software vulnerability that would allow for a crypto-heist... and the helicopter's destination.

"Look... Em and I have a problem here. If we don't tell you where Nicholas is going and how he's going to steal everything, you'll kill us. And if we *do* tell you... you'll kill us. And the important thing for you to know is... we'd very much prefer to be alive. Even if it means letting you get away with... well... murder."

"What do you propose?"

"First off, how are you going to kill Lyra and Achilles?"

Calypso scoffed. "I'm not going to tell you that."

"Bomb on the boat," Em said. When Callie narrowed her eyes at her, Em added, "I saw you arm something on your screen."

"Thank you for reminding me..." Callie retrieved the headset, keeping her gun trained on Boone and Emily. "Angler, this is Palantir. Are you aboard the boat?" She listened for a moment, then began carefully typing with one hand, eyes on the divemasters, with only occasional flicks to the keyboard. "Good. I am restoring power to the tender bay. Head toward the destination we discussed, but... I will be joining you at sea. I have Calypso."

Boone watched as Callie stifled a snicker, listening to her team's response before replying. "After Stallion died, I ambushed the bridge crew, that's how. Now... we'll want this rendezvous to occur over the horizon, so stay on the bearing you have for thirty miles, then drop your speed to five knots, understood?"

As she listened to another reply, Boone looked carefully at the briefcase. It seemed to be a cobbled-together assortment of devices, set into a homemade control panel. And there, to one side... little joysticks. A controller, like for a video game. *Or... a drone.*

"Of course this is outside of the plan! I will explain *why* once I reach you. Palantir out."

"Voice changer?" Boone surmised.

Calypso smiled but didn't reply. She put the headset and her smartphone back in the case before closing it and latching it, all the while keeping her gun on Emily and Boone. "You were about to offer me a scenario where you tell me what I need to know, and I let you live. Let's discuss options on our way to the boat. But first…"

Leaving the case where it was, Callie went over to Stallion's corpse and removed another zip-tie. She tossed it over to Emily. "You know the drill," she said to Boone. "Hands behind your back."

"Oh, for the love of…"

Calypso laughed. "Twice in one day. Hey, maybe you'll find you're into bondage by the time this is over. Besides, if I remember correctly, Emily's the better skipper. And I'll need someone to drive."

"I don't like it," Angler said after Palantir signed off.

"What's to like?" Potluck said. "Missing Othonos, missing helicopter, the beanpole got away, and Stallion's dead. FUBAR."

"At least he got Calypso back," Angler mumbled. "Three-quarters of the hostages is better than half."

"Lift is operational," Tolstoy said, his voice now sounding like someone with a nasty cold. On their way down, he'd popped into a bathroom to grab a roll of toilet paper, shoving wads of it up his nostrils in an attempt to staunch the bleeding.

"Hit it, then climb aboard," Angler ordered.

An angry claxon sounded. In moments, hydraulics whined as the starboard bay door slid up, revealing a placid sea under a starry sky. With a lurch, the *Castor* began moving sideways toward the opening.

Tolstoy cleared his throat. "I realize is... what is word... 'insensitive' for me to ask, but... since Stallion is dead, do we split his share?"

Angler glared at the Russian. "Line of duty, Tolstoy. His family gets it."

"*Da*, yes, of course. But on other hand... the extra half million for his separate boat trip? It seems to me..."

As Tolstoy droned on through his noseful of bloody toilet paper and the boat slid into the water, Angler looked up at the moon, laying down a pearl-white carpet on the waves. *I'm done with this line of work*, he promised himself.

◆ ◆ ◆

The moon was nearly full, the night sky devoid of clouds. *Good flying weather*, Nicholas thought, then laughed out loud. Here he was, thinking like a veteran pilot, when he had only begun his lessons several months ago. He checked the navigation screen, ensuring he was still on course. He was. Glancing out the starboard window, he spotted a ship below. Much like the *Apollo*, this one also appeared to be dead in the water, no wake behind it. And it looked familiar.

Nicholas laughed. *Oh, this is too good. Could it be?* He switched on the helicopter's marine band radio to pick up VHF Channel 16, home of 156.8 MHz, the international distress frequency.

Pan-pan, pan-pan, pan-pan, this is Nordic Starr *out of Cozumel, bound for Grand Cayman. We have suffered an engine breakdown and require assistance.*

Howling with laughter, Nicholas snapped the radio off. *They must have broken down over a day ago.* "Pan-pan" wasn't a distress call on the level of Mayday, but it likely meant they had tried and failed to fix the problem themselves, before caving and calling for help. Still chuckling minutes later, he flew on.

Ahead, in the distance, he could just make out the lights of George Town, the capital of Grand Cayman, situated on the western coast. But that wasn't his immediate destination. Checking the waypoint, he banked the ACH160 to the right, heading for the southwestern coast of the island. He would be in George Town soon enough. And by nine a.m., he would be one of the wealthiest people on the planet.

Emily walked behind Boone as Calypso ushered them down a passage that linked the internal bridge access with some of the family's private suites. Reaching a particular door, Callie called for them to stop. Using Tolstoy's keycard, which now hung around her neck, she opened the door and motioned for them to step inside.

"Welcome to Nicky's suite," Calypso said, looking around. Spotting an object in the corner, she stepped back and motioned Emily over. "Good, he left it. Pick it up."

Emily recognized the black hard case from their night dive. "That's Nicholas's UPC."

"Yes. Pick it up." Callie gestured with the gun, her other hand carrying her own, similarly sized case.

Emily picked it up. "What do you want this for?"

"Tell you on the boat. Hurry it up—they have enough of a head start already."

Emily did as she was told, throwing a glance at Boone, but his eyes were locked on Calypso.

"Come on, out to the hall. Stairwell at the end."

Boone led the way. "I've been thinking of a way we can all come out of this—"

"I'm sure you have," Calypso interrupted, a tinge of sarcasm in her voice. "But we're doing this my way. Down the stairs, both of you."

They did as they were told, soon reaching the bottom level and entering the tender bay. The air had a salty tang of seawater, and Emily noted the area around the closed starboard sidehatch was awash.

"Get aboard," Calypso ordered, nodding toward the sleek limo tender, the *Pollux*.

All three climbed the short flight of metal stairs to the side of the boat. Boone stepped in and Emily followed, setting the UPC's container down before turning to find Calypso handing her own case across. Emily took it.

"Set it down right there. Gently. Boone, go sit down by the bar and make yourself comfortable. Emily, go to the wheelhouse and take a look at the controls. You better hope you can drive this boat."

Calypso stepped back and flipped a pair of switches. A claxon echoed in the bay as she stepped across, gun leveled as she grabbed hold of a handrail. The sound of hydraulics echoed in the tender.

Emily turned her head to port, noting the massive bay door there rising up, gentle waves lapping up against the waterline. The *Pollux* lurched as the system moved her sideways along the rails, toward the night sky and the tropical seas. In the midst of all that was happening, a stray thought bubbled up: *I hope Brixton will be okay if we...*

Calypso's sharp tone, tinged with impatience, brought her back to the here and now. "How's it coming up there, Emily?"

"I can pilot it, no prob."

"Good. Once we're underway, I'll explain how we can both get what we want."

28

"You're serious?" Boone asked, wincing as the boat hit another wave top. Calypso had forced him to sit on the floor in the corner of the open-air wheelhouse. *If my tailbone isn't dust by the end of this, I'll be lucky.*

"*That's* your plan to let us stay alive?" Emily asked incredulously as she gripped the vibrating wheel. The *Pollux* skimmed across the waves, nearing its top speed of forty-eight knots.

"Yes," Calypso said.

"You're going to just drop us in the middle of the ocean?" Boone asked.

"The seas look quite calm. Nicholas's UPC scooter floats and it has a distress beacon. And once I'm back aboard the *Apollo*, I'll make an anonymous call to the various Coast Guards in the area. Someone will pick you up."

"And we tell you what you need to know… from the water?" Emily asked. "That's a bit barmy, innit?"

"What's to stop you from killing us then?" Boone asked. "Or using the controller... send the scooter to the bottom of the sea, like you tried to do with Nicholas."

Calypso looked wistful. "That was fun, I must admit. But there will be no need for me to kill you."

She stepped back just inside the main cabin, sitting in front of her open briefcase of gizmos, a clear line of sight to Emily at the wheel. "Anything ahead on the radar?"

"Nothing yet."

Calypso glanced at the screen inside her case. "No signal... we'll need to get closer." She lifted her phone from the briefcase and came forward, looking down at Boone. "You're wondering how it is I'd let you live, knowing you might turn me in for murder?"

Boone stared at her, waiting.

"Because *I'm* not going to kill Achilles and Lyra," Calypso said, then nodded at Emily. "She is."

"Okay, we are thirty miles out from the *Apollo*." Tolstoy said from the cabin cockpit. A black and gold cigarette dangled from his lips. Even as he'd cursed the divemaster for smashing his nose, his rage had been somewhat tempered by the fact that he'd ended up with a full pack of the cigarettes.

"Reduce speed," Angler ordered from the port dive bench.

"What is happening? Where are you taking us?" Lyra asked.

The Othonos hostages were sitting on the starboard bench, Achilles with his hands still tied behind his back. Additionally, the defiant man now sported some duct tape across his mouth. If the arrogant brat had said, "Do you know who I am?" or "You'll never get away with this!" one more time, Angler would've deep-sixed him.

"Please, tell me!" Lyra cried.

"We're taking you somewhere safe," Angler said. "And assuming your dad pays up, everything's gonna be fine."

"And my sister? You sent her away—where is she?"

"You'll be seeing her real soon," Angler rumbled, then frowned. He rose from the bench, mental gears turning. Everything he'd heard from Palantir had led him to think the guy was likely a code monkey and a desk jockey. The guy knew enough military lingo that Angler suspected he was in the service, but there had been phrases that rang hollow. *And now he tells us that he took out the bridge crew that had killed Stallion? And then he secured Calypso?*

He looked up to the flybridge. "Potluck? Anything?"

The Wisconsinite was looking toward the west-northwest with a night-vision monocular. "Nothing yet."

Angler paced. *The whole plan was flawed. Separating Stallion and Calypso from the rest of them was idiotic. Unless... unless it wasn't.* He stopped pacing. Turning on his heel, he went down into the hold in the bow, staring at the bulky case he'd delivered there at Palantir's insistence. *The man's drone. Said he would need this for reconnaissance of the safehouse neighborhood until the ransom was secured.* Angler took hold of the handle and brought the suitcase-sized container up on deck.

He set the case down near the stern and crouched, reaching for the latches... then halted. Stood again. "Potluck! Take over the wheel. Tolstoy, get over here. Bring your tools."

"I'm not killing anyone!" Emily cried, taking her hands off the wheel.

"Oh, you're no fun. Fine. You don't have to push the *actual* detonator, I'll handle that. You can use the remote control for Nicky's UPC and play 'let's pretend.' But you *will* push a button and I'm going to use my phone to film you doing it as their boat goes boom. Either that, or I do to Boone… what I did to Stallion. And he's much better looking than Stallion, so it will be far more tragic."

"You… you're evil!" Em cried.

"That's what they said about Machiavelli," Calypso scoffed. "I'm actually being quite practical. And I believe a combination of carrots and sticks will be best, to ensure you two go on your way and I never hear from you again." Calypso twitched the gun barrel at Emily. "Hands at ten and two. You're deviating from our heading."

Emily returned to the controls, making a course correction.

"That's better," Calypso said. "First, the 'carrot.' I will deposit one million dollars into your dive company's account. Isn't that generous of me? Guess what? That's also part of the 'stick.' The source account will be the same one that paid my merry band of guns-for-hire. If you ever return with wild tales of Calypso killing her family, the money trail leading to you will suddenly become visible. The same goes for footage of you using what looks like a remote to blow up the *Castor.*"

"Thought it all through, haven't you?" Boone muttered.

"Yes, I have, actually." She gave a bitter snort. "Everyone thinks Nicky is the smart one. I can run rings around the gimp."

"Unless he drains your inheritance down to practically nothing," Boone reminded her.

Calypso shot him a glare. "Good thing you'll be telling me how he's going to do it. Right?"

"I've got a blip. Four miles," Emily said in a hollow voice.

"Should be close enough. Kill the running lights, engage the autopilot, and come back to the main cabin. Boone... scoot your tight little buns across the floor and join us. Try anything... and I'll start with the kneecaps."

"Is drone. So?"

Angler had asked Tolstoy to check for any boobytraps on the latches to the case. Finding none, they had opened it. What lay within was just a large quadcopter drone, its four rotor-arms folded back against its midsection.

Angler chewed on his lip, holding a flashlight beam on the case. "Potluck? Gimme a look aft."

Potluck left the wheel and climbed halfway up the flybridge ladder. "Nothing y— wait! I see it! It's the *Pollux*. Quite a bow wave on her!"

Angler felt a sudden surge of urgency as he peered into the gloom astern. *No running lights...* "Tolstoy, can you see anything... I don't know... *wrong* with this drone?"

The Russian shrugged. "It look similar to ones we use in Wagner Group." He reached in and took hold of the main body, lifting it from the case. "Camera assembly should be on the bott— ooookaaaay... that not normal."

A pair of cables ran from the underside of the drone into the bottom of the case, disappearing into the foam padding.

"Don't move!" Angler reached out, gingerly taking the drone from him. "Where do those wires lead?"

Tolstoy removed a small flashlight from his bag and clamped it in his teeth. Between the toilet paper nostril-plugs and the mouth-light, the Russian made for a strange sight. He moved his face closer to the foam, parting it carefully with his fingers, then retreated and removed the flashlight from his teeth.

"Well?" Angler asked impatiently.

"Well... remember our fake bombs on doors?"

"Yeah...?"

"This one not fake."

"Shit! Can you deactivate it?"

"*Da*, no problem," Tolstoy said. He took the drone from Angler, replacing it in the case, before closing the lid and hurling it overboard. "Huh. What you know? It float."

"Fuck! Potluck! Floor it!"

"Showtime." Calypso kept her gun on Boone, positioning herself in front of her briefcase, which now stood open and powered up. "Open the UPC case and get the remote."

Boone watched as Emily retrieved the black case and removed the scooter from it, catching Boone's eyes as she did so. Emily's earlier tears had dried and he knew she was transitioning to anger. *Good.*

Boone had watched Calypso carefully as she had offered up the use of the UPC and its distress beacon, and then went through her whole "carrot and stick" schtick. He was certain it was just a deliberately complicated smokescreen to give them hope. He had seen it in her eyes: she would kill them the second they told her what she wanted to know.

"Hurry up!" Calypso shouted.

"Sorry, the remote's underneath." Emily set the scooter down near Boone's feet and gave him a meaningful look, then removed the remote from the bottom of the case. "Got it."

"Good. Get over by the window. I've got the original remote to the drone wired into my little box of fun." She tapped a few keys, then lifted her smartphone. "Now, Emily... hold your prop up a little—I want to get it in the light."

Emily raised the control unit, looking back at Callie questioningly.

"Good. Right there," Calypso said, eyes on the smartphone screen as Emily held the UPC controller up. "Look out the window toward the bow."

Boone quickly slipped off his dress shoes.

"Try and look a *little* bloodthirsty, for fuck's sake," Calypso cursed. "Oh, nice... *good*. Now pick a button, any button. And... on three..."

Boone extended a foot, sliding the UPC closer to Calypso.

"One..." Calypso kept her smartphone on Emily, but dipped her gun hand to the keyboard, extending a pinky. "Two..."

Emily mashed her fingers to the scooter's controls. A loud hiss and blinding strobe light filled the cabin, along with a zipping sound as a thin, black tendril whipped crazily across the floor. Calypso, startled, swung her barrel toward the sudden movement.

Boone struck. Planting his hands behind his butt, he tensed his muscles, rocked back on his palms, and snapped his long legs out, clamping his sizeable feet onto Calypso's gun hand. Twisting savagely, he tore the pistol from her grasp, sending it clattering into a corner. Calypso dropped her smartphone and punched a key in her briefcase.

"No!" Boone shouted from the floor, as a flash of light in the night sky flickered in the windows, followed by a distant boom.

Calypso's face lit up with rapture. "Two down, one to go!"

Emily was already moving. As Calypso turned to go after the gun, Emily stepped in close and hammered a picture-perfect haymaker punch into Calypso's jaw. The murderous Othonos crumpled like a puppet with its strings cut.

"Damn..." Boone breathed, impressed. "What happened to all the Krav Maga tricks Sophie taught you?"

"Sometimes you just want to punch the seven bells out of someone," Emily hissed, wincing as she nursed her hand. "God, I've been wanting to do that since the moment I met her!"

"You wanna turn that thing off?" Boone tucked his knees up toward his chest as he stretched his lanky arms out beneath him. He had always been freakishly limber and it only took a moment to bring his bound hands around his feet. *Wish I'd kept those clippers,* he thought. *But I wasn't exactly expecting a repeat.*

Emily lifted the remote for the UPC, tapping three controls in sequence. "Noisy little purge valve, and... emergency strobe, and... spooling antenna." In moments, the twitching, hissing, flashing object ceased its spectacle. "And actually... let's turn on the emergency beacon, yeah?" She did so as she watched Boone rise, his bound wrists now in front. "Look at you, Houdini. Well... half-a-Houdini." Suddenly, her face grew solemn. "Oh, shite... Lyra and Achilles! Come on!" She dashed forward.

Boone scooped up the pistol and went to the open-air wheelhouse. Tossing the gun into a cubby, he stepped up to peer over the glass, expecting to see the glow of flames. Instead, the only visible illumination was the moon overhead and its reflection on the waves. He looked down at the radar screen, looking for the dot that would represent the *Castor*. *There it is*. But it wasn't four miles out and it wasn't stationary.

"Em! We have incoming!"

Emily looked up from the wheel, taking control. "Where?"

A rattle of automatic weapons fire from the port bow answered her question. Boone thought fast, then reached over, tapping Emily's bare shoulder. "Cut the engine!"

Em killed the throttle, and in a moment, only the lap of the waves against the hull was audible, along with the distant burble of another engine. The *Castor* was visible in the moonlight, a black-clad figure with a raised weapon visible atop the flybridge. Then, a voice—gravelly and familiar—floated across the expanse between the two vessels.

"Ahoy the *Pollux*!"

Boone raised his long arms above the windscreen, waving them back and forth, zip-tied as they were. "Ahoy the *Castor*! VHF channel sixty-eight!" he shouted at the top of his lungs. He'd picked one that wasn't the go-to for emergencies or Coast Guard, in the hopes they'd realize he was suggesting a parley. Boone reached over and switched their marine radio to that channel. "Hold the mic," he said to Emily.

"Hope you know what you're doing." She grabbed the handset, keying it for him.

"This is the *Castor*, broadcasting on sixty-eight," came a voice.

"I read you, *Castor*," Boone responded.

"Palantir? That you?"

"Negative, uh… Angler? Do I have that right?"

There was a long pause, then. "Who is this?"

"Well, since you like code names… this is Beanpole. Or, uh… Dog Owner. Or 'Guy-who-headbutts-Russians.'"

Laughter was clearly audible over the connection. "Yeah, you tagged him good. What the hell are you doing over there?"

"I went from one hostage situation to another," Boone said. "Guess I'm just that kind of lucky. Look, Angler... I got news for you. You've been had."

"Yeah, I figured that much out," the voice said darkly. "Finding a bomb under our feet kinda clued me in. Put Palantir on."

"Well, I would, but..."

"She's resting," Emily said into the mic.

There was a long pause. "Say again. *She?*"

"She was using a voice changer," Boone said. "It's Calypso Othonos."

The radio went silent, but across the waves he could hear angry shouting. Boone nodded to Emily to open up the channel again.

"Angler, you there?" Boone asked.

The voice came back on, rage clearly audible in it. "I'm here."

"Listen, I'll give it to you in a nutshell. You were hired to kidnap the Othonos heirs... then Calypso was going to blow all of you up on the helicopter. Make it look like the kidnapping went wrong. When her brother screwed that up, well... you can figure out the rest. There was never going to be a ransom."

Emily tilted the handset her way. "But look, it's not completely bodged... you got paid something substantial up front, yeah?"

"Yeah."

"So leave Achilles and Lyra with us and go. Whatever the rest of the plan was... that plan never existed. You were s'posed to be dead by now."

"Stallion *is* dead," Angler said. "Calypso do that?"

Boone started to interject, but Em silenced him and continued. "There was a gun on the bridge. A grenade of some kind went off. It was chaos."

A female voice came onto the channel. "We want Calypso! You can have the other two."

"Look, Calypso is a young woman who has totally lost the plot," Emily pleaded. "She's going away for a long time."

Boone leaned in. "Plus... we set off an emergency beacon when we took Calypso down. Coast Guard is likely on the way. You get caught with any of the Othonos kids on board, that might be hard to talk your way out of. Leave them with us and go."

Voices across the lapping waves, then: "We're putting life vests on the hostages now. Pick them up after we're gone. There's been enough killing today, but if you come after us..."

"We won't," Emily said.

Boone looked back at the cabin. Calypso was stirring. "Hey, Angler... one request?"

"What?"

"You got any more zip-ties? And... something to *cut* zip-ties?"

29

"Callie... how *could* you?" Lyra asked in horrified disbelief, tears streaming down her cheeks.

The youngest Othonos made no reply as she sat upon the deck of the cabin, hands bound, glaring silently at her eldest siblings.

Ten minutes earlier, as the mercenaries aboard the *Castor* sped away toward Grand Cayman, Boone had used the multi-tool they had tossed over to free himself before diving in to bring Achilles and Lyra on board. The two had listened with growing shock and horror as Boone outlined what their sister had been planning. Now, with Emily at the wheel, the *Pollux* was nearing the *Apollo*. The others remained back in the interior of the limo tender.

"Monster!" Achilles glared at Calypso, his nostrils flaring, fists clenching. Then all of a sudden he sagged, his posture losing all of its aggression. "I've lost my baby sister." Moisture welled in his eyes. "What did we ever do to you?"

Calypso looked at the floor, her face inscrutable.

"And where is Nicholas?" Achilles asked Boone. "She was going to kill him too, right? So where did he take the helicopter?"

"You remember that weird waypoint your co-pilot pointed out to you?" Boone prompted.

"Yes..." Achilles thought hard. "Wait... Nicholas had been taking lessons lately."

"Quite a few lessons, according to Stavros," Boone said.

"Why did he run away?" Lyra asked with confusion. "Did he learn of Callie's plot?"

"No... he had his own plot."

At this, Calypso looked up. Boone sighed, shaking his head before turning to Achilles.

"Nicholas was resentful you were going to take over the entire business. He's planning on draining the family's finances using the... whatever they're called—Olympus's proprietary crypto-currency. He may have already done it."

"How do you know this?"

"Well... I don't. Not for certain. It's a hunch. But we met someone aboard who may be able to tell us if I'm right and do something about it."

As they approached, the *Apollo* abruptly lit up, its power restored. Achilles went forward, grabbing the radio to contact the ship. In moments, he was speaking with the bridge. He ordered them to find Stavros and have him contact the police on Grand Cayman, guiding them to the location of the helicopter's possible landing point.

"Wait!" Emily turned from the wheel. "Make sure he tells them there is a bomb on the helicopter!"

"Oh, my God, yes..."

"Also, tell the crew that the bombs on the dining hall doors are fakes." Boone quickly interjected. "They can go in and free everyone, if they haven't already."

"And ask the bridge to open up one of the bay doors for us, yeah?" Em asked. "And maybe have someone who knows what they're doing come down and talk me through the docking procedure?"

Achilles did so, and was instructed to bring the *Pollux* to the port side. Then Lyra made a request.

"Ask about Father! He fell ill when the attack happened."

The bridge crew quickly reassured her that Karras Othonos was stable and would be taken to the ship's medical bay. Achilles thanked them, informing the crew that he and Lyra would go to their father's side as soon as they were aboard, and to send Stavros down once the pilot had accomplished his task.

"Actually, may I?" Boone reached for the radio mic. "Hey, can you locate a guest and have her go to the med bay to meet us? Her name is Chloe... uh..." He looked to Emily.

"Bollocks, she never gave me a last name," Emily said. "But she's got short, red hair... and she used to be in software security."

In minutes, the tender had been secured and brought aboard. As a security man stepped into the cabin to deal with Calypso, Boone and Emily followed Achilles and Lyra up to the med bay.

In one particularly long passageway, Lyra slowed, then turned. She regarded Boone with her dark eyes, then shifted her gaze to Emily. "Once again, you have saved me. And Achilles. The both of you. We are in your debt."

Boone tugged the lapels of his jacket. "I got a free suit out of it. I think we're square." He looked down at it, the fabric still damp from his plunge into the seawater. "Gonna need a pretty serious trip to the dry cleaner, though."

Lyra smiled, blinking away tears. "I heard you on the radio... you saved Calypso, too. Many would have let them have her. I am so sorry about what happened. I always knew Callie was a little... different... but *this?*"

Boone reached out and drew her to him, Emily joining in from her side. Together, they shared a moment of comfort, broken by Achilles as he rushed back around a corner.

"They found the helicopter!"

"What are we gonna do, boss?" Potluck asked, as the lights of Grand Cayman came into view.

Angler had been thinking about that for the last half hour. Stallion was dead and all they had to show for this op were the down payments. All of the plans that "Palantir" had laid out for them—specifically, anything beyond boarding the helicopter—had to be considered worthless. Fortunately, he had done a little planning of his own. All three of them had ditched their tactical gear over the side and were now dressed as typical tourists from a stash of clothes Angler had stowed in the hold. Their larger weapons had also been gifted to the fishes, though they each retained a sidearm.

"Tolstoy, take us north around the coast. There are marinas in the bay on the north side. We'll pull in somewhere and pretend to gas up... then just ditch the boat and head into town. Lay low until we can arrange passage out."

"Ooh! I want to go to Hell!" Tolstoy crowed.

"What the *hell* are you talking about, Boris?" Potluck asked.

"Is little place on island. It has own post office! I want to get postcard with postmark for to send to Wagner Group bastards. Greetings from Hell!"

Angler laughed. He was going to miss his band of lunatics.

"The helicopter was right where the waypoint was," Stavros told them. "In a construction site. The bomb squad is there now. No sign of Nicholas."

They were waiting outside the med bay at the doctor's request. Karras had suffered a heart attack, and although the old man was stabilized, he had not yet regained consciousness. Lyra kept looking through the small windows in the double doors. Footsteps sounded from a neighboring corridor and a familiar pair of faces turned the corner.

"Keith!" Em called out. "Are you all right?"

The young man smiled broadly. "You're asking me? I'm glad to see you two are alive and well! You missed out on some Billy Joel. I had a truly 'captive' audience in that hall, and I made the best of it. Were you looking for this young lady?"

"Hey Chloe, good to see you," Boone said. The redhead looked a little shell-shocked, but none the worse for wear. "We could use your skills. Remember that little vulnerability you mentioned? I have a feeling it was put in there on purpose. By Nicholas Othonos."

Chloe's face lit up. "That would explain a lot. It was so minor, and so buried... you'd almost have to know it was there to exploit it."

"So, what do we do?" Achilles asked.

"The bank branch," Chloe began. "It probably has servers I can access. Contact the bank staff and have them meet us down there."

"I'll take care of that," Keith said, taking out a radio.

"And I'll stay here," Lyra said. "In case Father wakes up."

329

Achilles kissed her forehead. "He is a fighter. He will be all right." He turned and strode away, gesturing back to the group. "Come on!"

———◆·◆———

"Almost..." Chloe said.

Emily watched in awe as the redhead's fingers flew across the keys. The bank manager, William, had aided her in gaining access. He now stood nearby, looking nervous.

"He said he was patching a vulnerability... and not to tell anyone," William said.

"No surprise there," Chloe said, continuing to scroll through what looked to Emily to be a wall of digital gibberish. Suddenly, Chloe leaned back in the office chair, shaking her head. "There you are," she said reverently. "He actually did patch it... closed the trapdoor behind him, if you will. I must admit, I'm impressed. I almost missed it, but the devil's in the details... and he didn't completely clean up after himself."

"What did you find?" Emily asked.

"Well... all the people who have assets invested in these Croesid units—your family, half the guests on this ship, people all over the globe... heck, even me—all of our units—our 'shares,' you could call them? We still have them."

Boone frowned. "I don't follow. What's he stealing?"

"Well, he's not stealing units... he's stealing value." She tapped a line of code on the screen, then drew her finger across to another line of code. "What he's done... he's taken the original Croesids— I'll call them Croesid-As—and created a mirror group of exactly the same number of units. Let's call them Croesid-Bs. When he

330

created this 'split,' the new group had practically no value, just a tiny fraction of a cent. And I'm guessing he's got those in multiple accounts he's planning on accessing."

"I don't get it," Achilles said. "If those units are practically worthless, then..."

"They *were* practically worthless. But the value of cryptocurrencies fluctuates with supply and demand, market forces... even manipulation. And in this case..."

"Bugger me, he flipped their value, didn't he?" Emily leaned in, looking at the screen full of code. "Now the As are next to worthless, and the Bs...?"

"Billions," Chloe said simply.

"What do we do?" Achilles asked.

Chloe shrugged. "Flip them back."

"It can't be that easy," Em said.

"It can, if you're the one who designed the cryptocurrency from the ground up. But since I know how he did it... I can *un*do it."

"How long will it take?" Boone asked.

"About an hour. Pantheon is the caretaker of Croesus Coin, and they are headquartered in the Cayman Islands, right?"

"Yes," Achilles confirmed.

"Then I'm guessing he's planning to go into a linked Cayman bank branch when they open tomorrow morning at nine, and transfer the funds from multiple personal accounts into Swiss bank accounts that are not tied to the Pantheon system."

"Will we be able to see where he's making the transfer?" Boone asked.

Chloe smiled. "We can, if I code it." She started typing furiously.

"Wait!" Achilles said, grabbing a stack of Post-it Notes and scrawling something on them. "While you're in there… can you make one other change?"

◆ ◆ ◆

"Missed you too, buddy!" Boone exclaimed, as the overeager potlicker pranced around their feet. The sitter had just departed, and the dog was looking for some playtime and affection. "Easy, Brix. It's been a long day."

"Yeah… I am right knackered," Emily said, beginning to slip out of her dress.

Boone placed a hand on her waist. "*How* knackered…?"

"Mmm…middling…" Emily grabbed his tie and pulled him down for a kiss, then laughed. "I'm having a little déjà vu." She looked down at Brixton. "Where's your squeak toy?"

The potlicker looked up with adoring eyes, wagging his tail.

"Y'know what… let's just crash," Boone said. "We can always play dress-up another day."

"Fine by me. Besides, I don't know about you… but I want to be well rested, up early, and caffeinated by the time Nicholas tries to access the money."

Boone chuckled. "Good point. I'll set the alarm. C'mon Brix!"

Sleep time! The dog bounded past them and jumped up onto the bed. All three were asleep in minutes.

30

Nicholas Othonos strolled into the bank he had selected in downtown George Town, on a street situated midway between the ocean and the airport. Having ditched the black suit and tie he'd worn to Achilles's birthday dinner, Nicholas now wore a lightweight summer suit that looked more at home in the Caymans. Over the last six months, Nicholas had traveled to Grand Cayman five times, and had made sure to establish a rapport with this bank, moving a little money from here to there and making very sure they knew just how wealthy his family was.

An attendant spotted him and quickly brought him to a small, glass-walled office. "Mr. Othonos, so good to see you again."

Nicholas smiled, noting the man's name tag. "Thank you, Cedric." Nicholas set his briefcase on the man's desk and extracted a sheet of paper.

"What can I do for you today, sir?"

"Just a little housekeeping. A major transfer from Pantheon occurred a few minutes ago, into four of our accounts here. I need to move all of the Croesid units from these four accounts"—he indicated four account numbers up top—"into *these* four accounts."

Cedric's smile slipped when he saw the bottom numbers were for a bank in Switzerland, his face becoming crestfallen. "So many units. I hope we have not done anything to offend you, Mr. Othonos."

"Oh, no, no, no... far from it! This is sort of a... a cryptocurrency 'stock split,' if you will. A new feature we're trying out. We'll still be throwing plenty of business your way, not to worry."

Cedric nodded, reassured. "I'll be right back, sir."

Nicholas closed his briefcase and peered through the outer glass windows at the blue skies of a tropical morning. He would soon be looking at a different tropical sky, half a world away in the Pacific. *And I'll own the whole damn island when I'm through.*

Cedric returned, looking equal parts confused and relieved. "As you say, sir. The new units were deposited at nine a.m. and I've made the transfers to the destination accounts you requested." He handed Nicholas a printout. "Will there be anything else?"

"No, thank you, Cedric." Nicholas took the sheet and started to rise... then abruptly dropped back into the chair. The total U.S. dollar amount that had been transferred stared up at him: $1,066.11.

And the currency unit designation wasn't "Croesids." Nicholas crumpled the paper in his trembling hands.

"Sir, is something wrong?"

"Midas Bucks..." he rasped.

"Oh, my goodness!" Cedric suddenly exclaimed, as flashing red and blue lights illuminated the glass office, multiple police cars pulling up on the street outside.

Numb, Nicholas stood and shuffled out of the office.

"Sir... your briefcase! Sir...?"

———————◆•◆———————

"They got him," Achilles said after he ended the call and laid the phone beside him. He and Lyra sat at the long table in the Owner's Suite, with Chloe, Boone, and Emily seated across from them. Achilles looked over at Chloe. "You're good. You want a job?"

Chloe laughed. "I'm a guest who could afford this cruise… I don't work for anyone anymore."

"Well, then how about dinner?"

"Flattered, but… I don't think Lisa would approve."

"She can come, too!"

"Achilles…" Lyra warned.

"Actually, I should get back to her. Maybe we can get a little time poolside before this ship is swarmed with police." Chloe rose and went to the door, then turned. "I can permanently patch the vulnerability for you. In exchange for another cruise. Preferably one without so much drama."

"Done," Achilles said. "And thank you again."

As Chloe left, a rumble sounded from the helipad over their heads as the visiting United States Coast Guard helicopter took flight. The orange-red Dauphin briefly appeared as it became visible outside the suite's floor-to-ceiling windows before banking away, headed to an approaching cutter that lay a hundred miles to the south. There had been some question of jurisdiction between Mexico and the Cayman Islands, as the assault on the ship had occurred at the midpoint between Cozumel and Grand Cayman. When it was learned that one of the bridge crew fatalities was an American citizen, the United States offered to step in, taking Calypso Othonos into custody.

"It's okay, Brix!" Emily reassured the dog when the helicopter shook the windows, eliciting a whine from the potlicker. Wearing a casual sundress, Em gently clamped Brixton's flanks in her bare legs, comforting the dog even as she prevented him from crawling under the table.

"Thanks for letting him come with us," Boone said. He had retired the suit and felt more at ease, now back in his customary T-shirt and shorts. He had gone the extra mile and chosen a new Bubble Chasers shirt without any holes or sun fading.

Lyra smiled. "Of course. After all, he is family to you."

Achilles's phone rang and he looked down, snatching it up when he saw the number. "It's the med bay!" He tapped the screen. "How is he?" he asked without preamble, then looked to Lyra. "It's the doctor. Father is awake and asking for us." He hesitated, then continued. "And he's asking for Nicholas and Calypso, too. What do I say?"

Lyra gently took the phone, saying "Doctor, please tell our father that Achilles and Lyra are on their way. He can speak to Nicholas and Calypso later. Don't tell him why." She hung up, placing a hand on her brother's arm. "Another day. When he is stronger." She looked across the table at Boone and Emily. "Will you come with us?"

After a tearful reunion and many questions—not all of them answered—Karras gestured for Boone and Emily to approach. "You have saved the lives of my children... *again*. I can never sufficiently repay you."

Boone shook his head. "Sir, there's no n—"

"*But*," Karras interrupted in a surprisingly robust voice, "I *will* repay you. In some small fashion."

"It's really not necessary, sir," Emily said.

"*Paidi mou*... my child... to me, it is. I will say no more." He reached out for his eldest son's hand. "Well, Achilles... I'm afraid the company is not yours yet!"

"Father, I have been thinking... perhaps we should reconsider whether we should put everything under my control. I'm not the businessman that Nicholas was. Is!" he quickly corrected himself.

Karras didn't seem to notice. "My boy, you are my eldest... and as such—"

"Father, we live in a very different world than the one you grew up in. I believe the company will be stronger if you make use of all of our talents."

"That is a very mature, very wise way of looking at things, my son. Precisely why you should lead the company!"

Achilles looked over at Boone and Emily. "Well, I tried."

Later that afternoon, Boone and Emily sat at a waterside bar in downtown George Town, just in view of the cruise ship terminal docks where tenders from the ships discharged their passengers. In the bay, the *Apollo* and two other cruise ships lay at anchor. Far out on the horizon, another cruise ship was making its way in. Relaxing beside the water at a table Emily had selected, the two divemasters contentedly sipped their beers, their potlicker pup enjoying a bowl of cold water beneath the table.

The Royal Cayman Islands Police Service was questioning guests and crew from the *Apollo*, and Boone and Emily had come ashore after an hour-long interview with a pair of inspectors. With inquiries likely to continue into the following day, Boone had asked Keith where to go for a bite and a beer and he'd suggested Rackam's. After letting the ship know where they'd be, the two divemasters had made their way the short distance to the local watering hole.

The restaurant and bar was popular with divers and locals— at least, when it wasn't overrun with cruisies. Situated right on the water, Rackam's had a sizeable outdoor dining area; blue and tan awnings and numerous colorful umbrellas provided plenty of shade from the tropical sun, and the U-shaped outdoor bar boasted plenty of stools for imbibers who liked to be closer to the liquor source.

"Ah, *man* that's good," Boone said after taking a drink of his draft beer, setting the perspiring pint glass down on the waterside table. It wasn't often that you could find a good dark beer in the islands, but Boone had been pleased to see that Cayman Islands Brewing had one. He took another sip of the Ironshore Bock. "How's yours?"

Em had gone lighter, choosing a bottle of the local craft brewery's flagship beer, Caybrew. "Refreshing! Nothing better than a cold beer and a hot sun. And it plays nice with this jerk mayo!" She dipped another conch fritter into the spicy sauce. "Y'know, Maine lobster and prime rib paired with a wine that's worth more than your savings is all well and good… but nothing beats a conch fritter and a beer a stone's throw from the Caribbean."

Boone reached over and clinked her bottle. "You speak truth." He took another swallow, then set it down. "Although… we can afford that highfalutin wine, if you want it. And another pair of those funky shoes you lost."

Em held up a finger while she finished chewing the remainder of the fritter she'd crammed into her mouth. "If you'll remember... those magic cards stopped working once we reached the Caymans."

"I'm not talking about the cards. Karras Othonos said he would repay us, and... well... I guess he did."

Emily cocked her head. "Go on..." she prompted, before taking a sip from her bottle.

Boone took out his phone, hopping onto the bar's Wi-Fi and pulling up his banking app. "Not sure how they got hold of the routing and account number for Bubble Chasers, but..." He slid the phone over. Seconds later he was wiping Caybrew from his face.

Emily managed to clear her windpipe of lager and grabbed the phone, goggling at the screen at point-blank range. "Whoa. We... we can't accept this. Can we? I mean... maybe we can?"

Boone shrugged, sipping his bock. "I was thinking of refusing it, but it's a drop in the bucket to them. And if we wake up in a cold sweat, racked with guilt, we can donate it somewhere."

Emily nodded. "Okay... fair 'nuff."

"Hey, uh..." Boone squirmed a bit in his seat. "With everything that happened... especially on the *Apollo* bridge... do you need to...uh..."

"Spit it out, Boone."

"Well, if you need to call that therapist in Costa Rica..." Boone trailed off.

Emily looked out to sea. She tapped the neck of her beer bottle with a fingernail, making a series of soft pings. "I thought I might... but y'know what? I'm good."

"Boone, Emily?" a figure approached their table, setting something down as they looked up.

"Keith!" Boone rose from the table. "Have a seat, I'll get you a beer."

"Oh, thank you, no, I've got to get back. Have you spoken with the Caymanian police?"

"Yeah, about an hour ago," Boone said.

"We're becoming quite skilled at chatting up island coppers," Em said, tossing a smile at Boone. "So, what brings you to our little seaside table?"

"Lyra Othonos sent me. She said she thought the two of you should have this. Whatever 'this' is." He pulled out an empty chair and set a familiar black case atop it. "Will I see you two back aboard the ship tonight? I'll be playing at The Muse, and we'll be in port until tomorrow at least."

"Save us a table!" Emily said.

"Will do! See you then!" The young man quickly made his way back toward the piers.

Boone reached over and opened the case to reveal the contents: Nicholas's Underwater Personal Conveyor.

"That's mine, by the way," Emily proclaimed through a mouthful of her third fritter.

Boone grinned. "How you figure?"

"I drove it first. And also, I used it to… oh, what was it that I did? Oh yeah, I remember. I used it to frikkin' save the world."

Boone laughed. "Consider it yours."

"No consideration needed, it's mine. Right, Brix?" Emily stuck her head under the table.

The potlicker gave a flurry of tail wags, punctuated by a joyous "woof."

Emily came back up top. "See? Brixton concurs."

Boone settled back in his chair, flush with contentment. Sipping the Ironshore Bock, he glanced out to sea… and nearly did a spit take of his own. "You gotta be shittin' me…"

The cruise ship that had been on the horizon was coming into the bay, the Caribbean sun shining down on all its broken-down glory.

"Is that...?" Emily said, setting down her Caybrew.

"It is."

Emily's nostrils flared with anger—a look that Boone found equal parts arousing and intimidating. She reached out, beckoning with her fingers. "Put the scooter up here."

Boone lifted it from the case and set it on the table. Emily powered it up, then plunked her lime green sunglasses down beside it, perusing the controls for a moment.

"What are you doing?"

"If Nicholas used the video to blackmail them, then he must've kept the video, yeah?" She tapped a few keys and a menu of videos popped up. Selecting the most recent, she pressed play. Emily's beautiful lips curved into a wicked grin. "Gotcha," she breathed.

"You are *so* sexy when you're full of righteous anger," Boone said, only half-joking.

Emily polished off her beer, clunking the bottle down with purpose. "Get me another, would you? Raining down justice is thirsty work. I'm going to transfer this video to my mobile."

Boone smiled, taking the empty up to the bar and waggling the bottle when the bartender looked his way.

"Another, please."

"And I'll take a Strongbow," a voice said.

Boone glanced to the side as a striking woman in polarized sunglasses approached the south side of the U-shaped bar. A bit taller than Emily, maybe a few years older, the first thing Boone noticed was a dazzling pair of tattoo sleeves: a colorful reef scene on her right arm, a black-and-gray shark on the left. Her shoulder-length blonde hair sported purple highlights, and she wore a T-shirt from a dive shop, a mermaid astride an anchor and an old-timey dive helmet dominating the logo.

The bartender smiled broadly, clearly recognizing the woman who sidled up to the bar. "AJ! Good to see you! An ice-cold bottle from the back of the fridge, coming right up."

"Thanks, Frank."

"You want a menu?"

"No thanks, I'm just meeting Nora here," AJ said, an English accent readily apparent. She tucked her sunglasses into the neck of her dive shirt. "You be at the Fox and Hare later?"

"I will indeed," Frank said, bringing over a pair of bottles. "A Strongbow for you...and a Caybrew for the gentleman." With that, he hustled away to a group of cruisies that had just arrived.

AJ gave Boone a polite smile and lifted her bottle. "Cheers." She turned to go.

"You're British," Boone said.

"You're tall," she deadpanned back, before granting him another brief smile.

Boone had been around Emily long enough to see how often guys were hitting on her—"macking on her", as she called it—and the opening salvo was frequently about Em's accent. And this woman had a familiar "not looking for flirtation" look in her eyes. Green eyes, Boone now noticed. Much like Emily's.

"Sorry, it's just that my girlfriend Emily over there is a Brit." Boone gestured back toward Em. "South London."

AJ relaxed at that, appraising Boone more closely. "You a diver?" She gestured at Boone's Bubble Chasers T-shirt with her bottle of cider.

"Yeah... Em and I are divemasters from over in Cozumel. Bubble Chasers is our op." He nodded toward her. "Mermaid Divers... that's a cool logo."

"Thanks. Friend of mine designed it for me." She smiled, a more welcoming smile this time. "Mermaid Divers is *my* op." She extended a hand. "AJ Bailey."

"Boone Fischer," he said, shaking with her.

Boone was already planning on introducing her to Emily, but the fact that she was the owner of a dive operation on Grand Cayman gave him an even better reason to bring her over.

"Would you care to join us? Emily is gonna love you. Plus, we've got something you'll probably want to see."

AJ shrugged. "Sure."

Boone led her back to the table, where Emily was completely engrossed in her phone and the touchscreen atop the UPC. He set her beer down. "Em, got someone you should meet. AJ Bailey… meet Emily Durand."

Em waved her hand at him. "Just a tick, almost got it… boom! Uploading!" She looked up. Catching sight of AJ, her jaw dropped. "Crikey…"

AJ raised an eyebrow and Boone laughed nervously. "Em… you okay there?"

Boone's question rebooted her and Em gushed, "Ohmigod, I love your tattoos and your hair and I love mermaids!"

AJ burst into laughter. "Boone here tells me you're a Southie," she said, still grinning at Emily's outburst.

"You're English, too? Boone, can we keep her?"

Brixton came out from under the table, tail wagging furiously.

"And who is this?" AJ asked. "Looks a lot like my friend Reg's dog Coop. A local mutt breed called a Cayman Brown Hound."

"That's Brixton," Emily replied. "Brix for short. He's a Belizean potlicker pup."

"Hello, Brixton." AJ gave the dog her hand to sniff as she addressed Emily. "Are you from that neighborhood?"

"No, Deptford. But that would make for a terrible name for a dog. How 'bout you?"

"Sussex, originally."

"AJ here is a divemaster," Boone said. "Mermaid Divers is her op."

"I *told* Boone we should've put a mermaid on our logo!"

"Emily's got a bit of a mermaid fetish," Boone said.

"Don't embarrass me in front of my new best friend!" Emily admonished Boone. "Besides, it's more of a mild obsession. That, and the color green. Love your eyes, too, by the way..."

"Okay, okay, don't scare her off," Boone teased, offering a chair to AJ.

AJ gestured at the UPC atop the table. "Is this what you wanted to show me? What is it?"

"It's kind of a cross between an underwater scooter and a drone. But the scooter's not what I wanted to show you... it's the video Emily took with it."

Emily smiled, understanding where Boone was going with this. "AJ, how long has Mermaid been operating?"

"About five years, give or take."

"So, I'm betting you know some conservation types over here, yeah?"

AJ nodded. "Casey, one of my best mates, works over at the Department of Environment."

"Ace! Well, then... take a gander at this." Emily slid the phone across the table.

AJ watched the video, growing angrier by the moment. "This dumping... this was in Cozumel?" she said, as the video neared the end.

"Yeah," Boone replied. "Few days ago."

"Why are you showing this to me?" AJ asked as the video came to a close, the stern of the *Nordic Starr* frozen in the final frame.

"Because *that* ship"—Emily tapped the screen—"is *that* ship." She pointed out to sea at the Hygge Cruises vessel as it dropped anchor.

AJ's jaw clenched. "Can you send me that video? I'm going to call Casey, tell her to get down here."

Boone smiled, picking up his empty pint glass and rising from the table. "I'll get us another round. I suspect we'll need it."

The bar was quite a bit busier now, so Boone staked out a corner and waited patiently. As he did, his eyes took in the customers. A few locals, quite a few cruise ship passengers. Boone watched one older gentleman light up a cigar, reaching out a gnarled hand for an ashtray down at one end of the bar, sliding it closer. Boone stiffened. There, in the ashtray, were a trio of familiar golden cigarette butts.

Adrenaline surging, Boone stepped back from the bar, scanning the entire outdoor seating area. The face he was looking for was nowhere in sight. Frank, the bartender, came over.

"Another Ironshore?"

"Uh... yeah... and another cold Strongbow for AJ." As Frank started to turn, Boone continued. "Hey, weird question... that ashtray over there. It was sitting down at the end and it's got some cigarette butts in there from a black-and-gold cigarette. Did you happen to see who was smoking them?"

"No, sorry... we had quite a lunch rush from the ships, I was swamped. But I don't recall anyone smoking over there for the last couple hours at least. I'll get your beers."

Boone returned to the table, setting the drinks down.

"What's up, Boone?" Emily asked.

Boone shook his head and smiled. "Probably nothing. How'd you do with the video?"

AJ waggled her phone. "Got it. And Casey will be here at half five."

"That's five-thirty, Boone," Emily said slowly, as if instructing a toddler on his ABC's. She winked at AJ. "I'm training 'im 'ow to speak proper."

Boone laughed. "That one I knew." He sat back and took a swallow of his beer. "So, AJ... what's it like, diving in the Caymans?"

"Why, you thinking of coming over? Poaching my business?"

"Nah, we're quite happy over on Coz."

"Now, hang on," Emily said. "We've just had a little... investment. What's to stop us from expanding? Then I could hang with my new best mate!"

When AJ laughed, Boone leaned forward. "She's not kidding. She will stalk you."

"I could do worse," AJ said.

"But seriously, what's the diving like?"

"Well... first off, you've got three islands to choose from... Grand, Little, and Brac. The water is gin-clear, brilliant viz year-round. And enough dive sites, you could dive a different spot every day of the year! Now... here on Grand..."

As AJ launched into a passionate rundown of some of her favorite sites, Boone gathered Brixton against his leg, sipping his beer as he looked out at the sparkling sea. He smiled. *Why not?*

Keep reading for The Afterword, but first:
If you enjoyed this book, please take a moment to
provide a short review; every reader's voice
is extremely important for the life of a book or series.

Boone and Emily will return in

Deep Focus

If you'd like advance notice of their next
adventures, head on over to

WWW.DEEPNOVELS.COM
or
WWW.NICKSULLIVAN.NET

where you can sign up for my mailing list. If you're like
me, you hate spam, so rest assured I'll email rarely.

And check out other authors who set their tales on the
water, near the water, or under the tropical sun at

WWW.TROPICALAUTHORS.COM

Finally, if you were as intrigued as Emily was by a
certain tattoo-sleeved Grand Cayman divemaster, check
out Nicholas Harvey's *A J Bailey Adventure Series*.

AFTERWORD

It's a very strange feeling when you finish a book, then fire up a document called "The Afterword" and realize just how many aspects of your life thudded into each other to create the novel lying before you.

Cozumel has provided some of my favorite diving experiences, and I've visited there several times. The first trip, we stayed in the original Hotel Barracuda (before it was destroyed by Wilma) and dived with Dive Paradise. Here's a tidbit that's likely to be of interest. Guess who used to work there as a divemaster? I'll give you a hint: I narrate his audiobooks and his lead character had a cameo in *Deep Shadow*. Yes, action-adventure writer Wayne Stinnett used to work at Dive Paradise, pre-Hurricane Wilma. The world is a tiny place!

The second trip to Coz we decided to dive with Aqua Safari, lodging in a little room they had above the shop. I enjoyed that stay, being able to just cross the street to their pier—the same pier where Emily encounters the drone. And in a later trip, although we weren't staying there, my "crew" and I were happy to revisit the site of the new Hotel Barracuda and have some drinks poolside at the No Name Bar crew bar. But then we scuttled on back to our hotel, because there was a hurricane on the way. We've had odd hurricane luck with our Cozumel trips. Every time I've gone, a hurricane or a tropical storm has popped up: Hurricane Chantal in 2003, Hurricane Dolly in 2008, and Tropical Storm Barry in 2013. We'd batten down the hatches and ride them out, but on only one occasion did we miss a single day of diving.

During out first trip to Coz, there were a lot of Volkswagen Things. Our second visit, we didn't see a single one. But there were plenty of convertible VW Bugs! We rented a bright orange one, then headed off to the Mayan temple complex of San Gervasio, deep in the interior of the island. It was there that I actually saw a mated pair of cardinals! I thought that was so unusual, seeing a bird I associate with North America, that I put it into *Deep Roots*. Another crossover with *Roots*: you may remember "Boonemily" found a certain artifact associated with a Mayan goddess? San Gervasio was a center of worship for the goddess Ix Chel. And what Coz car rental day would be complete without a trip to Coconuts? Yes, those photo albums exist... we saw them, but we didn't "see" them. A cruise ship group had them. Also, when we were there, I don't remember much of a menagerie, but apparently there are a lot of critters there now.

Some of the best diving I've experienced has been on this beautiful little island. We always booked the fast-boats when available, the best sites being far to the south. And yes, much like the scene with the *Lunasea* racing the *Barco Rápido*, I remember "racing" other boats for prime moorings in the south. The currents can be tricky down there. It's the only time I've had to share my octopus with someone, when powerful currents at Cedral Wall led one of our number to burn through their air. The thing I remember about that day was how chill we both were, down there at a depth of seventy feet. The sequence of signals boiled down to:

"Hey. I'm out of air."

"Oh, you are? Okay, here. Hey divemaster, we're going up."

Staying calm and just following the training really pays off. Another fun memory: we shared a fast-boat with a couple and kept thinking one of them looked familiar, finally recognizing one of the pair as an actor from a hilarious show on Comedy Central, *Strangers with Candy*. Greg Hollimon, who had played the principal on the show, ended up joining us for dinner at La Mission. And another actor buddy whom I have dived with several times made it into this story: Matt Boston. Matt has never read my books. So I killed him. Well, his Greek doppelganger at least, "Mattaíos."

One of the great things about Cozumel is the plentiful selection of excellent restaurants. And I'm not talking about the ones that lurk near the cruise ship piers, where binge-drinking is the theme and waitresses blow whistles at you until you pound down a liver-killing amount of alcohol. No, I'm thinking of a number of spots where you can get some amazing local cuisine for not too many pesos. If you've read my other books, you know I can't stop myself from having Boone and Emily sit down to a meal or three. I didn't end up doing that so much in this book, so real quick, here are some of my favorite places to "grab a scrummy nosh," as Emily would say: La Choza: home of avocado pie… very chill, not touristy, great local food. Casa Denis: A venerable establishment, set back from the main square… fantastic seafood. La Mission: Another old standby, great place to get lobster and steak… wonderful atmosphere. And Pancho's Backyard: Lots of great dishes, and they had a jalapeño margarita I still dream about. Apparently, they've opened a second location down by the southern cruise ship piers, but that was after my last visit.

And on the subject of cruise ships: there are too dang many. Well, maybe not *now*, with COVID-19 devastating the cruise industry… but the amount of cruise ship traffic is reason enough— if you're thinking of visiting Coz—to consider some of the resorts further south. And if staying closer to the city, pay the extra for a fast-boat. You'll thank me when you blow past a cattle boat packed to the gills on your way south to snag the best dive sites.

Enough about Cozumel. How about another island that came into play? Nope, not Grand Cayman. When I was seven years old, my parents took my brother and me on our one-and-only trip to Europe. My father was a lover of Greek philosophy, so naturally we went to Athens… and from there, we took a ferry to Hydra; a tiny, arid island with a tiered town surrounding a beautiful harbor. We were met with a donkey, who carried our luggage up steep stone steps to our lodgings. And, being a child of seven, the foremost memory of that journey was that donkey pooping constantly all the way up to our destination. But last year, when I learned that Hydra had one of the oldest maritime colleges in the world, I knew I needed to bring it into play with Karras Othonos's background. I was also a huge fan of Greek mythology in my childhood, so the cruise ship company's theme was a no-brainer. Speaking of Greece… if any of you know Greek, then one of my plot's "surprises" might not have been as much of a surprise. Lovers of all things Caribbean will hear "calypso" and think of the musical style. But Calypso is a Greek name, and it means: "she who hides."

Another "life influences art" moment: after the release of *Deep Cut*, Wayne Stinnett convinced me to join NINC, Novelist's Inc., of which he was the current president. I had a wonderful time at the conference that year, down in St. Petersburg, Florida. Got to meet my editor, too. (Hi Marsha! Is this Afterword too wordy yet? Fight me!) Anyway, the tie-in. On my way to the airport after the conference, I was in a taxi with an Aussie driver, so with his accent I was already off to a good start. As we drove over a long bridge, headed toward Tampa, I remarked to the cabbie: "The water looks *really* shallow. Is all of the bay like this?" And he informed me that yes, much of it was extremely shallow, and that the biggest cruise ships couldn't go under the bridge we were crossing, and even the medium-sized ones could only go under...riiiiiight... here. And at that moment we hit the highpoint between the two towers of the Sunshine Skyway Bridge. Instantly, I imagined a ship passing beneath with baddies rappelling down and the opening scene was born.

A brief word about the *Apollo*. I learned a lot about cruise ships and mega-yachts writing this book. For one thing, the terms superyacht and mega-yacht are frequently used interchangeably, with even yachting associations arguing over exact nomenclature. The *Apollo* would fall under a category called "giga-yachts," and I based it on several of the largest yachts in the world, borrowing aspects from four amongst the top ten. I then combined those elements with several exclusive luxury cruise ships. You may have thought at some point, "Hey, the *Apollo* seems a lot bigger than the one on the cover." You would be correct! While I do strive to have cover images that tie into aspects of each book, the yacht on the cover of *Deep Devil* is a "superyacht" at best, but it had a helicopter, tender-bay doors, and the colors of the sunset were too good not to use.

A quick shout out to Cameron Akins of Caradonna Adventures dive travel agency for her assistance, and for pointing me to Jorge Marin of Cozumel Marine World. Thank you, Jorge, for answering my questions! I was very sad to learn of the passing of Dawn "Shelley" Snow, of Caradonna Adventures. Dawn put together nearly every dive trip I've ever taken, ending with my journey to Saba to research *Deep Cut*. She clearly loved the islands and was enthusiastic and knowledgeable about every adventure she planned for us.

If you are a fan of "Tropical Authors," I should mention a couple tie-ins here: A big thank you to novelist and occasional Cozumel resident Paul Mila, for providing Boone and Emily with a condo to rent. And to Nicholas Harvey—whom I sometimes call Brit Nick—for allowing a certain Cayman Islands divemaster to enter Boonemily's world and offer an endgame for the subplot of the sewage-spewing *Nordic Starr*.

On the subject of "Tropical Authors," if you haven't checked out our website, swing on over there and take a look. www.tropicalauthors.com. See some authors there you like? Then sign up for our newsletter! We will alert you to all new releases and any deals on books that come up.

Sadly, we lost one of our own last year: Author Ed Robinson, known for his Trawler Trash Series with its legendary waterman, "Breeze," passed away in November. He was nearly finished with his last Breeze book, and reached out to fellow author/boater Wayne Stinnett, asking him to finish it. *Cayo Costa Breeze* will be available this year.

Thank you to all of my beta readers: Chris Sorensen, John Brady, Kevin Carolan, Stuart Marland, Alan and Joan Zale, Mike Ramsey, Dana Vihlen, Patrick Newman, Drew Mutch, Jason Hebert, Glenn Hibbert, Deg Priest, Alan Fader, David Margolis, Bob Hickerson, Malcolm Sullivan, and Brooke Johnson. Many of you have extraordinary backgrounds in diving, boating, and writing and you all kept me on my accuracy-toes and made some wonderful suggestions.

A big thank you to Shayne Rutherford of Wicked Good Book Covers for taking a stunning photo of a yacht off the coast of hilly Croatia and making it look like flat Cozumel. And additional thanks to Martonio Paleka for that wonderful sunset photo, Marsha Zinberg of The Write Touch for her on-point editing, Colleen Sheehan of Ampersand Book Interiors for her pristine formatting, and proofreaders Gretchen Tannert Douglas and Forest Olivier for their error-seeking eyeballs. My thanks to Karl Cleveland for his work on my DeepNovels.com website, and thank you to everyone at Aurora Publicity, who are taking some of the marketing load off my shoulders so I can spend more time spinning words into stories.

A little Nick News... after giving Boone and Emily a rescue dog in *Deep Roots,* I decided I ought to follow their example. Last summer I adopted a seven-year-old pup named Momo. She can be a handful... and sometimes I refer to her as Momostopheles, Devourer of Souls. But she's been a welcome, fuzzy companion who *usually* lets me work.

And finally, as always, thank you to my readers (and my listeners, you audiobook fans). I know where "Boonemily" will be next—and having read this book, I suspect you may have a pretty good idea, too. Until then, stay safe, stay sanitary, stay sane... and keep seeking the sun.

ABOUT THE AUTHOR

Born in East Tennessee, Nick Sullivan has spent most of his adult life as an actor in New York City working in television, film, theater, and audiobooks. After narrating hundreds of titles over the last couple of decades, he decided to write his own. Nick is an avid scuba diver, and his travels to numerous islands throughout the Caribbean have inspired this series.

For a completely different kind of book, you can find Nick Sullivan's first novel at:

WWW.ZOMBIEBIGFOOT.COM

Made in United States
Orlando, FL
05 November 2023